Learning to Drive

1st gear

2nd gear

3rd gear

4th gear

MARY HAYS

Learning to Drive

A NOVEL

Shaye Areheart Books   New York

Published by Shaye Areheart Books, New York, New York.
Member of the Crown Publishing Group, a division of Random House, Inc.
www.randomhouse.com

SHAYE AREHEART BOOKS and colophon are trademarks of Random House, Inc.

Printed in the United States of America

Design by Lynne Amft

Library of Congress Cataloging-in-Publication Data
Hays, Mary.
Learning to drive : a novel / Mary Hays.
1. Accident victims—Family relationships—Fiction. 2. Christian Scientists—Fiction.
3. Vermont—Fiction. 4. Widows—Fiction. 5. Guilt—Fiction. I. Title.
PS3608.A985L43 2003
813'.6—dc21   2002156283

ISBN 1-4000-4780-3

10 9 8 7 6 5 4 3 2 1

First Edition

for my mother

ACKNOWLEDGMENTS

My husband, Stephen Long, has set what I believe must be an endurance record for listening, reading, commenting, and editing, and then doing it all over again (and again) with love and patience. I would not be writing this paragraph if it weren't for his help or the help of Judy Blume and George Cooper, my very first encouragers and steadfast champions to the very end. Thank you to Catherine Tudish, friend and fellow writer, who has so generously shared her insights and know-hows, and to my daughters, Sara Pinto and Francesca Pinto, who have given unstintingly of their goodwill and bright hopes for so long (and who love a good laugh—is there a more encouraging sound?). Many thanks to my experts, speech and language pathologist Penny Andrew, C.C.C., S.P., artist Dennis Grady, and Priscilla Connolly, M.D.; to Sally Brady for her enthusiastic support and her gift of time; and to Robert Brower for his acts of heroism in helping me to loosen the Porter's grip. I would also like to express my thanks to my agent, Timothy Seldes, and to my editor, Shaye Areheart, for their part in giving this story life on these pages, and to Marty Asher, who found a way to make it happen. I am deeply grateful.

Stand porter at the door of thought. Admitting only such conclusions as you wish realized in bodily results, you will control yourself harmoniously. . . . The issues of pain or pleasure must come through mind, and like a watchman forsaking his post, we admit the intruding belief, forgetting that through divine help we can forbid this entrance.

—MARY BAKER EDDY, *SCIENCE AND HEALTH WITH
KEY TO THE SCRIPTURES*, 1875

• • •

These porters do now become a porterage themselves, and those parts that were wont to bear the greatest burdens, are now so great a burden.

—J. SMITH, *OLD AGE*, 1676

The best way to get along with the Porter is to never look at him directly. What if he should see something in your face he doesn't like, a hint of corruption, a history of low scores? His list of forbidden passengers is ten feet long, twenty, forty . . . there's no end to it. At the top of the list is Death. Well, who wants Death sitting right up front? He's got a point after all; the Porter's not all hot air—it would be too demoralizing to sit behind Death and count the hairs on the back of his neck. And who wants to share a seat with Malice, Disease, Peeing in Pants, Deformity, Snits, Ignorance, Bad Manners, Sorrow, Rage, Puffery? How about Sloth? Would you like to share your hard-boiled eggs with him?

Or with Cranky? Cranky's nose is always running. When the Porter throws Cranky off the train and she lands on her bum, admit it, you're not disappointed. Weak Ankles is allowed to ride if she stays seated. Broken Bones, if on the mend. Some forms of suffering are allowed in the caboose—Disappointment, Discontent, Loneliness, Vague Fears, Bloat. But not Despair and his cohorts, not Madness, Old Age, Poverty . . . you name them, you know them. They're probably pushing at your own back right now, trying to shove their way in, but no, Despair and his cohorts don't get on this train; the Porter sees to that. He tells them to find another means of transportation. He suggests a bus, and he laughs in their faces.

Is the Porter male or female? Male. Definitely.

Where does the Porter get his authority? From God.

Where does the Porter live? In your mind, with his monkey. When the Porter sleeps, the monkey makes mischief.

The Porter's smooth brown face is blank. He checks his red coat for lint or signs of muss, polishes his brass buttons, reviews the passenger list, erases names. On his shoulder sits a little monkey wearing a stiff red hat decorated with black-and-gilt stripes; sometimes the monkey jumps off, looking for fun, but the Porter pays no mind, for he is a busy fellow.

The Conductor, whose navy-blue jacket is stained with his morning's cereal and whose pants are so long he steps on his own cuffs, shambles through the train without enthusiasm. He has given over his authority to the Porter, and it has left him weary. When he calls out the stops, he no longer bothers to enunciate, using the same weary melody for all the stations on the way to the city. Those who care about appearance and demeanor are hoping the Conductor will opt for early retirement.

As for the Flagman, he is more interested in demonstrating his command of semaphores than in performing his job with efficiency. He often delays the train through an excess of zeal. He went to semaphore school, and his young wife must patiently wait in bed for him every night while he swings his flags around their tiny apartment, leaving the broken vases and shattered cups for her to clean up in the morning. Still, he is handsome and she doesn't object. Later, perhaps, but not now.

The passengers, though, are not so patient, and they speak with irritation of his excesses, his pirouettes and jetés, his flamboyant and ridiculous signals. But at least they speak of him. Of the Brakeman they never speak. They hardly know he exists, yet he is the one who keeps them safe. The Brakeman keeps his eyes open, he makes sure all is well, he stays awake, and he stays off the bottle. Even while enjoying his thermos, he will pause to rework his stopping distances, taking account of the day's information: Is there a cow on the track? A loose rail? What is the speed of the wind on this sunny day? Is the train shaped like a peach? Nothing escapes him; in a flawed configuration, density is a deadly force. The passengers are too busy worrying about the Porter to think about the Brakeman. It is the Porter who rules the train, who gets to decide who shall ride and who shall not. It is the Porter we all fear and admire.

Punctuality is the Engineer. His complexion is pocked, he's twice divorced, he has a soft paunch. Watching from the tracks, waving, hoping for a blast from his horn, we can see only his smart cap, the set of his shoulders. His personal life remains unknown to us, his debts, his rotten molars, his bad temper, the hours he loiters in the adult-book shops, we know nothing of this. And why should we care? Why should we peer at his back teeth? His business is speed, performance, adherence to schedule. So what if he's no party wit, no bon vivant? He gets us there on time. He avoids collisions, he drives with a fine style. He is a friend of the Porter. Together they work hand in hand to maintain the reputation of this fine train.

In America's golden past she was known as the Queen of the Rails. She sped, she fairly flew, from one great city to another. She didn't go to Podunk then. She didn't sit on a siding for an hour while somebody straightened the seams of her stockings. Lately, she has begun to age; she has begun to crack and fray within. She has gotten a bit stiff; it is hard for her to bend down and view the back of her own legs. But her rubber seals are still intact; she still has style, chrome, speed, sex appeal; her jolts are felt only in the last few cars. Nevertheless, they are talking of junking her. The upkeep, the repairs, the incidence of vandalism, employee theft . . . these are the arguments used by those who want to scrap the great lady. They point to the quality of the passengers. Few of them eat in the dining car any longer, preferring to bring their own smelly fruit, their noisy snacks—the roar of snacking in the rear coaches is positively deafening. And they bring their disposable diapers. That is the absolute worst. The Porter does not allow them anywhere on this train, but somehow the passengers will sneak them on anyway. The cleaning crew finds them the next day, stuffed into every nook and cranny, full and fulsome.

Fortunately, even nowadays, the passengers who sit up front are a different breed, and it is still a pleasure to clean their cars. The kinds of things the Better Passengers leave behind are small and tasteful. Debris you could eat off. Loot you could treasure. Raincoats folded up into cunning little pouches, collapsible umbrellas with monogrammed handles, Modern Library editions of the unread classics, individually wrapped candies purloined from well-stocked candy bowls of the finest Waterford crystal. The Porter reviews the loot, tucks a few horehounds into his pocket. Only the very best passengers would eat such awful candy. The awfulness of what a person eats is a faultless measure of breeding. Think of tomato aspic, junket, puddings (especially when beige).

The Better Passengers are known by what they wear: thick cotton, pure wools, materials with substance, fabrics that drape and hold their own against time. They eschew blends; they loathe fabric that clings. They take good care of their clothes. They leave the instructions on the tags on their collars, and they follow them to the letter: "better not wringing"; "all bleach"; "not gnawing"; "no rub in cold rivers"; "unsoaking use solvents." There are so many instructions, and so incoherent! But this is the price of dressing well—wearing scratchy tags that make you want to scream at your loved ones, following insane instructions written in fuzzy print. This is the true sacrifice, taking orders from nitwits who don't know the first thing about parallel construction. The Better Passengers have a deep respect for good grammar. They have the best vocabulary. Many of them have won spelling bees. They took Latin in school; they probably spoke it at home—they have that sort of confidence, the confidence of having communed with their mothers in the ablative. And why wouldn't they be confident? They sit up front, they're in the right, they wear cotton, and they plan to live forever.

Syracuse, New York

DECEMBER 1952

Man, governed by immortal Mind, is always beautiful and grand.

—MARY BAKER EDDY, *SCIENCE AND HEALTH WITH KEY TO THE SCRIPTURES*

•　　•　　•

CHAPTER

1

Charlotte lay awake all night listening to the clock in the downstairs hallway. Every quarter hour it squeezed out a chime within a long and predictable sequence of sounds that became more distinct as the night wore on: a wheeze, a cough, a running start, and finally a pause and a failure of nerve, and then a little song—another quarter hour is coming, another is gone, another is coming, another is gone. She pictured the old, dead quarter hours piling up, then sliding off the pile and disappearing into endless Time where quarter hours didn't count. Quarter hours were mere human constructions, temporary units fabricated by mankind for convenience in daily life, like minutes, though more important than minutes, since clocks didn't chime every minute—and for that she was very grateful. There was an infinite number of units of time, as many as you could think of names for, each one folded inside the other, their inward progression stretching beyond the mind's eye, to the outer edge of knowing, all of them ticking, relentlessly beating, like her own heart.

She decided to drown them. She gathered them into Melvin's fishing net and lowered them into a dark pool, watching as the flimsy little units cascaded gently toward the muck at the bottom. Just before they landed, she reversed the net and whipped it out of the water. Success! None had stuck! They were all gone, or nearly all. Just one was left; it clung to the net, its delicate green wings twitching, ticking, relentlessly beating. . . . She was doomed; she would never sleep. Her skin prickled; her long, heavy braid pulled at her scalp. She listened to Melvin breathing peacefully beside her, to the quiet little snort at the bottom of each breath that signaled his blissful oblivion. Across the hall, their two small sons slept on, two soldiers of sleep marching through the night. It was always she, the lone female, who had to carry the whole nocturnal consciousness of the household, she alone who watched and prayed, and waited for the dawn.

Insomnia had been a way of life in Charlotte's family. Her mother and two older sisters were always prowling the house at night in search of sleep, a loosely knit pack stalking the same elusive prey. Their mother read from Mrs. Eddy's works, her flowered bathrobe tucked tightly around her legs as she sat curled up on the couch, head resting on her hand under the glow of the lamp. Rosey, the oldest, read romantic novels, while Kitty, the middle child, did puzzles. (Kitty was always alert and cheerful no matter what the hour and could easily do anagrams after midnight.) Charlotte, the baby of the family, was last to join in their forays. At first she snacked, like any child let loose in an unsupervised kitchen. Later, she got out her crayons and sat alone at the long, polished table in the dining room, creating the same little scene over and over again: a house with a high-pitched roof and a garden in front (always drawn from the same perspective), a standard lollipop-shaped tree (with nests), a row of tall flowers marching alongside the walkway through the garden, two happy clouds, and a flock of V-shaped birds in the far distance. After she had made a few of these pictures, so full of goodwill and brave resolve despite the dark shadows in the corners of the room, her fatigue would take over and her flowers would wilt, the tree would list, her birds in flight would start to wobble, and Charlotte would awake with her face on the paper. As she groped her way back to bed, feeling vaguely ashamed that her staying power was so slight, she would always vow to do better next time.

Their father was the only one in the family who had a normal relationship with sleep: Jerome Baird took it for granted, looked forward to it, cherished his sleeping garb. He would doze off after meals or during his daughters' impromptu recitals and incoherent dramas, waking up just long enough to announce his intention of retiring, yawning and stretching as he locked the doors and made his sleepy way upstairs, carrying a book they all knew he would never stay awake long enough to read, and inspiring them all with envy.

After her youngest child was born, Charlotte had suffered a bout of insomnia so severe that she actually became physically ill. It was a time in her life that she still looked back on with apprehension; nevertheless, she was grateful for it, too, because it had led her back to Christian Science. Baird was only four at the time, the baby just a few weeks old. She had truly lost her wits, hardly knowing who she was. (At one point she even considered the possibility that she was someone else, an older woman who suffered from numbness in all her extremities and who rode buses in endless loops around the city.) The children needed all of her attention, yet she found it impossible to focus. She would wander off in search of a diaper and find herself in the basement, looking for a broom, or wake up at night, ravenous, and begin baking, then leave the batter to collapse in the bowl while she went to look up the fifth monarch of England in her college history text. Perversely, a sinister idea began to take hold: She would die if she slept, if she let go. In the wink of an eye she would go from constant, unwavering, unblinking consciousness to absolute extinction.

She became painfully aware of her pulse, coming to regard it as a fragile lifeline. Her heart skipped beats. Her skin went from its normal lightly freckled pallor to a dead papery white. She grew thinner and more angular. Her small flat face, grown luminous with anxiety, became a white disk lost in a cloud of red hair; her fingernails cracked; she bumped into things. Her sisters called daily, asking for updates on her condition. She couldn't make decisions; she felt angry at the baby. She felt afraid. Melvin worried about her safety and the safety of the children, and he hired a girl, Gretel, to stay in the house with her when he was gone. He was just starting his souvenir business then and was spending a lot of time in Vermont taking his "scenics," which is what he called his seasonal photographs.

He claimed she was a hazard to them all, and she agreed, yet she couldn't seem to gain control of her actions. He even suggested that she cut her hair—she had never cut it, not once, not even when the craze for bobs overtook her sisters. It tumbled down over her back, a luscious coppery waterfall that reached well below her waist. There was so much of it, people turned to stare at her on the street, dazzled by all that hair. It influenced everything she did—the careful way she turned her head; the pretty way she perched instead of sat, with her back held straight; the peculiar way she walked, at the same time awkward and graceful, like a heron picking its way from rock to rock along a shallow river. And of course, wherever she went, she left it behind her—on people's furniture, on their clothes, in their mouths—and in her own house, on her own clothes. She came across the long red strands a hundred times in the course of a day, like her own secret tracks; if she ever committed a murder, she had once told Melvin, she would have to wear a hair net.

Cutting it, he had argued, would help her sleep; it wouldn't pull at her in the night and wake her up. It had frightened her, hearing him say that. When they were so in love—when they filled the whole world for each other, when it wasn't big enough to contain them—he had called her long hair his ocean, his heaven, his coppery earth.

At his insistence, she made an appointment with a doctor in downtown Syracuse. Young Dr. Jericho listened to her story, examined her cursorily, and concluded that she needed to relax.

"I'm trying to relax," she told him. "I'm trying to sleep. I'm trying everything."

He snapped her file shut. "Not everything, Mrs. McGuffey. You are a young and beautiful woman. Why not try enjoying life? Ask your husband to take you to the movies."

The movies! How dare he! Here she was, desperate, half out of her mind, and he told her to go to the movies! Walking back to the bus stop on Genesee Street after her appointment, she passed a Christian Science reading room and paused to look through the plate-glass window. She had not considered herself a Scientist since her marriage to Melvin ten years earlier, when she was a student and living at home with her sister Rosey and her father, a classics professor and the author of two slim volumes of poetry written in strict and regular recurrence of quantitatively long and short syllables.

The Bible and the *Science and Health* lay open side by side on a green velvet cloth. Passages from the current week's lesson had been underlined in powder-blue marker on both their pages. The underlined passage in the *Science and Health* was well known to Charlotte and featured the Porter, a curious figure who had accrued special significance in her imagination as a child:

> *Stand porter at the door of thought. Admitting only such conclusions as you wish realized in bodily results, you will control yourself harmoniously. . . . The issues of pain or pleasure must come through mind, and like a watchman forsaking his post, we admit the intruding belief, forgetting that through divine help we can forbid this entrance.*

Her father had had an ancient model train set that he kept hidden in his bedroom—perhaps not exactly hidden, but it had seemed so to Charlotte, since why else would a grown-up keep such a thing to himself? He kept it on his big desk in a corner of the bedroom, covered up by a woven white shawl of his wife's, along with his Science books and periodicals and stacks of "Home Forum" pages from the *Monitor*. When she was sure she was alone in the house, Charlotte had sometimes stolen into his room to look at the little figures, at the gloomy station house, the corroding tracks and bridges and railroad cars. The little figures that belonged to the set were dark and mysterious and made of a hard rubber material: Among them were a conductor, an engineer, a flagman, a flagman's wife (they had the same startled expression), and a porter, whose red trousers sported a military crease. His face was creamy brown, and on his shoulder was a curious lump of deteriorating rubber with a long cinnamon-colored tail, and in her imagination, Charlotte had construed it to be a sweet little monkey who whispered naughty things.

Standing at the window, feeling the mesmerizing pull of Mrs. Eddy's soothing, familiar words, made softer and sweeter by the velvet cloth beneath the book, Charlotte had been seized by a powerful longing for her mother. Charlotte was ten at the time of her mother's death; protected by her family's belief that disease and death were essentially illusions, and that the inevitable outcome of every sickness was the good health her family members took for granted, she had remained unaware of much of the drama taking place in the house during her mother's illness. Her mother's bewildering behavior toward the end was enveloped in mist. Only certain smells brought her mother back, and the image of her strong, beautiful hands.

Charlotte remembered the peace she'd felt as she sat with her family in the little church they attended on Sundays, the quiet rustling of people's clothes at the Wednesday evening testimonial services, the lilt in her sister Kitty's voice as she read aloud to her family from Mrs. Eddy's works on Sunday evenings.

When Charlotte was twenty and newly married and just barely starting on a life of her own, Kitty was already a licensed Christian Science practitioner. She had completed all of her classes at the Mother Church in Boston at the exceptionally young age of thirty-two and had started a small practice out of her home. Kitty had always had an advanced understanding. Even as a child, she had been a dedicated Scientist, performing healing ceremonies on squashed bugs and droopy baby birds, giving testimonies in church in her reedy little girl's voice, sitting beside their mother's bed in the dark and praying with her whenever she got one of her nervous spells.

The reading room was very clean and nearly deserted. A Mrs. Helen Wade Rounds was on duty that day, wearing an expensive-looking maroon suit with a loose-fitting jacket that was held in place by only one button, as if there were other, more ineffable forces at work to keep it closed. She had looked up, smiling, and handed Charlotte a copy of Mrs. Eddy's book. "Take this," she had said. "This will help."

After reading the first three pages on the living-room couch, Charlotte had fallen fast asleep. Hours later she woke in the darkness to the smell of baking potatoes as Melvin, in the kitchen with the children,

prepared their supper. She lay there a long time, enveloped in a delicious
drowsiness, and listened to their voices—Baird's high-pitched, childish
tones, Mel's low somber ones, Hoskins's erratic infant sounds—and was
filled with gratitude for God's power to heal, and for heavenly sleep.

When she went back to the reading room the next day to thank Mrs.
Rounds, the white-haired woman behind the desk said she'd never heard
of her. After the testimonial service Charlotte attended the following
Wednesday, the usher shook his head solemnly. No, he didn't know of
her. Charlotte took it as a sign and came to think of it as part of her healing: the visitation of Mrs. Rounds, with her one button, her soft, powdery
skin, her utter confidence. In her writings, Mrs. Eddy defined angels as
God's representatives, and that seemed like a perfect description of Helen
Wade Rounds: She had materialized out of nowhere at just the right
time, offering Mrs. Eddy's healing words at the exact moment when
Charlotte needed them, and then simply disappeared.

Charlotte sat up, quickly undoing her braid. When she lay back down
again, Melvin stirred beside her. She held her breath, listening intently
and willing all her muscles to be still. The last thing she wanted to do was
to wake him prematurely.

The Porter arrived at once, looking dapper in his red jacket. Surprisingly, his fingernails were dirty, and then she saw why: He had been
shining his shoes, or perhaps it was her shoes, or perhaps another passenger's. He held the dirty rag loosely in one hand and bowed slightly. Was
there something contemptuous in his little smile? They had a rocky relationship; sometimes it went smoothly, sometimes not.

She directed him to close the door against the images that had been
trying to invade her consciousness all night: Baird in the bathtub, his
soapy hair sticking up in comical shapes; Hoskins struggling in his
father's arms as they climbed the stairs; Melvin plunging him into the
bath; Baird's wild laughter. She had rocked Hoskins to sleep, rocking and
singing until her arms grew numb from the little boy's weight. When she
finally set him down in his bed, he sank into sleep like a stone in a

riverbed, without a twitch or a ripple. An hour later, when she went to check on him, he still hadn't stirred. He was lying on his back, palms up, fingers softly curled. There were faint dark circles under his eyes, making him look fragile and exhausted. She said a silent prayer before she left, asking God to comfort him and make him forget his moment of terror. Somehow, she vowed, she would make sure it never happened again.

When the faint light in the bedroom was uniform, she got up. She felt grainy and raw, weary to the bone. She put on her thick red robe, giving the belt an extra tug for increased purpose and strength, and peeked into the boys' room on her way downstairs. The closet door stood ajar, just as they always left it, so that the light would fall on the floor at the certain angle insisted upon by Hoskins before he would consider going to sleep. One of their parental chores at his bedtime was readjusting the closet door to his satisfaction. Sometimes Baird would move the door a little after they left the room, but not enough so that anyone but Hoskins could tell. When they got there in response to Hoskins's screams, Baird would be buried under the covers, feigning sleep. He was snoring lightly now, his arm thrust out over the side of the bed, and in the mysterious light of the bedroom, his arm seemed to glow a little.

Charlotte crept down the stairs and went through the swinging door into the kitchen, pausing a moment before turning on the light. Her eyeballs hurt. Her heart was fluttering. How was she going to make it through the day?

She let out the dog, standing in the cold air at the back door while he relieved himself against a mound of snow. Hannibal was an English setter, with belton markings; his silky coat was white with light orange ticking, and barely perceptible against the white snow. It had been snowing on and off for a week; more had fallen during the night. The spruce was laden, its branches drooping.

Hannibal hurried back into the kitchen, leaping lightly over the camera equipment Mel had piled by the door. Charlotte filled the thermos with hot tap water, started the coffee on the stove, searched in the back of the cupboard for a clean cup. It had been several days since she'd done the dishes, and most of them were in the sink, where a web of iridescent grease floated on top of the water.

Then she sat down at the table in the breakfast nook and rehearsed her lines while she waited for Melvin to come down.

His itinerary was propped up against the salt shaker: "Leave Syracuse at 7 A.M., Friday, December 12, 1952. . . ." He always dated even the most informal of notes—he loved keeping records. In his heart he was a scientist, though with a small *s,* of course. He dated all his shopping lists as well, and every picture he ever took, noting the time, the lens setting, and the position of the sun, or the absence thereof. Next to the dates on his itinerary he had listed the names of the places he intended to photograph, the most important being the church in Beede, the village where he had grown up. The members of the First Methodist Church of Beede always waited for him to come up and take his Christmas picture before setting up the outdoor life-size crèche, which was too modern for the traditional images he preferred. Leona Cake, who was the postmistress and generally the one who saw that things got done right, made sure that Mel got what he wanted. She liked to say that it was Melvin McGuffey who single-handedly had made Beede's First Methodist the most photographed church, not just in the state of Vermont, but in all of America.

Charlotte thought it might even be true. Melvin had photographed the church in every light, in every season, its graceful spire silhouetted against the hillside, the stand of sugar maples behind it variously aflame or dormant or ebullient with springtime buds. He always took his pictures from the same spot, a small turnoff on the road that led up to the old McGuffey place, which is what the local people always called the house on McCrillis Hill that Mel and Charlotte had inherited from Mel's parents some years earlier; it was unclear whether the *old* referred to the house or the McGuffeys. Since the village fire the summer before, which had wiped out the graceful old building that had housed the Weavers' store (quickly replaced by a hideous prefab from New Hampshire) and left painful scorch marks on the back of the Wyndams' house, Melvin had had to adjust his viewfinder to eliminate these eyesores—which he did, competently and creatively, with the same sure hand he used with all his photography.

He called his souvenir business the Vermont Scene Company of Syracuse, New York, which he had named partly in jest, hardly expecting the commercial success that would follow. He had a knack, as it turned out, for marketing as well as for capturing pristine beauty. His popular images appeared everywhere, on place mats, greeting cards, calendars, ashtrays, shot glasses, key rings, postcards, cardboard jigsaw puzzles, trays, clock faces, playing cards. When he saw his pictures on cheap tea towels and date books in souvenir shops, he was always embarrassed. But it was a lucrative business, and he was tired of babies and weddings, he told Charlotte, and anyway, he liked tromping around Vermont's countryside. The photographs he took before the war for the Farm Security Administration had been long in storage, and he never looked at them.

The radiators all over the house began their clanging. Charlotte heard Melvin get up, go down the hall to the bathroom, close the bathroom door. She monitored his footsteps as he returned to the bedroom with his toiletries, imagined him snapping the little brown case shut, buttoning his tartan shirt, pulling his favorite gray sweater over his head.

He came down the stairs, walked toward the kitchen. Her heart lurched as he came through the door with his suitcase. Her saliva had dried up, and she couldn't speak.

Melvin searched through the cupboard for a cup, found one in the back, and poured himself some coffee. His movements were brisk, energetic; he loved his trips to Vermont, at any time of year, in any weather. "Did you sleep?" he asked.

"Did I keep you awake?"

"I noticed some activity. You sat up."

"I sat up?"

"For a minute."

"I undid my braid. It was bothering me."

He leaned back against the counter with his coffee, smiling. "Really? What was it doing?"

She took a breath, and didn't answer.

"I was making a joke," he said finally.

She got up to feed Hannibal, who was watching Melvin's every move; he knew the signs of a trip, and knew he was being left behind. "Don't bother feeding him now, Charlotte. He knows I'm going, and he won't eat. You can feed him after I go." She sat back down, feeling defeated. He poured the hot water out of the thermos, filled it with coffee, capped it, set it aside. "I got through to Leona last night," he said. "Orrin's in the hospital again."

"Same thing?" she asked, trying to keep her voice light, and he nodded. Orrin Poole was their caretaker in Vermont. Orrin always had some calamity going on, a mysterious combination of arthritis, heart trouble, engine trouble, and what they thought he was calling "bad deeds," but which they had finally decided was "bad dreams." He'd looked after the place on McCrillis Hill for Mel's parents for years, and now he did the same for Mel and Charlotte. In the winters he kept the driveway plowed and the snow off the roof, but this year he had hardly been there. Too many bad dreams.

"Leona will try to get someone there today to plow. If Johnny can't do it, she'll try Eugene. She said there must be three feet of snow. . . . I may have to snowshoe in." He paused. "Are you sure you're all right?"

She nodded, feeling hopeless. "I'm fine."

"You're still angry about last night."

She shook her head.

"I'm sorry, Charlotte. I lost my temper."

He'd come to the doorway of their bedroom where she was rocking Hoskins and offered a kind of an apology. He was at his wit's end, he said. It was time to ask for help. She told him it wasn't the time to discuss it; it was never a good time for her, he said; she was forever avoiding such a discussion. After a while, when she didn't answer, he withdrew.

"It's not that," she said.

"Well, something's wrong; you should see your face."

She focused on breathing. Air in, air out; it was going in, but it wasn't reaching her lungs. All she had to do was say, *Something's wrong with us, Mel.* "The problem is," she said, speaking very slowly and carefully, "we don't have a tree."

"We don't have a tree?" he repeated, incredulous.

"A Christmas tree."

"That's why you look so distressed, because we don't have a Christmas tree?"

"It isn't just that."

"What is it, then?" He stared at her, waiting.

Another opportunity. *It's us.* Just two words. Her hair, which she had wrapped in a loose wheel at the back of her head, was coming undone in little spurts. Three breaths. Three heartbeats, booming. "It's us," she said softly. *Alea iacta est.* The die is cast. For a minute she thought perhaps he hadn't actually heard her, but his expression told her he had. There was no going back. Caesar crossed the Rubicon and headed toward Pompeii, defying the senate and so commencing the civil war. "I've made up my mind that we should separate," she said, heading toward the ancient city, finding the steady rhythm from her perch on the animal's back.

He stared at her, his gray eyes changing color, and she knew that he was already at work, building his own defenses. He had to, just as she had to go forward, to plow through, to reach the real battleground. "I've thought about it, and this is what I want," she said.

"What about the children? Have you thought about them?"

"It will be better for them in the long run."

"Is it someone else? Someone at school?"

"No, Mel, it's nobody else."

"What about that fellow with the roadster?" He spit out the last word, showing his contempt.

One day another student had given her a ride home after class, and she had invited him in while she searched for a book. Melvin had come home unexpectedly that afternoon and had interpreted her surprise as guilt. *No explanation necessary,* he'd told her, waving her away brusquely, but she knew what he thought. "There's no one, Mel, I swear. It's not like that. We live in a house divided against itself."

He exploded into a harsh laugh. "Oh, baloney, Charlotte! What a time to be quoting Abraham Lincoln!"

"It comes from the Book of Luke. It's from the Bible."

"So what! What difference does it make where it comes from?"

"Please lower your voice," she said quickly. "The children will hear you."

"And have you thought about them? You have no idea what you're up against with Hoskins. Getting rid of me is not the answer."

His tone was sarcastic, and she was glad for the little shove it gave her past her next moment of doubt. "It will be better for them in the long run."

"And for you?"

"I'm not trying to *get rid* of you."

"You're not?"

She felt herself teetering at the edge of a large open space. "It will be easier without all this confusion between us."

"Which kind of confusion is that? I'd be curious. Is it your principles or your feelings that cause you this confusion?"

She had to say *feelings*. Then he wouldn't argue, because she would have said she didn't love him anymore. "My feelings," she said.

"Somehow I doubt that you know what they are." He turned away, took his leather jacket off the hook, put his hat on his head. "If you want to reach me, you can call Leona at the post office and leave a message. I'll check in with her." He dropped his cup into the sink. "If you think about this a little more, you may change your mind—the boys will miss me, Charlotte, even if you don't. Maybe my absence will help. Then you'll see what it's like to manage alone." He went through the door. His cup bobbled around in the greasy water for a moment and then sank.

"Be careful," she whispered, watching him pick his way through the new snow, weighted down by his equipment. When he reached the garage, he opened the door and began loading his truck. She looked at the clock. It was seven exactly.

CHAPTER

2

An hour later Charlotte and Baird were playing their breakfast game with Hoskins. The younger boy was swirling the brown sugar around in his oatmeal with his finger, and Charlotte was trying not to notice. "How old is Hoskins?" she asked, keeping her voice bright and cheerful despite the ringing in her ears and a desperate thirst that water couldn't seem to quench.

Baird answered for him, loud and clear. "Three!"

"How old are you, honey?" she prompted. Hoskins looked away with a shy smile. He was a beautiful child. He'd had exceptional physical beauty from the moment of his birth—everyone commented on it, even the nurse as she'd handed him to Charlotte, his perfect features showing no signs of his long struggle to be born. Everybody said he looked like the Ivory baby, with his big blue eyes, his rosy complexion and golden-red curls, his lips sweet and full and perfectly formed, but Charlotte knew otherwise; the Ivory baby was simple, Hoskins was deep. The Ivory baby was easy to love, Hoskins was an enigma.

Baird held three fingers aloft in a Cub Scout salute. "Say three, Sniksoh."

"Please, Baird, you know I hate it when you call him that."

"But you don't hate anything!" he said, his mouth full of cinnamon toast.

"Of course I don't. But I don't like it, and you know it."

"It's just his name backward. It's the same name."

Charlotte took note of his smug look and decided to ignore it. Recently he had alerted her that when he called her Mom he just might be saying her name backward, making her wonder where a seven-year-old could possibly have learned about palindromes.

Hoskins had been named after Charlotte's maternal grandfather, T. E. Hoskins, the Boston manufacturer of ship hulls, and it was a nearly insurmountable effort to keep people from shortening it, or twisting it, or ignoring it entirely—Winston Berry, the minister at the Presbyterian church next door, and their closest neighbor, called him "Champ." Gretel called him "Buddy." Harry Clatter, Kitty's husband, called him "Spike."

"Say it, sweetheart, say 'three,'" she said wearily.

Hoskins held up the Cub Scout salute that Baird had taught him on his third birthday.

"No, honey, say it. Say 'three.'"

The boy took a big breath and held it. He smiled expectantly.

"Go ahead, sweetheart. Say *three.* You can do it."

His eyes shining merrily, Hoskins slowly lowered his head toward his cereal until his nose came to rest in the bowl. With a great satisfactory noise, he let go of his breath and blew out, splattering oatmeal everywhere.

Baird's school was only a short distance away, but it was across a busy street, and Charlotte always walked him there and picked him up, or else she sent Gretel, if it was one of the days when Charlotte was in class. Gretel had stayed on to work for the McGuffeys after Charlotte's bad time—her *grande crise,* Charlotte sometimes called it laughingly—though the girl now functioned as a baby-sitter. She was loyal, very dependable—plodding, actually—and ever vigilant. Nonetheless, Charlotte suspected that her experience as a guard had tainted her with a sense of superiority, and she was careful in what she said to Gretel, lest the girl take some silly remark seriously and report signs of another period of encroaching dementia to Melvin.

Hoskins followed a few paces behind with Hannibal, whom Melvin had trained to trot along at his side without a leash. Baird was talking excitedly about the Christmas party at school, which was four days away. His second-grade teacher, Miss Gallagher, would be choosing one of her students that morning to be Santa Claus and to hand out the packages at the party. He hoped desperately that she would choose him. "I think she might," he said, forging ahead over the ridges on the snowy sidewalk.

Charlotte agreed that she very well might, and Baird showed her a horse chestnut he'd had in his coat pocket. "It's good luck. Norman gave it to me."

Norman was Kitty's boy, a little more than a year older than Baird. "That's being superstitious, Baird."

"He got skates."

"Oh, honey! Norman got skates because your Aunt Kitty bought them for him! It had nothing to do with collecting chestnuts; that was just a coincidence. And it has nothing to do with your teacher picking you to play Santa Claus."

"You don't think Miss Gallagher will pick me."

"But I do!" Charlotte said brightly. "And I know how to make sure it happens!"

"What's that?" Baird asked suspiciously.

"Grow a beard. Then Miss Gallagher will be sure to pick you."

"I can't grow a beard!"

"Well, it would work, wouldn't ɪᴛ? Especially if it was long and white."

"How could I grow a beard?"

"I don't know," she said, picking up her pace and scooting ahead of him. "I've never been able to do it myself."

"You can't grow a beard; you're a girl!" Baird said, laughing and running after her.

When he caught up with her, she put an arm around his shoulders and urged him never to change, not ever, not one iota, no matter what. "Promise?" she said.

"Okay, not one iota," he repeated, and he let her keep her arm where it was until the end of the block.

As they approached the chain-link fence around the schoolyard, Charlotte reached for Hoskins's hand, holding it tight until the bell sounded and Baird ran into the building with the throngs of other children. As soon as the playground was empty, she released him and he flew to the fence, running silently along the top of the packed snow and racing along one side as fast as he could, then turning and running back, the cold air turning his breath into wispy little clouds. He ran swiftly and silently, intent on keeping an even pace; he was a graceful child and hardly ever stumbled or fell. He began his course again as Charlotte waited, gazing upward at the snowflakes falling lightly from the sky, allowing Hoskins the time he needed to express his exhilaration at life in his own peculiar way.

He was almost three and a half, and he still didn't talk. Or at least he didn't talk to his family. He talked to the dented green bucket Melvin had found for him while bicycling home from work one day, to the various objects he collected in it, to bugs on the sidewalk, to birds in the air—but never to them. He used words whose private meaning they couldn't fathom—*butter beans* and *Leviticus* and *mercy me*—words and phrases he used interchangeably for all manner of things, defying their ability to break the code. And all his road signs and traffic talk: *how to make a left turn; a red light is next; traffic proceed; traffic stop*—phrases from the 1952 New York State driver's manual, which he insisted someone read to him night after night. And if it wasn't that, it was the worn copy of *Small Appliance Repair* or the instruction book that came with Charlotte's sewing machine.

Baird claimed to understand his little brother, often acting as his self-appointed interpreter in order to communicate Hoskins's "requests" for ice cream or permission for both of them to stay up late. Every once in a while Hoskins would blurt out a word they were sure he could never have heard, like the time he said "Fenbendazole" very clearly and distinctly to his plate after supper. After a little research, Mel had discovered that it was the name of a new bovine wormer on the market.

Nearly everyone wanted to discuss his "problem" and to suggest a cure, or to speculate on the reasons for his odd behavior. Charlotte had to be constantly on guard against such thoughts, silently refuting suggestions of Hoskins's imperfection with prayers and reasserting his true identity as a perfect child of God. Privately, though, her heart ached. When Baird was Hoskins's age, he was always talking. He had wanted to know everything—the names of things, how they worked, what their purpose was. He wanted to engage her in talk; he wanted her attention. "What's happening?" Baird would ask in his babyish accent. "What are you talking about?" Whereas Hoskins wanted to know how things tasted, or how they felt when he rubbed them on his head. He wandered about with his bucket, carefully selecting objects for further study—they called these his "investigations," as if he were a young scientist going about the natural world gathering specimens, and wondered at his purpose.

He was clever about getting what he wanted. Either he led them to it silently, or else he waited and got it himself, without their permission. He was remarkably agile and could climb any kind of structure without falling. His sense of direction was excellent, too, and he could retrace the most complicated routes, which was a blessing in a way, since he so often disappeared without warning. One minute he'd be right there with them, and in the next, he'd be heading confidently toward the farthest tree or the highest hill. Or he would simply be standing behind a door, breathing carefully lest they discover him. He didn't want to be found.

Again and again, he demonstrated an almost reckless disregard for danger. The first time that a strange dog approached him, the hairs stiff along its back, Hoskins had clapped his hands and run toward it as if it were a long-awaited guest. Charlotte had lunged after him, calling out, and stopped short when she saw the dog licking his face. He had surprising affinities for people, too, like their trash man, Mr. Berks, a fierce little man with bent legs who talked loud enough to wake the dead and who had tufts of white hair sprouting out of his ears. The old man would cavort around in their driveway with trash barrels, heaving their contents into his truck as though they were as light as a feather. Whereas Baird shrank from any contact with the peculiar fellow, Hoskins would rush outside, or in bad weather he would rush to the window, waving and laughing with delight as Mr. Berks loaded up the trash.

He laughed at Mr. Berks, but not at the things most three-year-olds laughed at. He didn't like to be tickled, or bounced on his uncle Harry's knee, and he hated peekaboo games and jack-in-the-boxes and other sudden surprises. He liked to be sung to, but he was particular, and he would shake his head violently if Charlotte began a song he didn't like. He was especially fond of rousing war tunes, like "When Johnny Comes Marching Home," or "Praise the Lord and Pass the Ammunition," and he'd listen to them happily as he leaned against Charlotte's leg, absently patting her skirt as she ran through her repertoire.

His hearing was phenomenal; on summer evenings in Vermont, he would cock his head and listen long before the rest of them heard the hermit thrush at dusk, before they heard the thunder. He would sometimes press his ear against the wall and listen intently with that characteristically solemn expression of his, his blue eyes large and thoughtful, or sit for hours in the long grass listening to the noises of the field like an opera lover made ecstatic by the privilege of a private concert by Caruso. Longing to know what he was hearing, Charlotte made a set of watercolor pictures for him so that when he seemed to be listening to something she herself couldn't hear, she could show him the little stack of cards: a calico cat puffed up in alarm, a river rushing down a mountain, a little windup clock with a funny face, a happy-looking truck hauling gravel in the city. Instead of being delighted, however, he merely looked at them with disdain. *Why must I tell you?* he seemed to be saying.

Secretly, she hoped the cards would help him talk. It was her own way of intervening in the outcome, though she understood it was up to God. When she told Kitty about them, feeling actually rather proud, especially of the calico cat with its multicolored fur all standing on end along its back, Kitty had cautioned her to stand guard against the temptations of a mother's ambition—there was nothing that she, as his human mother, could do to improve on Hoskins's perfect spiritual nature. Her role was to know with all her heart that he was the perfect image and likeness of God, and to let go of the idea that he needed any human help. Only then would his perfection be manifested. But Charlotte was feeling contrary that day and had pointed out to her sister that if that were always the case and it was wrong to try to improve a child's mind with learning, then why was Kitty a teacher? Kitty had laughed, surprised, and said, *When in Rome, do as the Romans do*. It was simply a job, she went on to explain. Being on this earth, and with a family to support, she needed to work. Harry was working through something—whatever the label was, wasn't important—and in the meantime, she was the bread earner. Her work as a practitioner did not bring in the income her family needed.

Her too-patient tone had irritated Charlotte, and she had wanted to point out that Mrs. Eddy herself had apparently not been able to see her own child as perfect, since he had interfered with her work as a healer and she'd had to give him away. She had farmed him out and then forgotten him. But Charlotte's challenges to Kitty were always short-lived, and she held her tongue. She knew that Kitty considered Mrs. Eddy's act a sacrifice for a higher calling. But Charlotte couldn't think of any calling high enough for her to give Hoskins to someone else to raise. Mrs. Eddy had defined children as "spiritual thoughts," part of that harmonious flow between potter and pot, maker and creation, yet it was the material reality that made Charlotte love Hoskins, especially his sweet little eyebrows, so often crinkled into a studious frown.

When Hoskins turned three and still wasn't talking, Melvin insisted that they make an appointment with the elderly Dr. Ludlow to discuss the boy's language problem. *(Can't we call it a preference?* Charlotte had pleaded. *Why make it such a negative thing?)* Dr. Ludlow had seen the boys for routine checkups and inoculations since birth. Melvin wasn't a Christian Scientist, and he and Charlotte had long ago worked out an agreement about the children's medical care: Charlotte would in no way subject them to any risk. Melvin, in turn, would allow her to bring up the children in her religion and cease (as much as he was able) his critical remarks. Fortunately, both boys were blessed with natural good health and had rarely suffered any illness more serious than the sniffles. Baird had bouts of a raspy cough, but it didn't seem to bother him, and it always disappeared after a few days. Hoskins was the picture of health. Both had had light cases of the chicken pox and measles, which had required little more than commonsense treatment with bed rest and liquids.

To their great surprise that day, Dr. Ludlow had recommended that they take Hoskins to a psychologist. The boy was a physically healthy specimen, Dr. Ludlow claimed, and perfectly normal in his mental development, as far as he could tell. His problem was psychological and most likely had to do with his mother.

Both Melvin and Charlotte were stunned. Melvin rose to her defense in front of the doctor, but at home he announced a new regime: They would no longer give in to the boy's moods or overlook his wayward behavior. The key lay in their expectations. By not demanding that he talk, they were preventing him from growing up. Not so, said Charlotte. He was an unusual child with unusual gifts. He needed patience, not training; understanding, not discipline. They needed to recognize his sensitive nature; he kept his ear pressed to the pulse of the earth, and knew things they didn't know, heard things they couldn't hear. Baloney, said Melvin. He was spoiled. He needed what every child needed: structure, discipline, routine.

The new regime brought harrowing tantrums. For months, they had lived on edge, never knowing when he would erupt. It seemed even the slightest frustration could set him off. At other times, when they denied him something he clearly wanted, they would brace themselves and then he would surprise them by riding through the moment with grace, but the stress was the same, the exhaustion, the aftermath of alarm. After these episodes he always fell into a deep sleep, like a spent lover, as he had done the previous evening.

She'd left the dinner dishes to soak and had gone upstairs to wash Baird's hair while Mel read to Hoskins from the driver's manual. When she called down to say they were ready, Hoskins had started screaming.

Normally, he liked his bath. They'd been having a fine time, Mel had assured her later, or at least as fine a time as you could have reading about road signs and stopping distances. He had carried the struggling boy upstairs, Hoskins hanging on as though for dear life to the handle of his battered green bucket. It clattered against the stairway wall, and Charlotte had rushed out to see what was the matter. When she saw how upset he was, she'd shouted at Mel to let him go, but he'd insisted on carrying out his mission, and when they reached the bathroom he had plunged the boy into the water. Hoskins flailed away in his father's arms, then bit his wrist. Melvin had gasped in surprise and grabbed for the bucket, filling it with water and pouring it over Hoskins's head. The boy coughed and struggled to get free, and for a moment—for just a split second, but long enough to register—Charlotte thought Melvin was going to drown him.

After Melvin stopped in the doorway to offer his halting apology (and then had waited for her forgiveness, which she hadn't offered), Baird had soon appeared in his place. It had been his turn for reading with his father downstairs and in his arms he held his own favorite books, ordinary, lovable, familiar children's books like *Andy the Musical Ant* and *Tree at the End of the Trail*. His wet hair was parted cleanly on one side and combed into a little pompadour on top. His face was shiny and grave. Standing there in his felt slippers and tailored navy bathrobe, he'd looked like a sober little man. "Hoskins was bad," he said sadly, shaking his head.

"Not bad," she whispered. "He's not bad, Baird. You have to believe that."

"He makes a lot of trouble."

"He's little. He doesn't know any better."

"He's not so little," Baird said. "When we're in Daddy's truck, he can sit up tall enough to see out the window."

They walked home slowly, Hoskins trailing a few steps behind, the dog plodding along next to him. They came within sight of the big white church that bordered their property on Onondaga Hill, and then their own house, with green shutters and a row of dormers. It looked terribly empty. She had a final exam to take in just a few hours. She'd had no sleep. The brash light of a winter world hurt her eyes.

After helping Hoskins out of his snowsuit, Charlotte sat down at the rolltop desk in the living room and contemplated what she had to do. Hoskins came through the French doors with three cereal boxes in his arms. He liked to line up the boxes along the border of the carpet, working carefully and patiently, moving the first to the end of the line, then the second and the third, until eventually the entire border had been touched. He sat down, ready to begin. Hannibal lay down next to the shredded wheat.

Charlotte reached for her textbook—*Understanding Your World: Fundamentals of Science for Non-Science Majors*. She had to pass only this one course, which would satisfy her science requirement, and she would be done. She'd been waylaid in her academic career by various changes of major (from art to philosophy, history to English), then marriage and children. After reenrolling at the university, following Baird's birth, she'd ambushed herself with an alarming predilection for electives. She and Melvin had countless arguments about her erratic choices. He tore his hair at her random progress, her apparent lack of purpose. "Why don't you do one thing at a time?" he'd ask. "If you try to do too much, you won't do anything well."

She sometimes repeated this to herself unwittingly. She didn't like the thrust of the statement, but the words stuck in her mind, and she would catch herself applying them to herself throughout the day, as if she carried around inside her a critical little parrot trained by Melvin. She'd once called him "the Grand Panjandrum of efficiency." This cumbersome antiquity had rattled around their marriage for years, causing havoc.

He begged her to finish something—anything. She knew he was right; it was a lifelong weakness. The only thing that she had ever really finished, in a complete and absolute way, was the family tree she had embroidered at the age of eight, and that had been a disaster. It was a project of mythic dimensions, a finely wrought sampler illustrating the Baird family tree all the way back to Adam and Eve. It was as big as a bedsheet, and she carried it with her everywhere she went, wadded up into a ball and stuffed into a bag. The background material turned from white to ivory to gray as she worked her stitches, extracting from the bag only as much material as she needed at any one time. She never spread it out for anyone to look at. It took two years to complete and when she finished, she discovered that she'd misspelled the word *begat* throughout. She had been humiliated by her own ignorance and pride, and she had vowed to rip it out and start over. Her family pleaded with her to leave it be—it was fine, it was fine, nobody would ever notice. She had finally hidden it away in the attic behind the eaves; when she pulled it out many years later, she found that rust had accumulated in all the creases, moths had chewed through the embroidery thread, beetles had eaten holes in the fabric and then hidden in the folds.

When she'd chosen Dr. Gum's course in introductory physics, Melvin had groaned. She was being totally unrealistic. She professed to not even believe in the physical world. Why on Earth would she want to study the laws that governed it? "Why not botany?" he wanted to know. "Or Earth science? Why not volcanoes? Everyone understands volcanoes!" She'd laughed when he said that, and quickly apologized. She didn't really mean to, but she often hurt his feelings—though never to the grave extent she had this morning. She might as well have shot him through with poison arrows, and she felt sick.

She closed her eyes, remembering Mrs. Eddy's words: *Like a watchman forsaking his post, we admit the intruding belief, forgetting that through divine help we can forbid this entrance.* The intruding belief was fear. The bodily result was dry mouth, palpitations, dizziness. If she had made the right decision, wouldn't she feel better now? She imagined Melvin on his way to Vermont, his cheeks rosy, his glasses fogged as the old heater in the truck struggled to keep him warm. He was wearing the fedora that made him look so dashing. He was a handsome man, and he had beautiful eyes. She remembered the way they'd looked as he reacted to the shock of what she'd said. Her timing could not have been worse. Certainly she shouldn't have made her announcement just as he was on his way out the door, and right before Christmas. What a thing for her to do!

What if she phoned? She pictured his relief when Leona told him that she'd called. He'd ask to use the phone right away; he'd be nervous. She imagined them on the phone, each one waiting for the other to begin. It would be worse than the first time they went to the movies together, when they'd seen *You Can't Take It with You* and she'd spent the whole time worrying about setting her elbow on their shared armrest. Later, hearing that it had won an Academy Award, she hadn't been able to recall any of it.

He'd ask how her exam had gone. She would ask about the weather, the driving conditions. And then what? Silence. The post office in Beede, even if it was only Leona's front room, was a public place. The whole village could be listening.

Hoskins was shaking the Cheerios box, clearly delighted with the sound. She reached for it, and he deftly swiveled around out of her reach. She clapped her hands sharply. Hoskins ignored her, but the dog looked up, cocking his head quizzically.

What if she wrote? A letter would probably take four days to reach him. It was Friday; he would get it Tuesday, or maybe Wednesday. According to his itinerary, he would be in St. Johnsbury on Tuesday, returning to the village before dark, in plenty of time to stop at Leona's for the mail.

She felt nervous and afraid. The next instant, her Porter appeared, sensing her mood and her need for support. As he clicked his heels together, she noticed the tufts of white hair sprouting out of his ears, and marveled at the similarity to Mr. Berks. Was it something she'd never noticed before? Was it new? The unsightly tufts contributed only a small, but nonetheless disturbing, note to his otherwise unruffled demeanor. His appearance had always been impeccable—yet this morning, his fingernails had been dirty, and he had carried a dirty rag. Now, the ears.

He opened his mouth and then closed it again with a sharp intake of her breath. "You are engaged in wrong-thinking! Change your belief. Reverse the testimony of the senses. Tired? Bah! Nervous and afraid? Bah! Full of doubts? Bah! *You are a law unto yourself,* says Mother. You decide, and it shall be! *You will suffer in proportion to your belief and fear.* Reverse the case!"

"But . . . But what? But . . . what if . . ." She couldn't finish. Her tongue wasn't working. It was tied in knots, dry, swollen. . . .

"No buts! No ifs! No half-truths! No maybes, no don't-know-for-sure, no let-me-look-it-up. The Truth only, the whole Truth and nothing but the Truth so help you God. Admit it, you're afraid."

Yes, yes, he was right. She was afraid.

"Reverse the case! You're not afraid! You merely *think* you're afraid. And thinking makes it so—even that scoundrel Shakespeare knew that! Stand firm! Be true!"

Yes, that was her job, to reverse the case and counter false belief, not to doubt herself. Everything she needed to do, she would do with God's help. Melvin had said that she wouldn't be able to manage alone, but she wasn't alone.

CHAPTER

3

The lecture hall was still half empty, but Mr. Fan, Dr. Gum's graduate assistant, was already placing test booklets facedown on the tiered rows of seats that rose upward on the sloping floor. Dr. Gum, a recent scientific refugee from mainland China, liked to appear after the hall was full; like a theatrical pro, he would wait until the very last moment and then trot out from the wings toward the lectern in his crisp blue lab coat, beaming up at his students with an expression that was ripe with the expectation of their success.

Among the students beginning to filter into the hall was Irene Mason, a buxom and bubbly sophomore who had become a sudden celebrity after a panty raid on her sorority. In the photo that had appeared in *Life* magazine, the fun-loving Irene stood at a second-floor window with two other girls, laughing and showing off the knotted sheets the boys had used to climb up to their rooms. Wherever she went now, a crowd surrounded her.

At thirty, Charlotte was always one of the oldest students in her classes. Sometimes an ex-GI would join her in looking askance at the capers of their classmates, and they would form a loose but comfortable bond, exchanging wry smiles as the bobby-soxers in the front row broke out in giggles, or pampered boys in greasy pompadours swaggered into class with their dark looks and arrogant expressions, expecting to sweep the girls off their feet.

Mr. Fan started down her row. He handed her a booklet and made a V sign for *Victory*. She took the little blue book, smiling bleakly. He was wearing a truly awful argyle vest; an early Christmas present from his paper-thin wife, no doubt. Charlotte had met her because she had been to Mr. Fan's wretched student apartment, where he had tutored her for eight fruitless sessions.

A major part of Dr. Gum's course had to do with Newton's laws of motion and the pivotal concept of force as something that could be quantified. It was in this area that Charlotte faltered most profoundly. She labored away at home night after night, underlining all significant passages in her textbook. She memorized formulas and bought a slide rule, which she didn't know how to use. She bought a new notebook and copied all her notes onto its clean ruled pages, hoping desperately for enlightenment through transference. She pondered God as a force, the Divine Creator of all movement, whether quantified or not. Nothing helped. Whenever Mel asked how it was going, though, she would say, "Fine," with a breezy little lilt to her voice to indicate her surprise at the question itself. But inwardly, she was sure she would fail.

So she hadn't been surprised when Dr. Gum asked her to come to his office. They had just had their first quiz, and her grade, posted outside his office door, had been zero. Zero! He sprang up from his desk as she entered the small cluttered room, coming around and holding a chair for her. "Mrs. McGuffey," he said, giving her name an extra sibilant sound between the double *f*s. "It is a pleasure to see you." He paused significantly as she sat. "A very great pleasure." He sat down across from her, beaming. Lying on the desk in front of him was her examination booklet. She smiled at him, quietly waiting for the ax to fall.

"Mrs. McGuffey, if you will permit me, I wish to ask you a question."

"Of course," she said.

"It is about your motives."

"My motives?"

"You say 'motives'?"

"Well, yes, sometimes. It's a word." In the lecture hall, Dr. Gum often addressed his students this way, by calling for advice on his English. Usually the words themselves were correct, though the context made it bewildering.

"Very well. Now, let us acknowledge at once that you have beautiful hair."

She felt her face freeze. She had the insane feeling that he was going to ask to touch it. Occasionally, standing in the midst of a crowd, she would feel anonymous hands moving over her back; sometimes children asked to touch it, as if it were a pet in a petting zoo. Normally, though, grown-ups didn't ask. "Thank you," she said.

"It is heavy, perhaps?" he inquired politely.

"Sometimes, yes."

"Perhaps when it is wet, it is heavy because the water has weight?"

"I suppose so," she said.

"When it is wet, when it is dry, it has different weight."

Charlotte nodded.

"Do you agree?"

"I've never weighed it."

"But your experience tells you . . ."

"It *seems* heavier, yes."

He looked up, triumphant. "Yes? You agree?"

"I suppose."

"Good enough, Mrs. McGuffey! That is density, you understand? Very good!" He beamed at her.

"Thank you."

"Tell me, you enjoy Mr. Newton?" he asked, as if inquiring as to her opinion of some new radio personality.

"Somewhat," she said.

"Somewhat?"

"I like his wig." Seeing his puzzled look, she added, "There's a picture of Sir Isaac Newton in our textbook, wearing a wig."

"But his ideas? Are you not impressed with his ideas?"

"I don't know if *impressed* is the right word."

He took up his red pen and made a little row of dots on the cover of her test booklet. "Mrs. McGuffey, would you please tell me why do you take this course?"

It was hard to say, really. She had never believed in molecules as the foundation of matter, not from the first moment she'd heard about them—not molecules, or atoms, or neutrons, or any of those little things—yet she found the study of physics, its language and formulas, appealing in some way that was hard to explain. Its laws were so exotic, and so . . . *immutable* . . . or so she had discovered on the first quiz. One's answers, she had found, were either right or wrong—no discussion, no equivocation, no temporizing conditions or second thoughts . . . no excuses. No *arguments*. While he waited, Dr. Gum drew a line through the dots he'd made. Why, she asked herself, would most people take physics? "To better understand the laws of the physical world, Dr. Gum."

"That is a very, very good answer, Mrs. McGuffey!" He was thrilled, and she felt vaguely ashamed. "You perhaps have a keen desire to become a scientist one day?"

The bold words that came to her made her heart flutter. "I *am* a scientist, Dr. Gum," she said quietly.

"Oh! How is that?"

"I practice the science of the mind."

He looked at her blankly. "This is Mesmer? From Europe?"

"No. This is Mary Baker Eddy, from New Hampshire. Mrs. Eddy founded a religion that refutes the so-called laws of nature."

"'So-called.' What is this 'so-called'?"

"This world is not what it seems." Her heart was racing. She had never been so bold.

"This science you speak of, it is metaphysics, is it not?"

"It is science."

"It is founded on observation, and experimentation?"

"It is founded on the invariable laws of God. I believe that science is a tool for clarifying the truths of the spirit."

"Aha. Like the Englishman, Roger Bacon. He said that it is possible to believe both. Perhaps, only, you lack confidence in the physical world, and so you do not understand it. It is the same for me: When my wife asks me to boil the rice, I burn it, because I lack the confidence of a good cooker."

One rainy day, Charlotte had seen Dr. Gum hurrying across the campus with his wife. Dr. Gum was shoveling her along by the arm, more or less hopping on his short legs as he propelled her forward in front of him. She was holding a newspaper over her head, and Dr. Gum had the umbrella. "It's cook," she said automatically.

"You don't say 'cooker'?"

"No."

"But you say 'writer'; a writer writes, a dreamer dreams. But a cooker . . . no?"

"Not a cooker, Dr. Gum."

"Thank you." He took out a small notebook and wrote something down. "Now then," he said, smiling broadly, "you are very frank with me, Mrs. McGuffey, and I appreciate that. I wish to continue our discussion in the same spirit of candor." He picked up her test booklet. "I wish to discuss . . . well, it is a matter that perplexes me. Do you understand what thing I speak of?"

"I do know that I didn't do very well on my test. I mean, not very well *at all*."

"No, no, your grade is of no consequence; that is my failure as your instructor. The fault lies with me one hundred percent!" He hesitated. "You believe in percent?"

"Of course."

"Very good. The puzzlement is this, Mrs. McGuffey. On your exam you draw a picture of a man and woman dancing. This is Arthur Murray's technique?"

"Yes."

"Why do you draw it here?"

"Well, I had to put something. It just looked very blank. My answers were very short, almost nonexistent, if I remember correctly."

He waved her explanation away. "Mrs. McGuffey, is this perhaps a picture of us?"

She was stunned. "Dr. Gum! It's a *doodle!*" He cringed, flushing, and she apologized, clumsily, and was overridden by his counterapology. He had misunderstood her doddle, he said. It was most unseemly! *Doodle,* she said, again rushing to correct him before she could stop herself. "Doodling is just a friendly American habit," she said. "Like writing, 'Kilroy was here.'"

"Ah, yes, I have seen that. In the bathrooms," he added, and blushed.

Charlotte rose from the chair, mumbling something about working harder. Dr. Gum suggested a tutor. He would ask his graduate assistant, Mr. Fan. She opened the door.

"Unfortunately, Mr. Fan is an idiot." He paused. "Perhaps, you would like me to tutor you myself?"

"No, no! Mr. Fan will be fine!"

"Then I will arrange it." Dr. Gum bowed low and with great dignity. "Mr. Fan it will be."

Mr. Fan lived in a small student apartment off Clinton Square, which he shared with his pretty wife, also a graduate student in physics, and their spider monkey, Stu, a cinnamon-colored monkey who wore diapers and who was obviously greatly loved by his owners. Every once in a while the monkey would blink rapidly and bare his teeth, which, Mr. Fan told Charlotte, meant that he was smiling. Stu had free rein of the apartment, and during the sessions he stayed put by an ancient velvet couch, pulling the stuffing out and scrutinizing it as though looking for nits. When the lesson was over, Mrs. Fan always served cookies. As she entered the room with her lacquered tray, Stu would jump up excitedly and sail toward her in a beautiful arc, landing on her shoulder, and Mrs. Fan would whisper, "Our bad little monkey," and hand him a cookie from the plate, a sequence of events that baffled Charlotte.

At Mr. Fan's suggestion, Charlotte brought Hoskins and Baird to her last session so that they could meet the monkey.

Mrs. Fan greeted them at the apartment door, wearing a fancy blue silk dress. Mr. Fan was holding Stu, who wore a tiny New York Yankees baseball shirt as well as his usual diapers. Baird reached out tentatively and patted him on his head. Hoskins, wide-eyed, put his hands behind his back. Mr. Fan put the monkey down, and Stu skipped away to work on the couch.

Mrs. Fan sat the boys at a card table covered with a white paper cloth, which she invited them to draw on with the crayons she had laid out. In the center she placed her tray of cookies. Baird looked at Charlotte, and Charlotte nodded. *Yes, fine, help yourself.* Hoskins had already broken his cookie in two and was starting to construct a tower.

Charlotte and Mr. Fan sat side by side on metal folding chairs and went over her notes for the final exam. She listened as Mr. Fan painstakingly explained, yet again, that energy was the capacity to do work. When Charlotte made a face, Mr. Fan suggested they talk about their rock.

The rock they often discussed was large and heavy and was poised at the brink of a precipice—at the top of a waterfall, Charlotte insisted. ("A waterfall is good," said the agreeable Mr. Fan.) There, it had potential energy. Once it started falling, the rock had kinetic energy, the magnitude of which equaled the work required to raise it back to its original position. ("I see a man in his undershirt moving the rock," Charlotte would murmur. "He's completely soaked.") The work required to get the rock back up on the precipice was exactly *mv squared,* Mr. Fan would say, smiling politely as he waited for her to object.

"It is always the same: mass times velocity squared," he explained now. "That is the formula to remember."

"I just don't see it, Mr. Fan. I'm sorry. That's the part I don't get."

Mr. Fan sighed. "It is not necessary, always, to understand. It is necessary only to believe."

"To me, well, I can remember it only if I can *see* it. I can't *see* mass or velocity."

"We have agreed, I believe, that it takes more energy to move a rock than a feather—" Mr. Fan stopped, astounded, as the monkey flew through the air with a shrill screech, landing with a crash on the card table. Baird rolled to one side; Hoskins went underneath. Mrs. Fan ran into the room, calling Stu's name, but the monkey leapt away, dropping the plate and careening around the room from chair to couch to cage to bookcase, then back to the window where he clung to the curtains, hanging on to the thick material and chattering away as if scolding them all for his misdeed. Mr. Fan lunged and caught him, along with a handful of the curtain, and they fell to the floor together, wrapped in mountains of dingy brocade. Mrs. Fan ran over to help disentangle them, and Mr. Fan emerged laughing, still holding on to Stu, who was hiding his face under Mr. Fan's arm. Charlotte was amazed by Mr. Fan's good humor and even more amazed when Mrs. Fan came back from the kitchen with three bananas and offered them to Stu, who grabbed all three and leapt away, disappearing behind the couch. "Naughty monkey," Mrs. Fan called out to him in a pleasant, singsong voice. "What will these nice boys think?"

Charlotte was already hurrying the boys, both speechless, into their coats and herding them toward the door. "Mrs. McGuffey!" Mr. Fan called to her as he followed, his face lit up with sudden brilliance. "Remember this: Energy is the monkey!"

Dr. Gum entered the lecture hall with a flourish and took his place down in front. There was a collective groan as he clapped his hands and told them to begin.

The first question was about Bohr's law and the dependency of his theory on statistical probability. What relevance did it have to the behavior of atoms? Charlotte wrote, "None." Question number two was shockingly simple and had to do with a formula Mr. Fan had explained to her many times and succeeded in making her memorize. She felt almost giddy. Against all odds, she might *pass*. Dr. Gum would be very pleased for her, she thought. He always smiled at her when they met up, a bit warily, of course, as though acknowledging his foolishness over his embarrassing assumptions, and she had come to regard him with respect: He had faltered, he had recovered, and above all, he had been a gentleman.

Next came a set of true-or-false questions. She had a 50 percent chance of getting these right. *(Yes, Dr. Gum, I do believe in percent!)* She breezed through these until she came to number eight: "Electricity is a vibration like light and heat." Personally, she doubted it, but she also felt that it was so unlikely, it was probably true. She wrote, "T." The set of mix-and-match questions had to do with who discovered what. Charlotte marked them off with confidence, feeling better and better about the whole thing. Then came the essay question, worth 40 percent of her grade. She stared at the board, as if seeking answers on its dark surface. Everyone else in the room was writing frantically.

Melvin's face appeared suddenly on the blackboard, and her heart bumped against her chest. He stared at her with a pleading look: Couldn't she reconsider? Wouldn't she change her mind? He would try harder to be patient with Hoskins, to be more understanding of her beliefs. He would be more respectful, more patient . . . less argumentative. Or was she the argumentative one? She had acted willfully, rashly, and after so little sleep, when her mind was befogged and her instincts numb, when she was easy prey for the suggestions of mortal mind and the compulsions of human will. She had not consulted God. She had acted impulsively and on her own. She had not waited patiently for the still, small voice to speak.

She closed her eyes and tried to pray. In the background was the scratching of a hundred pens. "Our Father which art in heaven, *Our Father-Mother God, all-harmonious . . . Hallowed be Thy name, Adorable One . . .*" She opened her eyes; it was too late for prayer. Rightly or wrongly, she had chosen her path.

She returned to the essay question: "Explain the difference between kinetic and potential energy in terms of two objects having different weights." How simple! She and Mr. Fan had discussed this so many times! She envisioned the precipice, the man in the undershirt, felt the hardness of the rock, heard the roar of the waterfall. "Let's say there's a rock at the top of a precipice," she wrote. "At rest, the rock has potential energy. As it falls, it has kinetic energy, the magnitude of which equals the work required to raise it back to its original position. Now, let's take the difference between a rock and a feather, two very different objects. At the top of the precipice, their potential energy is the same because they're at rest." She wasn't absolutely, entirely sure about this, but she continued. "However, their kinetic energy is different. Because the gravitational pull is different. The heavier the object (the rock), the greater the pull. It would take more energy (MORE WORK! mv^2 = mass times velocity squared!) to get that rock back up to the top because the gravitational pull is greater than it is on the feather. Of course, we might want to know if the feather is wet or dry, as its densities would be different under those conditions, just as my hair, after I wash it, has a different density than when it is dry, but that is another matter entirely, Dr. Gum. I have enjoyed this course very much."

CHAPTER

4

On Tuesday morning, four days later, two policemen came to her door. Baird was at school being Santa Claus, with a wad of cotton batting glued to his face. Hoskins was taking his nap. Charlotte was sitting cross-legged on the floor of the living room, sorting Christmas lights and trying to untangle the strings. One of the officers was a young man with rosy cheeks, whose expression showed his desperate longing to be elsewhere. The other was an older, heavyset man with black thick eyebrows that met at the top of his nose. The two men stood on the doorstep with their hats in their hands and asked if she was alone. Yes, she said, knowing they weren't interested in hearing about her little boy napping upstairs. They wanted to know who was there in case she fainted.

The accident had taken place three hours earlier, in St. Johnsbury, where it was snowing heavily. Her husband had stepped out into the street from between two parked cars and was struck down by a young boy driving his mother to the beauty parlor. He was taken to the hospital by ambulance and died en route.

The older of the two men insisted on staying until she called a "dependable family member or type of relative." They waited patiently, the snow on their boots slowly melting into the hallway carpet while she sat in front of the phone in the living room. She felt paralyzed, her mind impaled on the older man's phrase, with its odd implication that she was too flighty to know whom to call.

On a Tuesday morning, Kitty would be in her classroom at the South Holyoke grammar school, perhaps writing out an assignment in her perfect cursive at the blackboard. Charlotte could get through to her only by going through the school secretary, a bossy woman who always asked you to "state your business." It would be better to call Kitty's husband, who stayed at home all day, cleaning; Harry would at least be able to get past the woman without breaking down into tears. The phone rang and rang at the Clatter house. She asked God to let him be there, but no one answered.

"No one home," she called to the men in the hall.

"Is there someone else?"

Rosey, of course, but Rosey always got hysterical in any crisis. There were the Berrys at the parsonage next door—Winston and Bunny understood these things, knew exactly what to say and do, yet it didn't seem right to call a neighbor before a sister. She felt desperately certain that she had to do things just right, that she had to follow the right protocol, whatever that might be. Protocol would save her.

Rosey answered the phone with the little affected cadence she used at work: "Kingston Ball Bearing, president's office"—up on the *Ball,* dip, up again on *pres.* Carefully, trying to enunciate clearly, Charlotte spoke into the mouthpiece. Rosey cried out in alarm; Charlotte hung up.

Out on the street, an elderly man walking a little black-and-white dog was picking his way along the snowy sidewalk. The little dog trotted along confidently, pausing every once in a while to wait while his master negotiated a patch of uneven ground.

"Any luck?" The policeman's voice was neutral, deep, not a hint of impatience. She felt like a criminal whose every move was being watched. The phone rang, a jarring sound. It was Rosey, crying. Charlotte listened for a moment, then quietly cut their connection. "It's all set," she called out to the men in the hallway, pressing the receiver against her flowery skirt, which she had chosen that morning to help counteract the dirty snow and the leaden, overcast sky. "They're on their way."

"Are you sure?"

"I'm sure."

"Do you want us to stay until they come?"

"No, thank you."

"Ma'am?"

"Yes?"

"I'm leaving the report here on the table."

"All right."

"We'll let ourselves out, then." The door closed. She watched them walk out to the street, then turn and go down the sidewalk. The police car was somewhere else, perhaps tucked away out of discretion: Don't let her see the car first, don't alarm her. Seeing them disappear, she took a breath—her first, it seemed, since the knock on her door. Her arms and legs felt numb.

The man and the dog returned, discouraged perhaps by the difficult terrain. The man would be eager to get back home, where it was safe and warm. He would take off his coat, hang it on the hook, rub his hands, call out to his wife, pull his galoshes off his shoes. He would be excited at the thought of his hot soup, the tidy table set by his faithful wife. Charlotte felt a burst of envy for his dull, predictable life, for his old galoshes, his plain tomato soup.

Was Melvin so distraught that he had stepped out in front of the car? It was completely unlike him to be so careless. He'd taught Baird how to cross a street—looking both ways, using all his senses. He held drills and made sure that he always provided a good example. But if he were sufficiently distraught? A picture emerged in her mind: whirling snow like hard little pellets landing on the tops of cars, lampposts, metal signs. Melvin squinting as he crossed the street, hands plunged into his pockets—he was rattled; he'd left his gloves behind in his truck. Perhaps he'd been drinking the night before. She could see him sitting in the rocker

beside the stove, brooding as he stared at the glass of whiskey in his hand
and replayed their parting scene in the kitchen. She'd just said it would
be easier without all the confusion between them; he'd asked in return
what kind of confusion she meant. *Is it your principles or your feelings?*
Perhaps in replaying, this time he'd imagined a different response from
her: *Not my feelings, Mel. I'll always love you.* Perhaps he would have
started a letter and then thrown it in the fire, remembering her coldness,
her obstinate resolve, her pretentious quote. It *had* been pretentious. And
she had been cold; yes, terribly cold.

She put her head down on the desk and wept.

CHAPTER

5

When the phone rang, Harry was sitting on the kitchen floor in his overcoat, digging away with his pocket-knife at a gummy brown mark on the linoleum. He let it ring, assuming it was the school secretary wanting to send Norman home with yet another fabricated stomachache. (What Norman really wanted, Harry knew, was to come home and make sure his Ted Williams card was safe. From whom? Harry, obviously. Neither of his children trusted him.) When the secretary had called the day before, Harry had asked her how come she didn't just tell Kitty, whose third-grade classroom was right down the hall from the principal's office, and Miss Pissy Priscilla had said, "When our teachers are at school, we expect them to be teachers, not parents. We prefer asking those at home to take care of the child." *The child,* she had said, as if she were holding something stinky at arm's length. This was not just an expression of ignorance and ill will on Pissy Priscilla's part; it was a special message for him, the goof-off parent, fucking off while his wife worked. She wanted to bother him. She wanted to ruin his day. Thus, he let the phone ring. When it finally stopped, he bellowed, "CAN'T GET ME! HA-HA!"

Sometimes he enjoyed being a real idiot. Most people didn't appreciate just how satisfying it could be.

It was Tuesday, Harry's day for washing floors. Washing floors was his favorite household task because it meant he could run his tests on the various new cleaning products he'd bought at the A&P during the week. Today he would test for Erasing Gummy Brown Marks. Harry did all his housework on Tuesdays through Fridays; on Mondays, he cooked his soups and casseroles for the week. He didn't like to have to cook in the evenings because when Kitty got home, he liked to be able to sit down with her and chat about the day and read the paper, like, as he joked, "a regular guy," though if he were a real regular guy, he told her, he'd have a couple of beers. Kitty was firm on the alcohol issue: Nyet. Not even cooking sherry. Instead, he ate a lot of desserts.

Harry had just returned from driving Norman, age nine, to school because his sister, Roberta, had once again flounced off without him. She was only fourteen, but she was one tough cookie, and Norman liked to use her as his personal bodyguard. According to Norman, there were bullies on every block, all of them wanting to steal his baseball cards, though Harry suspected their bullying had more to do with their contempt for Norman's plump frame than his baseball cards. His son had the bulging midriff of a little old man and many of the mannerisms, including a habit of boring his listeners to death with minute preoccupations, such as a litany of facts about the Boston Red Sox. When Norman found Ted Williams's card in the pack Harry and he had bought at Phil's Variety Store on the corner, he'd been ecstatic. That was six months earlier, when Ted took off for Korea. Since then, each and every Clatter had heard about Ted's batting average, height, weight, and hometown, his prospects for the future, and his heroic flight missions.

Harry and Roberta had had a row at the breakfast table, the same one they always had when she came downstairs dressed for school like some kind of suffering refugee. It was the Left Bank look, she told him when he inquired about the heavy black eyeliner, and he ought to be glad she aspired to be an intellectual and not some silly adolescent. "But you *are*," he'd the poor sense to say that morning. "And you can't be an intellectual at the age of fourteen—you'll have to wait at least until you're sixteen. Anyway, Bobbie," he said, using his baby nickname for her, which he suspected she secretly liked, "adolescents aren't supposed to wear black eye paint. They're supposed to be *bright-eyed* and *eager to learn from their elders*." She gave him an *Oh, Dad* look, a quickie she tossed off by rolling her eyes—as opposed to the long, painful ones that came with a lot of commentary—and announced that she wouldn't be home until five. She had a club meeting.

"Which club is that?" Harry asked, confused. She seemed to belong to a lot of clubs, and none of them were the Girl Scouts.

"The Young Writers Club. We meet every Tuesday."

"Every day it's something else. Sometimes it's just a little hard to keep track of what day is what."

"It's Tuesday, Dad, the day after Monday, the last day of school before Christmas vacation. Only six shopping days until Kris Kringle's visit."

"You can't be expecting Mr. Kringle to fill the stocking of a young revolutionary, can you?"

"I need ballet shoes."

"Young writers study ballet?"

"Oh, Dad, everyone wears ballet shoes. It doesn't mean they're ballerinas." She laughed at the absurdity of it and looked down at her white bucks, which were carefully scuffed. She agonized over her footwear, it seemed, mortified by what was outmoded, which meant she was in nearly constant anguish. The rest of her apparel stayed the same, apparently not subject to the same fickle dictates of fashion: army-green trousers, black leotard, droopy black hair (made blacker, he suspected, with evil chemicals), droopy black eyes. She'd wanted to pierce her ears, but Kitty had objected ("Like some *gypsy?*" she'd asked in alarm). Harry sometimes wondered aloud where this child had come from, but Kitty's answer was always the same, and always unsatisfactory: from the same place we all come from, our Divine Maker.

The phone started up once more. Pissy again, refusing to take no for an answer? One of Kitty's patients in the grip of a spiritual crisis? In either case it was better not to answer.

When Kitty announced that she wanted to become a Christian Science practitioner, he'd been worried it might mean she'd take on more of an official CS party line, but, in fact, her vocation hadn't changed her. It hadn't ruined her sunny nature; it hadn't undermined her common sense; it hadn't compromised her lovely buoyancy of spirit in bed—when in Rome, she'd say gaily, do as the Romans do! But although he teased her about her spiritual calling and her elevated status as a practitioner (*Would you please move that mountain for me?*), he had more or less concluded that she was a brilliant healer. How else could he explain her successes? He wasn't a Christian Scientist, but he'd seen Kitty's curative powers work. But how did they? Was it her faith? Was it her patients' faith? He'd suggested once, once being enough, that her healing talent might work equally well were she a Muslim, or even a Catholic. What a hue and cry went up then! What? A papist? With all their hocus-pocus?

He knew firsthand, of course, the long history of healings in their own family: the mumps averted, the infection that cleared up, the fever that broke, the broken arm that healed so quickly the surgeon was astounded. (Broken bones were beyond her, Kitty told him. Even Mrs. Eddy had called a doctor at certain times.) And "demonstrations"—everything was a demonstration: lost car keys recovered, the perfect dress waiting on the rack, the traffic ticket forgiven. But as for the Harry Problem, she couldn't seem to help. His fuckups were royal and flamboyant. His paranoia was crippling. The FBI was on his tail; he wanted to lob grenades at the mailman. They'd told him at the sanatorium, where he checked in from time to time, that when he started to lose it, he ought to lie low, to stay on the beaten path and avoid people in uniform. And keep taking the little white pills he'd hidden upstairs in the pocket of his old golfing sweater. Well, he was trying. He was lying as low as he could, and the closest he came to uniforms nowadays were the smocks people wore at the A&P.

The phone was ringing again. Whoever it was *really* wanted to talk to him. He picked up the receiver with a curt *Yes?*—hoping to forestall any personal questions.

At first he only noticed that Charlotte sounded wobbly; it took a while to hear what she was actually saying. She spoke very carefully, the way a person walks over unfamiliar terrain in the dark, expecting an abyss to open up at every step. She wasn't making much sense. Finally the grim picture began to emerge. "It was snowing," she said, and stopped.

"And?" he prompted.

"He walked out between two parked cars and got hit."

"You said a boy was driving?"

"He had his learner's permit."

"Then his mother was legally responsible." Harry wasn't sure why he'd said it. What difference did it make?

"He might have been distraught," she whispered. "I'm not sure it was an accident."

He decided not to ask her what she thought it might be. "You said it was snowing."

"That's what the police said."

"Well, then, there was a visibility problem."

"But why, Harry? Why did it happen?" He couldn't tell if she was crying or not—she was making funny, squeaky sounds. "There has to be a reason."

"No, there doesn't, that's what accidents are all about. Things happen without a reason, you're in the wrong place at the wrong time, things don't work out right."

"But why?" she asked again in a small voice.

"There's no *why*. I've been to St. J— didn't we all go to the museum there last summer? They have diagonal parking on Main Street. It's very dangerous when a person walks out from between cars that are parked like that. The pedestrian can't see what's coming. The driver can't see the pedestrian."

"How could it happen, at this time of all times? I just don't understand."

"You shouldn't be trying to understand. This is not a time to try to think." She was out-and-out crying now. "I'll take care of everything, don't you worry. Just let me handle it." He was amazed at how calm and knowledgeable he sounded, whereas he'd never actually been in this position before. No one had ever asked him to do anything like this. And now he was volunteering—it was close to suicide. He'd go get Kitty and the children at school immediately, he told her. If they left Holyoke right away, they'd be in Syracuse by suppertime. In the meantime, Charlotte should get somebody to come over, maybe those people from the church next door, the Peppers.

"The Berrys," she said.

For a split second he wanted to argue. He was sure they were the Peppers. "Look, I'll take care of everything. Just tell me who to contact in Beede, and I'll take care of all the arrangements." Who was he kidding? He knew what the arrangements were: They were the funeral directors, police, probate judges . . . the people in uniform.

She talked fast, as if racing against an oncoming wave. He didn't have to go to Beede itself. Leona Cake in the village could get her husband to close up the place. The water didn't need to be turned off because Melvin wouldn't have turned it on, not just for four days, as it turned out. . . . Here she paused, trying to collect herself. "But you'll have to go to St. J and see to . . ." A small strangled sound.

"See to things there," he offered.

"Yes. To things there. You can take the Budline from White River when you change trains; it goes straight up along the river. The truck is still there, I don't know where. You'll have to find it."

"I'll do my best, whatever it takes. Don't you worry about anything." Harry couldn't believe the zingy little note of confidence in his voice. He was talking about traveling, negotiating, chatting with strangers, making demands, asking questions. He'd be in a strange place. Kitty wouldn't be there. He wouldn't know the routes, the twists and turns, the hiding places, the safety zones. Vermont was way off the beaten path.

Rosey whipped around her apartment getting ready. After finally getting through to Charlotte, she had raced home from the office, packed her suitcases, and assembled her traveling kit: deviled ham sandwich on thin white bread with mayo and a dab of relish, moistened washcloth for freshening up, and *Thirty Days to a More Powerful Vocabulary*. She liked to keep the washcloth close beside her as she drove, neatly folded on top of a piece of waxed paper so that it wouldn't damage the upholstery. Whenever she felt fatigued, she could reach for it and pat her wrists. The vocabulary she intended to study at stoplights.

After everything else was ready, she still had to make her final decision about the nested casserole dishes she'd bought for Charlotte as a Christmas present. She'd picked them up at a tag sale for a song, and only two of them were cracked. Somehow, though, kitchenware didn't seem appropriate in this time of tragedy, smacking as it did of a pleasant sort of domesticity. But what, then? Something for the funeral? She imagined Charlotte standing beside the casket, looking very, very sad and very, very beautiful; a tall, slender redhead in black, bravely holding her little boys by the hand. They would be dressed in little suits and grown-up shoes, hair combed and neatly parted, faces scrubbed. They would be so adorable—especially Hoskins, who looked like an absolute angel, though they all knew his naughty side well enough, had all chased after him down the street, listened helplessly to his screaming, watched, dumbfounded, as he climbed into the empty washing machine and agitated himself like a load of wash. Baird, pale and worried as usual, would be scowling as he tried to understand the puzzling thread of events that had put his father in a casket.

Very puzzling indeed. In the long run, though, it was probably all for the best. Melvin's view of the world was too gloomy, just like his father's had been. He wasn't even a Scientist; he was a scoffer, an *iconoclast*—one of Rosey's new favorite words—which had made it hard for Charlotte to practice her faith. As far as Rosey was concerned, Christian Science was simply a beautiful way to look at the world. She herself didn't have the kind of inner strength necessary to be a good Scientist—she left that up to Kitty and Charlotte—but she felt she benefited from their greater understanding, in some overall and rather vague way. It was a very brainy religion, very mental, and called for great self-discipline, which Rosey admitted she didn't have, and actually didn't even want. She remembered when Charlotte was taking philosophy in college and was so excited about the Greek Stoics. Where was the thrill in self-denial? Christian Science made things go better, Rosey believed, and in some general way, she felt she was happier and more content because of Mrs. Eddy's writings. But when it came to getting sick, she always said, it was time to see a doctor.

In time, Charlotte would remarry, and this time around she might make a better choice, perhaps a well-to-do, well-dressed, well-spoken, cheerful businessman with a positive outlook who could look after her properly. (Rosey would have liked one of those for herself.) In the meantime, Charlotte was free to enjoy her status as widow while she searched for Mr. Right.

Rosey and Kitty had tried to tell her that marriage to Melvin was a mistake, but of course she wouldn't listen. And she could have had anybody! She was only nineteen when she met him, a tall, graceful girl with long red hair and blue eyes as wide and bright as a doll's. Men gawked at her as she floated past with that peculiar gait of hers, which Rosey could tell the men found fetching.

Charlotte was at the university, majoring in one of her many enthusiasms, when she found him, though Rosey never knew how. He wasn't a student, or a serviceman—or even patriotic. The story was that a heart murmur had kept him in civilian clothes, though there were many who whispered that Mr. McGuffey was a holdout from Lindbergh's America First Committee, which most everybody had abandoned after Pearl Harbor. There were no flags flying at his photography studio on University Place, no placards in his windows.

Rosey had been shocked when she found out Charlotte was seeing him. It was the spring of 1942, and Rosey was a volunteer hostess at one of the service centers in Syracuse. It was her job to round up girls and bring them to the mixers on Saturday nights. She always invited Charlotte (who she hoped might meet some very nice young commissioned officer) to come and bring her college girlfriends, and Charlotte always refused. Rosey said it was her duty to go. Charlotte got her back up, as she was wont to do when opposed, and told Rosey scornfully that she did not intend to be some little cuddle bunny for a drunken sailor.

"How can you talk like that!" Rosey was outraged. "Congenial gatherings encourage national unity!" she cried, quoting one of the many billboards around the city. "We're trying to bolster the spirits of the men who are keeping us safe!"

Finally Rosey succeeded in getting their father to intercede. He hated to intercede. He hated to take sides or be involved in any kind of domestic fandangling; he wasn't interested in any of the events normally associated with what he called the "corporeal realm" at all, particularly those having to do with the emotional life of women. *I'm sure it will all work out, Rosamunde,* he would always say, withdrawing. *Pray over it, and you will find your answer.* But Rosey couldn't sit around waiting for an answer while her little sister was busy falling in love with such an unlikely prospect as opinionated Melvin McGuffey, ten years older than Charlotte and an avowed agnostic, if not outright atheist and card-carrying iconoclast. Besides, he had a sharp tongue, and he frightened Rosey.

Worn down, Jerome Baird had asked Charlotte to please go with her sister to one of the mixers. He rarely asked anything of her; she acceded at once to his request and invited her friend Jane Owen to go with them the following Saturday night. Jane was a sweet little blonde who showed up at their house that evening wearing a very nice powder-blue sweater set, a tweed skirt, and saddle shoes. She was a perfect party girl and would have been adorable except for her dark horn-rimmed glasses, which Rosey unsuccessfully tried to get her to remove.

The three of them arrived at the center loaded down with party cups and apple cider, doughnuts and cold cuts. Oh, how the men swarmed around Charlotte! After refreshments were served, Rosey's male cohost announced that it was amateur night and handed out cards bearing the names of famous radio duos, telling everyone to find their corresponding partners. Charlotte drew the Jack Benny card. The Mary Livingston card was held by one Ensign Robert Zyrcyk, whose ears stuck out like a teddy bear's. His cheeks were red—maybe a little too red. Jane drew Abbott, and teamed up with Costello, a young army lieutenant named Jerry Watson, who looked like Leslie Howard in *The 49th Parallel.* Oh, why couldn't Charlotte have drawn the right card!

The game called for the couples to recite gag lines from their designated celebrities' shows, and the rest of the crowd was supposed to guess whom each pair was impersonating. Rosey observed Charlotte and her partner conferring. When it was their turn, Ensign Zyrcyk called out "Jell-O again," and right away someone guessed the show. Jane and her partner, the dashing Leslie Howard look-alike, offered, "If I do, I det a whippin'! I dood it," and everybody roared with laughter, especially Charlotte's partner, who appeared to be getting drunk, despite what should have been a cup of cider in his hand. "That's Red Skelton's line," he yelled out, "not Abbott and Costello's!" He repeated it twice, raucously, and threw his arm around Lieutenant Watson's shoulders. His friend turned, and Ensign Zyrcyk lurched backward into the crowd, falling into a mess of arms and legs.

Charlotte slipped away, and, before long, Melvin came to pick her up. It had been a complete failure—in fact, more than a complete failure. A rout. A disaster. Rosey had managed to create a danger for Charlotte from which Melvin, the hero, could rescue her.

After they left, Rosey went to look for the disgraced Ensign Zyrcyk and found him passed out in the hallway. What a fool he'd been. Jane Owen stayed on for the whole evening, playing game after game with Leslie Howard. By the end of the evening, she was in his lap and they were smooching. Much later, Rosey learned that he was shipped out to sea a few days after that, never to return. Still, somehow, in the back of her mind, she had always regretted it wasn't Charlotte who had drawn Costello.

When Charlotte told Rosey she intended to marry Melvin, Rosey pleaded with her to reconsider. Why? she asked. Why him, when she could have anybody? Charlotte had just laughed and said, "You mean, like that sailor?" It had hurt, but not as much as what she said next. It was love, she said solemnly, and meant to be. "You just don't know what it's like. You'd understand, I'm sure, if you'd ever experienced it."

Oh, thoughtless youth! Rosey certainly did know what it was like! And she'd given him up for Charlotte herself!

When Lillian Baird died, Rosey had given up her own life (and prospects) and moved home to help their father look after little Lottie. Jerome Baird had been bewildered by the clutter of females in his household even when his wife was alive, and he hadn't the foggiest idea what to do with a ten-year-old girl left alone in his care. Kitty was married by then and living in Holyoke, Massachusetts. She had her hands full with Harry, who had slipped out of his regular self like a loose jacket soon after the wedding and was a worry to them all. Rosey, who was twenty-four at the time, was working at one of the state offices in Albany, with a hopeful eye on the governor's secretarial pool. She had done what was expected of her and returned to Syracuse, giving up her wonderful job, her smartly dressed friends, her cute little apartment with the pretty bay windows. And adorable Duncan, with the dark chocolate curls.

By the time Rosey finally moved out of her father's house, after his death and Charlotte's departure as Mrs. McGuffey, she was irrevocably single and it was too late. Now here she was at forty-four, still going to other people's houses for Christmas, still sending presents to other people's babies. Few eligible bachelors ever crossed her path. Her boss's business associates in Kingston came and went, never even looking her way except to remark on how lucky he was to have someone like her running his office. And then they closed the door firmly behind them. *Someone like her,* they said. Not even her specifically.

Even her boss treated her like a generality. Howard Sample was a family man, of course (who wasn't?), but he perspired in a certain way that made Rosey feel he was not fulfilled. He seemed overwrought much of the time, and she did her best to soothe him. She protected him from awkward encounters. She kept his appointment book up to date, with hardly any erasures, and she bought him coffee mugs whenever she went on vacation. He had his Florida mug, his Statue of Liberty mug, his Mardi Gras mug, his saguaro cactus mug. The latter contained a slightly obscene suggestion, an aspect of the mug she hadn't noticed until Howard pointed it out to her with a little pat on her shoulder. The warmth of his hand had lingered on her upper back for several hours. When he offered her champagne at the modest little cake-and-cookies affair she had organized for him on his birthday, she had accepted, poured herself a second glass, and let it go to her head. Then he had driven off in his immaculately waxed Cadillac convertible for a gala evening with his wife, and Rosey had drifted out onto the lawn in the moonlight, in her bare feet, singing the "Indian Love Call." The grass, which looked as soft and perfect as the illusory lawns in children's books, turned out to be soft only from afar. When she walked through it, it prickled her feet.

Rosey drove the thirty-five miles from Kingston to Cairo, New York, in a haze of slippery snow and then another hundred yards along a shallow ditch, coming to rest on a snow-covered lawn next to a red and white miniature windmill that had been frozen in midmotion sometime in early November. It was six o'clock and pitch dark when she landed, just six days before the winter solstice and the darkest day of the year. Fortunately, the Malverns were standing at their picture window, peering out at the snow, as she arrived on their lawn. They called the wrecker and made tea, and the three of them watched as the big truck appeared out of the darkness, blinking its yellow lights, and dragged Rosey's car off the lawn and into the Malverns' driveway.

Then they disappeared into the kitchen to prepare supper, and Rosey called Charlotte in Syracuse. "The important thing to remember," she told Kitty, who answered the phone, "is that I'm not badly hurt. It's just my back."

"What about your car?"

"What about my back?"

"You said you drove your car off the road."

"It's my back that hurts."

Though she was clever enough to cloak it in sympathy, Rosey thought, Kitty could be truly heartless. "I went into their yard. About a hundred yards, the tow-truck man said."

"Is it working?"

"I can't get back in it now, no more than I could get back on a bucking bronco. Please don't ask me to. I'm going to spend the night."

"Oh, Rosey."

"Don't worry, please. I'm going to be fine. I'm standing here looking at a sweet little framed needlepoint of a one-room schoolhouse. Mr. Malvern is a retired schoolteacher."

"You're spending the night at a stranger's house?"

"I don't feel well enough to travel."

"I don't think you should spend the night with strangers."

"They're very nice! They couldn't be nicer, and they just love card games. We're going to play cards after supper."

"I don't like this."

"I *knew* you'd be mad at me!"

"I'm not mad, Rosey. But I don't like it."

"Just tell me one thing. Is Charlotte all right?"

"She's fine."

"What's she doing?"

"She's reading to the boys."

"Did she tell them?"

"Yes."

Rosey's voice quavered. "Poor thing. I wish there weren't any death, it's so awful. Are they really sad?"

"I don't think they quite understand yet."

"I keep thinking of how much those boys are going to miss their daddy. They say everyone needs to grieve; it's the healthiest thing. Everyone needs to be expurgated, especially children. I can just see them at the funeral in their little suits and their little grown-up shoes. . . ."

"We're not having a funeral, Rosey. You know Christian Scientists don't have funerals."

"Then how about a little memorial get-together? I'll organize it, I'll take care of everything, you don't have to do a thing. We'll have that neighbor of Charlotte's officiate—Dr. Berry? And you, too, of course. Do you remember that poem of Daddy's called 'Oh, Lonely Star-Gazer'? I was thinking I could read that; it would set a nice tone."

"I think we're doing all right, Rosey, as is."

"Are you saying you don't want my ideas?"

"Of course not, it's just that we're doing fine. I don't think we need to stir things up."

"Stir things up! With a memorial service?"

"Please, Rosey, let's not argue. We'll talk when you get here."

"I don't understand how you can be so cheerful."

"I'm not being cheerful."

"You *sound* cheerful."

"How am I supposed to sound?"

"Well—a little sad, I would think."

"I'm just doing what has to be done." Kitty paused. "Without you here to help me, I might add."

"I knew it! I knew you'd be mad!" Rosey began to cry. "I just feel so sorry for the children!"

"Rosey, please, you need to bear up like everyone else, and help Charlotte through this."

"But what about a little get-together? I don't think that's asking too much."

"I could use some help, Rosey. There are three young children here who need a lot of attention, not to mention Charlotte herself. She feels very bad. Roberta is sequestered in the guest room, writing her autobiography. It's her homework assignment, she tells me, and apparently it takes precedence over all family business, no matter how pressing. Harry is in Vermont, looking for Melvin's truck, and trying to take care of some very complicated business there. The only person not here or not helping is you."

"But I've been in an accident!"

"Yes, indeed, and Charlotte doesn't need to know anything about it. I don't expect you to say a word," said Kitty, speaking very slowly now. "This is not a time for you to take center stage. It is not your place to be the most emotional one here, or the most injured. Or the most distraught. Flaunting your grief is not going to help anyone."

"Flaunting?"

"You've already flirted with taking center stage by driving off the road instead of arriving here in an orderly manner like everybody else. Your job is to *help*, Rosamunde Baird, not to cause problems."

"You see? I knew you'd be mad!"

"All right, fine. I'm mad. Now do you feel better?"

"Much better! See you tomorrow!"

CHAPTER

6

Kitty awoke on the couch at 5 A.M., put on her robe and slippers, and went into the kitchen to make herself some cocoa. Everyone else in the house was asleep; she wished she also could have afforded a few extra minutes of sleep. She had whisked everyone to bed early, reserving the living-room couch, and the privacy it offered, for herself. The house was full. Roberta was in one of the twin beds in the guest room; Rosey would take the other when she arrived. Charlotte was alone in her room, and Hoskins in his own bed (and what an ordeal to get him there!). Norman had been put to bed on a pile of blankets in the boys' room; within minutes, Baird had joined him on another pile of blankets, leaving his own bed empty. Kitty heard them talking for a long time after the lights were out. There had been a fair stream of talk, and it seemed like a good sign—Baird had seemed quite fragile to her when she first arrived. The busier he stayed, the better.

She stirred the milk slowly with a wooden spoon so that it wouldn't stick to the bottom, watching for the telltale bubbles that would appear around the edges of the pan.

She had a lot to do, even before the rest of the family was up. First, she would do her work for her patients back in Holyoke, and then the day's Lesson, which was a selection of readings from the Bible with interpretations by Mrs. Eddy. By then, Charlotte might be up, and they could talk again.

Kitty had four patients at the moment. One of them had suffered a disfiguring stroke; another was facing progressive blindness. The third, Mr. Matson, was very worried about having a second heart attack. She took a moment and directed a brief message of encouragement toward the little house in Holyoke where nervous Mr. Matson slept in a tan corduroy La-Z-Boy, the little table by his side cluttered with crossword puzzles and Christian Science periodicals. His wife worked as a butcher at night, and he spent long lonely hours at home alone in his chair, afraid to move.

Kitty's fourth patient suffered from inordinate lust. She had never met Mr. Bixby face-to-face; he had told her his sad story over the telephone. Compelled by a tyrannical lust to go from woman to woman, he had lost everything meaningful to him: his wife—two wives, in fact—his three children, and, since being discovered in a compromising position in his office with a female client of the firm, his latest job. He had wanted to go into some detail on the latter, and Kitty had assured him it wasn't necessary. It was only the big picture she was interested in; excessive concern with the details would inhibit his healing. "Mr. Bixby," she had said as kindly as she could, "perform your office as porter and shut out these unhealthy thoughts."

She could apply Mrs. Eddy's words to herself as well. *A sick body is evolved from sick thoughts. Sickness, disease, and death proceed from fear.*

Hannibal, who had been patiently watching her at the stove, followed Kitty as she carried her cup and saucer to the living room. The dog circled a spot on the rug in front of Melvin's leather armchair and flopped down with a long sigh. She shut the French doors to the hallway as quietly as she could and set her steaming cocoa on the low table in front of the couch. The dawning light had reached that stage when objects seem to be lit from within, making them glow with a kind of silvery, metallic light. In another minute they would turn solid and familiar. Dust balls would appear. Spiders would depart. There were signs of Melvin every-where: the worn armchair guarded by his handsome dog, his many books on the bookshelves, framed snapshots of the family on the mantel above the fireplace. Kitty peered at one of them more closely: Melvin and Charlotte and the boys were on the big granite steps of their front porch in Beede, Melvin squatting down with his arm around Baird's shoulder, Charlotte in a sundress looking down at the baby, her long hair covering her face.

Kitty quietly tucked the photograph into the drawer of an end table. There was no need for such a painful reminder.

She unzipped her briefcase and took out her Bible and her *Science and Health,* both bound in a soft, nubby leather, so pleasurable to touch, and laid them gently on the table's glass surface. She leaned back against the couch's soft pillows, closed her eyes, and prayed, *All is infinite Mind and its infinite manifestation.* Kitty loved that word, *manifestation*—as had Mrs. Eddy, apparently. Healings were manifested. Man manifested his true nature as the perfect image and likeness of God. Matter was a man-ifestation of error. Spiritual understanding was a manifestation of Divine Mind. A simple, five-syllable word. Kitty had once wallpapered a whole room under its influence. She had gotten it fixed in her mind while she was mixing the paste, and it had stayed there all day, right up to the last moment when she was applying the sweetly flowered Victorian trim around the edges of the ceiling.

There were other words in Mrs. Eddy's lexicon, however, that weren't so friendly, such as *mellifluous.* She'd had a terrible tangle with it. In fact, it had been more than a tangle; the truth was, she'd ended up struggling with it just as Jacob had wrestled with the angels.

The first time she came across it, she looked up its meaning, but as soon as she closed the dictionary, she forgot it. She looked it up again, and again its meaning withdrew, like a snake departing from its skin. Then one day, when Kitty was running off some Dittos in the teachers' room, the word started going around and around with the drum as she cranked, and it came to her with a sudden, blinding light that the purple ink flow-ing out of the mimeograph machine onto the white paper was like a mellifluous river of God's love, flowing smoothly like the sweetest honey. The mimeograph machine was in fact manifesting the very meaning of *mellifluous,* a word like all the rest of the words in Mrs. Eddy's vocabulary—elegant, sweet-tasting, ephemeral, rare. Divine Harmony was being demonstrated by the mimeo machine just as it was demonstrated everywhere in the workings of the so-called material world. That was the demonstration being offered her. After that, she understood the word perfectly. It had been a private sort of healing, a revelation designed for her alone; besides, who except another Scientist would understand? There were secrets that had to be kept and this applied nowhere more aptly than to one's work with Science. Mrs. Eddy cautioned her followers against too eagerly proclaiming difficult concepts to an uncomprehending world. In the words of Christ Jesus (never Jesus Christ, which would make *Christ* into a last name, like *Smith,* making for the ludicrous possibility, *Jesus Smith*): Do not cast your pearls before swine. It sounded a little harsh, but she knew what he meant.

When Kitty left Charlotte the night before, she was sitting up in her bed, light on, face pale and puffy. She had looked like a drowned person.

The house had been in a shambles when Kitty and her children arrived. Charlotte had stood in the doorway wearing a wrinkled kimono, her hair in a long, dispirited braid, watching as they tottered forward through the snow with their suitcases and bags of groceries, stiff from spending six long hours in the car. Bunny Berry was in the kitchen, cleaning up and making supper. Charlotte had been sitting at their mother's dining-room table, fingerpainting with the boys. She'd left a jar of discolored water sitting on it, among the papers and paints; when Kitty picked up the jar, she found a white ring on the beautiful old table's polished surface.

Charlotte had been eager to review the facts: the time Melvin would have left for St. Johnsbury, the chores he would have done at the house before he left, the scene he would be hoping to shoot, whether he might have had to walk down to his truck, the probable depth of the snow. She showed Kitty the police report, repeating the brief, heartless phrases written there. They'd had an argument before he left Syracuse on Friday, she told Kitty. Kitty said she didn't want to know about it and advised Charlotte not to dwell on it. All married couples have their differences, she reminded her. The sooner she stopped thinking about it, the better she'd feel. Harry and Kitty had little spats all the time. It was perfectly normal.

"It wasn't a little spat," Charlotte had said, staring hard at Kitty. "It was a scene, an awful scene, and now he's dead. We were a house divided against itself—that's what I told him the morning he left." She covered her face. "Oh, when I think of it . . ."

"Charlotte . . . please . . ."

"I told him I wanted a separation. Then I never spoke to him again." The skin around Charlotte's eyes was a pale, violet color.

Kitty had been shocked, and had suggested—because in fact she couldn't think of anything better at that moment—that Charlotte take a hot bath.

"It won't change what happened."

"I wouldn't dwell on it, especially right now," Kitty told her, but Charlotte had turned her attention to a spot on the wall across the room, above Kitty's head, letting her know that she was finished with the conversation.

During the day, Charlotte had taken Hoskins upstairs to her room to read to him. Roberta was camped out in the guest room, working on her autobiography. After a while, Roberta came downstairs to ask Kitty what her aunt was reading to Hoskins—she had heard some of it through the wall. "It was all about driving a car: 'How to park on hills. How to make a right turn. A red light is next. Traffic proceed. Traffic stop.' It was weird." Roberta had not seen Hoskins or Baird since the summer, when the whole family had been in Vermont together—and she had forgotten how strange he was, she told her mother. "He doesn't smile at all."

"He smiles sometimes, just not very much."

"Mom, he never smiles!"

"He's a darling little boy."

"There's something the matter with him, Mom."

"You know very well that if you're seeing a flaw in Hoskins—"

Roberta interrupted. "My English teacher says, always use nouns, and the more specific, the better. If something has a name, name it."

Up until a year ago, Roberta had been a sweet little girl. And a good little Scientist. She'd even given testimonies at church about the demonstrations and healings she'd experienced—her cocker spaniel's recovery from a terrible flea infestation, the earaches that had plagued her when she was younger. Now, all she did was argue.

"I need to know, Mother."

"Are you writing about your family?"

"Of course I'm writing about my family! I'm practicing my listening skills. Mr. Corington says the most important thing is to make your writing authentic, and the best way to do that is to write down what everybody says."

"This Mr. Corington has some funny ideas."

"He knows what he's talking about. He's a brilliant teacher. I'm supposed to listen in on conversations."

"Is that what he told you, to listen in on your family's conversations?"

"I have to get the hang of dialogue."

"Your personal life is none of your teacher's business."

"It's *homework,* Mother."

"It's *snooping.* It's not right to pry, Roberta. This is a very difficult time, which makes it doubly important for you to respect people's privacy. This is a very difficult thing for your aunt Charlotte to have to go through. For you to think about it as an experiment is callous. You may be precocious in many things, Roberta, but you are sorely lacking in compassion. Try to imagine how what you say will make others feel."

"But I need to know the truth."

"You don't need to know anything! You're just a child!" Kitty had told her at a higher pitch than she'd intended, and Roberta had stomped away in a huff.

Kitty needed to work on Roberta.

The brass doorknob on one of the French doors turned with a small noise. The dog looked up, watching the knob intently. The hallway was in shadow, and all Kitty could see through the small panes of glass was the outline of a child. The door opened slowly, inch by inch, and Hoskins slid in, wearing his slippers and his plaid pajamas. She patted the cushion next to her on the couch. "Come sit with me, Hoskins, dear." He stared at her, his expression solemn. She patted again, repeating her invitation, and he withdrew.

With only a week to go before Christmas, Kitty and Rosey did their best to create a normal holiday atmosphere despite the sad circumstances. Kitty spent hours in the kitchen with Hoskins, making sugar cookies in Christmassy shapes; Norman and Baird made tree decorations out of construction paper and wads of glue. Rosey took Roberta to see *High Noon,* hoping to inspire her to act more like Grace Kelly. (Afterward, they went shopping at a department store—Rosey wanted to buy a new robe for Charlotte, something elegant, she told Roberta, something sexy. "Wow," Roberta said, regarding her aunt with admiration. She'd never heard her use such a word. Rosey reached for a short black-and-white-striped number on a rack. "She always had a lot of admirers, you know, before she married your uncle Melvin." Rosey held the silky robe up to herself and asked Roberta what she thought. "I think it's really sexy," Roberta told her, thrilled to be talking like that to someone in her own family.)

Kitty and Rosey rolled up their sleeves and cleaned the house from top to bottom, removing Painful Reminders as they went. The telephone rang constantly. Kitty tried to intercept the calls, which she felt would be distressing for Charlotte, who was sequestered in her room, working on the boys' holiday presents. One of the phone calls was from the postmistress in Beede, another from a man with an accent—a Professor Something, Kitty couldn't quite understand him. She told all callers that Charlotte was fine, that she was resting and doing well. And the boys were fine. Everything was fine, thank you. She didn't want to encourage them to call again.

The Berrys were very helpful. They seemed to know just what to do and say to make everything easier. They stopped by at least once a day, bringing cakes and cookies and casseroles. Winston sent the fellow that shoveled their walk to do Charlotte's. Kitty had always liked the Berrys. They were a robust white-haired couple, both short and compactly built, with the kind of pink, elastic skin that advertises a brisk circulation. Kitty remembered Melvin's nickname for them—"the Pods," he called them, as if they were merry pranksters with tasseled caps. Like most Protestants, he'd once proclaimed within her hearing, the Pods were a pedestrian lot, always flocking to committee meetings and panel discussions and in general confusing religious doctrine with *Robert's Rules of Order*. Protestants had an unrelenting missionary zeal and an insatiable need to proselytize—at least Christian Scientists didn't pass a cup or pray for conversions of the heathen, he said; they just squeezed their eyes shut and silently *willed* the rest of the world to join them. Saying that, Kitty remembered, he'd laughed.

Kitty managed to find some time to spend alone with Baird. She told him she knew he was sad and assured him that his daddy was safe and sound. "We say someone has passed on because we can't see him, but that doesn't mean he isn't still with us." Baird picked at a spot on his pants. "Your daddy was a fine man, and he loved you very much, and he still loves you. He will always love you. And you will always love him. And in that way, you'll always be together."

He looked up at her, his gray eyes thoughtful, and Kitty decided he looked a lot like Melvin. Same high cheekbones, same sandy-colored hair and pointed chin. "Our Father-Mother God would never want any of His children to suffer, Baird. God doesn't want us to feel sad."

"Mommy's sad."

"It's hard for her, and it's hard for you, too, but everything's going to be all right. She knows that God is All-in-All, so there's no room for sadness, not if God takes up all the room, right? There's no room for anything that isn't God."

"Can I go now?" he asked.

"Of course, dear."

He darted out of the room, and after a while Kitty heard him arguing with Norman about who was the best, the Yankees or the Red Sox.

Rosey continued to lobby for a memorial "get-together." Charlotte was moribund and needed to expurgate her grief, she said, offering two of the words she had learned on her trip to Syracuse, and which she hadn't had a chance to use yet. (You had to use words five times in order to make them yours, the book's author said, again and again.) "Roberta agrees with me," she told Kitty. "She thinks it's important to have some kind of service."

"She thinks it's important to take notes," said Kitty. "I know what that's about."

"I think that was Daddy's problem," Rosey continued, ignoring Kitty's comment. "He never got a chance to grieve outright."

On Sunday the three sisters gathered all the children and trooped off to church. After the service, the First Reader, who was wearing a long, sparkly dress, came up to Charlotte and pressed her hand, then turned to her sisters. "Isn't Charlotte brave and good?"

"We just love her," Kitty agreed, touching Rosey's sleeve.

"We treasure her," said Rosey.

"Oh, Rosey," said Charlotte, embarrassed.

"Well, we do!"

"We must remember that if God is eternal and changeless," the woman said, ignoring the little interruption, "then man is also eternal and changeless. Death is the illusion; life is the reality. At times, though, it's a difficult concept for us."

"Sometimes you just have to break down and grieve," said Rosey, darting a look at Kitty. "In the proper setting, of course."

In the evenings the sisters and the children gathered in the living room and talked of Lazarus rising from the dead, of what Jesus meant when he said that death was the last enemy to be destroyed. There was no such thing as an afterlife, Kitty reminded the little group. That was a sentimental idea, and a limited one: Why would you want to limit the glories of eternal life to life as it's known to humans? There was only Life Harmonious. "Life *is*," she said. "We're the same after as we are before; we're God's perfect ideas."

"What about an afterbirth, do we believe in that?" Roberta asked, and the little group waited while Kitty assessed her daughter's intentions. She was, after all, only fourteen. What would she know about such things? But her face was flushed, as if she were fully aware of what she'd said.

"That's different," Kitty told her. "It doesn't have anything to do with anything."

Rosey wanted to talk about the new, happy Lazarus, the one they never heard much about. "Just think," she said brightly, "one minute he's dead and the next minute he's fine! Why, who knows what happened after that? He's never mentioned again. He could have gone on to a career in sports, for all we know."

Roberta, intrigued by the interesting possibilities of such a discussion, wanted to know which sport he would have chosen. Soccer maybe, she said, because of his experience with rolling heavy stones. "Baseball," said Norman, "he'd play for the Red Sox."

"Why not the Yankees?" Baird asked. It took Charlotte, acting as referee, to clear up the ensuing argument by suggesting that Lazarus was clearly meant to be a golfer; they all looked at her, shocked at her playful tone. Hoskins busied himself at the periphery of their evening discussions with his new cache of pennies, which Rosey had brought from Kingston for him. He lined them up along the designs on the carpet, first in single file, then by twos and threes, and so on, always keeping his soldiers ("What else could they be?" Rosey asked the others) in a strict mathematical array.

One evening the talk turned to a passage in the *Science and Health* that Kitty particularly loved, and had found effective with some of her patients. It involved a sort of story that Kitty thought would be helpful for the children, as it would allow her to translate Mrs. Eddy's metaphysics—at times too abstruse for them—into a simple story about the illogic of death. It involved a whistling boy on a bicycle, delivering the wrong telegram and thus causing a dear friend's mistaken grief. Kitty quoted the passage: *A blundering despatch, mistakenly announcing the death of a friend, occasions the same grief that the friend's real death would bring. You think that your anguish is occasioned by your loss.* She paused dramatically. "Not true," Kitty explained cheerily, "for here comes the boy again, wobbling a bit as he turns the corners, holding another telegram aloft in his hand. *Another despatch, correcting the mistake, heals your grief and you learn that your suffering was merely the result of your belief. Thus it is with all sorrow, sickness and death.* Our Beloved Leader is saying that although your grief feels absolutely real, it's only a mistake, a misunderstanding of what life is. That's all death is—a misunderstanding. You *think* you should be sad. But that's not so."

"Why was he riding a bike?" asked Norman.

"Western Union boys always ride bikes," Rosey explained.

"Maybe it was a motorbike," Roberta suggested.

Charlotte shook her head. "Not in Mrs. Eddy's day."

"Why are we focusing on the bikes?" asked Kitty. "There are important truths to be learned here."

"It's easier to talk about bikes," said Charlotte sadly. "And more fun for the children."

Three days before Christmas Eve, Harry called from St. Johnsbury. He was on edge, talkative, nervous. The wallpaper in his motel room was giving him the creeps, he told Kitty. "It has thousands of eyes."

"Eyes?"

"Eyes and feathers."

"Peacocks," she said. "It's only peacocks, honey."

"But what are they doing on the walls!"

She was relieved to hear him laugh. He was eager to read her an article from the local paper about Melvin's accident. She wasn't going to believe it, he said. It was a mishmash of ludicrous mistakes. Without waiting to hear whether she was willing to listen, he launched forth.

> *A pedestrian was struck and killed by a motorist on Tuesday while crossing Main Street in St. Johnsbury. Melvin McGuffey, 42, a photographer and owner of Vermont Scene Company of Syracuse, New York, was taken by ambulance to Barton Hospital, where he was pronounced dead. The driver, Boyd Eppleman, 18, stated that the victim suddenly appeared in his path and that he was unable to take defensive action.*

Mr. Eppleman was not cited, although he asked to be cited. Witnesses said that the victim stepped out into the path of Mr. Eppleman's two-toned shell-blue Plymouth from between two parked vehicles in the middle of the block, one of them the truck belonging to the victim. Mrs. M. T. Mahoney, who was visiting her sister in St. Johnsbury for the holidays, said she believed the victim didn't see the car, which she described as "eggshell blue." Mrs. Margaret Eppleman, the driver's mother and a passenger in the car that struck the victim, was taken to Barton Hospital for treatment of minor bruises and released. In a statement made from the hospital in a phone call to this newspaper, Mrs. Eppleman described the victim as "roaring up" suddenly in front of the car. She said she believed her son was an excellent driver. The car he was driving had been a gift to her son from his father when Mr. Eppleman left to join American troops in Korea. Sgt. Eppleman died in the siege of P'anmunjŏm.

Harry stopped. "So? What color tank do you suppose Sergeant Eppleman was driving in P'anmunjŏm? Might that have been an eggshell blue? And would that be a *dark* shell blue and a *light* shell blue on the lad's two-toned shell-blue Plymouth? And what about Mrs. Eppleman's call to the newspaper, in which she casts suspicion on the victim by saying that he *roared* up? And Mrs. M. T. Mahoney? Who exactly was she buying a Christmas present for? And what about the other witnesses, what were they wearing?"

"Harry, it's just a small-town newspaper. It's not the *Monitor;* you can't expect good reporting. Please, Harry, you don't have to get so upset." It wasn't a good sign, his focusing like that on the newspaper article. Sometimes, when he was nervous, he would cut out pieces from the paper and carry them around to read aloud to people until the clippings finally fell apart along the fold lines.

"Well, I'll tell you, my assignment isn't easy. I don't like the people over at the mortuary. I don't like their looks, their attitude. And I can't find the truck. The police here rent spaces for their impounds, and

Melvin's truck is locked away in some fellow's garage—and he's somewhere else."

Kitty tried to speak calmly. "Harry, God is taking care of you. He is ever-present. You are not alone."

"I know, that's the problem. I'm not the only motel guest. There's also this other guy."

"*There is no life, truth, intelligence, nor substance in matter. All is infinite Mind and its infinite manifestion, for God is All-in-All.* Maybe you could say that to yourself."

"Maybe I could. And maybe I could change motels."

"You don't need to change motels. You need to change your thinking."

He lowered his voice. "The funeral director brought me Melvin's clothes in a paper bag. They give you what's called a family room to wait in—about the size of a grave, naturally, with a picture on the wall of Jesus patting some lambs. Well, I don't know if they're lambs; they're kind of peculiar-looking, like some kind of hybrid animal, if you ask me. The pencil they leave for you in the room has been sharpened with a knife. Don't you think that's kind of odd?"

"Odd?"

"Sinister."

"Oh, Harry. This is not a good way of thinking. What did you do with the clothes?"

"I took the wallet and told them to burn the rest. I was tempted to keep the leather jacket, though. I've always liked that jacket."

"Did you?"

"No. I was worried what Charlotte would think. It's a shame, though."

"And the ashes?"

"I told them to ship them to Artie Perkins; he's the sexton of the Beede Cemetery Association. That's what Leona Cake told me to do. He'll keep them until the ground thaws. She's quite a gal, that Leona. Seems to know how to do everything. She wanted to know, did we want a service up there in the summer."

"I don't think so. I don't think we want any service at all."

"What should I do about the truck? I mean, if I ever find it."

"Leave it there."

"Well, I don't know. I think Melvin really liked it. I don't see how I can just leave it."

"Charlotte has the DeSoto. How many vehicles can she drive? See if you can sell it for her."

"I thought I was supposed to bring it back. She seemed worried about it."

"She doesn't want Melvin's truck."

"Are you sure?"

"I'm positive. What did you find out about the insurance?"

"It was in force. She won't lack. He carried personal insurance and insurance on himself as head of his business. She's sitting pretty."

"You're doing so well; you're being so helpful. We all appreciate everything you're doing. I love you, Harry. And I miss you."

"I love you, too. I wish I was there."

"Will you try to get here by Christmas?"

"It all depends on what this guy in the other room does."

"No, it doesn't, Harry. It all depends on God."

"And the pills."

"You're taking them again?"

"Got to, sweetheart. I'm too far from home."

C H A P T E R

7

Charlotte was in her bedroom making a wizard's wand for Baird for Christmas. Kitty had been helping her to finish her present for Hoskins, a pea-green corduroy jacket and matching hat, lined, and with a hand-embroidered label on each pocket: "Hoskins McGuffey" on the left and "Please return to sender" on the right. Kitty was sitting at the sewing machine by the window, putting in the zipper, when they heard Rosey sound the alert downstairs—Hoskins was missing! Charlotte could still hear them calling to one another as they went from room to room. She wasn't worried—there were a lot of people in the house. After a while, she heard Roberta come out of the guest room next door and yell, "He's here! He's in my closet!" Charlotte smiled to herself. For several days he'd been going around the house with a screwdriver, pretending to take doorknobs off closet doors. He so loved anything mechanical in nature.

In any case, it had been quite a job to figure out how to wrap the wand itself—her yardstick—so that the pretty silver paper wouldn't wrinkle. Her first attempts had been disastrous, and Rosey had had to return to the store twice for more paper. The key was building an inner base of tissue paper to create the shape of a wand instead of a club, but after that was done, it was relatively easy to continue layering the paper until the shape and size began to look right.

Kitty had read the Bible lesson aloud to her that morning in her sweet, calm voice. When she came to a certain interpretive passage of Mrs. Eddy's, she had stopped to discuss it with Charlotte: *Under divine Providence there can be no accidents, since there is no room for imperfection in perfection.* Then she had written it down for her on an index card and stuck it into the frame of the mirror on Charlotte's dresser. She'd written "imperfecton" instead of "imperfection," and Charlotte considered fixing it while Kitty was out of the room. Charlotte remembered writing out another quote on another index card, years ago, which she had taped to the mirror in the bathroom she shared with Melvin: *Sorrow has its own reward. It never leaves us where it found us.* The next day she saw that Melvin had scrawled "Not a new idea" underneath Mrs. Eddy's words. It was easy to scoff, to criticize, to amend and improve. What took courage was to believe.

No one would talk about the accident; no one would talk about why it had happened. Baird had asked why, of course. She had wanted to say, *I don't know,* which was the truth. But she hadn't. Instead, she'd recited the Lord's Prayer with him the way they always did: He said Jesus' words, and she said Mrs. Eddy's. "Give us this day our daily bread," he'd said, and she'd followed with, "Give us grace for today; feed the famished affections," and he'd stopped her, as he always did, and asked, "Why famished?"

"Because you need more kisses," she said, as she always did, and he'd smiled.

Seeking understanding herself, Charlotte had been reading and rereading Mrs. Eddy's chapter on marriage during the last three days and had been alarmed by a certain passage: *Husbands and wives should never separate if there is no Christian demand for it. It is better to await the logic of events than for a wife precipitately to leave her husband or for a husband to leave his wife.* She studied the phrase *logic of events*. There were two ways to take it. According to the first, Mrs. Eddy was saying that everything happens when it's supposed to happen. You can't rush the order of events by imposing your own will—your human will is too puny, and your understanding, as a mortal, too limited. Possibly she was referring to the many men of her day who were terrible drinkers and who tended to keel over early, or she could have been alluding to a spouse's early death through natural causes. That was the benign interpretation.

The other involved the power of Charlotte's own mind. The mind was very powerful—it could stop a train hurtling toward disaster; it could manufacture money for the impoverished; heal the sick, feed the hungry, unwrap Lazarus if necessary. It could put the right person in the right place at the right time—or the wrong person at the wrong time. It could push him into the street.

She thought she heard a soft knock on the door. It opened, and the Porter entered. "You are harming yourself with your destructive thoughts," he said with his tight little smile. He cleared his throat several times and adjusted his chin strap. Chin strap? Was he wearing the monkey's hat? *I'm not strong enough,* she thought. *I can't do this. Please.* She raised the wand in an instinctive gesture of protection. The door opened wider and Roberta entered with a florist's long white box.

The Porter was gone.

"Are you all right? You look . . . funny."

Charlotte put the wand down. "I'm fine. I was just thinking."

"What's that?"

"It's a sort of wizard's wand, for Baird. I have presents for him, including a wonderful dump truck your uncle Mel and I bought . . . but I wanted to make him something. . . ."

"Does it work?"

"What do you mean?"

"Well, does it do anything?"

Charlotte smiled at her. "You mean, like, beep? Or light up? No, it's just something to play with, for the imagination."

"Somebody brought you this," Roberta said. "You want me to open it?" She was already lifting the top and unfolding the lilac-colored tissue paper. "A Chinaman left it. He rang the doorbell and left."

"That must be Dr. Gum, my professor. He and his wife had to flee mainland China after the revolution. They came here to start a new life."

"Neat."

"I don't think you're supposed to say 'Chinaman.'"

Roberta put her hand over her mouth with an anguished look, and Charlotte hastened to tell her it was all right, really. She hadn't done anything wrong. People said it all the time; they just didn't realize how it sounded. But she was particularly fond of Dr. Gum. He was a very nice man. "I think it must have been very hard for them at first, being such important people in their own country, to come here where nobody knew how important they were. They didn't even know the language, and you know how stupid people appear to be when they don't know the language—even when they're brilliant."

"I'm mortified."

Charlotte sat down next to her on the edge of the bed. Roberta was wearing her mannish trousers and a white, short-sleeved shirt that made her look young and innocent, like an anxious camper far from home. "But what's in the box?"

"Maybe it's not from your professor," Roberta said, cheering up. "Maybe it's from an admirer. Aunt Rosey said you used to have a lot of admirers."

"Dr. Gum is sort of an admirer, in a way."

Roberta grinned mischievously. "In what way?"

"Not that way. Let's look."

Roberta lifted out a dozen miniature pink roses and handed them to Charlotte, and then the card, which Charlotte read silently. Roberta leaned toward her, reading it over her shoulder. "What exam?" she asked.

"Fundamentals of Science. I passed. Isn't that amazing?"

"I thought they would be sympathy flowers, like all the others downstairs."

"Well, they are. But he adds a message: 'Congratulations, my dear Mrs. McGuffey! You receive a passing grade!' I'm going to graduate!"

"What will you do?"

"I don't know. I've always been in school, in one way or another. I don't know what it's like to be . . ." She raised her arms in an expansive gesture.

"Sprung," said Roberta.

"Yes, sprung. Melvin would be so surprised! I finished!"

"I need to tell you something." Roberta looked very grave.

"What is it?"

"I'm really sorry about Uncle Melvin."

"Thank you. I know you are."

"*Really* sorry."

"Yes."

"I think it's horrible."

"Thank you."

"And it's sad, too."

"Yes. But we'll be all right; don't worry. We'll be all right."

"Do you think Hoskins is sad?"

"I don't know, really. He doesn't show his feelings."

Roberta screwed up her face and hunched over a little. "Aunt Charlotte?"

"What is it?"

"Nothing."

"Nothing?"

"I was wondering . . . never mind."

"Maybe you'll ask me later."

"Maybe," Roberta repeated doubtfully. "There's something else. I need to warn you that we're going to HoJo's for lunch tomorrow and they want you to come. Well, I mean, Aunt Rosey wants you to come. She's the one who's planned it. At first, I was glad because of the opportunity it will give me to study human nature. My English teacher says I have to observe human nature in all its guises. But now I'm not so sure. It could be gruesome. Aunt Rosey says it will be an 'agape,' which she told everybody is a ritual practiced by the ancient Greeks. Or something. We're going after the memorial get-together for Uncle Melvin." It was sort of like a funeral, Roberta explained in a rush, seeing Charlotte's expression, but more informal, because Christian Scientists didn't believe in funerals—not that *she* was a Christian Scientist—her friend Elaine had told her it was a cult, and it was very, very embarrassing. She was going to study the world's religions and pick one of her own—after she was an adult, of course. She didn't know enough yet. "The get-together is supposed to be a surprise," she added. "I hope you don't mind if I spoiled it. Aunt Rosey says it will help you expunge your moribund condition."

"That would be good," Charlotte said, tossing her heavy braid onto her back and offering a small smile. "Or maybe we could just wave this magic wand and it will go away on its own," she said, and Roberta laughed.

The waitress at Howard Johnson's showed the little party of mourners, dazed and chilled to the bone, to the nearly deserted dining room. "I saw Mommy Kissing Santa Claus" was playing on the loudspeaker; in the far corner, orange lights blinked on a plastic tree. There was a brief scuffle as Baird and Norman dove for the same chair while the adults were occupied with shedding their snowy overcoats and hats. Winston Berry found a high chair for Hoskins. "There you go, Champ," he said, lifting the boy into it and giving him a little pat on the head. Hoskins dodged away.

Charlotte sat down next to him and handed him a bowl of sugar cubes from the table. He began opening them, giving each one a methodical lick as he took it out of the paper and placed it in a train of cubes on the tray in front of him. He was perfectly calm, perhaps even more angelic-looking than usual. He had had a full-blown tantrum upon leaving the snowy, windswept city park, which Rosey had chosen as the site for the memorial. No one had been able to fathom why she had chosen the place, and she hadn't explained, though as they left, Kitty had asked her if she had perhaps been imagining it on a summer day, filled with happy families picnicking on the grass.

The experience had left everyone dazed and disoriented. They had plunged through the snow toward a cluster of snow-laden picnic tables at the far side of the park, plummeting through the hard layer of crust at each step with little cries of dismay and stopping every few yards to recover boots or shake the snow out of gloves and mittens. A thin sun came out briefly in between snow squalls, but the wind was bitter, whipping coats open and sending hats flying. They gathered into a dispirited circle around the tables, and Dr. Berry read a few somber passages from the Bible, followed by Kitty reading from the *Science and Health* in a quavering voice. She concluded with a little homily. "There is no cause for lamentations. Man *is,* not *was* or *will be.* We are the same before birth as after. As our Beloved Leader reminds us, it is life that is real and death that is the illusion."

Rosey then recited Jerome Baird's poem, her voice straining as she tried to override the wind, and Norman and Baird crept away to a trash barrel nearby to examine its contents. While she shouted out the words in which the poet called upon the lonely stargazer for help in finding his way in life, likening the heroic figure to sailors of old who might steer the weary traveler away from the reefs and shoals of inward-turning souls, the boys pulled out the bottom half of a frozen squirrel, cut off cleanly at the midpoint. Winston Berry leapt toward them, whisking the carcass away, but not before Hoskins caught sight of it. He reached out for it, straining to get out of Roberta's arms, and let out a bloodcurdling scream when Dr. Berry dropped it back into the trash can. Charlotte hurried back to the parking lot with him, and the others followed in their wake, stunned into silence by the utter ferocity of Hoskins's outburst. It took half an hour for Charlotte to calm him down, sitting in the car with him with all the windows rolled up while the others stood around awkwardly making small talk.

The waitress came to take their orders, and Rosey ordered a round of hot-fudge sundaes. It was going to be on her, she added gaily; it was her treat. The adults remained silent, looking at one another for clues. Baird and Norman wanted hot-fudge sundaes, with cherries. Roberta said she wanted fried clams. Rosey laughed. They weren't there for dinner, she told her; they were there for sundaes. "Forget it, then," Roberta said. "I'll just have ketchup."

"Well, Hoskins will have a sundae, I know that."

"He likes plain ice cream," said Baird. "He doesn't like gooey stuff."

"He doesn't like *sundaes?*" wailed Rosey. "I never heard of such a thing!" She was very disappointed, she said. She had wanted everybody to have a nice time. She had looked forward to this for a long time, especially out there in the park, with the cold wind blowing. This was their treat. It was to be a kind of modern kind of agape. Rosey looked around. When nobody asked her to explain, she shrugged, clearly demoralized by their lack of enthusiasm.

Winston and Bunny said they would have sundaes. Roberta took out her notebook and began writing.

"Wonderful! Kitty?"

"I'll have water."

"I'll have tea, please," said Charlotte.

The waitress regarded them sadly. Her little cap, its brim decorated with a drooping holly sprig, was stuck to her thin hair with hundreds of hairpins. "Well, I want a hot-fudge sundae," Rosey told her. "Is the fudge really hot?"

The waitress nodded. She hadn't written anything down.

"And lots of whipped cream. Is it real whipped cream? I don't like the kind they have now in those cans. It just isn't the same. I don't think it's real."

"Could you bring me a plate for my ketchup?" Roberta asked as the waitress was leaving. The girl turned around and gave her a look.

"How old is our young fellow now?" asked Bunny Berry.

Charlotte started to answer, but Baird interrupted, loudly repeating the question. "How old is Hoskins?"

Hoskins looked up, as if on cue. "Tree," he said, clear as a bell.

Baird grinned. "He said it! He said he was three!"

Charlotte turned to the others, excited. "Did you hear what he said? Say it again, Hoskins. Tell us how old you are." He placed another sugar cube at the end of the train. They all watched expectantly.

"How old is Hoskins?" Baird asked again in a shrill voice.

"Tree," he said softly, smiling shyly as everybody clapped.

"Isn't this wonderful!" said Kitty.

"It's a miracle!" yelled Baird.

Kitty laughed. "Not a miracle, Baird. It's what we *expect,* isn't it? Hoskins is a very talented little boy."

"He sure can scream," said Norman.

When the waitress came with their orders, Rosey dove into her sundae with exclamations, offering spoonfuls all around. Roberta poured a mound of ketchup onto her plate, then stirred it with her fork. Rosey asked Kitty how her water was, with a wry smile, and Kitty said, "Wonderful; very fresh," with grand enthusiasm, as if she didn't understand she was being teased.

Bunny Berry asked Charlotte if she thought she would be spending the summer in Vermont again this year, and Baird piped up between mouthfuls before she could answer. "We always go to Vermont!"

"Always, for Baird, is four summers, you have to understand," she told Bunny.

"But when you're seven," Bunny said, "that's a lot of your life."

"It's half," said Norman.

"Wow," said Roberta, "math genius at work," and Norman stuck out his tongue.

Winston explained that they were looking for summer rentals. The Presbyterians were having a Worldwide Convocation the following year, and they needed to call in their brethren from the foreign missions this summer for planning sessions. "You might want to consider it, Charlotte. If you do go."

"What a fine idea," said Bunny. "You know the Swayzes, don't you? They always rent out their house to our people in the summer. You could ask them how we do as landlords."

Charlotte had never seen her neighbor Genevieve Swayze's exotic tenants, only the house gifts they left behind: tribal baskets, wooden flutes, beaded bags, ivory dogs. From these, Genevieve had told Charlotte, she had imagined the diligent craftsmen at work around her house—colorful African princes fashioning tribal baskets; short golden-skinned Peruvians carving flutes; Dutch theologians thoughtfully planting bulbs; silent Lapps tying knots. Genevieve knew her tenants spent a lot of time out on the lawn because of all the badminton birdies she found in the grass, and the many copies of "Amazing Grace" in French and Swahili left under the porch. Other than that, they left no trace; the Berrys were meticulous, and so were their guests. The church paid very well, too, Genevieve had told Charlotte.

"Our rental period coincides with school vacation in Syracuse, for obvious reasons. You usually leave after Baird gets out of school, don't you?" Winston licked the last bit of fudge from his spoon.

"I'll think about it," said Charlotte. "I haven't really made any plans."

"Of course not," said Bunny, "it's much too early for you to be making plans. We should know by March, though, if you want to rent out your house. We furnish the linens, if that's a consideration. Otherwise, you can leave everything just as it is. I'll even hire your girl to keep her eye on things here for you, if that would make you more comfortable."

"Charlotte has a lot to think about," said Kitty.

"Of course," Bunny agreed.

"The house in Vermont is so gloomy!" said Rosey. "It would be a big mistake, in my opinion. At this time in your life. You'd be so lonely! The people in the village are very nice, of course, but they're not your type. Besides, it would be too sad for the boys."

"It wouldn't be sad," said Baird.

"Sad," Hoskins repeated. "Morebun."

"My goodness!" exclaimed Rosey. "What did he say?"

"'Moribund,'" said Roberta. "It's on your week's list. Remember? We were going to expunge Aunt Charlotte's moribund condition."

"For goodness' sakes, Roberta, I wouldn't talk like that in public," Rosey said good-naturedly, and everybody laughed.

Harry arrived by taxi from the train station at the last minute, looking fit as a fiddle and loaded down with presents. Kitty said he looked wonderful—energetic and in command and oh, my goodness, so handsome! He was wearing new clothes, a good-looking, slimming pair of chinos and a crisp white shirt, which he said he'd gotten at a little haberdashery on Main Street in St. Johnsbury. Rosey complimented him extravagantly. He looked just like Cary Grant, she said. When Kitty found a private moment with him, she gave him a big hug. She was so proud of him! "I got a refill on the little white you-know-whats," he whispered to her, grinning, and despite herself, Kitty laughed.

As soon as he could, Harry took Charlotte aside and told her that everything was done and there was nothing for her to worry about. She thanked him, leaning her head against his shoulder. He put his arm around her waist and hugged her. "You *are* looking good, Harry," she said. "Maybe you should travel more often."

"I was able to sell the truck," he said, furtively removing a strand of her hair from his mouth. "All the papers were right there in the glove compartment."

"You sold Melvin's truck?"

"Isn't that what you wanted? Kitty was sure."

"I guess I'm just surprised," she said, thinking about how careful Melvin was with his truck, how hard he worked to keep it running. He would be so upset! Harry seemed pained, on the verge of an abject apology. "I suppose it was impractical for me to think of keeping it," she said, trying to help.

"At least it will be a little cash for you. The fellow gave me fifty dollars."

"Oh, Harry!"

"Was that too little? He said the defroster didn't work. Oh, boy, I've made a royal mess, haven't I?" His shoulders sagged, his face fell. "Oh, boy, what have I done now!"

"That's all right, Harry; don't worry about it. You did your best. Please, let's forget it."

"I don't know if I can."

"Of course you can. Let's talk about Christmas. And your daughter—she's looking beautiful, isn't she?"

Roberta had come downstairs wearing a dress, a sort of a purple concoction, it seemed, too tight in the waist, too big in the shoulders. Her expression was of one who had just been run through with a sword. "Dad bought it," she announced miserably to the room. "What do you think?"

Christmas morning was a big success. The tree was perfectly decorated; the children's stockings bulged with treats. It took a long time to open the presents, which the adults drew out by imposing a one-present-at-a-time rule. Norman showed off his Ted Williams–model Little League bat, reminding everyone that his hero's career batting average as of the end of the '52 season was .361. ("He might be in Korea," he reminded everyone, "but he'll be back—you wait and see. And then he'll hit four hundred again.") Baird waved his magician's wand around, touching people's heads and calling them by silly names. It lasted almost an hour before Harry sat on it. Charlotte praised the casserole dishes Rosey gave her, pointing out that most of them were in good condition. Hoskins, dressed in corduroy coat and hat, methodically tore all the wrapping paper into small bits. Roberta paraded around in the silky black-and-white-striped robe Rosey presented to her, making her gasp in surprise. Later, Harry handed Roberta a tiny package labeled "TOP SECRET—OPEN IN PRIVATE." She opened it in the bathroom and came out to give him a hug. "Thanks for the pierced-ear earrings, Dad," she whispered. "I won't say a word."

"Just don't make the holes too bloody," he told her. "And don't wear them around the house. Try to be discreet for once."

While Harry was making his rubbery pancakes for their late-morning brunch, Mr. Matson called Kitty from Holyoke to wish her a Merry Christmas and to say that he'd been feeling so good, he'd been bowling. (In a burst of lightheartedness, he referred to his heart as his "ticker.") When they were all seated, Kitty suggested an orange-juice toast. "To a wonderful family and a wonderful Christmas," she said, raising her glass. "Maybe the best Christmas ever." A long silence followed. "Well, maybe not the best ever," she added, "but very nice."

CHAPTER

8

It was a bright, sunny Saturday in late March. The pussy willows were out, and the last of the ugly mounds of blackened snow were almost gone. Genevieve Swayze had telephoned Charlotte to say she'd seen a robin; crocuses had been sighted in people's yards. There was a general feeling in the air that something was about to happen, something was about to give way, and the long winter would finally let go.

As soon as Gretel left with the children for the movies, Charlotte went upstairs to sort through Melvin's things and make decisions. Her sisters had tried to help her with that after Christmas, but she had told them she wasn't ready. She didn't feel particularly ready now, either, but the sunshine helped. She took a green tweed jacket out of the closet and set it on a chair, then another jacket, a pair of trousers, a belt. She emptied one of the small drawers in his bureau: pencils, matches, handkerchiefs, socks. A key, a film canister. A snapshot of Hannibal as a puppy, loose change. More socks.

The strength began to drain out of her. She sat down on the bed and reached for a book from the bookshelf—*The History of Bandstands in America, Volume I*—and started leafing through it. Books were easier. Would somebody in Africa want this? Bunny Berry had told her that the missions could use just about anything. She picked up another, *Ships of the Desert*. She gazed at the sphinx on the cover, its eyes glinting in the reddish-gold of a setting sun. Maybe. *The Illustrated Digest of World War II*? Possibly. Algeria had seen the war. When she took the next one off the shelf, a little wave of dread washed over her. It was the book that included one of Melvin's photographs, *The American Barn: 1850–1950*. She turned to his picture of the Wyndams' barn, which had been partially destroyed in the village fire the previous summer. It was a bright day, and Melvin had heightened the contrast to the dark interior. One of the Andoulette boys, shirtless and barefoot, was just visible in the shadows.

Melvin had worked as a photographer for the Farm Security Administration before the war, taking the kinds of pictures a person could pass by a hundred times and never notice: a farmer cutting hay with a team of horses; a barn struggling against gravity and neglect; an empty street of fine houses; farm women passing buckets; men lined up at the quarries, ready to work. The people in these photographs were stoic, and the air around them was thick and grainy. When the war was over, he had told her, people weren't interested in those kinds of old-fashioned pictures, the ones showing people working hard and pinching pennies; they wanted a world that was new and shiny. His souvenir photos offered all that. They were picture perfect, images from everywhere and nowhere.

Charlotte looked around the bedroom at the books scattered across the floor, the sad little pile of clothes. She'd done nothing since her sisters left, had done nothing to help herself, or the children. Hoskins had made no progress at all—the hope they'd all felt about his starting to talk had soon evaporated. Baird was sad. She hadn't been sleeping. Ever since the policemen had come to her door, she had been carefully navigating a path around the rim of a blackened hole. Had she not said anything to Melvin the morning he left for Vermont, the hole would in time have closed up like any ordinary wound. As it was, it had stayed open and gaping and charred, and after three months she still couldn't look down inside. She was poised on the edge, and she couldn't move without falling. Sometimes she felt she couldn't breathe, either, and then she would clench her teeth and hear the distant beating of drums.

The valves of the heart, opening and closing for the passage of the blood, obey the mandate of mortal mind as directly as does the hand, admittedly moved by the will. Charlotte had inadvertently memorized Mrs. Eddy's words; after constant repetition, they had taken on an increasingly sinister tone, conjuring up a group of natives with strange haircuts, like rooster combs, sitting around in a circle and beating drums in the smoky twilight. The phrase *mandate of mortal mind* had a certain hypnotic rhythm, especially when repeated endlessly, and against her will. It was Mrs. Eddy's point, of course, that the involuntary responses of the body were misnamed, that there was no such thing as involuntary action because all actions of the body were governed by the so-called mind of man. In this case, her own so-called mind had distorted the meaning of the words and turned them against herself, which would mean she was practicing self-inflicted mental malpractice, a metaphysical impossibility but probably true nonetheless.

She realized that she was staring at the sphinx with the red eyes, and she put the book in the pile of things to go to the missions.

When Gretel returned with the children, she called upstairs to say she was taking Hoskins to the basement with her to do the laundry. Baird ran up to tell her about the movie. They'd seen *Snow White and the Seven Dwarfs* and Gretel had bought them candy and Hoskins had sung "Heigh-Ho-Heigh-Ho" all the way home and when Gretel had pulled the car into the driveway she'd told him to shut up and then she told him she was sorry and then she cried and she told Baird not to tell. "Are you mad?" he asked.

"Sometimes people lose their patience with him, Baird. I know she means well; she's very fond of you both. It's probably why she's doing the laundry, because she feels bad. I'll talk to her. I'm sure she's very, very sorry."

Baird was looking around the room. "What are you doing?"

"I'm . . . cleaning."

"Those are Daddy's clothes."

"I know. I'm giving them to the Berrys, for their people in Africa."

He sat down on the bed. "Why?"

"Because I don't know what else to do with them. I know it must be distressing . . ."

Baird shrugged. "I don't care." He picked up the book about bandstands. "Why are you giving away this book? I like it."

"Oh, I didn't know that."

"And this." He picked up the book with Melvin's photograph in it.

"I'm not giving that away, don't worry. Did you ever see your daddy's photograph of the Wyndams' barn? Here, look." She found the page and handed it back to him. "Do you recognize that boy? I think it's Axel, when he was little. That picture was taken a long time ago, back in 1940, even before I knew your father."

"I think it's Amos."

"Amos is too young."

"Let's bring the book with us this summer and we can ask Mrs. Andoulette."

"I don't know that we're going."

"Why not?" His voice was brittle, the way it was before he cried.

"I've told you, I'm not sure we should do that. We've never been up there alone."

"I'll help, I promise. I won't be annoying."

"You're never annoying."

"Then why can't we?"

He made her want to laugh, the way he'd reduced their only obstacle to something under his control. She thought of arriving at the house on McCrillis Hill, seeing Melvin's coffee cup in the drainer next to the black sink. She thought of what her sisters would say.

"Please, Mom?"

She wondered what she might find. It was possible that he might have left a note—she'd thought of it before. Or might not have. Why would he, anyway? He certainly intended to come back to the house. His death wasn't premeditated. But he might have started a letter to her, or jotted down some thoughts, or he might have said something to some-body. She would learn, certainly, in what condition he'd left the house that day. She could see what he'd been reading. (There were shelves and shelves of books in the library; he always found one there to read. Odd books, old-fashioned, unusual things.) The boys could run around. She could make jam. She could find out if he'd talked to Leona or Beatriz—somebody might be able to tell her something. She might even be able to look down into the hole, and perhaps this black, charred feeling would go away.

Baird was jumping up and down on the bed, gaining momentum with each spring. "We're going, I know! We're going! Hooray! Hooray! We're going!"

"Wait, I never said so, Baird," she said, trying to look stern. Jumping on beds was a completely forbidden thing to do, and it looked glorious.

"Please? Please?" A *please* for every jump. The mattress was begin-ning to slide off the frame. "We are, I know it! We're going, we're going!" and he leapt off the bed into her arms, his weight hitting her all at once and making her sprawl backward into the chair. They landed on the pile of clothes, the handkerchiefs and socks. The chair went flying, and they erupted in helpless laughter. Baird sped out of the room and down the stairs, yelling for joy. She heard him go into the kitchen, down the cellar stairs.

Bunny Berry was delighted when Charlotte called. "What luck! We're desperate for rentals! I'll help you get ready. I'm sure we can make this work." They came over right away. Winston was wearing a striped apron. (He was making a torte, he explained. He'd been a pastry chef in his youth—Charlotte might not have known that, he said proudly—and he'd found that making a nice dessert on Saturday afternoon helped him work out the snarly places in his sermons on Sunday.) Within an hour they had settled on all the arrangements, and Winston trotted back to the parsonage to roll out the crust while Bunny stayed to help Charlotte fin-ish the task she had started earlier.

"Oh, it's a wonderful feeling to finish a job," Bunny said gaily as Charlotte handed her the teapot. "We'll be done in a jiff." Charlotte found herself buoyed by Bunny's spirit, which she found suddenly charming. She'd always been leery of her; perhaps she'd never given her a chance to shine.

They found boxes in the basement and began heaping everything in them—Bunny would sort it all later, she said; it was not something Charlotte should be doing herself, and especially not alone. The job was to clear everything out that Charlotte didn't want to keep, and Bunny would do the rest. The trick was not to get bogged down in what would happen to things on the other end. When the bedroom was done, Bunny began putting the books back on the shelves before they moved on downstairs. "You'll want to keep these for the boys," she said. She picked up the bandstands book. "Melvin certainly had eclectic tastes, didn't he?"

"He was interested in a lot of things."

"Like you," said Bunny. "No wonder you got along so well."

Braiding her long hair for the last time, Charlotte felt as though she were dressing the dead. Though she'd never done such a thing, she was sure that the slow, ceremonial nature of the task was the same, with the same careful avoidance of regret, the same concentration on doing things right out of respect for the momentous occasion.

She worked carefully, looking in the mirror propped up above the kitchen sink and concentrating hard on her task. The boys were asleep upstairs. The dog lay on the small braided rug, his chin flat on the floor.

The first braid was the hardest to do. She first tried the kitchen shears, which were stout enough for broccoli but not for one of her braids, and then ran for her sewing scissors. She started cutting at the lowest point on her jawline. The scissors made an unpleasant grinding sound as they labored through the first of the braid's three strands. When she got to the last strand, the cut ends of the other two swung out grotesquely, like helpless climbers having lost their footing and dangling alongside the cliff by a rope. She quickly cut through the remaining strand and the heavy braid fell with a thud into the sink. She stared at it for a moment in shock and wonder.

The second braid was easier to do: She was practiced, and there was no turning back. Still, the awful noise of the scissors made her skin crawl. She set the second braid down in the sink next to the first and shook out her hair. It sprang out all over in confused directions. When she combed it out, she could tell that one side was clearly longer than the other. She began clipping, first on one side, then on the other, trying to feel the length in back with her hands. Her ear showed on one side—nothing to do but show her ear on the other. By the time she finished, her hair was very short. Short, and still uneven. She looked about twelve.

She washed it quickly in the sink and rubbed it dry with a towel, elated at the ease and quickness of it; it still stuck out in different places but it was better. It would curl, and take the shape of her head. If not, she would try hats.

She laid the braids out side by side like two corpses on a clean dish towel and studied them. Detached, their animal natures had suddenly come alive; the little sprouts of coppery hair below the rubber bands extended out into space as if groping blindly to feel where they might go next, like the ends of earthworms seeking a path into the earth, unaware that their other ends had been hacked off. Her first thought was to put them in a paper bag and stash them away in a closet somewhere. She opened the drawer next to the stove where she kept the hammer and nails and rubber bands. She slipped a rubber band around each of the cut ends and set the braids, intact, into the drawer, thinking of what Cal McGuffey had once said to Melvin about her hair.

When Melvin first brought her to the house on McCrillis Hill to meet his parents, it was July of 1943. Gas was rationed then, and they used up all the coupons they had on the trip. That first evening, they sat out on the tilted porch with Cal and Adele after supper, waiting in silence for the fireflies to come out in the field below the house.

The smell of cooking onions had followed them outside and soon mixed with the smell of Adele McGuffey's Old Golds and the sweetish tobacco in Cal McGuffey's pipe. Adele sat silently in her small rocker, holding the glass ashtray in her lap. She was a small, dark-haired woman who wore her thin, knobby braids wrapped around her head like pop-corn strings, and she was so shy, Charlotte had at first wondered if her future mother-in-law was mute; Melvin and his father talked over and around her, ignoring her completely, to all intents and purposes treating her like a chifforobe. Melvin's father was small and wiry. He was, by turns, both garrulous and taciturn, and it was hard to know what was going to happen when you spoke to him. Charlotte was already a little bit afraid of him. He had strong opinions, and when he blurted them out, it was hard not to feel attacked.

Finally, Melvin spoke up. Late in June every year, he said, the field down there was ablaze with lupines. They bloomed all at once so that people from miles around came just to see them. He knew it was hard to imagine, now that the flowers had passed and the field had reverted to grasses and weeds, but it was a wonderful sight.

Adele and Cal nodded. Charlotte said, "I'll bet they're lovely."

His father had planted them for his mother when they were first married, Melvin said. It was his wedding gift to her.

Cal McGuffey knocked his pipe against the railing. Charlotte murmured something indistinct.

After a long silence, Melvin announced that they had some news.

"About the war?" Cal McGuffey asked. The Third Reich had just made its third assault on the Eastern Front. Calvin McGuffey was a fervent supporter of America's role in the war and was still suspicious of the reasons his only son wasn't helping.

"It's personal."

There was a long pause.

"Charlotte and I plan to be married." Neither of his parents said anything, and Melvin finally added, "That's why we're here. I thought you'd like to meet her."

"All right," his father said. After a while, he turned to his wife. "They're getting married, Mother. Did you hear that?"

She turned her head and looked at him—not at Charlotte or Melvin. "So they say."

Did she doubt it? Charlotte wondered. Did she know something they didn't know? In the ensuing silence, Charlotte decided it must be a country expression, like "Aha" or "What do you know?" At least, when they'd told Charlotte's father, he'd managed to say, "Fine." Rosey, on the other hand, had wept.

Later that night, when Mel sneaked down the hall and into bed with her, he surprised her by saying he thought his parents liked her. She wondered how he knew that. Had they said something? she'd asked him. "The only thing Father asked about was your hair," he told her. "He wanted to know if it was real."

"He thinks it's a wig?"

"I don't know. He said it was an awful lot of hair for one woman to carry around all day, and he wondered what you did with it at night. So I told him you took it off and put it in the drawer." They had laughed off and on about it all night.

And here she was, finally putting her hair to rest in a drawer, with no one to enjoy the joke but herself.

A Chink in His Armor

*The Porter doesn't care for challenges, so be forewarned—you'll
lose any battle you try to wage with him. He may puff up like
a bullfrog and sing into your ear for longer than you can bear it,
or he may simply turn on his heels and leave; not, of course,
without a biting remark designed to deflate you. If you want to
stay and fight, watch out. When he curls his lip in a smile, you
will find that you want to strike him. Your heart will beat a little faster as you realize the mess you're about to get into, and
you will probably feel that involuntary tightening of the muscles in the chest that invariably signals the onset of saying something stupid. Not a good idea. He sneers and oozes through your
pores, making you want to wring yourself out. Your fingers itch
for his neck. Watch out! They say apoplexy is caused by a hem-
orrhage to the brain, a rush of blood in the wrong direction. It
causes paralysis, insensibility, floundering. A cathartic must be
administered at once. If the limbs become paralyzed, strychnine
is called for. If you can't find any of these remedies, a pot of mustard will do. Dip your feet in it. Put ice on your head. Send out
for leeches, shout, plug your finger into the nearest socket.
Reverse the flow of blood, and send it somewhere else; get it out
of the brain before it explodes.*

*The monkey will be sitting on his shoulder, watching atten-
tively. He's bored, but this little hubbub has perked up his interest. His expression is tranquil; his dark almond-shaped eyes are*

soft and sweet—there's nothing more innocent-looking than a bored primate. He takes a peanut out of the folds of the Porter's collar, scrutinizes the shell, cracks it softly with his teeth, extracts the nut, and tucks it into the Porter's ear. And then pooof! *Out flies the peanut! The monkey leaps down off his shoulder, landing on the carpeted aisle as easily as a butterfly. He scoops up the nut, examines it intently, and puts it in his nose. The Porter snaps his fingers. "Not in the nose!" The monkey pays no mind and skips off down the aisle, chattering to himself like a merry, innocent child.*

This might be the chance you've been waiting for, a chink in the Porter's armor—he's got an Achilles' heel! You look frantically around the dimly lighted coach for help. Most of the passengers appear to be unconscious. They're dozing in the stiff, bristly seats, hunched in that way that signifies the onset of sleep, shoulders slowly folding down around the rib cage, chin descending into neck, jowls loose and flapping at each exhalation. You recognize Cranky at one end of the coach. How did she manage to stay aboard today? She's dressed to kill in a capacious dress and matching maroon hat, reading a paperback by the dim light of an overhead lamp. UFO BRIDE! *the cover screams. Across from her is Disappointment. His seat mate, Weak Ankles, is looking lovely today in a shirred blue dress with matching pumps. Adolescence is sprawled in a seat across the aisle, the cuffs of his moth-eaten reindeer sweater riding rapidly toward his elbows. His hands are too big; his feet look like snowshoes. He's watching the murmuring couple intently, trying to learn the secrets of love.*

The monkey leaps quietly to the top of Cranky's seat. In the blink of an eye, he has grabbed at her hat and pulled it off. Then he grabs at her breast. Whomp! *She strikes the monkey in the chest. He backs off, chattering and scolding, trying to enlist the sympathy of the other passengers. He leaps into the boy's lap, leaps away, springs into your arms. You're very frightened. His little teeth are very sharp. He's not wearing diapers. Everyone in the coach is suddenly awake, watching to see what the Porter will do. The train whizzes past empty fields, ramshackle build-ings, dry, sandy roads. You're nowhere. The monkey puts his long arms around your neck and hugs you tight.*

Beede, Vermont

If mortals would keep proper ward over mortal mind,
the brood of evils which infest it would be cleared out.

—MARY BAKER EDDY, *SCIENCE AND HEALTH WITH*
KEY TO THE SCRIPTURES

. . .

CHAPTER

9

Once they were out of Rutland, the rain let up and a pale disk of a sun struggled to shine through a white sky. They came over Mendon Mountain and down the other side, away from the ski chalets and curio shops and wholesale baskets and into the sparser, more rugged landscape of central Vermont, through green and narrow valleys shaped by winding rivers, up and over densely wooded hills. The soil here was thin and stony; every inch of arable land was in use. Rows of ankle-high corn grew on nearly vertical slopes; Holsteins grazed sideways on precipitous hillside pastures. The narrow road wound in and out, around sharp curves, past tidy white farmhouses, tilting barns, tarpapered shacks, retirees' havens with silly names, vegetable gardens, shabby-looking roadhouses.

It was a warm and humid day in early June. Charlotte drove with her skirt bunched up around her knees, leaning forward like one of those courageous innocents of old attached to the prows of ships, aiming their cargo toward an unknown horizon. Baird, in the passenger seat beside her, remained upright and vigilant, ever alert for familiar landmarks.

Hoskins was asleep in the back, his face pressed into the car's upholstery, his golden-red curls plastered flat to his scalp in the moist air. The dog sat bolt upright next to him and stared out the window as if counting miles.

When the rain stopped, Charlotte rolled down her window and let the wind mess up her cap of curly hair. It was one of the many pleasures of having cut it—she felt lighter, freer, deliciously different. She liked the boyish, rather mischievous effect and the way her red curls clung to her head, showing off the curve of her ears and the nape of her long neck; her eyes seemed brighter and surprisingly bold.

It was one of the most daring things she'd ever done. She hadn't consulted with a soul. Both her sisters had been appalled. "It was your whole *personality,*" Rosey wailed. "You look like . . . someone else! No one will know who you are!" And they didn't. Acquaintances ignored her. Strangers on the street no longer turned back for a second look at her splendid hair. She was a chameleon disguised on a branch, free to observe without being seen. When they'd stopped for lunch at their traditional halfway stopping place, the proprietor of the Dinosaur Hut hadn't recognized her, giving her only a cursory nod as she stepped up to the counter to order Stegosaurus burgers for herself and the boys and a rare T-Rex for Hannibal.

They rounded a curve and came up behind a puttery old tractor driven by a boy not much older than Baird; the boy looked neither right nor left, studiously ignoring the traffic collecting behind him. When she finally passed him on a brief stretch of straight road, Baird folded his arms against his chest and assumed an important expression before announcing that this was the summer he was going to learn to drive. His father had promised to take him to the fairgrounds in the truck and let him practice.

Charlotte expressed surprise. He had just turned eight; he was going into third grade. As far as she knew, third-graders didn't drive.

"Daddy said I have to practice, so when I'm older, I'll know how."

"You don't need to practice. When it's time for you to learn, you'll pick it up quickly. Don't worry, Baird. When the time comes, I'll teach you."

"In this car?" he asked, as though the DeSoto were a famous ruin.

She was about to launch into an arithmetic problem for him about his age and how old the car would be by the time he was ready to drive, but then he announced that he was willing to learn only on the truck, and she stopped. She should have known what was coming. He blamed her for letting his uncle Harry sell it, though she'd tried her best to explain that it was out of her control. It had wrenched her heart, seeing him sob with such abandon. He'd been talking about the truck ever since the accident, and about *the boy,* which is how he referred to Boyd Eppleman, making her wonder if he'd heard *boy* instead of *Boyd* the day he overheard Roberta reading the police report aloud to her mother in the kitchen. Was the boy in jail? he'd ask out of the blue. And, Was the boy in jail *now?* She'd found pictures Baird had drawn of him—big head, stick body, big eyes looking out through bars. But the expression was always Baird's, the eyebrows, the ears, the anxiety.

"Amos Andoulette drives. He's not very old."

"That's different. The Andoulettes are farmers."

"We're farmers."

"No, we're not. We're from the city."

"Daddy was a farmer."

"Your daddy was a photographer. A very good photographer, but not a farmer. He loved Vermont very much, but he still wasn't a farmer. And his father was not a farmer; Grampa Cal was a salesman." He asked her what Grampa Cal had sold, though she knew he'd heard it all before. "Just about everything," she said. "He sold tombstones for a while, then later he made up something he called McGuffey's Famous Cal-Oric Tea and made a lot of money selling it through the mail. It was supposed to help people lose weight, though your father always said there was nothing in it but tea." She looked over at Baird. "But it's the belief that counts, we know that, don't we? Grampa Cal was a very smart man, but possibly not as honest as he could have been. His inventions were . . . well . . . questionable." There were others, too. Cal-ipods, for one, special shoes that supposedly helped lame people walk, and Cal-iphones that helped deaf people hear. He'd made a lot of money on his schemes and lost it when the government closed him down for fraud. Melvin had never opened the boxes in the barn left over from his father's business but one of Cal's advertisements, printed in fancy bold letters, was tacked to the barn wall: NEW CURE FOR OBESITY! it proclaimed to an unsuspecting public. DRINK MCGUFFEY'S FAMOUS CAL-ORIC TEA!

It had not been a smooth departure. Both Rosey and Kitty had called early in the morning, while Charlotte was running back and forth between the house and the car and trying to get the loading done before the boys were up and in the way. Hannibal would need most of the backseat. He required enough room to turn around several times before lying down, or else he'd stand the whole way and tremble.

She was on her way back to the house at a fast clip when she heard the phone and rushed pell-mell to intercept it. It was Rosey again, pleading with her to change her mind and look for a beach house somewhere so that the boys could at least swim and not be cooped up all summer in a damp, depressing farmhouse with nothing but sad memories to keep them company. And Charlotte definitely—*definitely*—should not take the dog. The dog was lot of trouble, a lot of responsibility, and what if he ran away? Couldn't Charlotte leave him with the Berrys?

Kitty was more evenhanded with the call that followed and said only that she hoped Charlotte knew what she was doing. She'd gotten up early that morning to do some work for her on the spiritual meaning of journeys, she told Charlotte. "Just as the Lord guided Moses and the Israelites safely through a hostile Egypt and past the sterile shores of the Red Sea, parting the waters and allowing them to cross over on dry land, I know that you and the children will be guided safely to your temporary home."

"We'll be fine," said Charlotte, clutching the dog's bowl in her hand. "And we don't have to cross the Red Sea," she said, laughing. "We just have to get through Schenectady."

At eight o'clock, a little band of well-wishers had gathered at the curb in the early morning mist to say good-bye: Winston Berry, with his handmade banner on a yardstick; Bunny Berry, with a check made out to

Charlotte for three months' rent; and Gretel, with an oozing rhubarb cobbler, still warm from the oven. Charlotte had been touched to see the girl marching toward them in the early morning drizzle, baking dish in hand. She had wanted to come to Vermont with them, but Charlotte had said no. She told her that she needed to stay in Syracuse and help the Berrys keep the house tidy between tenants (the first set was coming from Dakar in a few days, followed by a contingent from Praetoria). She didn't say that she didn't want her along because she didn't want to take any informants with her. Her sisters were sure to be keeping track of her in Vermont, and she didn't see any reason to make it so easy for them.

Before driving off, Charlotte had wrapped the cobbler in a paper bag and set it on the floor at Baird's feet. She could see it already leaking onto the bag, and, a few blocks from the house, she stopped next to an empty lot and threw the whole thing, dish and all, into the wet underbrush. A man, happening by, scolded her. What an example she set for her children, throwing trash into the woods! When she got back into the car, Baird wanted to know what the man had said.

"Good morning, Missus, and have a good trip!" she told him, and he laughed at her attempt at a cheerful brogue.

A few miles before they reached the township line, the sun broke free of the clouds and they drove the rest of the way on a wet tar road that sparkled in sunshine, passing through a string of hamlets and settlements all named after Silas Beede, a Revolutionary soldier who was paid for his military service to his young country with tracts of land. In time they became Beede Center, Beede Corner, East Beede, South Beede, Beedeville, and the more substantial village of Beede itself.

The bigger farms along the way boasted proud names: the William A. Smith Farm; Robert Henley & Sons; Bruce Atkins, Polled Herefords. The women weren't mentioned, of course, though they worked as hard as their husbands and sons. On the last curve before the village, a mailbox in front of a modest Cape equitably proclaimed its owners "Ed & Nora Thrush," but the Thrushes ran a vacuum-cleaner distributorship and not a farm, and the only animals in their yard were brightly colored wooden cutout figures. Charlotte thought the life-size red dog might be new, as well as the row of bright green cornstalks along the driveway. Nora Thrush, wearing an apron over her Bermuda shorts, was standing on a step stool at her front window; she turned as the DeSoto approached, a roll of paper towels in one hand. Charlotte tapped the horn lightly—she didn't know if Nora would recognize her, but she didn't want to be unfriendly. Nora leaned toward her as the car passed, frowning, and Charlotte thought she saw her fall into the bank of spirea at the front of her house.

Baird began calling out the landmarks in a wild, wobbly voice. "*Sandpit!*" he yelled. "*Crooked tree!*" Hoskins, his pink cheeks bearing the clear imprint of the car's upholstery, stood up next to the dog in the backseat and waved with a faraway look, like a politician in a motorcade.

When they reached the village limits and the small black-and-white sign solemnly announcing its unincorporated status and its population of seventy-eight, Baird shot up in his seat and shouted, "The McGuffeys are here! Make that eighty-two!" just like his father always had. Charlotte looked over at him to see if he knew what he'd said. She knew he could count.

On they sailed, past Eugenia Sissy's and Ada Poole's matching immaculate pink houses with flawless cream-colored trim, and the sad mess of tar-papered shacks across the road from them; past the Moose Garage, which was what everybody called Bill Furst's crowded repair shop because of his sister Georgia seeing the moose; past the boarded-up school that had not exactly burnt down in the mill fire the summer before but had been seriously singed, and next to it, Mabel Coffin's ancient blue gas pumps, so miraculously spared; past the empty spot that had been the post office, built in 1813 and written up in the historical register as the only government building in the state of Vermont with a beveled palladium window over the front door, and the generous lot that had been the site of Eugene Wyndam's big barn with its well-known and well-loved cupola in the shape of the Vermont Statehouse; and finally, just before they reached the First Methodist Church, the empty space where the bob-

bin mill had been. As they passed, Baird hunched over expectantly, prepared to see what he could see. The fire had been the highlight of his life
so far, and as they drove by, he reported that he thought he could see
embers and that, possibly, after a whole year, the fire was still burning.

Baird had been the first to hear the whistle and to see the column of
smoke. He'd been down in the field below their house looking for moles
when he heard the mill whistle sound at the wrong time of day. The wind
was fierce, flattening the grass and swirling the long branches of the huge
white pines that bordered the field. When he saw the funnel of black
smoke break through the tops of the trees from the village below and billow into the sky, he'd raced to the barn to tell his father. A moment later
his mother came running across the lawn with Hoskins in her arms. His
father wiped his hands on his mustard-colored overalls and told her to
get the keys to the truck that were hanging on the board there in the barn.
For a long moment his mother had stayed frozen in place in front of the
board and his father had stepped forward calmly to point them out, saying, "Try to stay calm, Charlotte. That's the best thing you can do in an
emergency."

They piled into the truck with Hannibal in the back and took off,
hurtling over the bumpy lawn and down the dirt road to the village,
arriving barely in time to see the last of the shooting flames from the
mill's explosion. The wind whipped the flames eastward from the mill,
and within minutes the Wyndams' barn was engulfed. The fire leapt
over the Wyndams' house and headed across the road to the school,
where it stayed only long enough to blacken the clapboards and take a
chunk out of the bell tower. To the west were Mabel's gasoline pumps
and beyond them, the Wyndams' store. To the east, the Moose Garage.
The crowd held its breath while the fire made up its mind. With a
mighty roaring sound it struck westward, leaping over the rusted blue
pumps, leaving them unscathed, and went for the store, which it took in
one gulp. From there it passed to the post office. It roared through the
building, spitting out the huge granite blocks that served as its foundation, then recrossed the road to its place of origin, where it paused to
reconsider the Wyndams' house, a forgotten piece of work. It wasn't

enough that it had taken their store of fifty years, their barn and their milking stalls and pitchforks and their sow and the three hundred bales of rowen that Eugene had just gotten in and their famous cupola, but it wanted their linens and rockers and silverware as well, their family photographs and yellowed books and shoehorns and doilies and jellied preserves and every reminder of their past. For a full minute the fire burned in midair, like a spirit in a bottle, making everyone guess its evil intent. The Wyndams' house? Back for the gas pumps? More school? It wanted none of those things. Instead, it turned its back on mere human concerns and went for the church.

By then the line of people handing buckets up from the river had reached the road; the volunteer firemen were crippled by the lack of one of their trucks, which was down for repairs. Their hose was faulty, too short or too weak, with reinforcements from the surrounding towns just barely arriving. The crowd cried out when a shooting star of flames plopped down on the church's asphalt roof. Walter Turley's sons, Fred and Barry, were up in a flash, propelled to the roof by superhuman means. (No one could say they saw them climb. They used no ladders. They had no ropes.) They crawled up over the pitch in furnacelike heat and stamped on the flames that licked at the spire, dousing them with buckets passed up from below.

Later, a man named Hollins wrote an article about their daring deed for a national magazine called *Unnatural Events* and everyone in Beede kept a copy on their coffee table. When Anna Wyndam sent a sympathy card to Charlotte after Christmas, she included a copy with the following passage underlined: "All hands set to work to douse the raging flames. Even the summer folks up on McCrillis Hill rolled up their sleeves and joined the bucket brigade along with everyone else. It was this kind of spirit that put out the worst fire in the Town of Beede's history." In the margin, Anna wrote, "This Mr. Hollins doesn't seem to know that your husband was a native son." And then she had tacked on a little postscript. "Eugene has sold his cows and gone into the insurance business and is quite miserable."

"Wait," Baird shouted, "you missed our turn!"

Charlotte was preparing to turn into Leona's dooryard. A flag hung from the porch and a new, hand-lettered sign read POST OFFICE, BEEDE, VERMONT.

"We're supposed to go up to the house first," he said.

"I need to talk to Mrs. Cake about getting the phone hooked up."

"But we never stop at Mrs. Cake's first."

"We are today, Baird. This is the new post office, right here at their house." Charlotte got out of the car and smoothed down the front of her skirt. "Don't worry; this will only take a minute. You stay here and look after Hoskins. I'll be right back."

He watched her go inside.

Hoskins made a little moaning noise, and Baird ordered him to be quiet. A face appeared at an upstairs window of the Andoulettes' house across the road. It disappeared and then quickly reappeared at a downstairs window. The same face appeared and disappeared several times, much faster than anyone could run up and down the stairs inside the house. It was Alphie's twin sisters, Baird decided, playing a trick. Alsina and Almina were ten years old and identical twins, and they were always trying to fool people as to who was who. They dressed alike and wore their hair the exact same way, with their braids sticking out at the sides of their heads like popsicle sticks. Even the freckles on their faces were arranged in identical patterns.

Baird admired the Andoulettes very much. There were a lot of them, and they wrote on trees. In his own family, everyone treasured trees. They talked about their favorites and said how noble they were, but Alphie and his brothers and sisters wrote on them. They had an apple tree in their backyard that was scarred with messages, but it was still alive and it bore fruit, too. The Andoulettes ate applesauce at every meal, and for dessert they ate it on bread.

When he inherited the earth, Baird wanted a tree just like Alphie's, a tree that he could scar and it wouldn't die. *Blessed are the meek,* the Beatitude said, *for they shall inherit the earth. Meek,* his Sunday school teacher had explained, meant "mild-mannered," kind of timid, like himself. He didn't know why somebody who was timid would get picked, but he was glad. Hoskins wasn't meek; he was spoiled and he did whatever he wanted, but Baird was meek and because of that, he was fit to rule the earth. And when he did, no one in his kingdom would treasure trees.

Baird didn't know exactly how many brothers and sisters Alphie had. Their names all started with the same letter, and sometimes he got them mixed up. There was Amarita, who was bossy and who rode Peter the pony around the yard bareback with her legs hanging down to the ground, and there were Amos and Axel and the twins, but there were older ones, too, who lived in Colby and they had children, which meant Alphie was their uncle. Some of his nephews and nieces were older than he was, and it was very confusing.

Colby was Baird's favorite place in Vermont. Baird's mother didn't like to go into the store there because there was always somebody drunk in back, she said, lounging around by the cheese, but Baird found the store thrilling. Also, there was a good hill there, very, very steep, steeper than McCrillis Hill, and when they drove to Quarry City, his mother always asked him to help her chant *I think I can, I think I can,* until they got to the top.

Baird had already decided that when he grew up, that's where he wanted to live, on top of the steepest hill in Colby, in a bright blue house with lots of hunting dogs.

A gray-and-white-speckled hen rowed herself around the corner from the back of the Cakes' house, followed by a whole string of hens, some brown and black and rust, some speckled, some white. They paraded proudly around the dooryard in a tight group, heaving first toward the shed, then the barn, then back to the doorstep, sometimes one in the lead, sometimes another. Baird leaned out the car window and yelled "Hey!" but they paid no attention and continued their collective swaying back and forth around the yard. He opened the car door cautiously—the Cakes' rooster had chased him once. He got out, leaving the heavy door ajar, and warily crept around the corner of the house.

Hoskins slid out, and Hannibal jumped down after him.

Hoskins yelled "Hey!" just like his brother had, and a hen took a pretty little hop in the air. He yelled "Hey!" again, and the hen hopped again, this time clucking loudly.

The chickens formed a long wavy string and headed toward the road. Hoskins followed them over the lawn, taking little hops as he went and spreading his arms wide like wings. They stopped at the edge of the road, milling around and trying to decide where to go. Hoskins stood in their midst, watching intently as a car approached down the straightaway through the village, traveling east. The driver slowed and waved as she passed, and Hoskins flapped his wings and clucked.

A logging truck followed, entering the straightaway just as the first of the chickens strutted across the road. Hoskins stood poised at the edge, unsure whether to follow, then Hannibal began barking behind him, and the boy turned to look. The truck driver sounded his horn as he passed, a piercing rumble that seemed to rise up from the road itself, and the little boy sprang back. In its wake the truck left a blast of hot air that stung his face and made tears spring to his eyes. Then it, too, disappeared around the bend to the east. When it was gone, the chickens were on the other side of the road, parading proudly around the Andoulettes' yard.

Baird came around the corner of the house and ordered the dog back into the car, then took his little brother by the hand and led him inside.

CHAPTER

10

Leona Cake was a magnificently efficient woman who could accomplish more in one day than most people could in a week. Besides being postmistress for the village of Beede, she was a lister and a justice of the peace for the Town, recording secretary for the Minervas, president of the Women's Home Dem, prime mover and organizer of Old Home Days, chair of the church's Christmas committee, assistant to the village sexton, Artie Perkins, and author of a weekly column for the *Beede Opinion* called "A Hundred Years Ago Today." Everyone depended on her to keep things running smoothly, and for the most part, everything did. Occasionally, though, in her haste and with so many pans in the fire, Leona blundered, as she had the previous September when the McGuffey family left their summer place on McCrillis Hill to return to Syracuse.

In order to make her newspaper column more interesting to her readers and to herself, Leona wrote about the ordinary goings-on in the Town of Beede and its various rural settlements from a historical perspective, using interesting bits of history to spice up not-so-interesting local affairs, and always taking pains to keep the two in a nice balance. Sometimes it took a little juggling; sometimes it took more than a little juggling. She made two separate lists on the backs of envelopes that her post-office patrons left in the wastebasket. On one she itemized historical facts pertinent to the date, which she gleaned from research conducted in her spare time; the other was composed of local news furnished by her neighbors. When the two lists were long enough, Leona would stop and stare at them, trying to see a connection. This was the delicate moment; either a connection fell into place, or she had to force one. If it came on its own, then the lead, and therefore her whole column, practically wrote itself. If it didn't, then she had to "work it," which was what she did with her dough when she didn't have quite enough to cover the bottom of the pan.

"Mrs. Jack Baker was visited last weekend by her son Mike and his new wife, Lara Jean, from New Bedford, Massachusetts," her column would begin. "A hundred years ago today, Beede had another visitor, a deadly tornado. . . ."

But the previous Labor Day, after the McGuffeys left Beede, she'd written this: "Mr. and Mrs. Melvin McGuffey and their two young sons left their summer home on McCrillis Hill today to return to Syracuse, New York, and we're sad to see them go. Likewise, a little less than a hundred years ago, villagers said good-bye to Major George Wells of East Beede as he left to join his fellow officers of the 100th Battery Division of the United States Army Corps in Frankfurt, Kentucky. Major Wells never returned from the Civil War, but we hope the McGuffeys will make it back next summer."

At the time she wrote it, Leona had been mildly dissatisfied with the "little less than" business in her comparison, but after Melvin's accident in December, knowing that the McGuffeys subscribed to the *Beede Opinion* back in Syracuse, she was downright horrified. It was the first thing Leona thought of when Linette Turley called her with the news about Melvin. Linette stayed tuned to the radio in her front room all day and had already called Leona twice that morning, once to report on the weather (more snow expected) and once to ask her did she know a Spanish word for *friend* that had five letters and started with *a*. She called again just as Leona was putting the last of her Jell-O molds into the fridge to set up for the Grange Christmas party, and she had felt a wave of impatience at hearing Linette's voice. "They just said Melvin McGuffey was killed over to St. J," Linette told her without preamble. "A boy run him over on his way to a basketball game. And you know something? I could've saved him. If I'd've waved him down when he drove past this morning, and if we'd've entered into a little conversation, it might've delayed him, and the boy would've been somewheres else and Mel McGuffey would be alive right now."

Linette was by nature melancholy, and the idea that she was somehow to blame had taken hold of her and had its pernicious effect: On New Year's Eve, after doing up the supper dishes, she'd put her head in the oven. Fortunately, Walter Turley had come into the kitchen to get some string and pulled her out just in time. They kept her in the hospital overnight and discharged her in the morning with a diagnosis of "holiday syndrome." "Like I was some fool that's afraid of Christmas," Linette told Leona. "It'll be in the newspaper, too. I'll be embarrassed half to death." She asked Leona to write something in her column that week that would set things straight, and Leona told her she would do her best. "Mrs. Walter Turley of Beede," she wrote, "was released from Mercy Hospital in Quarry City last week, where she was recovering from the shock and sorrow she suffered on learning of the sudden death of the son of her longtime friend Mrs. Adele McGuffey of McCrillis Hill. Likewise, a hundred years ago, Miss Susie Moffit lowered the flag that waved above the schoolhouse in memory of her pupils' beloved pony, Dixie, who froze to death during bitter night temperatures. Apparently, the young students had braided Dixie's tail for the Labor Day parade, in which Dixie always rode, and had not thought to unbraid it for the long winter she would spend in Carrie Wyndam's field behind her barn. Her long tail, made heavy by an accumulation of ice from recent storms, brought Dixie to her knees. Unable to rise and seek shelter on the lee side of the building, she succumbed."

After it came out in the paper, Linette called to say she didn't get it. What did her hospital stay have to do with a horse? Leona told her it was subtle. "It has to do with human nature. Those schoolchildren felt bad, and so did you, but who's to know? Maybe that horse would've died of a heart attack even if her tail wasn't braided. Maybe Mel McGuffey would've gotten run over somewhere else even if he'd stopped to talk with you. It's hard to know why these things happen. It's pride that makes us think everything revolves around us."

"I'd say those schoolchildren were thoughtless fools," said Linette. A few minutes later she called back to ask if Leona had ever studied for the ministry, and for a moment Leona felt flattered, thinking she might have caused Linette to feel spiritually uplifted, but it turned out Linette only needed a five-letter word beginning with *v* that stood for an "evening church service."

When Charlotte walked in, Leona hardly looked up, assuming that the woman with very short red hair was just another tourist on her way somewhere else who'd forgotten to mail her electric bill back home. Tourists didn't actually stop in the village. There was nothing to do, nothing to buy, unless they wanted to stare at Walter's cows grazing behind the parsonage or pick up some canned goods over to the store. When Leona finally realized who it was, she was momentarily rendered speechless. "Why Charlotte McGuffey, you've cut your hair! For a moment there, I was sure you was Mary Martin stepping out from *South Pacific*. You surely do look different."

"And so does your front room, Leona. It looks like a real post office now," Charlotte said, gazing at a philodendron's brownish leaves with a wistful smile.

"I'll tell Johnny you said so. He'll be pleased to hear it." After the fire, the government had wanted to consolidate the Beede post office with the post office in Colby, which meant Leona would lose her job. What with Johnny's crushed leg, and him being too proud to ask for government assistance, they knew they wouldn't be able to make ends meet. Then he'd gotten the idea of turning their front parlor into a post-office lobby, and Johnny had convinced the higher-ups that it would save them money. After some dithering, they'd agreed to his proposal, and Johnny had set to work, doing everything by the book, making sure every *i* and *t* in the government regulation book was dotted and crossed. Johnny had gone to great lengths to make the place look authentic. He'd replaced their brass ceiling fixture with cheap fluorescent lighting, laid imitation wood over every horizontal surface (including the cherry dry sink Leona used for her ivy collection—it still smarted when she thought about it), put down yards of rubber carpeting over the wide plank floors, and installed a drinking fountain with a defective spout. Then he'd hauled in an aged philodendron and let it go dry, a last-minute decorating touch he referred to as the "lace on the bride's pajamas." He liked to claim that anyone could walk into what had once been their front room and not see a single reminder of their lives as human beings except for a glimpse, when the door to their part was open, of an Ethan Allen colonial rocker and a small braided rug on a spotless green linoleum floor. Nor would they see Benson, Leona's Scottie, who had made the old post office his home despite all government rules to the contrary. When the fire broke out the summer before, Leona had run straight to where Benson liked to sleep on the W-2 forms, and for once he wasn't there. It had been a terrible blow to her when they brought her his frizzled collar.

Charlotte clasped her hands together in a funny little gesture, halfway between wringing and praying, and Leona got the idea that she was nervous.

When Melvin first brought her to Beede to meet his folks, they'd come to Old Home Days in the schoolyard, and Charlotte, who was just a young girl, really, no more than nineteen or twenty, had come dressed up as a pioneer woman, complete with a bonnet, and everyone was impressed. She'd made the dress herself, Melvin announced, obviously so proud of her, and then Charlotte had turned around and you could see the dress was held together in the back with safety pins. She'd always been friendly, and Leona was hoping that her friendly streak was wide enough so that she might forgive Leona for her awful blunder. "I sure am sorry about what happened," she said delicately. "It was an awful shock to all of us."

Charlotte nodded in acknowledgment, a practiced nod, Leona thought. How many times since Mel McGuffey's accident must she have nodded like that? What a terrible thing for her—no warning, no time to say good-bye, no rhyme or reason. You expected accidents on a farm; there were perils everywhere: pitchforks buried in the hay, rivers that swelled and wells that beckoned, animals inflamed with hatred of the human race. And then there was the known malevolence of farm machinery. Men were cut up, hacked up, mutilated, dragged to oblivion, cut in half, cut in quarters. Sometimes it was the operator, sometimes it was the Lord. Sometimes, as in Johnny's case, it was a mix. He'd had no business going back out after dark set in, and when he was so tired, too, but at least he hadn't just walked straight *into* the baler, like it seemed Melvin had just walked into that boy's car.

"I've got one of his pictures on a hand towel in my kitchen and I think of him every time I wipe my hands." Leona nodded at the wall calendar open to the month of June. "And, of course, I look at that every day." The caption underneath the photograph only said "Summer Day," though it was clearly Perry McDonald's stone wall and one of his big maples that was dying from the load of salt they put on the roads all winter long.

Charlotte said she was sure Melvin would have appreciated hearing that.

"I don't suppose we'll have another calendar as good as that ever again. I don't know what we'll do come December, without next year's picture of the church."

Having already embarked on the perilous slope of delicate matters, Leona forged straight ahead to another. She knew Christian Scientists didn't believe in doctors, but she hadn't known, until Kitty Clatter's husband called Artie Perkins, that they didn't hold with funerals. After Melvin died, Harry Clatter had called Artie from St. J to let him know that the funeral people were sending Melvin's ashes to him and he was to put them in the ground whenever it thawed, no ceremony necessary. Artie had called Leona, wondering what to do. He didn't feel right being the one to select the day, he told her. It was a matter of some moment, and he didn't think it should be up to him. She didn't bother to ask why it should be up to her—people just expected that kind of thing from her, and in a certain way, it was all right with her, too.

"Let's do it the day the pussy willows bud out," she'd told him, and that had settled it. But she hadn't told Charlotte, and she knew she ought to have. It was her husband, after all. Leona had devised a sort of service despite the lack of instructions, or perhaps even in direct contradiction to the instructions, such as they were or weren't. She had lugged her great big family Bible to the cemetery, and after Artie placed the ashes in the hole, she read out two of her favorite psalms nice and loud to the silent stones around them and sprinkled a handful of dried rose petals on top of the dirt. She wasn't sure how Christian Scientists viewed the afterlife, so she didn't say anything extra in case she said the wrong thing.

"We took care of the ashes," she said, and Charlotte nodded and thanked her. She waited for her to ask *when,* but she didn't, so Leona told her. Charlotte said it was a good day for her to have chosen. The last Saturday in March had been a nice sunny day. She remembered because it was the day that the baby-sitter had taken the boys to see *Snow White.* And then Charlotte smiled at her very sweetly, just like the angel in Leona's childhood *Illustrated Bible Stories,* who smiled no matter what scene she was in, even the one where Mary Magdalene was being pelted with stones.

The door opened, and Charlotte's boys walked in and headed straight for the drinking fountain, which Leona had learned had a kind of magical appeal for people of all ages. "What a handsome fellow the little one is," she said, fishing for his name, which she could never remember. "I imagine he's talking a blue streak by now."

"Hoskins isn't talking much yet, but Baird does his best to make up for it," Charlotte said, and smiled. She looked very tired.

Baird turned the fountain knob, and the water shot right over his brother's head and onto the floor. Leona assured Charlotte that it happened every day and she was used to it, explaining that although she'd been disappointed at first to see her front room modernized so ruthlessly, and those ugly rubber mats put down all over her beautiful floors, she had to admit that Johnny had a point about wear and tear.

"I stopped to see about getting the phone hooked up, Leona, if you wouldn't mind making the call for me."

"Not at all."

"And to see about the mail."

"Well, there's not much during the year, you know. Sometimes a flyer or something."

The anxious look returned to Charlotte's face. "I suppose Melvin came by when he was here?"

"Oh, yes. He stopped in a number of times." Charlotte was looking at her expectantly. "We talked about erasers, mostly. He asked me if I remembered the time we was in first grade together and he swallowed an eraser. It was just a little gum eraser. The teacher stepped outside, and Melvin stood up and asked if there was anyone who thought he couldn't swallow an eraser. Of course, no one spoke up, because all of us was always eating erasers. He had to go through with it. He didn't really want to, he told me. He said he'd dreaded it." Leona could tell that this was not what Charlotte had hoped to hear, so she added, "There's a good chance we talked about the weather, too. It would be hard not to, with all that snow."

"Did Melvin ever mention to you that I might call here, looking for him?" Charlotte was clearly hoping the answer was one way or another, but Leona had no idea which. She didn't remember anything about it; Johnny was in the thick of remodeling at the time, and there was plaster dust everywhere, and the post-office people down to White River were pressing them on the deadline, and it was Christmas to boot. Leona wavered a moment and settled for a *yes*. She felt relieved, seeing Charlotte's expression. Then she asked Leona how he'd seemed when she saw him, how he'd acted, and Leona had to guess all over again.

"Well," Leona told her, "I guess he seemed about like he always did, kind of grumpy and pleased at the same time. You know how he was. You might ask Beatriz. I know he called on her."

Leona dialed the phone company. A woman whose voice she didn't recognize asked her to hold. "They've modernized the whole telephone operation over here," she told Charlotte. "They're plugging us in way over to QC now, and nobody knows anything. Fired all the operators. They've got a robot instead. They've gone *automatic*," she said grimly, making it sound like *crazy*.

When she hung up, Leona announced that Charlotte would be hooked up the next day by the close of business. And if there was anything else she could do, she hoped Charlotte would let her know. Orrin was back in the hospital again, and she didn't think he'd done much for her up at her place. What with all the rain they'd been having, her lawn might've grown up to a forest by now. "I know Beatriz will be glad to have you up there on the Hill with her," she said. "Ben Hightower walked out on her on Thanksgiving Day. I don't know if you knew that, just walked on out without a word. Bea's taken it real hard; she's gained an awful lot of weight, and now she's got varicose veins as well. That's not the only thing she's got, either. Her list is awful long, as I'm sure you'll find out for yourself. Poor old Bea. You can imagine what it's like for her losing Ben after losing little Homer Grant just two years ago. I know she'll be happy to see you. Course, you've got to be careful; she can drive a person crazy—you know how she is—she loves to talk. She might be shy around strangers, but if it's somebody she knows, she can talk a label off a can."

"Charlotte's here," said Leona.

"I know it. Nora called."

"She's on her way up now."

"I know. Anna called to say she was just leaving your place."

"What else do you know, Bea?"

"I know that little boy of hers strayed on down to the road and nearly got run over by one of Turley's trucks. Anna was hulling strawberries at the kitchen sink and says she didn't even have time to wipe her hands before it was all over. I'd hate to think Charlotte would have to go through what I've been through, losing my little boy. Anna says it was awful close."

"I hope you won't go telling her that."

"Oh, I won't. I've got some sense, Leona Cake. You suppose she'll stay the whole summer?"

"I don't know, Bea."

"What all did you talk about then?"

"This and that."

"I don't see how she's going to manage by herself up here, with two children and all." Beatriz sighed deeply.

"You been outside today? Didn't Dr. Zetterling tell you to get some fresh air every day?"

"I'm not feeling so good today."

"You ought to use a little of Charlotte's medicine yourself, Bea. Maybe you should see if she can help you. Those Christian Scientists know how to look on the bright side of things."

"It's the sister that's the healer."

"I don't know as you need to be healed, Bea; it's more like you need to be prodded." Though Beatriz's list of ailments included some frightful-sounding conditions (varicose veins, sciatica, glandular enlargement, goiters, neurasthenia, neuralgia, and something called hyperchlorhydria, which sounded to Leona an awful lot like Johnny's old friend acid indigestion), Leona nonetheless believed that many of her friend's problems originated in her head. Beatriz found a lot of ailments in her worn *Merck's Manual of the Materia Medica,* fifth edition, which she kept next to her bed and read at night when she should've been reading *The Power of Positive Thinking.* Dr. Zetterling, who ran the health clinic in West Beede, had given Bea a copy of Dr. Peale's book to see if she couldn't improve her attitude, but the patient clearly preferred Merck's gloomy forecasts. "Charlotte will be paying you a visit, I'm sure, and when she does, she'll be asking you about your conversations with Melvin while he was here. She won't want to hear any of your gloomy premonitions."

Beatriz said she wouldn't say a word about any of that.

"What will you say?"

"I'll have to give it some thought."

"You do that, because she'll be asking."

"Her little one talk yet?"

"Doesn't look like it. I wouldn't say anything about that, either."

"What can we talk about?"

"What about the weather?"

"Well, it's starting to heat up." Beatriz sounded doubtful. "You think she plans to sell?"

"I don't know as I know."

"It'll be awful melancholy for her at the house, knowing her husband was there all alone his last few days on Earth. She must be awful sad."

"I'd say she probably is. One thing, though, Bea, you better be prepared—she's cut her hair."

"No!" She paused. "Can I mention it?"

"Sure you can, just as long as you keep it positive. Tell her it looks real good."

"I'll do that."

"Don't be saying, 'Boo-hoo—how could you cut your beautiful hair?' or anything like that."

"That's a lot of things not to say, Leona. You think I'll remember all that?"

"Make yourself a list."

"All right. What was the first one?"

CHAPTER

11

Charlotte turned the DeSoto up the narrow dirt road across from the church and headed over the wooden bridge that spanned the west branch of the Molson River, swollen now with the recent rains. On the other side of the bridge was the turnout where Melvin had always taken his pictures of the much-photographed church. A dark sedan with out-of-state plates was parked in the turnout—another photographer, no doubt, walking around in the nearby woods while he waited for the late afternoon sun to get positioned right. As they passed, both Charlotte and Baird turned to stare. She pressed the accelerator, and they began to climb. Hoskins scooted closer to Charlotte on the front seat. His damp scalp smelled faintly vinegary.

"What's varicose veins?" Baird asked.

"It's a condition people are afraid of. That's what all disease is. People talk themselves into it. That's what gossip does. Everybody's got troubles here, honey, you'd better get used to it. Do you know what a miasma is?"

"No."

"Do you remember when we went to Florida to see Grampa Cal and

Gramma Adele and they were staying in a little cabana with jalousies on the windows and you got bit by a spider?"

"Sort of."

"Well, that place in Florida was a swamp. People used to call the air in a swamp a miasma, and they believed that it was the cause of all disease. That was a long time ago, and a lot of the ideas they had at that time were very silly, but this was not such a bad idea because a bad atmosphere does make people sick—it makes them have unhealthy thoughts. So in a way, they were right to think that a miasma causes bad things to happen. And that's what gossip is. It's a miasma, and we have to constantly stand guard against it, or it will drag us down and make us feel bad."

"I hope I don't get them."

"Don't worry about it, Baird. As long as you remember that God loves you, you won't have to worry about varicose veins."

Charlotte carefully nosed the heavy car up and over the little rises in the road, peering anxiously over the wheel lest she meet up with Betty, Beatriz's errant ewe, who wandered unattended up and down the hill all summer, transporting pounds of stickers and burdock and other debris in her unsheared fleece. People said she was a maverick sheep; Leona said she wasn't a sheep at all, but some kind of davenport. Every so often, on an irregular basis and when driven to it by pity, Leona would oil up the shears she kept in her laundry room and go after Betty, wrestling her to the ground and giving her a shaggy-looking clip. In the wintertime the ewe stood under Beatriz's carport, nibbling on the hay Eugene Wyndam brought up to her whenever he happened to think of it.

After the first little burst of houses near the bottom of the hill, the narrow dirt road climbed straight up through dense woods. At the very top was the McCrillis Copper Mine, sold to a group of Canadian investors after the war and shut down by a breach-of-contract suit. The issue of clear-and-present danger to the community became clouded by issues of ownership and priorities, claims and liens. Ruin set in; entrances to the mineshafts crumbled; posted signs toppled and lay stricken in the dirt. The property remained a dangerous place, and many children, seeing the copper-colored runoff, had grown up believing that the mines leaked blood.

"Betcha he's out," said Charlotte.

"Betcha he's not," said Baird.

They were almost to Hallam's tiny house, and it was time to predict whether or not he'd be out on his porch, reading a book in his wheelchair. His arm always shot up in a blind salute when a car passed. Hallam had run away from home as a boy to fight in the Spanish-American War and had lost his legs in the battle of Santiago Bay. President McKinley had personally awarded him a medal, which people said he kept in a mayonnaise jar full of water, for reasons that no one knew.

Hallam wasn't out, and Charlotte reached over and ceremoniously shook Baird's hand. "Looks like you won this time. Will you keep track for us this summer?" Melvin had kept track of their guesses in one of the little spiral notebooks he always kept in his shirt pocket. On their way back to Syracuse after Labor Day, he'd read off the number of times each of them had made a correct prediction and make his announcement with great fanfare. Somehow, Baird always won.

"I don't have a notebook." Baird's voice was unsteady.

"We'll get you one," she said, knowing she'd made a mistake. But when she wondered aloud whether the pair of rubber boots by Hallam's door meant he might have gotten wooden legs, Baird regarded her with sudden awe. "What?" he exclaimed excitedly. "Wooden legs?" And when Hoskins repeated it, pronouncing it "wooden eggs," they both laughed, and Charlotte silently thanked God that children's feelings were so transient.

They watched for Hale Wheel's geese as they passed his place and then turned left at the fork. The right fork went on up to the Nest (also known as the Artists' Place), a rambling old farmhouse that was home to a motley group of people and owned by Francis Roux, a sculptor who put rusty-looking spiral staircases in unexpected places. There was a staircase in Walter Turley's hay field that you could see from the road to Quarry City, but Charlotte was never able to look quickly enough after the big curve and had only seen it out of the corner of her eye. On the way back it was hidden by Walter's silo. Francis Roux was brash and loud and full of himself—he was either a big fish in a little pond, or a big fish in a big pond, she didn't know which, but he didn't seem like a little fish in any case. He had coal-black hair and light blue eyes—he was handsome, there was no doubt about it, and it was clear he knew it, too. He talked and laughed a lot and didn't seem to care much what people thought of him. Whenever Charlotte saw him in the village, he was deep in conversation with someone, excited about something, or laughing and pushing his dark hair out of his eyes, having a good time. People in the village said he was an ex-drunk; Melvin said he was a Lothario. She'd once asked Melvin what a Lothario was, anyway, and he'd said, "A flirt, Charlotte. I know you know what that is." And he'd glanced at her quickly and looked away.

There were only two other houses on the left fork—the Roons' and Beatriz's. The Roons' house was squat and little and emanated a grim kind of loneliness, a little like the Roons themselves. Ted and Jeannie and their teenage son, Philip, came from Petaluma, California, every year and spent their vacation working in the yard or around the pond below their house. Ted Roon was a musician (Rosey called him Red Tune). When mowing the lawn, he wore khaki Bermudas and thick workman's socks and boots, as if engaged in mighty tasks, and was of a cheerful disposition. His wife, Jeannie, was built like a spinet piano—in a solid rectangular block, with spindly legs—and had a way of keeping her elbows bent and slightly back, which furthered the spinet effect and added a pugilistic element. Their son, Philip, spent his days at the pond, or if it was raining, he stayed on the porch and stared morosely out at the road; when Charlotte drove by, he looked up but didn't wave. Leona had once found a picture of Ted Roon in *Life* magazine that showed him shaking hands with Dean Acheson on the White House lawn. Underneath the photo, the legend read, "Dean Acheson welcomes representatives of the music and arts world."

Next was Beatriz Sissy's small yellow Cape and the three-sided shed where she'd parked her car for good when her baby died. Little Homer Grant was only a few months old when Charlotte saw him, but he'd had dark circles under his eyes even then, like a tired old man. His skin was white and papery, and when Charlotte picked him up, he'd felt weightless, as if he were made of parachute material. Beatriz declared she had no use for a car anymore; she wasn't about to go anywhere now that Homer Grant was gone. For two years, the back end of the little brown Plymouth had been exposed to the elements and its paint had gone from a milk-chocolate brown to the variegated, iridescent color of an oil slick.

The McGuffeys' house was the last one on the fork and at the top of a long dirt driveway. Each spring, when the earth gave up its frost and the water bubbled up through the air pockets in the roadbed, the driveway rutted out. After a while, the weight of cars smoothed it over again, but the first trip up in the summer was the roughest. A dignified row of maples bordered the dirt road and followed along the edge of the field that would be ablaze with lupines in just a few weeks. Then people would start coming to see the flowers, parking down at the road and walking up to stand in clusters at the edge of the field while they gazed with a kind of reverence at the riotous mass of blooms. In the four years since Adele had died and Charlotte and Melvin had been spending their summers here, Charlotte had never known anyone to pick them or in any way violate the family's privacy.

The house came into view, and Charlotte's heart leapt with excitement. They were here. They'd really done it. The roof line sagged a little more; the screened porch listed at a greater angle; the white paint had continued to peel and weather, but there it was, intact and waiting. Its beauty was faded, fragile. It needed a lot of work. A bank of old lilacs just losing their blooms separated the house from a large barn, which had started its descent back to the earth many years before; Melvin had propped up one side of it with what he called buttresses, but which were really just long boards. In front of the house was an ancient maple, half of it lost to lightning long before Charlotte's time; in back was a steeply sloping pasture growing up to woods again. To the east of the house was Cal's ancient apple orchard, and to the west, the overgrown and weedy patch where last year's garden had been.

Charlotte pulled the car up, and the dog bounded out, followed by Baird and Hoskins, who raced across the lawn, trying to be the first to find the key under the rock. Across the valley the green hills were shrouded in mist; it was a familiar and beautiful sight, and for a moment

Charlotte forgot why she had come and what her task was, and the dread she had felt for weeks drained away and became relief. Then slowly, weary from the trip, she got out of the car and followed the boys through the grass, which she was puzzled to see had recently been mowed.

The house smelled of damp earth, the way it always smelled when they first opened it up. She went through the house, opening all the doors to the outside, letting the warm air in. Stepping up through the low door to the laundry room from the kitchen, she remembered to duck; she had trouble with the lock on the back door and had to bang on the metal rod to get it to move at all. When she finally swung it open, she saw that the grass in the back had been cut, too.

She moved cautiously from room to room, looking for signs of Melvin's presence, but there was little to see. The boys were shouting with excitement in the parlor. They'd gone straight to the corner cupboard where the toys and games were kept and were pulling everything out and greeting it anew. She heard Hoskins shouting something that sounded like "Varicose veins! Varicose veins!"

Melvin always kept the whiskey bottle on the clock shelf above the kitchen sink. Charlotte examined it to see if the level had gone down, but she couldn't tell. The only thing it told her was that he hadn't polished it off—unless he'd bought a second bottle. She doubted it. She'd never once seen him drunk. She lifted one of the round plates on the cookstove and looked inside: a piece of charred wood in a bed of ashes. The breakfast dishes had been done up and left in the drainer; Melvin would have expected to be back that night, so he wouldn't have put them back in the cupboard. There was a coffeepot on the cookstove. She lifted the lid and looked at the grounds still in the basket, hardened into black dirt and covered with white mold. The refrigerator door was propped open, the way they always left it when they closed up the house—Johnny must have done it when he came in to turn off the electricity. She had a sudden thought: What if everything had been a mess and he had picked up, feeling sorry for her? She doubted it. Johnny was a thin, laconic man with a bad limp who always wore the same dark green Dickies. She could hardly picture him cleaning her house.

She realized with a thud of disappointment that of course the water wasn't on. She wished she'd thought of it when she was at Leona's—she could have brought some up. Melvin had drained the pipes the previous September when they'd returned to Syracuse, and she had no idea how to reverse the process. She still had some drinking water left from the trip, and they could use the old outhouse for the moment. In the morning, she'd ask Johnny to come up, though she hated to start asking favors right away.

Melvin would have slept in the little spare room next to the kitchen, which was the only room small enough and close enough to the cookstove to keep warm in the winter. At the moment the door was closed. She went down to the basement.

She took the flashlight and hammer they always left hanging just inside the cellar door and crept down the wobbly steps. Their basement had a dirt floor and was packed as firmly as the coffee grounds; she was shocked to see that it, too, was covered with sheets of a stringy white mold. She searched for the fuse box—Melvin was always the one to do these things and she had never really paid attention. She shone the light on the switches, turning the one labeled "Main Switch" to On. That was easy enough. She chose the closest window and wiped away the cobwebs, then worked on the two big nails on either side. When they were both out, the window still wouldn't budge, and she struggled a while before she had success; as she lowered it on its hinges to the bottom of the outside window well, she felt a mighty surge of hope. When the sun came out in the morning, the house would start to dry out.

She went back upstairs and plugged in the refrigerator. It immediately began to hum, a brisk, cheerful sound. She turned on a light. A tidy glow suffused the room.

It was time to look.

The two small windows faced north, and it was the darkest room in the house. Adele McGuffey's crocheted coverlet was neatly folded at the bottom of the narrow iron bed, her handmade braided rug on the pine floor next to it. There was a book on the bedside table and Charlotte stepped forward to look: *Hiawatha*. Surely Melvin hadn't been reading that. His hairbrush and shaving case were on the dresser, a bottle of Old Spice, a book of matches, change, a camera lens. She looked in the dresser drawers: underwear, socks. There was a corduroy shirt in the closet, a pair of pants.

She had hoped for more. Then she remembered his wallet, his camera, all his equipment. Where had it gone? His gray sweater was neatly folded over the back of a chair—it was the sweater he'd been wearing the morning he left Syracuse. She picked it up and laid it on the bed, carefully refolding it so that the sleeves were perfectly matched along the back. There was a moth hole in one sleeve; he'd asked her to darn it, and she'd put it in her mending basket and left it there. They didn't discuss it, and he finally started wearing it again.

When the sweater was perfectly folded, she smoothed it out, drawing her hand over its rough surface again and again until there wasn't the faintest indentation.

Darkness came on slowly. Charlotte served peanut-butter sandwiches on the porch for supper, and the boys ate in their pajamas, then ran around barefoot in the yard, looking for special stones. She thought of the evenings when she and Melvin would sit out here with Cal and Adele, watching the mist settle into the valley and listening to the sound of Adele McGuffey stubbing out her Old Golds, rubbing them in the saucer until the tobacco fell out of the paper.

When it was finally dark, the fireflies came out, and Charlotte and the boys stood at the edge of the porch calling out to the hills on the other side of the valley, trying to make them answer back. Hoskins, tired all at once, took her hand. She put her arm around Baird's shoulders, and they watched together as the night deepened in silence.

She doubted that she had ever been so lonely.

CHAPTER

1 2

During the early morning hours, a cold front moved in from Canada and met up with the warm moist air of the Champlain Valley, forming a rolling bank of fleecy white fog that moved down through the state, touching the tops of everything four feet high: ponies, fence posts, pickups, stop signs, pristine bathtubs sheltering Catholic saints, rusty bathtubs thrown out and forgotten, tedders, threshers, wagons, scarecrows, picket fences. The farther south it traveled, the more cunning the objects it touched—polished antique carriages, white-washed picket fences, cast-iron valets in obsequious poses gracing meticulously close-cut lawns. A thick bank of fog hovered above the ground, wondrous white cotton that expanded as it traveled to fill up meadows, hillsides, valleys, roads, and riverbeds. Outside the puffy white cloud, the sun was shining gloriously; inside, the world was damp and gray. Guernseys, tall enough to have their heads in the clouds, closed their eyes and quivered against the shower of cold droplets. Dark horses standing motionless in fields turned darker. Drops of water hung suspended from the tips of leaves. Gradually, as the day grew warmer, the fog lifted, and the last of the wisps sailed up into the wet green hills and disappeared.

.   .   .

After the quiet little ding that signaled the telephone service coming on, Baird sat down and prepared to make his first call of the summer. He lifted the receiver and dialed. Mrs. Andoulette answered. He asked to speak to Alphie. She said Alphie wasn't there, and Baird hung up. He waited while he worked on what to say next, but when he picked up the receiver again, someone was talking. He listened for a while until he heard the woman say, "I believe someone is on the line," and then he put the receiver down very quietly.

His mother came down the narrow stairs with her arms full of blankets. She passed through the room and out through the kitchen and laundry room into the backyard. He could see her through the pantry window laying the blankets out on top of the grass. It seemed like a funny thing to do. She didn't often clean the house, and he wasn't sure she was doing it right. Ever since she cut her hair, he'd been uneasy about what she might do next. She could change things around in a minute. On her way back upstairs, she asked him whom he was trying to call. Baird said he was just listening, and she told him not to be a pest.

As soon as she was gone, he dialed Alphie's number again. Mrs. Andoulette answered, but this time she sounded mad. He hung up without speaking.

Baird studied the wallpaper for a while and then got up and went to look for Hoskins. He was supposed to be watching him, which meant he was supposed to make sure he didn't vanish. He had already vanished once that morning. They found him behind the mops and buckets, wedged into a corner in the laundry room. "How on Earth do you *vanish* so quickly?" his mother had exclaimed, sounding kind of pleased, in a way. Baird guessed it was better to vanish than to just disappear.

Baird found him in the parlor on the floor behind the couch, turning the pages of the big dictionary; only he wasn't *looking* at it, he was *listening* to it. He had his ear down close to the paper as he turned the pages, and he had a funny expression on his face, like he was praying. A chair was pulled up to the wall of bookshelves, and there was a space where the book must have come from, but it was too high for Hoskins to have reached it from the chair—he had to have flown up there. Baird knew that was true of ghosts; they could fly or walk through walls and go anywhere and get anything they wanted. When they went up and down the stairs, they didn't even have to touch the steps. They just kind of floated, bobbing a little at each one. And that's just the way Hoskins did it; he kind of rocked his way up and down, doing a little dance and shaking his fanny as he went. It was possible that Hoskins *was* a ghost, or that he had turned into one because Baird had told God he wished Hoskins was a freak—but that was only because people were always saying how handsome his baby brother was and Baird was fed up. He hadn't meant it to last.

He opened the corner cupboard and took out the puzzle he and his father had done the summer before. There were a thousand pieces, and they had not lost one. It was because of Baird himself, primarily, because of his sharp eyes. The puzzle picture was of three rowboats tied up in a little cove on a lake; it had been easy to find the pieces of the bright blue boat and the man's green shirt, but the rest of the puzzle was hard, and it had taken them nearly a week to do it. His father liked to call him a "puzzle whiz" because of his sharp eyes. He had worked on it at night after Baird went to bed. When Baird came downstairs for breakfast, he found whole new sections put together, but he never said anything, and his father never said anything, and they pretended together that it was always the both of them working on it side by side, and every little triumph was theirs to share.

"Well, for Lord's sakes, look who's here. I thought you was never coming to see me! Charlotte, what have you done to your hair!"

"I know it's a shock."

"What on Earth possessed you?"

Charlotte had just about decided to leave when Beatriz opened her door. She'd been standing on Beatriz's porch with her water container in her hand, watching as the boys investigated Beatriz's car, parked in the open shed. Hoskins walked slowly around the mottled brown Plymouth, kicking the tires. Then he bent down to look underneath it while Baird tried the door handle on the driver's side. "I don't really know. I guess I just wanted to try something different. My braids and I have parted company for good."

"You can sell hair like that, you know; for wigs, I suppose. I don't know what they do with it." Beatriz pulled her flowered housecoat closer around her. She was a short woman, and the extra weight she'd put on during the year made her look like a little round barrel. On her feet she wore dainty black Chinese slippers. "I'll tell you, though, I believe I'm getting used to it already."

After the young McGuffeys started spending their summers on McCrillis Hill, it was Beatriz who adopted Charlotte and tried to make her feel welcome, taking her around to meet people in the village and advising her about different people, whom she could trust and whom to look out for. Beatriz was full of life then and so happy with her tall, handsome Ben Hightower, and then with her little Homer Grant. Charlotte couldn't imagine what it would be like to lose a child.

"I see the boys is grown like weeds."

"Oh, yes, they're growing, all right."

"I suppose the little one's talking by now."

"He's got some favorite phrases," Charlotte said, thinking specifically of *varicose veins*.

"You wait; you'll get your miracle. Once he starts talking, you'll be praying for release. I'll open up the car for the boys. They can get in and pretend to drive if they want. I won't give them the key. They won't hurt nothing, Charlotte. Don't you worry. They'll have a fine time." Beatriz returned with the key and trundled out to the car, unlocking it. Baird immediately scrambled for the driver's seat; Hoskins dove over him to the other side. "Don't worry, the horn don't work," she told Charlotte, dropping the key into the pocket of her wrapper as she returned. "They love it here, don't they? I believe I heard them shouting over at your place the night you got here. They was making all kinds of ruckus."

"We were shouting for echoes."

"I'd say you was probably shouting for joy."

Charlotte laughed. "I'd say you're right."

"Come on in. We'll set for a minute while the boys have their fun."

"I thought I'd get some water while we're here." Charlotte followed her into the house, and down the narrow hallway into the kitchen, noting how Beatriz seemed to tiptoe delicately in her little shoes.

There were dirty dishes everywhere: in the sink, on the floor, on the table. Half a loaf of bread in a bread wrapper lay on a foldaway bed next to the gas stove. On the other side of it was a yellow dresser decorated with dancing-bear decals—probably little Homer Grant's, Charlotte thought.

"I've been sleeping in here," Beatriz explained sheepishly. "It just seems easier." She pulled out two chairs from the table. "I got to keep off my feet, you know. I got vein trouble. It's the extra weight." She said it as if it were an inevitable burden she had to accept. Dr. Zetterling had told her to hoist her legs up whenever she sat, she explained, and promptly did so, pulling out a second chair from its place at the littered table and putting up her feet. When she lifted her short legs, Charlotte averted her eyes. There was a lot of refuting of error to be done, she realized, if she was going to spend any time with Beatriz this summer.

Charlotte cleared away a few of the dishes in the chipped sink and set the container down under the faucet. The window shades were drawn, and the light in the room was a sickly color.

"I sure am sorry about your Mister," Beatriz said while Charlotte ran the water. "It's an awful thing. He was a nice man, always good to me. He was a real American. They're saying the Russians are coming, you know. Could be just about anybody is pink. Senator McCarthy is doing his best to rout them out, but I doubt he can find them all. I do know the new people down at the store are saying all them up at the Nest are pink, Francis Roux and all his people."

Charlotte turned off the water and sat down across from Beatriz. "Hasn't Francis Roux been here a long time?"

"People change," said Beatriz. "Look at Alger Hiss. I suppose he was a decent man once." She sighed, and her whole being seemed to sag. "Ben left me, you know."

"Leona told me. I'm sorry."

"I should have known he wouldn't last. One thing you probably don't know is, he didn't have a ring finger. That should have told me something right there, wouldn't you say? A man without a ring finger? He worked down at the bobbin mill one summer just long enough to cut it off. Then he was back to trucking. Said it was safer."

Ben Hightower was a slim, handsome trucker from Ontario who wore expensive-looking cowboy boots with long, narrow toes. He'd stopped at the village store one day on his haul to Boston, and young Beatriz had been standing there in her best pink pantsuit, looking all aglow. On the way back, Ben left his suitcase at her house on the Hill. Gradually, trip by trip, he moved in. They'd never actually married, but after seven years, the state of Vermont considered Ben her common-law husband.

"He was too handsome, that's the conclusion I've come to. A man as handsome as Ben Hightower has always got a wanderlust you can't control." Beatriz took a hankie out of the pocket of her wrapper and wiped her eye. "Our relationship was never meant to be, like little Homer Grant himself."

"Oh, Beatriz. You talk as if you and Ben were doomed."

"We *were* doomed. As was H. G. It's a good way to put it. Doomed." She looked around at the chaos in the kitchen. All was bathed in a hopeless yellow-green wash of sorrow. "But do you want to know the worst of it? It's Ben Hightower I miss the most, not Homer Grant. I know a mother ought to care more about losing her baby than her man, but it's not my baby that makes me feel this dark clawing thing in my heart like I do, like it's going to break." Beatriz raised her head and gasped, pressing her trembling lips together as she dabbed at her eyes with her handkerchief.

Charlotte tried desperately to think of something comforting to say. What she really wanted to tell her was to open the shades and get that bed out of the kitchen; it was obvious that that was where she spent all her time, sleeping and eating on those wrinkled sheets.

"I'm so sorry, Beatriz. It's going to be all right, I know it will."

"You think so?"

"I do, I really do."

"The last I saw of him was the day before Thanksgiving. Got one postcard since then, back in April. I don't suppose you'd want to see it."

"Of course I would. I'd love to see it."

Beatriz heaved herself up out of her chair and went into the other room. Charlotte heard Hoskins shouting outside, "Red light ahead! Traffic proceed! Traffic stop!"

Beatriz returned holding a soiled and tattered white card, the plain kind sold at any post office. "There's no picture," she said sadly, and handed it to Charlotte: "Greetings from Alabama—have new route through Mobile and Birmingham, two interesting cities. The weather is humid and not to my liking—Ben." Charlotte looked up, trying to smile reassuringly. "Well, that's wonderful, Beatriz."

"You think so?"

"I'm sure he'll come back."

"You are?"

"He might. I know that things always work out, eventually." Charlotte read it again. Surely there was something there to latch on to, to give Beatriz hope.

"What do you see?"

"He doesn't like the weather."

Beatriz leaned forward, anticipating Charlotte's next words. "Go on."

"Well, why would he complain about the weather if he was going to stay? He's telling you something, maybe that he's dissatisfied with his decision."

Beatriz nodded, brown eyes shining. "He's asking me how I feel about his coming back."

"In a way, yes," Charlotte said, worrying now that she might be getting in a little too deep. "Of course I don't know. And he didn't give you an address, so you can't actually reply. But maybe he's thinking it over."

"He's thinking he might come home?"

"It's just a thought."

"You said you were sure of it."

"I did?"

"You said, '*I'm sure he'll come back.*' Just now."

"Well, he might. If believing that helps you change your attitude, then that's good. You'll feel a lot better."

"Leona says I have a bad attitude. So does Dr. Z. The both of them are always after me, saying I should get out more, that I got to think positive." She smiled tentatively. "Who knows? Maybe I'll try. Dr. Peale says being positive is everything. I got his book right here in the house. Isn't that what you folks believe, you got to think your way through your troubles?"

"You mean in Christian Science?" Beatriz nodded and Charlotte continued cautiously. "Christian Science is a little different. It's not really a . . ." She didn't want to say *fad*. "It's a religious system."

"Oh, yes, I know that. I might be taking it up."

"Wonderful," said Charlotte.

"I might even go to church with you sometime."

"All right."

"If you think that would be okay."

"Of course."

"You have them healing meetings in QC, don't you?"

Charlotte nodded, trying to look enthusiastic. It was hard to picture Beatriz at a Wednesday night service. They weren't *healing* meetings, she wanted to tell her, like in some revival tent. She could imagine what Beatriz envisioned: people waving their crutches, calling out, sweating with excitement. The church in QC was hardly even a church, just a little room with white walls and polished floors in a made-over house. Generally there were only a handful of people in attendance, sitting in folding chairs that creaked a little as they shifted their weight, rehearsing lines they probably wouldn't say.

"They say Christian Scientists can heal over the telephone."

"Well, yes."

"If I get real low some day, you think I could call you for help?"

"I'm not a practitioner."

"Oh, I know. I just thought you might be able to cheer me up some. I get so low."

"My sister Kitty is a practitioner, but I'm not."

"But you can look into the future."

"Oh, no! I can't! You mean about Ben? Oh, no. I'm not a fortune-teller! I'm just *guessing*."

"Well, I think that's what fortune-tellers do. They guess, don't they? And then they charge you fifty cents." Beatriz laughed, and her whole face changed.

"You have a beautiful smile, Beatriz."

"Why, thank you. I guess I've got some reason to smile, now you're here."

Charlotte got up to go. She screwed the cap on the water container and lifted it out of the sink. "I wouldn't worry about the Communists too much, Beatriz. I don't think there're too many around here."

"Could be some of them at the Nest. They've got new people coming and going all the time, could be any of them. Could be Stodge." Stodge was a poet and as tall and skinny as a broomstick. He walked up and down the road all summer trying to sell his poems to people for a quarter apiece. Charlotte had bought one, written in pencil on Big Chief tablet paper. She hadn't been able to make head nor tail of it. "Could be those women Francis has up there. His ex-wives is there most of the time—they come and go like it's their own place, bring their friends and whatnot. Who knows what all's going on. Then there's the Great Bellini, of course. He's living there now, I understand. Well, we'll see how long that lasts. You know Paul?"

Charlotte remembered Paul Bellini from the old store in the village, where she'd often seen him buying candy and beer. She thought of him as a disheveled dandy. "I believe I do."

"The man's a drinker. You got to be sober to stay at the Nest. Of course, there's always miracles. He stacked my wood one year, and the whole woodpile fell over. It's lucky no one was standing there, or they'd've been killed. Of course, he was drinking then."

By then they were out in the yard, but Charlotte still hadn't asked her question. Baird's engine noises drifted out the car window, peppered with traffic alerts from Hoskins. She listened, rehearsing her question and reminding herself to keep her tone light. "Did you see Melvin when he was here?"

"Well, yes, I did."

"How did he seem?"

"Well, he seemed all right."

"In what way?"

Beatriz frowned. "Let's see. He looked healthy. Didn't seem to have a cold or anything. You know how colds seem to go around that time of year. Everybody's sneezing."

"Well, I didn't think he had a cold, Beatriz. I meant, his mood. Did he seem . . . I don't know . . . worried? Or preoccupied? Was he bothered by something?"

"That I wouldn't know. I don't recall him saying anything about being bothered."

"Is there something you think you should tell me, Beatriz?"

The boys were tussling in the front seat. It was time to get going.

"I can't."

"You can't?"

"Leona said not to mention it."

"Oh. Well, you can tell me. What is it?"

"I had a funny feeling."

"What kind of funny feeling?"

"I thought maybe something was going to happen."

"You mean you had a feeling about something bad happening?"

"I had a premonition. But Leona said I shouldn't tell you. She said you wouldn't want to hear it. But I been thinking about it, and maybe if I'd've said something . . ." She paused. "It might've changed his plans and he would've been somewheres else when that boy was driving his mother to a card party."

"You didn't know."

"No, I didn't."

"It wasn't a card party," said Charlotte.

"Oh, have I got that wrong?"

"He was taking her to the beauty parlor."

"Oh, yes, that was it." Beatriz shook her head sadly. Charlotte asked her what they had talked about and Beatriz said she was pretty sure they must have talked about the weather. And Ben, too. "Must've," she said.

"Your husband was surprised, said he'd always thought Ben was a decent fellow. And so fine-looking. He wondered what got into him. I says, 'Well, to tell you the truth, I imagine it's another girl. Another girl in another port.' And he agreed with that. 'Yes,' he says, 'that makes a lot of sense.'"

It didn't sound at all like Melvin. "Did he seem, well . . . sad?"

Beatriz thought a moment. "That's hard to say. I think he felt bad for me, because of my situation, you know. So he was pretty solemn."

"Of course."

"Let me think about it a while. Maybe I can come up with something."

"That's all right. Don't just try to come up with something to please me."

"Well, I don't know why not. You've done me a world of good already. I don't see why I couldn't return the favor."

CHAPTER

13

There was a man in the yard when they returned, standing in the shade of the lopsided tree and chewing on a piece of grass. He had an insouciant look, as if he owned the place himself. Hoskins was laboring up the driveway behind Charlotte and Baird; Hannibal plodded along beside him. When they reached the yard, she set down the water container and waited for Hoskins to catch up.

The man seemed steady enough as he stepped forward, though he had a sort of glazed look. Charlotte didn't know if it was drink, or his eyes, which were large and dark and seemed slightly out of focus. She recognized him then. Despite the heat, Paul Bellini wore a suit jacket flapping open over a once-white shirt; a carefully folded red bandanna peeped out of the jacket pocket. He had shiny penny loafers, complete with two shiny copper pennies. "I come to see the lady of the house," he said, grinning and showing several missing teeth.

"That's me. I'm Charlotte McGuffey."

"Didn't you used to have a heck of a lot of hair?"

"Yes, I did," she told him very formally. "A heck of a lot."

"No, seriously, are you the Missus? I thought maybe you was the big

149

sister!" He threw his head back and laughed. "You could pass for one, I'll tell you." Hannibal was slowly wagging his long feathered tail. The man held out his hand. "Nice dog."

"He was my dad's," Baird said loudly.

"Real nice." He gingerly patted Hannibal's big head, and Charlotte got the idea that he might be afraid of him.

"He's a hunting dog," Baird said.

"Is that so? What's he hunt, elephants?" He grinned at Baird.

Baird's expression was deadpan. "Birds."

"I had a huntin' dog once; a beagle, name of Rebel. Used to bark all night."

"Dad trained Hannibal not to bark except at dangerous people."

Paul laughed. "Don't worry about me. I'm harmless as a kitten." He took a step back and bowed in a grandiose, goofy gesture. "Paul Bellini here. The Great Bellini, some call me."

"How do you do?" said Charlotte stiffly, though she couldn't prevent herself from bowing slightly in return.

"I do just fine, thank you, ma'am, I do!" He threw back his head and roared. He was really tickled. When he recovered, he turned to Baird. "You like magic?"

Baird nodded solemnly. "I used to have a magician's wand, but it got crushed."

"You don't say! How'd that happen?"

"My uncle sat on it. It was made of paper."

"Well, don't you worry. I got more than a paper wand, I'll tell you!" He gave a loud hoot.

"Mr. Bellini . . . ," Charlotte began.

"Paul is fine. I don't stand on no ceremony, despite being known throughout the area as the Great Bellini. And you know why I'm great? 'Cause I'm a man of talent. Now, does that surprise you?"

"No," said Baird.

"You ever heard of the famous Howard Thurston and his rising-card trick? I call that child's play, is what I call it. I have amused thousands with my card tricks, coin tricks, you name it." The Great Bellini paused.

"I got a treat in store for you, and your mother, and your little brother, too. I know all Howard's secrets. Plus, I got my own feats of dexterity and skill that will leave you faint. Some folks say the Great Bellini's got airs—well, I say back, 'There's nothing wrong with a little pride in a man, no matter what his station.'"

The dog wandered off, looking for shade.

"Is there something in particular you wanted?" Charlotte asked.

"I come to see if you like your lawn. Figured you'd want to see my work."

"It was you that cut it?"

"Yes, ma'am, front and back both. Ain't you the one looking for a caretaker?"

"Who told you that?"

"Little birdie," he said, laughing.

"Thank you for stopping by, but I'm afraid I don't need a caretaker."

"I beg to disagree with you, Missus. I'd say you was in desperate need of some help around here. You see your porch? See how she's tipping? Get enough rain, she could go at any time if the sills is rotten. You got to get your garden in, too, and pretty darn quick. It's already too late for peas. I'll bring some plants over and jump-start you. They've got more tomato plants over to the Nest than they know what to do with."

"I can manage the garden myself. And the grass."

"Not with that mower," he said.

"You used our mower?"

"Course, grass gets used to one kind of handling, you don't want to take it by surprise with another." Seeing her expression, he added quickly, "I didn't touch nothin'. It was just sitting there in the barn, waitin' and willin'. These mowers, they *like* to work. Like them workhorses, they *live* to work. Same with mowers." Then he turned to Baird. "You know Mike and Mack?" he asked. Baird shook his head, still making up his mind about the man. "Eugene Wyndam's team. Nice team. You mean your mother don't take you to the fairs?"

"My dad took us to the Barton Fair last year."

"There you go, then you seen Mike and Mack in the horse pull. Nice team. They always place." He turned to Charlotte. "You tell me you're going to turn over all that ground for a garden by yourself?" He shook his head at the folly of it. He was working hard at convincing her she needed him. "Can't be done. You got to have a machine—or an able man; able and sober. We got to till, it looks like. I'd say that's our best route."

"How much do I owe you, Paul?" The sooner she paid him, the sooner he'd leave.

"You don't owe me a ding-dong thing. I done it on spec. Customer don't pay until she's satisfied."

Hoskins came out of the house carrying the nearly empty jug of water left over from their trip. He descended the big granite steps carefully, his eyes glued to the jug in his hands. When he reached the grass, he set the jug down with a little sigh and went back into the house.

"Cute," said Paul.

"He's not cute," Baird said.

"What is he, then?"

"He's a handsome fellow."

Paul grinned. "Well, la-tee-dah!"

Baird shrugged, letting him know that he was just reporting the facts; it wasn't necessarily his opinion. "That's what everyone says."

"All right then, handsome he is! What's his name?"

"Sniksoh."

"Snickers?"

"Hoskins," Charlotte said.

"Hawken?"

"HOSKINS!" yelled Baird.

"Nice name," Paul said mildly. "Never heard it."

There was no car in sight, and Charlotte asked him if he'd walked. "I live at the Nest, right on the other side of that rise there. I came through the woods. You ever been to the Nest that way?"

"I've never been to the Nest."

"You'll have to come over sometime, bring the kids; there's always something going on. But no drinking, no sir. Francis used to be a drinking man himself, and he knows you can't fool with the stuff—he don't allow no alcohol on his property whatsoever, of any stripe."

"That's all right. I don't drink much."

He looked at her, not sure if she was kidding. "Me, neither. I don't drink nothin' now but soda pop. I am on the W-A-G-O-N, and I'm stayin' on it, I swear to it. I do Francis's welding, learned it in the navy. He makes them spiral stairs, you know? The ones you see going up? Well, I suppose they come down, too, if there was anybody to come down 'em, but who's gonna do that, one of them little angel babies, you know what I mean?"

"Cherubim."

"You got it!" He laughed happily, as if they were sharing a joke. "And what do they need stairs for? They got wings!"

"So you help Francis Roux with his art?"

"That's right. I'm his sidekick, you could say, kind of like Tonto." Baird looked at him curiously, and Paul asked him if he liked the Lone Ranger. Baird admitted with a little nod that he did. "You think about it," Paul told him, folding his arms and adopting a man-to-man pose. "Kemosabe wouldn't be where he is today without Tonto. Tonto solves all his problems for him. Couldn't do a thing without him."

Hoskins came out again, this time lugging Charlotte's dishpan and his green bucket down the steps. The bucket was filled with the stones he'd been gathering the evening before. He squatted down on the grass, intent on his task. He dumped the stones out of the bucket and very carefully filled the bucket with the last of the water from the jug.

Paul went over and squatted down next to him. Hoskins began dropping the stones into the water, one by one. "Hello, there, handsome fellow." Hoskins dropped another stone in, ignoring him.

"He doesn't like strangers," Baird said.

"I'm no stranger, been here in Beede all my life, born and raised here. My dad worked down at the mill. He was a sawyer. You know what that is?"

"Does he saw?"

"You got it! A sawyer saws! Ain't you a smart one!"

Hoskins slowly swished the stones around in the water. Paul handed him a small white one flecked with gray and asked him if he liked it. Hoskins took it, looked it over carefully, and discarded it.

"Don't he talk?" Paul asked Charlotte.

"He repeats words, but he doesn't actually talk. He's a mimic."

"He can say 'Leviticus,'" Baird said. Paul asked him what it meant, and Baird said he didn't know.

"You do so, Baird. It's a book in the Old Testament."

"You sure there's nothing you need me to do?" Paul asked her. "You need anything moved or fixed or whatnot? Just say the word and I'll do it, whatever it is. I'm mighty handy, mighty willing."

And plucky, she thought. He'd plowed through her cold reception unabashed, tried his best to ingratiate himself with the children, tried his best to charm her into hiring him. "Do you know how to turn the water on?" she asked.

"We just need to find the pump, and the switch, unless the system is gravity-fed. You ever noticed a well house, anything like that, up on the hill there behind the house?"

Baird said he remembered seeing a pump in the breezeway next to the kitchen, and Charlotte and Paul went to look, with Baird trotting along, excited about seeing the old pump work. Not this kind of pump, Paul told him when they got there. It was just an old hand pump, anyway; you needed water to prime it, and there was a mystery for Baird to solve, needing water to get water. "How are you going to do that?"

Paul scratched his head in an exaggerated stage gesture, but this time Baird laughed. "I know! I'll get Sniksoh's bucket!"

"Sniksoh?" Paul asked as Baird ran off.

"*Hoskins* backward."

Paul opened his eyes wide and struck himself on the forehead. "How come I didn't think of that!"

When Charlotte insisted again on paying him for his work, he told her a different story. He'd come because Francis had told him to. "He said I ought to try to find some work, says there's too many people at the Nest relying on him, he's sick of it. He's got big problems, I'll tell you. He's making one of them stairs for some guy in Toronto, and Francis hates it and he can't work. The guy ordered some special kind of stairs, and Francis says it's stupid. He's in a real bad mood. He's got the sugar disease—when his sugar's off, oh, boy, you never know what'll happen."

It seemed everyone in Beede had some complaint. "And do you have a disease, too, Paul?"

"Hives," he said, grinning, "but only when I drink schnapps."

She asked him what it was like, living at the Nest, and he told her a lot of people came and went. A lot of women, he said. "Francis's friends from the city. The ex-wife was there for a while, and her girlfriend, and some kid, I don't know whose." He shook his head sadly. "He has terrible trouble with women."

Charlotte smiled at the earnest way he said it, making it sound like a condition a person couldn't possibly overcome.

Baird came careening around the corner. "Sniksoh's gone! I looked in the barn, and he's not there, either!" As Charlotte started around to the front at a run, she heard Baird giving Paul some advice: *Just stay calm, that's the best thing you can do in an emergency*. It was what Melvin had told her the day of the fire, when she couldn't find the key.

They found him, finally, perched in the upper branches of the lop-sided maple. The tree's trunk rose up three or four feet before the first handhold, and Paul expressed amazement that Hoskins could climb it. Charlotte tried not to appear concerned, but when Paul offered to climb up and get him, she whispered that he might get upset, and then he was quite a handful.

"He screams," Baird told him matter-of-factly.

"I'm sure he'll come down on his own," Charlotte said, loud enough for Hoskins to hear.

"Too bad he don't talk," Paul said. "He could tell us what his plans are."

Paul offered to go to work on the water problem while they waited to find out if Hoskins would choose to come down on his own, though he'd need some pipe wrenches, he told her, adding that he'd understand if she didn't want to let him use her tools; it had been a mistake to take the lawn mower out of the shed, and he was sorry. Charlotte countered his apology with her own, saying she shouldn't have been so . . . She couldn't find a word, and he supplied it. "Huffy," he said, and she laughed.

It turned out that their water came from a dug well up the hill and ran down to the house through a series of underground pipes. To keep it from entering the unheated basement in the winter and then freezing and bursting the pipes, someone had installed a shutoff valve in a wooden box built onto the side of the house. Charlotte had noticed it before, but had never known its purpose. Paul opened up the box, removed the insulation, and found the valve that he was looking for.

Back in the basement, all they had to do was turn on a faucet. The air was expelled in a series of hisses and burps until a gush of rusty water exploded into the pail they'd placed below the spigot, and the water gradually ran clear. Charlotte told him she felt much better knowing all this now; it made the house much less of a mystery, and she planned to write it all down.

Paul said he'd be glad to show her how to turn the water off, too, and how to drain the pipes when the time came, which he hoped wasn't any time soon, of course, but he could see she was a very curious person and liked knowing how things worked. He admired that in a woman, he told her seriously, in a tone that implied that he had a very reasonable set of standards for his women and it made him sad that a lot of them didn't measure up.

They found a garden fork in the barn and went out to the garden. Paul hung his jacket on the fence and began turning over the ground, working away in his slippery loafers, stepping on the fork as it sunk into the ground and leaning his weight forward to make it sink deeper before jarring a clump of grass loose. He talked as he worked, making his way slowly along the edge of the garden plot, shaking the dirt out of the weediest clumps and throwing them over his shoulder. Baird brought out his dump truck and hauled away the clumps of dirt and grass Paul discarded.

Charlotte watched him while he worked, listening to his stories and keeping one ear open for sounds of Hoskins descending the tree. He had an ex-wife, she learned, named Billie, and two children, Paul Jr. and Tanya, ages nine and fifteen, and both of them with a smart mouth just like their mother. They lived in Colby with Billie's boyfriend, who was a bully and a drunk. And that really got his goat because that's why Billie

left him in the first place, because of his drinking, so where was the justice in that? Billie was drinking now, too, he'd heard, and he feared for
his children. Sometimes he thought about kidnapping them, just driving
over there and putting them in the backseat and speeding away. Where
to, though? And who would pay for the gas?

Hoskins came down from the tree at lunchtime as quietly and
quickly as he had gone up, materializing in their midst without fanfare.
Charlotte tried not to show her relief and told Paul and Baird loudly and
pointedly that she was "trying not to notice any visitors of the young variety" and would appreciate it if they didn't appear to notice, either. Paul
said, "I don't see nobody," and winked broadly.

"Try to stay calm," Hoskins said solemnly, and Paul collapsed laughing. Hoskins lay down in the dirt next to him and laughed just like he
did. Their laughter infected Charlotte and Baird, and they didn't stop for
a long time.

Before he left, Paul said rather awkwardly that he had something to
tell her, something he just thought of and he wished he'd've thought of it
earlier and could he talk to her alone?

She sent the boys away, feeling a little trickle of alarm.

He made a little indentation in the dirt with his shoe. "You know
how I said Francis told me to come over here and help you out?"

"Yes."

"I think maybe your husband talked to Francis when he was here.
You know, in December. I think he might've told Francis he needed
someone to look after the place."

"Why would he ask Francis?"

Paul shrugged. "Maybe you should ask Francis. I wasn't party to the
discussion." He paused again. "Francis paid me already."

"I see. So that's why you didn't want any money."

"I guess I should've said something before."

"At least you were honest. You didn't let me pay you, too."

He gave her his best smile. "Hey, yeah, I was being honest. But he
didn't tell me to help you out with the water, or the garden. I did that on
my own."

"It was nice that you made Hoskins laugh."

"Anytime," he said happily. "Maybe next time I'll show your boys how to make a magic coin disappear."

"I suppose you ought to come back prepared to work."

"You're willing to hire me?"

"I am."

"You don't want no references?"

"Why, do you think I should ask around?"

"Better not," he said. "No telling what people might say."

"I don't care what they say. You're honest, and you like to work. And you like the boys. I can see they like you."

"It's a deal. I'll be here tomorrow."

She watched him climbing the hill behind the house with a jaunty gait, his jacket slung over his shoulder. She almost thought she could hear him whistling. She went into the house, feeling ashamed of the way she'd greeted him in the yard, with so much suspicion in her heart.

CHAPTER

14

Charlotte awoke in the night, certain she heard footsteps. She listened for a while, then got up to look out the windows. There was nothing to see but a clear night sky, a waning moon, and bright, isolated stars. She examined the shadow of the lopsided maple, its good branches waving lazily in a gentle breeze; something white lay on the ground. Perhaps a mushroom had sprung up on the damp grass. The longer she looked at it, the odder it became. She awakened Hannibal from his post in the boys' room, and he padded down the stairs after her. He wasn't much of a guard dog, but at least he could tell a mushroom from an intruder.

As she walked out on the porch, the white object in the grass turned into her own dishpan.

Something, though, had awakened her. She checked out the rest of the downstairs, then poured herself a glass of water at the kitchen sink. Fear, Mrs. Eddy warned, was a great temptation. We are tempted to feel afraid because of messages from our corporeal senses, messages that are false in the first place and arise from a mortal, fearful, and limited mind.

Our senses tell us there is a noise in the silence, an odor in the air, a stranger in the basement. It is even possible to imagine a thing so completely that it becomes real. In some cases, said Mrs. Eddy, fear itself actually makes the fearful result manifest. That, in fact, is how people got sick: It was the mind that carried the infection. *Change the belief and the sensation changes. Destroy the belief, and the sensation disappears.*

It was all up to her. She was in absolute control of the palpitations she was experiencing at that very moment   all she had to do was change the belief. The same was true for Beatriz and her varicose veins. In her overwrought imagination, her enlarged veins—or perhaps it was her constricted veins—carried too much blood to her feet, or not enough; Charlotte didn't know exactly which. She hoped never to know, and she hoped Baird would never know, either, though she wasn't sure if men ever got varicose veins. At any rate, by imagining them so clearly, Beatriz was punishing herself by calling up the fearful result. It was no different from the way Charlotte felt now, imagining someone in the basement.

She pictured a man's leg thrusting itself through the open basement well window. A little trickle of fear ran around the inside of her skull.

The realization of what she was imagining stunned her and made her sit down hard in the kitchen rocker. Water from her glass splashed onto the floor.

When Baird asked about Beatriz's varicose veins, Charlotte had told him to think about how much God loved him, and that was what she needed to do for herself. She was made in God's image and likeness and was a manifestation of His perfection, which meant: no flaws, no fear, no holding of breath and straining to listen to whatever was, or wasn't, down there on the damp dirt floor. God was Love, and God filled all space. There was no room for anything else, no beginning or ending of time or anything else, just God existing in one endless, ongoing present that went on forever. It was very hard to imagine, given one's limits as a human being. The best she could do was to think of a flower expanding from a bud to a blossom, never going anywhere, always staying on the same stem.

A second leg thrust itself into view through the narrow cobwebby opening. She was surprised by the footwear—the shoes were soft, almost like slippers. You'd expect boots from an intruder—she clutched at the idea: Would someone with sinister motives wear slippers? Feet, legs, torso, arms . . . he dropped to the ground soundlessly, covered in cobwebs. He wore a little bellhop's hat ajar on his head—it was the Porter, wearing his monkey's hat! The Porter was in her basement!

He was suddenly beside her, his uniform stained and covered with debris, his eyebrows dark and dangerous. A bit of sticky spiderweb stuck to his nose. *Look at yourself, quivering with fear in the dark, imagining monsters! Your mind is a sinkhole, a writhing mass of morbidity! I've been listening, I've been watching: Did you see my husband? How was he? How did he seem? Was he upset? You shouldn't have come, and you know it. You're getting nowhere, you know nothing, it's done no good except to make you look foolish. And look at the people you're asking!*

*Have you done your lesson since you got here? No, you're too busy. You read the paper, you read the COMICS; I see you! You can't wait to find out what Daisy Mae is up to, but do you do your Science reading? NO! What do you fill your mind with? Your little troubles, your self-indulgent feelings. I've seen you cry, like a sniveling human, because you feel so sorry for yourself! You're supposed to PROTECT yourself from these things with right-thinking, not INVITE THEM IN AND WALLOW. I gave you some latitude when you first arrived—*give her a week, *I said to myself,* let her pull herself together.

His breath smelled bad, and she tried to lean back as far as she could, out of range. His brow vibrated rapidly with a nervous twitch.

You're treading on perilous ground; you're dabbling in morbid preoccupations. Or moribund, *shall we say? Even Hoskins knows the word, and how dangerous it is! You know what happens to morbid people, don't you? They get sick! Look at Beatriz! You're just like her. You've swung wide the gates, letting in poisonous thoughts. You don't even call me anymore to shut the door. I have to sneak in to help, crawl through cobwebs, ruin my uniform. Look, I'm missing a button! And these slippers, I had to borrow them from Johnny Cake!*

She could see now that he was wearing worn sheepskin slippers. He'd walked over the dew-soaked grass, and they were a mess. She wondered if it would be up to her to replace them—she didn't know what the protocol could possibly be for this. Was she responsible?

And what about that CLOWN you hired? You're afraid to even tell your sisters what you've done, how far you've strayed, who you're associating with. Have you even talked to them? No—and why? Because you don't want to admit what a mistake you've made by coming here!

She wanted to say he was being unfair. She wasn't wallowing. And she'd done her best to get in touch with her sisters (well, her second best). She'd only read *Li'l Abner* once, and not because she craved the comics, as he seemed to imply. She'd bought the *Beede Opinion* when they went down to the store for groceries because she wanted to see if Leona had written anything about their arrival in her column. She'd written about their departure in the fall and made what Charlotte's father would have called an "unfelicitous comparison." The McGuffeys subscribed to the paper in Syracuse, and at some point after the accident, she'd remembered Leona's reference to the poor soldier. She was certain Leona must be mortified.

He laughed. *Unfelicitous! How erudite! And do you suppose these people here know the meaning of that word? These are not your people! They know nothing about discipline, reason, hard work. They're common. They know nothing of metaphysics. They live from day to day, from one melodrama to the next. Daisy Mae, indeed!*

She struck him on the mouth, and he was gone.

In the morning, Charlotte rolled up her sleeves and attacked the pantry. Every summer she mounted a full-scale attack, and every summer she was defeated, routed by overflowing drawers full of loaf pans and whisks and strainers, rusty frying pans and slotted spoons, iron cornbread-muffin trays too heavy to lift, pans without lids and lids without pans, bewildering wooden implements whose use she couldn't fathom. There were jelly jars and mismatched dishes, parts of double boilers, spoons without handles, timers that didn't work, and an occasional mustache cup (valuable if it had had a handle) or a little Hummel figure (worth saving if its nose wasn't smashed). In among the larger items were little colored vials that looked vaguely medical in nature, and measuring devices that could have been pharmaceutical—relics, probably, of Cal

McGuffey's forays into the lucrative business of medical quackery. Everything was in such a jumble that it was always hard to assess what was important, which things were worth saving, which things should be thrown out.

The heaviest burden, perhaps, came from the fact that these things weren't hers—or even if they were, literally, because the property had in fact passed to her, she didn't feel that she really owned them, or the house and its history, or the objects in it. She had inherited them, and now she was their guardian, whether she liked them or not.

At first she started in her usual way, which was to empty one shelf at a time, clean the shelf, and put back only those items that appeared either valuable or useful. Soon, however, she saw the folly of her method: The potential to be cowed by a single colander was much greater than one among many. The single colander cried out, *Save me! Look at me again! Others have cherished me!* By comparison, one colander among others was a puny, helpless thing. She should deal with categories, not individual items.

She began putting like objects together on the floor in separate piles: kettles in one pile, then lids, graters, ladles, strainers, frying pans, and so forth. It soon became clear, however, that except for lids without pans, there wasn't enough of any one kind of thing to make up a sizable category. She ought to be arranging things by function and size. But this was tricky: How big is medium? Is a colander a container, since it lets liquid *out?* After a while, Charlotte began to sense the beginnings of a familiar weariness; she was getting nowhere. She had waded right back into the same tidal pool of slotted spoons and muffin tins. The jelly jars swirled around her, pulling at her and undermining her resolve.

She had never been a good housekeeper. She sometimes wondered if her mother had suffered the same lack of enthusiasm for domestic tasks. There were piles of things in the upstairs hallway, she remembered, and things on the basement stairs, but what they were or how long they stayed there, she didn't know. Her mother hadn't liked to iron, she knew that. "Just a lot of wrinkles," her mother had said one day as she moved a pile of clothes out of an armchair. Charlotte had been—doing what?

Just standing there, watching? Did she laugh? Lillian Baird was a tall woman with a tired, handsome face; she wore her red hair up. Charlotte could imagine her letting the dishes go, sweeping around the table and not looking under. But she could only really remember her reading, and once, snapping green beans in her lap. She would have liked to think she shared her indifference to housekeeping with her mother. Her sisters painted such a perfect picture of her, she didn't seem real.

Charlotte kicked off her huaraches and sat down on the floor, letting her skirt billow around her. These were merely objects, she reminded herself, over which she ought to have dominion.

The scowling face on the mustache cup on the counter in front of her, with the dried glue running down its cheek, had an odd familiarity. She stared at it for a while and decided that it looked like Cal McGuffey.

He would not have trusted Paul Bellini with his lawn mower. The problem was, she didn't know if she should, either.

She picked up the cup and threw it in the wastebasket, where it landed with a lovely ring of authority. She looked around for other things to pitch—anything with a chip or a crack or streaks of rust—and as she tossed them one by one into the basket, she heard remnants from one of Cal's impassioned speeches in her head.

The poor, he liked to say, were only poor because they liked it that way. They liked their old cars and scrawny chickens and their feuds and all the other parts of their soap-opera lives. They enacted their melodramatic scenes again and again, day after day, generation after generation, for one reason only—because they loved the excitement. It was as simple as that. But they weren't content with just being poor, they had to cause trouble. Why? Because they liked trouble. They didn't care that people like Cal and other taxpayers had to pay for it out of their own pockets: paying to pave over roads the poor rutted out with their hell-bent driving; paying to build jails to house the ornery and the wicked; to build hospitals to amputate the gangrenous limbs of the dumbfounded and the woe-begotten; paying to assist in the delivery of incestuous issue; paying to treat the victims, and the perpetrators, of that plague, venereal disease. The taxpayers paid and paid again, and all for what?

The poor, he'd say, shaking his head with the enormity of their usurpations, used up more than their share of the common good. They overgrazed, in every sense of the term.

Charlotte threw a rusty strainer into the basket. Cal McGuffey was a crook. He lied to people. He sold them false goods and took their money, and then he railed against them.

The previous owners of the village store had been, if not actively warm, at least moderately friendly, but the atmosphere in the new store, which had been set on the old store's foundation and still smelled like smoke, was a grim one. Minna was at the counter, studying the cash register and looking generally furious. She was wearing a pastel duster, a shapeless cotton dress that emphasized the pearlike shape of her body and the sticklike shape of her legs. She didn't look up.

Minna and her husband, Waldo, were from across the river in New Hampshire, and when they came to Vermont after the fire to start up a new store, they brought their politics with them. They were fanatical patriots and used the place as a forum in which to promote their views about the Red Menace, which, to hear it from them, was breathing down Beede's neck. One of the first things they did after stocking the shelves was to install a suggestion box just inside the door, where they asked their customers to insert the names of possible Communist sympathizers in the area. Charlotte had no idea how often people left suggestions, but everything was all set up for them to do so: pad of paper, pencil, hand-lettered sign with an arrow saying DROP HERE.

Charlotte went up and down the aisles looking at the merchandise. She'd already been there several times, but this was the first time Minna, and not Waldo, had been on duty in the store. Waldo was even harder to talk to than Minna.

The boys were at the candy display, where Hoskins was starting to rearrange things. She wouldn't linger.

Minna waited until Charlotte set her groceries on the counter before she spoke. "I still got some of your husband's souvenir plates. Nobody seems to want them. I gave him the rest of his money when he was here. We sell on consignment only—that's our practice—we don't put the money up front. You want 'em?"

Charlotte said she did and then asked if Melvin had come in to shop. "Sure he did."

"He bought some things?"

"Bought some milk."

"Is that all?" she asked gingerly.

"I make it my business not to notice."

Rebuked. "Of course. I just wondered."

Minna leaned toward her over the counter. "If I was you I'd think twice about hiring the Great Bellini, as they call him. He's nothing but trouble. Of course you know where he's living. You know what they're all about." Minna let her opinion take an awkward shape in the space between them and then waited until it hardened into resin.

Baird handed her two O-Henry bars. "I'll take these, too," Charlotte said.

"You might want to tell your Mr. Bellini he's got an unpaid bill here"—Minna looked up, stone-faced—"when you see him."

"How much is it?"

"His bill?"

"Isn't that what you're complaining about?"

Minna stared at her for a minute, then covered her thumb with a rubber cap and very deliberately thumbed through the receipts. "Eight dollars and fifteen cents. Unpaid for over six months."

Charlotte handed Minna a fifty-dollar bill. "You can add that amount to my groceries."

"You're paying his bill?" Minna looked at her as if she were out of her mind. "I'll have to get change in back." She moved away, still talking. "I'll get those plates for you while I'm at it. I don't have the room to keep everybody's things here, I've got a business to run." When she was gone, Charlotte quickly filled out one of the slips hanging off the "Commie Box" and wrote "MINNA BEAL."

•   •   •

Alphie Andoulette wasn't home, and Baird was bitterly disappointed. He was over to Colby staying with his nephews, his older sister Amarita said. He'd be back the next day. "You want to play with the twins?" she asked Baird. "They're out back, getting into mischief probably."

"Go ahead," Charlotte told him. "I'll wait here." Baird went off reluctantly and Charlotte told the girl that Baird hadn't had anyone to play with for quite a while. "I'll just wait here for a few minutes while he gets reacquainted."

"Fine by me. I ain't doing nothing. You want something to drink?"

"I'm fine, thank you, Amarita. Is it Amarita, or Rita?"

"Don't matter," she said, perching on the porch railing. She was about thirteen, all elbows and knees, a beanpole with dirty feet. Her green eyes were set close together and rimmed with long, thick lashes. She fiddled with her sandals, the cuffs of her shorts.

"How come you cut your hair?"

Charlotte decided that one day she would like to answer, *None of your business*. "It just came over me."

"I wouldn't've."

"Well, then, you can grow yours."

"It don't grow out good. It just gets all raggedy." She touched her ropy brown hair. She had a noticeably crooked face, but with those eyes, Charlotte thought, she'd be very striking when she was older. "Mr. McGuffey said I should let it grow."

"What did you say?"

"He said if I was going to be a model in New York City, I should let it grow."

"Are you talking about my husband?"

Rita nodded.

"When did he tell you that?"

"When he was here in December. He took my picture."

"How did that happen?"

"He was over there, getting ready to take his picture of the church." Rita pointed at the turnout across the road. "I asked him to take my picture."

"What did he say?"

She shrugged.

"Did he *speak* to you? Did he say anything?"

"What would he say?"

"I don't know. I'm asking you."

"He said, 'Go get your sled, and I'll take your picture.'"

"After you asked him?"

"Yup."

"I'm surprised. He never put people in his pictures of the church."

Rita shrugged. "I guess he wanted to try something new."

"I guess he did."

"He wanted me to change my clothes."

"He said that?" Charlotte asked, astounded.

"I was wearing my sister Alice's coat with the fur collar, and he didn't like it. He said it was too grown-up looking and I had to go home and put on my ugly old snowsuit that's ripped in back."

"Did he say that, 'Go home and put on your ugly old snowsuit'?"

"I guess."

"Did he smile?"

"At me?"

"At anybody?"

"He kind of laughed at my coat. He said it was too big for me. He said, 'Where'd you get that thing?'"

"Was he making fun of your coat?"

"Maybe," said Rita, growing less sure.

"I just can't really imagine my husband making fun of your coat."

"You think that picture'll come out in a magazine?"

"I don't know how it could, Rita. The film is gone, the camera's gone. Everything is gone."

"Where is it?"

"I don't know, that's what I'm trying to say."

"Damn," the girl said, frowning. Then she brightened. "You need some help up to your place this summer?" Rita was holding out her hands, showing Charlotte how strong they were. She was milking for Mr. Turley, she said. "You got to have strong hands to milk, even with them machines. I can houseclean, too. You need someone to clean? I can find things, too."

Charlotte asked what sort of things. She couldn't imagine.

"Anything, and I don't charge extra for it, either." She smiled out of one side of her mouth, like someone recovering from a stroke. "And I can see in the dark. You want me to come up sometime?"

"I'll let you know when I bring Baird down to play with Alphie."

"I got to know quick," the girl said, brushing her raggedy hair away from her face as if batting a pesky fly, "or else I got to go back to vacation Bible school for another whole week."

"All right, we'll try it on Monday for a few hours. Would that help?"

"Sure would," said Rita, and she gave Charlotte a big lopsided smile.

On the way back up to their house, Charlotte took a detour on impulse to the Nest, but the place was deserted; she hadn't expected it, with its local reputation as such a busy place, such a well-known center of dangerous un-American activity. She did not believe that the Red Threat had come to Beede and wasn't even sure that it existed at all. Melvin had called Joe McCarthy an irresponsible fearmonger. Even Millard Tydings, appointed by President Truman to investigate McCarthy's charges of disloyalty in the State Department, had recognized his lies and exaggerations, and labeled his charges a fraud and a hoax, but not before many careers were ruined. If Melvin himself were still working for the FSA, he'd told her, he, too, would be investigated, given the whiff of treason that had lingered after he hooked up with pacifists before the war. After Eisenhower's election, he believed, McCarthy would feel empowered and be even more dangerous. The new, improved McCarthy would have power behind him. Charlotte ought to be careful about what she said to her fellow students, he told her. "You mean, the bobby-soxers and the frat boys?" she'd countered. "Do you think they care about world events?"

She wished now she'd asked him more about it instead of dismissing his ideas so quickly. He might have known something she needed to know. It happened a lot; he took a position and she immediately dug her heels into the opposite point of view without waiting to listen—what he was for, she was against. It made things so simple.

The housekeeping practices at the Nest were obviously very casual, as evidenced by the sagging cot on the front porch, a broom with a stump of a handle, a heap of swollen books left out for the dew to ruin, one desperate geranium in a broken pot. The yard was full of ragweed. Charlotte and Baird took a quick walk around to the back, leaving Hoskins happily engrossed in the Vermont driver's manual Beatriz had given him. He had found it in the glove compartment of her car, and she had insisted he take it, prevailing over Charlotte's objections.

The backyard offered signs of more activity: a hammock hooked up between two trees, seed packets, a haphazard collection of garden tools, a scrawny cat with kittens in a cardboard box. A welder's mask and gloves lay on the flagstones in the hot sun. There was an outbuilding Charlotte assumed was Francis's studio, and she peeked in the window. The framework for one of his staircases lay on its side in the middle, surrounded by a jumble of tools and electric cords. She picked up a book lying on a wooden bench against the outside wall. *The Varieties of Religious Experience,* by William James. *My! A thinker!* Unless it was one of the ex-wives people talked about.

Baird brought her two nondescript tabby kittens, their eyes barely open. "No," she said before he could ask, "we can't."

"The Andoulettes have kittens."

"Baird, we can't take on kittens. What would we do with them when we left?"

"We could take them with us."

"No."

"Or we could stay."

"It will take more than kittens to make me stay here, Baird. Grampa Cal's house needs a lot of work to make it livable."

"I thought it was ours."

"Well, it is, technically. I'm just used to calling it that."

"Let's call it ours now," he said. "Or Daddy's."

Of course, she thought, and she was sorry.

Baird put the mewing kittens back in the box with the skinny mother cat, and they walked around to the front. Hoskins had gotten out of the car and was sitting on the porch steps. From his expression, he'd clearly been anticipating their appearance. "Hi," he said, looking rather proud.

"Hi!" Charlotte and Baird both called in unison, smiling happily at each other. "Well, isn't this is a lovely surprise," she said. "What are you doing? Are you waiting for us on the steps?"

"No."

"You mean yes," Baird told him. "You're supposed to say 'yes.'"

"No," he said more emphatically, shaking his head.

"You mean, you're not waiting for us," said Charlotte.

He shook his head again.

"Well then, what *are* you doing, Hoskins?"

Hoskins stared at the ground a few feet in front of him, at a scraggly plant. It was the geranium, planted now in the ground.

"I'll bet he learned to plant things from Paul," Baird said.

Charlotte was delighted. "Oh, isn't that lovely, Hoskins. What a nice thing you've done for the people who live here! I'll bet they'll be awfully pleased."

"Do you think they'll notice?" Baird asked, looking around at the unkempt yard.

"They will if we leave them a note," she said, and went to the car to find something to write with.

CHAPTER

1 5

Everyone in the little church was very still. The evening was warm, and the windows were open to the sound of a chorus of crickets chirping on the shadowy, close-cropped lawn. Beatriz sat on a folding chair at the end of the aisle, leaning sideways and presenting a melancholy picture of a ship listing in shallow water. Every once in a while she sighed audibly. Hoskins and Baird, their faces scrubbed and wearing white shirts and ties, sat on the other side of Charlotte.

Against her better judgment, Charlotte had finally acquiesced to Beatriz's desire to attend a testimonial service, which Beatriz still insisted on calling a *meeting,* with the implication that anyone could, and would, get up and talk—a prospect that made Charlotte very nervous. A few weeks ago, she had lent Beatriz a copy of Mrs. Eddy's book, and since then, Beatriz had called her many times with the kinds of questions that made Charlotte cringe. ("What should I do if I have a nightmare about being murdered? You think it may come to pass?" and "You think Mrs. Eddy could help me lose some weight?") It would be very embarrassing if she should share those thoughts aloud during the service, but Beatriz had pressed and Charlotte was loath to continue making excuses. She had never really seen anyone like Beatriz in a Christian Science church. Most everyone was very well-dressed and looked as though they had everything they needed—or if they didn't, they didn't let on.

On the way over, Charlotte had tried to explain exactly what would happen during the service. There was a First and a Second Reader who would stand at the front of the church and read selected passages, first from the Bible and then from the *Science and Health*. After that, the room would fall silent. Eventually somebody might—or might not—rise to speak. Beatriz interrupted her. "So I don't have to testify."

"No, no, not at all; it really isn't necessary." There were plenty of people, Charlotte assured her, who were loyal members of branch churches all over the country who had never once, in years and years, gotten up to testify. It probably wasn't a good idea the first time. Charlotte didn't advise it.

"What if I should be moved to speak?"

"Moved?"

"If I feel the spirit."

"You might want to suppress it," Charlotte said, and smiled at her, seeing her worried look. "At least for the time being."

"While I'm a postulant?" Beatriz said.

"Postulant! Where did you hear that, Beatriz?"

"Mrs. Eddy. Or it might have been Linette Turley and her crossword puzzles. It means you're thinking of joining up."

"For goodness' sakes." *How amazing,* Charlotte thought. You just never knew what was going on in people's minds.

She had described the kinds of things Beatriz would hear people talk about in their testimonials—thoughts about God that had occurred to them during the day, healings and demonstrations of the power of Christian Science that they were grateful for. Charlotte tried to stress that these were not traditional prayers, that Mrs. Eddy did not encourage her followers to make requests. All prayer was *mental,* she explained carefully, except for the Lord's Prayer, and the reading aloud of the *Science and*

Health. There were no orations or confessions, no loud praising of the Lord. Finally, after the last person had spoken and a certain allotted time had passed, the First Reader would say, "Let us pray," and everyone would bow their heads. Then a basket would be passed around for contributions—Beatriz didn't have to make any, she should know that—and the organist would play to let them know it was time to go home. There was no fellowship hour or reception with cake and coffee in the basement, as there was after most Protestant services. And there was no preacher. Mrs. Eddy was the preacher.

"Is that so! Still? I thought you said she passed away!"

"Well, yes. What I mean is, the preacher is her book. She thought it best not to let—well, human beings—do the preaching. They might misinterpret her words."

"They could, you know."

"Yes, they could. It's sometimes a difficult belief to understand. It would be easy for people not to get it right." Charlotte thought of Mrs. Eddy's penetrating gaze.

"All right, then," Beatriz had said, clasping her purse to her chest as they turned the corner and headed toward the little church, "I think I'm ready."

The four of them comprised nearly half the people in the sparsely furnished room that Wednesday evening. The First and Second Readers, a man and a woman, were seated perfectly still in the left front row. Across the aisle from them, also very still, was a woman in a navy-blue suit and pillbox hat crowned with a nest of navy-blue veiling. Behind her sat a large, big-boned man in a tweed suit. His nose, which was also large, was disfigured by a growth of the same shape and texture as those sometimes seen on maple trees. On the other side of the aisle, behind the Readers, a gangly teenage boy wearing a plaid sweater vest sat alone, his head bowed. There was a well-dressed, middle-age couple in the back row, behind Charlotte and her little group.

At length, the First and Second Readers rose in a graceful, practiced manner, and walked with great dignity toward the two lecterns at the front of the room. The First Reader was a white-haired man with a kindly face. He reminded Charlotte of her father, who in fact had been the First Reader for a while in the branch church the Baird family had attended in Syracuse. The Second Reader was a somewhat portly woman with a thin puff of hair arranged on top of her head. Her stiff taffeta skirt whispered as she moved. They took their places and smiled confidently at the few people seated in folding chairs before them.

Written in stenciled gilt letters on the right-hand wall at the front of the church were the words DIVINE LOVE ALWAYS HAS AND ALWAYS WILL MEET EVERY HUMAN NEED—MARY BAKER EDDY. Written in the same lettering on the left wall was THE TRUTH SHALL SET YOU FREE—CHRIST JESUS. These two quotes could be found at every Christian Science church in the land.

The Second Reader opened the service by reading several passages from the Bible. Afterward the First Reader read Mrs. Eddy's explanation from the *Science and Health*. Charlotte remembered overhearing her father practice reading the new week's selected passages in the years he was a Reader. He always went into a different room, which she assumed was because he felt self-conscious.

When the Readers were finished, they closed their books and gazed out over the room in a way that suggested they were waiting for something that they were confident would be very pleasant. It was time for testimonies.

After a long period of silence, the Second Reader disengaged herself from the lectern and stepped to the side of it, signifying that she had left her special role as Second Reader and whatever spiritual authority and wisdom it conferred, and entered the more human and temporal realm of the congregation. She began by thanking God for answering her prayers about a "difficult personal matter," which she didn't name, but which, she said, had been resolved beautifully and "in an unexpected way." "Which shows us," she ended by saying, "that we can't predict the mysterious ways in which God moves."

Charlotte stiffened as she heard Beatriz say, "Amen!" The Second Reader looked startled briefly but immediately recomposed her face into benign neutrality and moved back to her former position behind the lectern. There then commenced another deep silence in the room.

Looking very serious, and scowling a little as if he were engaged in an important task in which he didn't expect to be challenged, Baird dug into his pants pocket for the toothpick wrapped in cellophane that he had brought to the church service as part of his personal arsenal. It was a favorite due to its apparently innocuous nature and its many covert uses. It was an item that, in the past, he had been able to use successfully in public to clean his fingernails, play Soldier, and poke Hoskins in the soft flesh of his arm. But as he dug for it, he spotted a much greater source of entertainment enter the room in the shape of a large horsefly. He nudged Hoskins, and the two boys watched, enthralled, as the fly cruised the little ball of navy-blue veiling at the top of the lady's hat. Baird and Hoskins watched it land; Baird made a hopeful buzzing noise, and Hoskins followed suit. Charlotte reached across the two empty chairs and quietly clasped both their knees, signaling her orders: *You will behave.* The boys waited breathlessly, but the lady made no attempt to swat the fly and it disappeared into the veiling, where it apparently became enmeshed. After a few minutes of intense effort, accompanied by sounds of engine trouble, the fly freed itself and took off. Baird giggled, followed by Hoskins's precise imitation.

The teenage boy stood up. "My mother couldn't be here tonight because of her nerves," he said, speaking very carefully, as if to the slow-witted. "She has a nervous condition. I try to help her understand that God is All. Sometimes we visit cemeteries on Saturdays; it's my mother's idea. You might think this is a sad thing, but it's not; we like reading the tombstones and wondering about these people. Some of them sound very interesting. I won't go into any details on that. But last Saturday I couldn't go because I had a sore throat. That's what I thought; it was my belief. Then Mother said, 'Here now, let's pray together,' and we read the *Science and Health*. She went off, and I stayed home and thought about what Mrs. Eddy said. I thought, 'It's only my belief.' When she got home, I felt a lot better. I'm very grateful." He sat down abruptly, as if hit by birdshot.

A long silence rocketed around the room. People shifted in their chairs. The man with the growth on his nose made a little tent with his fingers, on which he propped his chin, looking thoughtful. The boy in the vest hunched down. Beatriz leaned over, and in a loud whisper told Charlotte she knew that boy. He was a sacker at the Grand Union in QC. She thought she might know the mother, too, but she couldn't think of her name. Charlotte whispered, "That's all right," and patted her soft arm, trying to let her know that she should just forget the woman and her name.

The lady in navy blue stood up, facing the lectern with a piece of paper in her hand. "Our Beloved Leader, Mary Baker Eddy, the Discoverer and Founder of Christian Science and inspired author of the *Science and Health with Key to the Scriptures,* said this: *It is Love which paints the petal with myriad hues, glances in the warm sunbeam, arches the cloud with the bow of beauty, blazons the night with starry gems, and covers Earth with loveliness*. I find this very inspiring."

"Amen, sister!" Beatriz called out, and Charlotte froze.

The speaker turned around so that she faced Beatriz. "I'm not finished," she said flatly.

"Oh, I'm sorry," said Beatriz sweetly, "I thought you was through."

"*Harmony cannot be disturbed by inharmony,*" the sister continued. "Perfection cannot be marred by imperfection. Not when we know the Truth. *Love never loses sight of loveliness.* Mrs. Eddy tells us that we must turn our gaze in the right direction. We must form perfect models in thought and look at them continually. If we hold them in our mind, we will always know the Truth." She sat down, ramrod straight.

Charlotte could feel Beatriz starting to rise and tried laying a restraining hand on her arm, but to no avail. She had it in her head to speak, she'd always had it in her head to speak, and nothing Charlotte had said to her had made a dent in that earnest, consuming intention. Beatriz continued to rise, grasping the back of the chair in front of her, and Charlotte let go.

"I am thanking the Lord in advance for the return of my fiancé, Ben Hightower, who walked out on me the day after Thanksgiving. I am trusting in the Lord and praying every day for his return. Life is hard but love is true." Beatriz looked around the room to see how it was going.

Everyone was looking straight ahead. "I have good reason to believe he'll be back, and I'm counting on it, I'll tell you that. If he does, it will be the good Lord's doing. If he don't, well, I suppose I will get used to it eventually. I have a good neighbor—well, she's sitting right here and I'm grateful for all her help. She's a fine woman. I'll tell you, if it weren't for her, well . . ." Tears welled up in Beatriz's eyes. "My little baby died last year. As if that wasn't enough troubles, well, off walks my Ben!" Beatriz hesitated, apparently casting around for an ending. "I miss my man!" She sat down, flushed, and gave Charlotte a look of great despair.

No one else spoke after that. There was an extended period of silence, some throat-clearing, some rustling. The man with the growth on his nose retrieved a pretty little basket from a small table at the side of the room and began to pass it around, averting his eyes delicately as money was put into it. Baird dropped his toothpick in as it passed in front of him; Hoskins reached in and took it out.

The First Reader looked at the Second. She nodded, and asked the congregation to join them in silent prayer.

"It's over?" asked Beatriz, sounding bewildered, as the organist began to play. "We didn't sing no hymns."

Charlotte prodded the boys forward down the aisle, hoping to gain the door before talking to anyone. As she passed the boy in the sweater vest, she thought she heard him asking the man with the growth on his nose if he thought he should put his mother in a home. The man seemed surprised. "Is she that needy?" he asked.

The Second Reader caught up with them before they got to the end of the center aisle. "Lovely to see you tonight," the woman murmured. "You've been here before," she told Charlotte, and Charlotte nodded and said yes, she'd been there last summer several times.

"We're from Beede," Beatriz announced proudly. "You know where that is?"

"I'm afraid not," said the woman.

"We got the most photographed church in the state."

"Really. Isn't that wonderful."

Charlotte didn't believe the woman thought it was wonderful at all;

she thought it was the kind of thing an ignorant person would say—it showed in her face, plain as day. She had the sudden impulse to shield Beatriz from her, to erect a barrier between them so that Beatriz wouldn't see the woman's expression. But she just stood there helplessly, waiting to hear what Beatriz would say next.

"Not to say that this ain't a fine church, too, little as it is. It's real clean."

"Yes," the Second Reader said. "We have it cleaned every Saturday."

"And your flowers is nice."

"Thank you."

"The one thing that made me curious, though, was the lack of singing."

The woman smiled at her. "We have a quiet way of doing things."

"You think I shouldn't've gotten up?"

"You might want to wait a few times and see how the others do it. Sometimes that's best."

"Well, I'm sorry. I guess I was just feeling kind of grateful to the Lord for being out. I been shut up in my house for a long while. And then, my sadness just kind of rolled on out, and lots of feelings with it."

"That's fine," said Charlotte, trying to move her along toward the door, where the boys were waiting for them, "you did fine."

"I don't know what come over me. Charlotte here made it perfectly clear I shouldn't get up and talk."

"They're just not used to people saying 'amen' aloud," Charlotte told her when they were back in the car.

"I know you made it perfectly clear—" Beatriz tried to say again, and Charlotte stopped her. She hadn't done anything wrong, she said, and she didn't want her to keep apologizing. Anyway, it had been too quiet in that little room with so few people there. You could hear the floorboards creaking. Beatriz had simply livened things up and made the whole service more interesting. As she spoke, Charlotte began to believe it. Beatriz had made things more lively. She was very sincere, after all, and the Second Reader ought to have done more to make her feel welcome. She ought to have been glad that they were there.

From the backseat, Hoskins shouted, "Amen!"

"Oh, brother," said Baird, and they all laughed.

"I suppose they sing on Sunday," said Beatriz. "They used to say I had a good voice. Of course there ain't been nothing for me to sing about until you come."

"I haven't done anything remarkable, Beatriz."

"You don't know. You done me a world of good already, and Ben ain't even back yet."

Charlotte had to admit Beatriz seemed to have cheered up quite a bit since she'd been there. Leona had noticed it, too.

"But I'm expecting him. You told me he's coming back, and I believe you. You think it'll be long now?"

"I don't know, I really don't."

"I have to tell you, while I was speaking there at your little church, I had a feeling he was getting closer. He may be on his way. I suppose that was a good part of it, why I had to speak out like that."

The sky was still light as they drove back through Quarry City. Clusters of teenagers stood on the corners; the Lobster Claw was doing a booming business. On the road out of town Charlotte pulled over at the Brown Cow, the ice-cream shack where Melvin and she had often stopped. Baird shouted out "Waahoo!" from the backseat as she pulled in, followed by another "Amen!" from Hoskins.

Charlotte and Beatriz ate their cones in the car while the boys sat on a bench outside the brightly lit shack, watching a group of older boys horse around in the warm summer night. "You going up to St. J?"

"Oh, no! Why would I go there?"

"Oh, I don't know. I thought you might. You might learn a thing or two, get the answers you need."

"What a funny thing to say, Beatriz. I don't need anything in particular. I'm just spending the summer with my children in this beautiful place."

"Maybe." Beatriz carefully licked the chocolate swirl around the outside of her vanilla. "I suppose you're looking forward to your sisters coming."

"They're coming at the end of July." In the past, they'd come at the end of June, as soon as the McGuffeys were settled, but Charlotte had managed to stave off their visit. Rosey had wanted to come sooner; fortunately, Kitty seemed to be busy with some Science business in Boston and had readily agreed to the delay.

"I know you're lonely."

"Beatriz, you don't have to analyze my situation. I'm fine."

Beatriz didn't reply, and they finished their cones in silence, watching the little scene in front of the shack. One of the older boys was showing off by punching his friend in the arm, trying to make him drop his cone. Hoskins stood up on the bench to get a better look. As Beatriz was wiping her fingers with her napkin, she said, "I imagine your little one will be talking real good before the summer is over. You'll have your miracle, Charlotte, don't you worry."

"I'm not looking for a miracle," she told Beatriz, still feeling cross about her earlier remark, but the minute she heard herself say it aloud like that, in that dismissive way, she knew it was a lie. She wanted nothing more than to wake up one morning and hear Hoskins chatting with Baird about some simple, ordinary thing, the kind of conversation between children that other mothers would take for granted. In the meantime she had to content herself with celebrating single words as milestones and tiny advances, like his planting the geranium among the ragweeds at the Nest and waiting for her to praise him.

Charlotte let Beatriz off at her house and waited until she'd gained the front door and turned on the outside light. It was finally dark.

She put the children to bed after only one story instead of two, and walked wearily down the narrow hall to her bedroom, thinking about not brushing her teeth—what did it matter? The door to the little bathroom was ajar, and she hesitated as she passed. She smelled stale cigarette smoke first, and then realized it wasn't the bathroom at all, it was the club car. The Porter had his feet propped up on the arm of an empty plush seat; he was in his stocking feet. The only other person in the club car was a prim and tidy lady dressed in a dark bombazine dress with a high neck-line and a white corsage pinned at her shoulder. She was scowling. She had white hair done up in ringlets and remarkably bright, deep-set eyes. It was Mrs. Eddy, reading her Bible.

The heavy door at the other end of the car opened with a hissing sound, and in walked Leona Cake wearing speckled lavender glasses, yellow culottes, spanking-white gym shoes. She hurried past Mrs. Eddy and approached the Porter. "The water on this train is brackish," she said fearlessly. "And we're out of cups."

The Porter responded with a dismissive wave of his hand. He was on his break; the matter could wait.

"I'll be sure to take a different train next time," Leona told him sharply, and turned on her heels.

"How about a bus!" he hissed as the pneumatic door struggled to close behind her and the noise of the wheels on the tracks subsided again. "Well?" he asked Charlotte, half-turning his face in her direction. She was still standing in the hallway. "How's it going? You satisfied yet with what you've accomplished? Which is what?" He took a package of Rolaids out of his pocket and popped one into his mouth. She gasped. The Porter had heartburn!

Mrs. Eddy was rummaging around in the tapestry-covered bag she held in her lap. She brought out a sheaf of papers and a fountain pen and began writing furiously, her pen scratching away against the paper, build-ing an empire.

The next day Beatriz called, ecstatic. She'd received another postcard from Ben Hightower saying, "Hauling steel to Lake Erie. Many interest-ing sights." It was postmarked "Altoona, Pa." He was on his way!

CHAPTER

16

It rained for three days straight, a relentless steady rain that kept up its monotonous rhythm day and night, there being no periods of waxing and waning or moments of imperceptible brightening, or hope. The world turned green and greener, a dripping rain forest of glistening leaves and blackened tree trunks. Water rose to the surface everywhere and rushed downhill, entering ditches and declivities, flowing through cluttered basements, damaging roadways. It ran off roofs, cartops, hats, the backs of creatures seeking shelter. Swollen streams met swollen streams; smaller rivers churned along toward bigger rivers, already filled to the brim, and continued their headlong race to the sea.

Hoskins spent the first day sorting through his indoor stones, patiently lining and relining them up along the cracks in the floorboards, occasionally pausing to press them up against his ear and listen intently. Baird had woken up with a list of vague complaints. He dragged himself around the house from one unsatisfactory occupation to the next before finally settling on the idea of working on his puzzle outside on the porch in the blowing rain. Charlotte objected; it was too cold and damp out there. Baird said it wasn't—and if he couldn't play with Alphie, who'd been in Colby all week at his married sister Alma's, and he couldn't help Paul, who wouldn't come because of the rain, then there was no other way to have fun and he might as well sit around watching his brother sort his stupid stones.

Charlotte relented finally, though he'd had the sniffles for a few days. The cause-and-effect relationship of all so-called disease, she told herself, was only a misunderstanding. Especially, she shouldn't assume that sniffles inevitably led to something more serious—that was laying the groundwork for it, assuming it, naming it, inviting it. *Array your mental plea against the physical,* urged Mrs. Eddy. Still, it wasn't smart to abandon common sense, and she made him put on a sweater.

Baird and Alphie had played together several times over the past few weeks. Rita brought Alphie with her when she came to clean on Mondays, and Charlotte had left Baird at the Andoulettes one morning while she did her errands in the village. When Charlotte took Beatriz into QC to shop for a new dress, she'd invited Alphie to go along and keep Baird company. On the way home, they had stopped at the Brown Cow, where Hoskins dropped his ice-cream cone in the dirt. Alphie, not quite understanding that you had to be very careful not to upset Hoskins, had at first offered him his, then retracted his offer. It was an awkward scene, and confusing for Hoskins, and by the time Charlotte purchased another cone for him, he'd started in on a tantrum. As they got back in the car, Charlotte heard Alphie tell Baird that if it had been *his* mother, she would've smacked Hoskins good.

Paul had come nearly every day. He was most obliging and slow as molasses. He talked about scraping the clapboards and repainting the house and pruning the lopsided tree and leveling the porch, but when he finally took off his jacket and hung it up on the nearest fence post— the sign he was getting ready to work—he went directly to the garden. He planted what he wanted. He'd argued when she asked for lettuce and spinach, saying they would bolt in the heat, it was no use trying, and it was way too late for peas, and he didn't care for cabbage, it was so wormy. He planted corn, although she explained she'd be gone by the time it ripened. One day he brought a tray of six tomato plants; when she asked where they'd come from, if he'd gotten them at a store and how much they had cost, he turned vague. They didn't look like they'd come from a store; they looked like they'd been dug up from somebody's garden, but she chose not to ask further. She remembered the day he'd first appeared and how he had offered plants from the garden at the Nest. But mostly it was just pleasant to have someone around, especially someone who let Baird help and who listened to Hoskins's nonsense words as if he were really talking. She had to make herself scarce, though. If he saw her, he'd stop everything and lean back on whatever was handy and launch into another long story. The man loved to talk.

From what he said, it sounded like things at the Nest were a shambles. The man from Toronto who had ordered the sculpture was threatening to sue Francis. He didn't just want his deposit back, he wanted compensation for "breach of promise," Paul told her, delighted with the phrase. Francis was being stubborn. He was saying he wasn't going to do it; the whole idea was too stupid, plus he'd already spent the deposit. Some of it he'd spent on materials and the rest of it, well, Paul guessed he must have given it away. "He's got women trouble," he told her. "He's too softhearted. He's got two ex-wives that's always asking for money—he just hands it over, then he has to borrow from his sister. It's a sad thing seeing a man that can't stand up to a bunch of women."

Rosey had called several times to tell her she was worried sick about Charlotte being there alone. During their last conversation, Charlotte had been trying to assure her that her fears were groundless, and in the process had let it slip that she'd hired a caretaker. So, she wasn't alone. There was someone else around.

"But not at night," Rosey had said in alarm.

Of course not at night, Charlotte told her. He wasn't *living* there, he lived at the Nest—and that led her to say that the people up there were helping to keep him on the wagon, an even bigger mistake.

"Are you talking about a man who DRINKS?"

"Used to drink," said Charlotte, wincing. Rosey could turn information into ammunition with the speed of light.

"But he could be a drifter!"

"Well, I think he is a drifter."

"Charlotte! What's come over you!"

"He's very earnest and well-meaning, and the children like him. He's quite entertaining."

"What do you mean?" Rosey asked suspiciously.

"He's funny."

"He entertains you?"

"Inadvertently," Charlotte said.

There was a long pause. "Do you lock your doors at night?"

"If someone wants to get in, they can find a way, lock or no lock," she said, thinking of the Porter. She had asked Paul to put screens on the two basement well windows, though she knew it was a token gesture.

"I don't like the sound of it," said Rosey. "I'd say you're playing with fire. I know all about the Nest. You'd better be careful, Charlotte. You're a woman alone now. Believe me, I know what that's like."

Charlotte settled down on the floor to work on the word cards with Hoskins. She showed him the calico cat. "What is this?"

"Cat."

"What kind of cat?"

"Calico cat," he said, making it sound like *cattaco cat.*

She showed him another card, this one of the elephant.

"Clumsy elephant." *Cumsy elefant.*

"That's right." She felt very excited—he might be reading rather than remembering. She found the hermit thrush. "And this?"

"Bird." He pronounced it *bhurrd.*

"What kind of bird? It's a thrush, one of the ones we hear in the evening, one of the ones you like. But there are so many thrushes! What kind is this? Yellow? Spotted? Nervous?"

He picked at his corduroy pants.

She took out a card that she'd recently made of a blue birthday cake. His birthday was coming up soon. "What color cake?"

He shook his head with his typical, sweetly stubborn look. Could he say "blue"? No, again. Could he say "Mama"? He smiled, saying nothing. She found the mother card. In the illustration, she had given herself long hair. She thought she might let it grow again, but not as long—she didn't think she could stand all the weight.

He picked up a stone and whispered something to it. She picked up a different stone. He was giving her clues. They could play telephone! "Hi, sweetheart," she whispered to the stone, "this is Mama. Call me back!" She listened carefully but couldn't make out what he said. "Can't hear you! Have to talk louder! Bad connection!" She could tell he liked the game, but he wasn't doing his part. "I'm waiting to hear from you! Speak up, please, sir. What was that? Your birthday? Did you say 'ice cream,' sir?" She wished she'd made more cards, ones he hadn't seen before. Then she would be able to tell if he was actually reading, rather than remembering. She turned a card over and quickly drew an ice-cream cone. She printed the words clearly underneath and held it up.

"Ice cream," he said.

"Yes! Ice cream!" Was he reading the words? She wrote "STOP" on the back of another card. "What's this?"

He looked at her, eyebrows raised in a funny little quizzical expression.

She grabbed the stone she'd been using as a microphone. "Can you tell me what this word is, sir?"

He stared at it for a moment and then flopped over on his stomach and covered his ears. He was done. She couldn't force him. She couldn't make him do anything he didn't want to do, and he knew exactly how to tell her that without bothering with any words.

On the second day the wind came swooping out of the west; it sent the rain whirling, lashing at the big white pines that bordered the field below the house and making the branches dance and sway. It blew onto the porch in gusts, forcing Baird to give in finally and let his mother help him transfer the puzzle pieces to the dining-room table. Hoskins was stationed at one of the windows, watching the pine boughs swirling in their mad dance; he moved his hips as he watched—a beat, a syncopated double beat, a quick pelvic twist—as if he could hear the branches singing.

Meanwhile, Baird's puzzle was getting harder. He'd already found all the edge pieces, and the other ones all looked alike. It was boring; he needed someone else to work on it with him. He watched his brother swaying at the window. You couldn't work on anything with Hoskins; he didn't know how to cooperate. His mother was always saying he had to cooperate with Hoskins, but Hoskins never cooperated with him. No one tried to make him mind; he just did whatever he wanted. He watched Hoskins moving his hips this way and that to the wind's music, humming a long tuneless chain of mumbly sounds, and after a while, Baird got up and quietly removed his precious bucket of stones and shoved them under the couch in the parlor.

A hue and cry went up when Hoskins discovered his bucket was missing. He hunted throughout the house, his little body pitched forward as he examined every corner of every room. Charlotte noted Baird's self-conscious, nonchalant look and took him aside, demanding the bucket's return. At first he denied all knowledge of its whereabouts ("What bucket?" he asked, his voice high-pitched, reeking of guilt), then admitted he'd moved it ("But only for safekeeping," he added). When he returned it to Hoskins, forestalling what looked like might turn into a prolonged shrieking episode, she asked Baird to come sit with her on the couch. She put her arm around him, and he leaned against her. She asked him to promise her something, and he asked, "What?" with a little smile that showed he already knew. "Promise me you'll never change," she said, "not one iota."

"Okay. I won't."

"All right, that's settled. Now, tell me what's the matter."

"Nothing," he said.

"Not true, Baird. What is it?"

"God is mad at me."

"God doesn't get mad! Why, because you hid Hoskins's bucket? You gave it back to him, and everything's fine. It's over." She could tell from his troubled expression that that wasn't it.

"Remember when he was little?"

"Which part?" she asked.

"Remember how everybody used to say, 'Oh, what a handsome baby!' and things like that? Well, I got sick of it, and I told God I wished he was a freak—and now he's a freak!"

"He's not a freak, not by any means, Baird, and God would never hurt him, you know that. And anyway, you can't boss God around. That's not the way it works. Otherwise, well, we'd be in charge." *And look what happens when we're in charge,* she thought.

He was silent, and she kept on going, trying to make him see that he wasn't responsible for Hoskins's behavior. He nodded, trying to agree with her, but she could see he wasn't persuaded. Maybe the problem was all the rain, she told him. It would be easier to understand when the sun came out again.

His head hurt, he said, and his neck. And his elbows and hands and legs. His skin felt funny, all prickly.

It's just the dampness, she said, giving him a kiss. The rain will stop soon and everything will dry up and the sun will come out again and everything will be all right. What if it doesn't stop, he wanted to know. It *has* to, sooner or later, she told him. Why? he asked. Because it always does. Even when it rained forty days and forty nights and Noah built his ark for all the animals, it eventually did stop raining, and then the bird appeared with an olive branch in its beak. What bird? Baird asked. A dove. Or maybe it was a passenger pigeon, she added, already on her way to get the Bible.

"How do you get to be six hundred years old?" Baird asked when she had finished reading.

"You just keep on going."

"But just some people?" He regarded her intently. "Can anybody live to be six hundred years old?"

"Not anybody, I don't think. Just the people God chooses."

"Too bad God didn't pick Daddy," he said.

•   •   •

He came to the side of her bed during the night and told her he couldn't breathe. She pulled him into her bed and when she felt the heat of his body, she leapt up. She filled a basin with cold water and brought it back to the bed with a washcloth and towel and started wiping his face and arms. "There's nothing to be afraid of," she whispered. "Think about how much God loves you. God loves you very, very much. He wouldn't want you to be sick."

"Okay." His breath was labored.

"You are a perfect child of God." She took off his pajama top and wiped his back and stomach. He flinched whenever she touched a new place. She kept refilling the basin with cold water and wiping him down with the cool wet cloth, and gradually his skin grew cooler. She sang and patted his back and waited for him to fall asleep, and then she carried him back to his bed in her arms.

In the morning the wind died down, but the rain kept up a steady pace, drumming on the tin roof over the breezeway outside the kitchen and dripping off the sagging gutters where they had been broken by the weight of the snow during the winter. She fixed Baird hot tea with lemon and honey, and he sat at the kitchen table sipping it, watching her with dull eyes. He had developed a bright red rash under his nose.

Hoskins was in his youth chair, carefully turning the pages of the big dictionary. He paused, looking at an entry under the guide words *wallaby/war*. Baird wearily stirred his tea and lay his head on the table. Charlotte suggested he go lie down on the couch, and he drifted out of the room without argument. Hoskins looked up briefly as his brother departed, then turned another page, scrutinizing the small print like a young Jacob Marley reading his ledgers.

It was cold and dark and damp, and Charlotte decided that the only way to take the chill out of the house was to make a fire in the old Majestic cookstove, which she'd done only a few times before and always under Melvin's watchful eye. But it didn't seem too hard; she'd just follow his procedure and do what she'd seen him do many times. He always started with a foundation of carefully crushed newspapers, then added small pieces of kindling, then the hardwood bobbins they got from the mill in the village (though the mill was gone now, they still had a good supply in the wood box), then the bigger chunks of firewood stacked in the breezeway outside the kitchen door. Melvin always ordered a cord of wood at the beginning of the summer, then spent a week stacking it. She'd have to look into that.

She wadded up the newspaper, carefully laying out six pieces in an evenly spaced row on the kitchen table. She used the small iron tool with a spiral chrome handle to lift two of the round stove plates and the bridge-shaped plate that rested in between them and stirred the ashes at the bottom. Now Melvin was ashes, too. The thought arrested her hands in midair; she took a deep breath and laid in the twists of newspaper with three pieces of kindling on top. A little flick of flame ran along the edges of the paper as she held a match to it. What happened to the body when it burned? Did it crinkle like the paper? Her mother had been cremated, too; she'd never had the nerve to imagine it. But by then, the body was pure matter, no longer the veil through which we see the spirit, only the useless veil itself, ready to be discarded as soon as possible. It was irrelevant, really. But what if, in fact, it took some time for the body and spirit to disentangle? What if that moment of separation took a while? What if God needed a little time to overlook the moment in order to see that it went well? Many cultures sent the spirit off after long days and nights of ritual celebrations. But of course, there it was, the folly of thinking in terms of human time.

When she replaced the stove plates, Charlotte was dismayed to see that smoke was curling out from the cracks around the burners, and she suddenly remembered the draft. She turned the handle on the stovepipe and the smoke quickly subsided. She waited a few minutes, staring at the ceiling for a while just as Melvin always had, and then added the hardwood bobbins.

Of course, he would have closed the stove down before leaving the house so that his fire would last, hoping that the house would still be warm when he returned. He would have left the house expecting to have a normal day. That was the sum of all she knew about his state of mind that morning, the absolute sum. She had hoped at the very least to come across one of the little notebooks he carried everywhere. He never noted his feelings in it, only business reminders and arrangements, money spent, places to photograph, but she might have extrapolated a few facts from what he wrote.

At least she knew he had photographed the church. Rita might have fabricated their conversation but probably not the whole event. He might have told her to go get her sled, but Charlotte doubted that he would have been so interested in having her in the photograph that he would send her back home for a change of clothes. He had talked about erasers with Leona, of all things. She hadn't a clue what he might have talked about with Beatriz, but it probably wouldn't have told her anything anyway. Beatriz had tried to bring it up several times, offering little comments of Mel's that she said she'd just remembered, about the weather or the scenery or Eugene Wyndam's insurance business. And, of course, Ben. She was fishing for what Charlotte wanted her to say, and it was meaningless.

Charlotte didn't really know anything at all about his last moments at the house except that he'd closed down the draft.

She got the can of Crisco out of the fridge and went into the pantry to start a pie crust. Hoskins slid down from his youth chair and followed her. She picked him up and set him on the counter while she measured out the flour and salt and worked the lard into the flour bit by bit. Then she turned the dough out and handed the rolling pin to Hoskins. He worked very intently, rolling the same piece of dough over and over until it was firmly glued to the rolling pin. She scraped it off with her fingers and pasted it into the pie plate until the bottom was more or less covered—not any worse of a crust than she usually made, she decided. Hoskins ate the scraps that were too small to use.

When Baird began to bark, she could hardly believe it was a human being making that noise. She rushed to the couch, asking herself what whooping cough sounded like. He lay there pale as a sheet; when she touched his forehead, she discovered he was burning up.

Her first thought was to call Kitty. She imagined the sound of her own panic-stricken voice, and Kitty's quiet, confident one. Too confident, too calm, too far away. This was an emergency; there wasn't any time to waste, she had to act. There was a woman doctor over at the clinic in West Beede. She could call and ask her what she thought—she would at least know whether it sounded like whooping cough—but it was the weekend; the clinic would be closed. She felt profoundly frightened.

The phone rang, and Charlotte grabbed the receiver. It was Beatriz. Wasn't it some rain? she said. It was just rolling off her roof. Was it ever going to stop? Charlotte held the receiver in the direction of the parlor and asked her to listen. Beatriz didn't hesitate for a second. "He's got the croup. You got to get him in the bathroom and get some steam going. Keep him there as long as you can. The steam will loosen up the phlegm. He's probably got a big wad of it in there. You got to get it out. You got any mustard powder?"

"What would I do with that?" Charlotte asked, remembering the dark little vials on Adele's pantry shelf. None of the little brown jars were labeled. They were all old, anyway, and for all she knew, they were poisonous.

"You make up a paste with water. Spread it between two old dish towels—you want them thin kind. Make a pillow out of them, then lay the whole thing over his chest. But you got to watch it 'cause mustard will burn the skin. My mother let it stay on too long one time, and I got a nasty burn."

"I'll use the steam," Charlotte said.

"You do that, and he'll come through all right. You want me to come up?"

"I'll call you if I need you." Charlotte turned on the faucet and let the hot water start filling up the bathtub. She closed the door to keep the steam inside and listened to the terrible sound of Baird's barking in the next room.

While the water ran, she tried to pray. All forms of sickness were *pictures drawn on the body by a mortal mind.* It was Charlotte's mind that was drawing the pictures on Baird's body and making him sick. The problem was in her, not Baird. But what if she couldn't overcome her fear?

The steam began curling up from the water, and the Porter's head emerged wearing a white bathing cap.

"No," she said aloud. "No, go away."

Sickness is a temporal dream, he said. *You'll pay for this.*

She thought about pushing the head down into the water and just holding it there.

You have no time to waste on prayer, you say. Too busy to know the Truth.

The front of the bathing cap came way down on his forehead, wrinkling it up like a pug dog's. It seemed impossible that he could still smirk, given the folds of skin lapping over his eyebrows.

Go ahead, draw pictures with your mortal mind, and listen to him bark. Why not mustard plaster, indeed? How about a voodoo dance?

It was hard to hold the head under the water; it wanted to bob up, and it took the whole strength of her arm and her shoulder and the long, aching muscles of her back to keep it under. And then it was gone, and she realized that she was on her knees on the hard floor, leaning over the tub, her face in the steam.

She rummaged through the shelves and found a bottle of aspirin and brought two to Baird with a glass of water. He asked who was in the bathroom. "No one," she said. "There was no one there. I was probably talking to myself. Just your silly old mother," she said, smiling, but he didn't laugh. She fetched a little stool from the laundry room and made him sit down beside the tub with a towel wrapped around his head like a hood and waved the steam toward his face.

It took four hours for the crisis to pass. When the hot water in the bathroom ran out, she brought him into the kitchen and closed off the doorway with a blanket. She kept water boiling on both stoves, using every kettle and pot, steaming up all the windows. She hauled in a chair for Hoskins—who stood at the sink, washing pots and pans—and a rocker for herself. Baird lay against her, limp and hot, as she plastered his forehead with an iced washcloth. She gave him two more aspirins and rocked him slowly back and forth while the kettles churned out their healing condensation. Her blouse stuck to her back, and perspiration trickled down from her armpits. Hoskins dripped buckets of water onto the floor.

The afternoon wore on and the rain stopped, and at last Baird's fever started coming down; she knew it because, although she hadn't been able to find a thermometer, the washcloth didn't get so hot between changes. The sun came out—wanly at first—and gradually the air warmed. Baird's cheeks resumed their normal color.

"Could you sing?" Baird's voice was unsteady.

"What would you like to hear?"

"'Daddy's Whiskers.'"

"Of course," she said and she sang all the lyrics of it she could remember to the rousy sort of sailor tune:

> *We have a dear old daddy*
> *Whose hair is silver gray.*
> *He has a set of whiskers—*
> *They're always in the way.*
>
> *Oh, they're always in the way.*
> *The cow eats them for hay.*
> *Mother eats them in her sleep,*
> *She thinks she's eating shredded wheat,*
> *They're always in the way.*
>
> *We have a dear old mommy,*
> *She likes his whiskers, too.*
> *She uses them for cleaning*
> *And stirring up a stew.*
>
> *We have a dear old brother,*
> *Who has a Ford machine.*
> *He uses Daddy's whiskers*
> *To strain the gasoline.*
>
> *Oh, they're always in the way.*
> *The cow eats them for hay.*
> *Mother eats them in her sleep,*

She thinks she's eating shredded wheat,
They're always in the way.

There was a knock on the kitchen door, startling them all. The outside world had long ceased to exist, and when Charlotte opened the door and found Francis Roux standing there in his bright yellow shirt and tall boots on the hard-packed dirt of the breezeway, she experienced the shock of a new reality. A warm breeze was blowing through the poplars, gently rippling their leaves. "Nice tune," he said, smiling up at her.

"It has lots more verses, one sillier than the next," she said, unaccountably happy to see another human being.

Shards of steam sailed out the door toward the breezeway rafters and dissipated in midair above his head. "You've been in a steam bath, it looks like."

"My son had a bad cough." Baird stood at her side, looking dazed, still wearing his pajamas. "He's feeling better now."

"Is he well enough to come outside? There's something I'd like to show you." It was as though it were his place and he was welcoming her to it. "The grass is still wet, though. You'd better get your boots."

Charlotte grabbed their rubber boots, lined up neatly behind the Majestic, and they went outside into the warm air under a dazzling blue sky.

"I got your note," he said, "and I came as soon as I could."

"My note?"

"The geranium. It's doing fine."

"My brother did it," Baird said. "All by himself."

They marched down the drive behind the Impresario of the Nest, in his springy gait, and stopped to stare in wonder at what he'd come to show her. The lupines had opened all at once in the sudden warmth after the rain, a gorgeous mass of purple and pink and blue and white blossoms covering the whole wide beautiful field. He turned to her with a delighted smile. "It's glorious, isn't it?" he said, and she agreed. The air was sparkling and the sun was shining and everything in the world seemed new.

CHAPTER

17

This is how it went: By the time they were done admiring the extravagant beauty of the flowers and debating what it meant that their beauty was ephemeral, she had changed her mind about him—not full of himself, but full of ideas; not cocky, but confident; not loud, but full of life. The lines on his face were partly from smiling; the somewhat dissolute look was worldly, exciting, pleasantly dangerous. This Lothario—this libertine, this seducer of women, this carnal soul—was courtly and charming, fun and funny.

They watched, laughing, as Hoskins broke free and plowed through the flowers and the wet grass, arms raised, dancing and twirling, falling and jumping, his wild hooting peppered with his current favorite phrases: When Francis heard "Sciatica!" and then "Amen, brother!" he roared with laughter. Baird looked uncertain, then roared, too, but when Hoskins suddenly disappeared in the midst of the flowers, Baird worried aloud about his catching a cold. "Like me," he said. "I got soaked on the porch." Charlotte told Baird not to worry, who was to say that the drenching was the reason he'd gotten sick? Hoskins would be all right—

everything would be all right. And it suddenly did seem like that, and not just all right, but grand.

Hannibal trotted down from the house to join them, and Francis told Charlotte and Baird that he'd had a setter once, with reversed belton markings. He was orange with white ticking instead of white with orange. He'd called him Fox. Imagine that, he told Baird, calling a dog Fox. Baird laughed.

And kind to children, she told herself.

He stayed and stayed. It was clear he was enjoying her company, too, and he didn't want to leave. They talked about Paul and his long history of failures. Bellini had terrible women troubles, he told her. "That's just what Paul said about you," she replied, and he laughed. "You suppose it's me or the women?" he asked. She smiled at him. "It's probably you," she said. They were both being outrageously flirtatious, but she forgave herself, recognizing her longing for simple male attention.

They tromped around outside in the wet grass looking at everything: Paul's work on the garden, Cal's ancient and scraggly apple trees, the juniper bushes growing up in the tired pasture where Eugene had once kept his cows. They were taking a tour of the estate, he explained to Baird, a pale and happy Lazarus in flannel pajamas, caught up in the promise of a new life now that his heavy stone had rolled away. "It's important to review one's estate periodically and check on the serfs' work—a serf being a servant who doesn't get paid."

"Like Paul?" Baird asked.

Francis turned to Charlotte, surprised. "You don't pay him?"

"Of course I do. Twenty-five dollars a week!"

"A royal sum," he said, and she wondered if he was being sarcastic. Did he expect more? What if the two of them were setting up some kind of scheme to dupe her and get her money? It was an alarming idea; instantly the insidious serpent Doubt took his place beside them. But then he continued. "Any money Paul ever had went for booze," he said, sounding sad, and the snake quickly withdrew. He was concerned only for Paul's welfare. "Here we are, you and I together, trying to set him straight. What do you suppose the chances are?"

"I'm hoping for the best. He's a very happy person."

"Like you."

"You think I'm a happy person?" She was amazed.

"I do, and it's a lovely trait. Where would we be without hope?"

What a nice thing to say!

"I can see that quality of brightness even better, now that you've cut your hair," he said, looking at her with a dazzling brightness of his own. "One of the reasons I came was to see for myself what all the fuss was about. The Woman with All That Hair chopped it off. I especially like the way your ears stick out. Women don't show their ears enough," he said. "They don't know the power of ears or a long neck like yours."

"Too long," she said, laughing.

"Not long enough," he countered. "Check out Botticelli's Venus, if you will: Her neck's a mile long, yet she's been a paragon of Western beauty for centuries."

He was going too far, but it was all right.

They looked through the barn, guessed at the number of mice nesting in the piles of hay still up in the loft, opened up a box of McGuffey's Famous Cal-Oric Tea. They examined the delicately tinted glass bottles, the elegant labels promising ease and elegance and a figure like the ancient gods and goddesses. "A genius!" Francis exclaimed. "You could lose weight just reading the label!"

Baird climbed up the series of ladders, wanting to show them how he could jump from the third to the second tier by swinging out on a stout rope and letting go at just the right moment. It took several swings before he got up the nerve to let go. Charlotte had witnessed Alphie doing it the summer before, while Baird hung back, watching, too timid to try it himself. She closed her eyes; his apprehension—and hers—was too much to bear. When Francis shouted "Hooray!" she opened her eyes to a triumphant Baird, grinning at them from the pile of hay on the second tier. From the look on Hoskins's face, she knew he would soon be trying it himself. Francis saw it, too, and before she could speak, he was climbing up the ladder that led from the ground floor to the second tier to join Baird. They would find a place to keep the ladders in storage, he said, then when Baird wanted to do his acrobatics, they could bring them out. Of course it would be hard work, hauling the ladders back up. How about a pulley? Wouldn't that be good?

He and Baird worked for an hour, devising a pulley system that could be secured in a way Hoskins couldn't get at it. Francis found a chain and a few boards; Charlotte brought them a rope and hammer and nails. Francis climbed up and down, and Baird fetched tools, which he handed to Francis from various vantage points. Francis began calling him "Big Baird."

Walking back to the house with her, the job finally done, Francis said very quietly, "I like pulleys," and though it required an odd and embarrassing leap of the mind, she found herself blushing, as if he had suddenly said, *I like you*. Modestly, she said nothing in reply.

At suppertime she set out crackers and cheese and paper plates and told the children they could have a picnic in the yard. He followed her around as she gathered what they needed and helped her haul it out of the house, saying he was hungry, too. He needed to eat, in fact. Quickly, too.

She was taken aback. *Quite the demanding guest!* "I wasn't expecting company," she said, but he didn't seem to notice her peppery tone, and he plopped down next to the boys on the blanket on the grass, saying that he loved crackers and cheese, it was nearly his favorite meal—and if she had any mayo and peanut butter, it would be a veritable feast. *But flexible, too,* she said to herself.

When it was the boys' bedtime, Francis read *Mike Mulligan's Steam Shovel* to both of them, discussing all the steam-shovel parts very seriously with them: dipper stick, hoist lever, turntable, smokestack. "Dipper stick," Hoskins repeated under his breath as Charlotte led him upstairs, "smokestack." As she tucked the boys in and told them a story, she heard Francis prowling around downstairs, pacing. He hadn't said a word about leaving.

They sat out on the porch and listened to the evening thrushes as it got dark. She brought out one of Adele's ashtrays for him—he smoked strong-smelling French cigarettes. She remembered the smell very keenly, she told him. When Charlotte was a fine-arts major, a tall, dark-haired girl in one of her drawing classes had smoked Gauloises; she was a horrid girl, very superior, very smug. Pretentious.

"And what happened to your art career? God knows, it's clear enough what happened to that girl, probably working away at this very moment on a book called *How to Draw Horses,* or *How to Draw People.*"

"How unkind," she said.

"Didn't you say she was smug and superior? Don't you believe those kind of people deserve what they get? But what about you and your art career?"

"I decided against it."

"Just like that?"

She knew it would sound like false modesty. She would say, *I wasn't good enough,* and he would say, *I bet you were,* and she would be left unable to say what she really meant, that she'd finally been overcome, her imagination vanquished, by the specter of Beauty and her own inadequacy as an imperfect mortal, flawed, careless, impudent. "I switched to music and studied voice."

He smiled at her. "And?"

"I had a small range, my teacher said. I would always be limited in what I could sing."

"But not 'Daddy's Whiskers,' you can sing that. I want all the verses. Will you sing it for me?"

"Now?"

"What could be a better time?"

He was large and took up a lot of room, and she decided that she had been living for a long time in a very small space. She went to get the song-book with all the verses and in her loudest and fullest voice she sang to the tops of the hills, their outlines blending into the night sky, of Daddy's whiskers in the soup, in the bath, being fashioned into braids by little Ida Mae, and when she was done, she sat down and they laughed together for a long time.

He told her about his lawsuit and that idiot Louis Thexton, who had climbed one of his stair sculptures in Toronto; he'd fallen off, twisting his ankle, and filed a complaint. When Francis got wind of it through his agent, he'd written the man a long letter. First off, he told him, he never should have climbed the stairs. They weren't meant to be climbed; they were meant to be looked at out of the corner of the eye, a fleeting shock to the brain, to the assumptions. If he wanted to climb one, he'd build one especially for him—a foolproof staircase outfitted with safety devices, harnesses, parachutes, railings, treads, bells that went off, sirens that sounded, but pointless in a utilitarian world. Now *that* was a real study in contradictions. A man should have constant friction, constant unrest, he told Thexton. We are only what we really are in the nexus of our contradictions.

Thexton wrote back positively cringing with gratitude. He'd never been in a dialogue with a real artist before, he said. He did *not* know what Francis was talking about, and he was absolutely thrilled. He asked if he could buy a piece of art such as Francis had described so that Thexton could present it to his mother on the occasion of her ninetieth birthday, knowing himself to have been the inspiration. Francis's agent had written back to him, naming a figure with a mess of aughts; Thexton had responded, bravely, by announcing that nothing was too good for Mum.

That was the previous September. Francis had spent most of the time since then fighting revulsion. The whole *idea* was messy. It was a contraption, a purely mental construct, an irony—in a word, it was embarrassing. He couldn't do it. It was a joke; it had always been a joke. And now he had a lawsuit pending. "When the deposit came, I couldn't wait to get rid of it. I gave it away. Now Thexton's lawyer is talking about taking my house—let him take it; I'd rather live under a bridge."

It didn't sound quite right. Even someone as blustery and bold as this man wouldn't just give it away. Live under a bridge? She didn't think so. "You're exaggerating."

"Of course I'm exaggerating."

"I thought artists needed to see things accurately."

"Those are accountants," he said, and they both laughed.

It was dark now and hard to see his face. She asked for a cigarette, and he lit one for her. She inhaled, and her vision instantly blurred. "I went to your house, but no one was home," she said when she'd recovered. "I went looking for you."

"I wish I'd been there."

"I wanted to ask you something."

"Ask away."

She paused. "I thought your place was always teeming with people."

"Is that why you went, to count the eggs in the Nest?"

"No," she said, hesitating. "I went because Paul told me you saw my husband in December."

"Yes, I did."

"Did you see him here?" She lay the cigarette down in the ashtray carefully so that it would burn freely.

"It was down at the store. It was bad weather that day, that sleety stuff. He said he was looking for a caretaker. Orrin wasn't able to help out anymore, and he was worried about the snow on the roof."

There was no moon, no shred of light, no reflection, only the outline of a man and the glowing tip of the cigarette. "Do you remember what day that was?"

"It was Monday. The day before his accident. Of course I thought about it afterward, how I'd just seen him the day before."

"How did he seem?"

"He was upset."

Her heart leapt at her throat. "Why? Did he say?"

"He said his defroster was clogged and he was on his way somewhere and he couldn't drive with it like that. I went out and looked at it with him, and we got it going again."

"Was that all?"

"You wouldn't say that if you'd been there that day. It had warmed up suddenly, then frozen again, leaving a layer of ice on the snow. It was hell driving."

She could see Mel complaining, his mouth bunched up. Upset, but not about her. Upset about a clogged defroster. She felt disappointed and was floored by a sudden idea: Did she *want* him to be upset about her?

"I think he said he was on his way to photograph someone's fence. He said that for a fence shot, a little sleet wouldn't hurt."

"Contrast," she said. "Edges."

"He was a very talented man."

"But unhappy with the kind of work he did."

"He's not alone," Francis said with a little laugh. "I know how that feels." Then he surprised her totally by asking if it had been hard for him, being married to her. "That's all right. You don't need to tell me. I know, though. I saw him with you, when you had all that hair, when you tossed it around. When you flaunted your beauty."

Tossed? Flaunted? What was he saying?

"Do you know what it's like for a man," he continued, "being married to a beautiful woman? I was, for about thirty seconds—one second of pride and twenty-nine seconds of torture. Every friend of Anne-Marie's was an enemy of mine, especially if she went off with them and didn't come back until morning." He paused. "Of course I deserved it. She's the one I gave Thexton's deposit to. She needed it and I didn't."

"You're exaggerating again."

"Okay, I owed it to her."

A liar?

"Can I ask you a question?"

"Shoot."

"When you gave it away, were you intending to give Mr. Thexton his sculpture?"

"I'm not sure I ever intended to."

"You mean, you weren't honest with him?"

"Right. It's complicated, but basically, you're right—I was dishonest."

"Oh."

"Bellini says you want him to prune that tree," he said as cheerfully as if they hadn't just had a difficult exchange. "It won't look right if you do that, you know; it'll be lopsided, and you'll spend all your time trying to adjust the angle of the hills to make it seem straight. It's hard to adjust the hills; it takes millions of years. It'd be easier if you just took the tree down and let me put a sculpture in its place for you. I'll use the frame I made for Thexton, without the damned contraptions, of course. It will look about like the others. Rusted steel, et cetera. What do you think?"

"You mean right there, in front of this house?" *He was trying to sell her something! That was it! All this time he'd been wooing her as a customer!*

"I wouldn't want money for it, you understand. The materials are already paid for. The design would cost nothing. It would require a few loads of cement, that's all, a couple of days of digging. We'd leave off the first few steps so that the children wouldn't try to climb it—your handsome little philosopher and your brave one, swinging out on the rope to show us he wasn't afraid. Did you see Baird's face? How proud he was?" He sounded worried. "May I come back tomorrow?"

"Yes," she said, her heart contrite.

CHAPTER

18

For a while she believed she ought to fight against the spell he cast—and it was a spell, she had no doubt about it. He tried to create the impression that his actions were spontaneous—impromptu improvisations inspired by a dazzling infatuation—but he knew what he was doing. He'd done it before, and he would do it again, only it would be somebody else then who succumbed to his powerful charm. She tried to analyze his techniques as a way of staying objective: He lavished attention, danced away, was at her side again before she could assemble enough distance to defend herself. And he began to call her "Charley." He *made* her want him, and she did, with her entire being. His physical presence produced in her a painful aching that nearly made her mouth water; the more she resisted, the more consuming it became. A little bit of her mind remained at attention throughout the duration of the spell, but when she fell, it, too, caved in.

At times she even pondered whether the whole business of falling in love might not be a modern form of animal magnetism, an arcane but fascinating subject that had preoccupied Mrs. Eddy throughout her life-

time, though she had called it Malicious Animal Magnetism, or, speaking
in a kind of code in the presence of believers, M.A.M., a mental state she
equated with hypnotism and esoteric magic. It was a bizarre notion, and
Charlotte had never paid much attention to it, dismissing it as one of the
many peculiar beliefs of the times in which Mrs. Eddy lived. In those days
everyone was fascinated with hypnotism, and many believed quite seriously that anyone with such intent could wreak havoc from afar with evil
thoughts, and do grave mental harm. Like many visionaries in history,
Mrs. Eddy had a streak of paranoia herself, believing that many of her
former students and formerly trusted advisers were trying to do her
harm. When stricken, she called in her staff members to help her combat
these malicious thoughts with prayer. She even claimed it was malicious
mesmerism that killed her third husband, Asa Eddy. Her ideas had
caused great scorn among many of her contemporaries, and Charlotte
could see how she could easily have felt persecuted. But she had never
seen how it could apply in modern times.

The feelings that had taken possession of her now were very animal,
very magnetic. And very pleasant. There was definitely a mental inva-
sion, though, if she counted the number of times she thought about him
in a single hour, thought of the way he looked in crazy shirts and faded
dungarees, or the way he looked at her when he was looking for fun, his
black, black hair, his amazing blue eyes. All this time, they'd barely
touched except for once, when Charlotte removed a splinter from his
hand. She stood close with a magnifying glass and needle and leaned over
him, her insides turning over. She knew that his did, too, because of the
way he looked at her when she moved away, his eyelids slowly closing
over those blue eyes. How could she resist this mesmerist? Hypnotized,
she would lose control, do foolish things, lose her way. Or find her way.
Wasn't that what all the love poetry was about, discovery? And longing.
If you were truly falling in love, you were beset by longing, like she was,
for instance, whenever Francis didn't show up.

It was a glorious time. The sharp edge of daily troubles melted away.
Future concerns didn't exist. Things that would have bothered her in the
past seemed inconsequential. She became more patient, more observant.

She made new cards for Hoskins and worked with him every day without the slightest sign that it was doing any good. She took the boys for
long walks in the early mornings, marveling at the intricacies of leaves
and insects, bird songs, the way trees reached for the light in whatever
direction they could. She saw lovely things all around her that she'd never
seen before: the glowing patina on the rush seat of a rocker, the sweet
carving on the back of a chair, the swirls of grain in the marble of the
upstairs dresser. She sang, she daydreamed, she listened for his car.

She was sure it was no secret in the village. At the store, Minna's glare
seemed more acute. Whenever Beatriz called she would start by asking,
"Is this a good time?" by which she meant, "Is he there?" Leona offered
veiled references to trouble ahead.

"That Francis Roux is *besieged,*" Leona said offhandedly one day
when Charlotte stopped in for her mail, as if they had just been talking
about him. "He practically runs a hotel up there—can't get any work
done with all the old girlfriends and ex-wives running around, and all
their friends. Was in here the other day to pick up his mail, and he told
me he had fifteen people up to his house over Memorial Day weekend
and he only knew about half of them." To which Charlotte responded as
if she were being told something about a stranger. "He must be a very
generous person," she said evenly.

She tried, somewhat feebly, to maintain some objectivity and mar-
shaled out his faults like an ascetic practicing a daily flogging: He was
impractical, impulsive, temperamental. He was excessive. It wasn't hard
to imagine him drunk and roaring around, careening through his two
marriages (two!), leaving his poor wives flattened and gasping. Now he
only smoked too much, and ate too little—he was oddly careful about
what he ate, with a list a mile long of things he wouldn't touch. He didn't
talk about it, but she noticed. It was an oddity because he was careless in
so many things, riding over things without paying much attention, forever creating unnecessary problems for himself—like the artistic huff
over Thexton, which he obviously enjoyed. He talked a lot, and most of
it was about himself—his ideas, his career—and his mistakes; he seemed
to love his mistakes, his old drinking self, his old dissolute life. Inspired

by his lack of concern about what she might think, she reciprocated with her own stories—about her childhood, her lonely time after her mother's death, her father's aloofness, the things she'd never finished, her life as a mother and wife—though circumspectly, of course, blaming herself for her and Melvin's habitual arguments and saying only that things were bad when he died. She didn't discuss their final conversation.

They talked about religion, too. She was cautious about discussing her own beliefs; she'd had plenty of experience that had taught her to be careful, and besides, she knew her mind was fuzzy from sheer exhilaration. She had one foot in metaphysics and the other on Earth, and was in danger of losing her balance. She asked about the William James book she'd found at his house, and he told her it came from a series of lectures the author had given at the University of Edinburgh on what he called man's religious appetites, from rational to mystical to utilitarian. It was hearty fare, James's book, and he would lend it to her if she liked. He was sure she would find it fascinating. James believed that the evidence for God lay in inner personal experience rather than in abstract philosophical systems. "In other words, it's impossible to prove God's existence rationally. Any attempt to use logic leads straight to the absurd. I like his point of view. He leaves plenty of room for unorthodox modes of enlightenment. He thinks we have more life in our soul than we're aware of or willing to admit, and that's where genius resides. And although he points out the flaws in history's creeds and theories, he maintains that religion as a whole is mankind's most important function. So he doesn't dismiss it, yet he can expose history's quacks."

Paul showed up first on those brilliant summer days. He worked in the garden and mowed the lawn, edging it with an ancient tool he'd unearthed somewhere, and prowled around with clippers, fighting back the encroaching vegetation. Everywhere he went, Hoskins silently followed, sometimes carrying his bucket, sometimes lugging the tools Paul handed him. Paul looked happy to have him around and chatted away as if engaged in a real conversation, as if Hoskins's traffic directions and erratic outbursts were pertinent remarks giving Paul a new perspective.

Rita came on Monday mornings and left a sparkling path in her wake. Hoskins followed the vacuum cleaner around, shouting, "Low clearance! Pavement narrows! Bump! Stop sign ahead!" Rita didn't see the humor in it. One day she complained to Charlotte that he had broken a charm on her bracelet. She said her brother Amos had given the little charm (a tin heart) to her for her birthday, and it was special. Charlotte suspected that she was lying, but she didn't know for sure until Rita told her, without blinking an eye or seeming embarrassed by her own presumption, that she would like Charlotte to buy her a new charm. She'd seen a teeny-tiny piano at a jewelry store in QC. Charlotte said maybe she would, but only if Rita would tell her the truth: Was it really Hoskins who had broken her heart? she'd asked, and paused. Or was it some other boy? Rita had laughed, getting the joke, and they had agreed, in the end, that Rita might have lost it.

She was, as promised, good at finding things, though her methods were peculiar and involved forked twigs and crossed fingers and all sorts of incantations and recitations. She thoroughly believed in luck, both good and bad, pinning great meaning on horseshoes, wishbones, first stars, new moons, spilled salt, wagons hauling hay, and countless other things. She was worried about what Charlotte had done with her hair when she cut it—you can't leave it around in case somebody fools with it, Rita told her, and Charlotte laughed. She counseled Charlotte to whip her eggs clockwise and not lose her nail parings. If she lost an eyelash, she had to quickly lay it on the back of her left hand, close her eyes, and make a wish, then place the back of her right hand under her left palm and hit it with three hard blows. If the eyelash was still there when she opened her eyes, the wish wouldn't come true. But if any of the three blows had knocked it off, then the lash had gone off somewhere to bring back her wish. Charlotte told her she wasn't sure she'd remember all that, and Rita said, "Okay, then just burn it." In any case, Charlotte shouldn't leave an eyelash lying around, or someone could use it to work magic against her.

Charlotte told her that she wasn't worried about those things because she wasn't superstitious. Those were ideas that had come about because people hadn't known any better. Long ago they hadn't understood the causes of things and had drawn the wrong conclusions. A black cat might cross your path before you touched something hot and burned your hand, but it was just a coincidence. And she wasn't afraid of walking under a ladder unless someone was up on top of it holding a hammer—in fact, she sometimes walked under a ladder on purpose. Rita had been horrified to hear her talk like that, and the next time she came to clean, she brought a handful of dried peony seeds for Charlotte to carry in her pocket as protection against bad luck. Charlotte knew it was a sign the girl liked her, and she took them and thanked her. When she was alone, she threw them away.

Francis, Paul, and Charlotte had a big powwow over where to put the sculpture. They tried standing here and there around the property, trying to get the right view. As they traipsed down the driveway, to get a better perspective from below, Francis put his arm around her shoulder, drawing her close. Baird walked on ahead, but Hoskins stayed put in the yard, watching them leave. "He kind of looks like he might be thinking of pulling a fast one," Paul told Charlotte, and he went back to get him. Francis gave her shoulders a little squeeze that seemed to say, *Everything's all right, we're looking out for each other.* And she put her arm around his back.

The problem, Francis explained when they had gathered at one spot again, was that if they put it where the tree was now, it would conflict with the roofline. All the lines would cross, and they'd have a visual mess. Charlotte suggested putting it in the space between the house and the barn and then changed her mind, deciding it would look too crowded. Paul said they ought to put it out back. Francis scoffed. What was the point of that? Charley might as well not even have it.

"Sounds good to me," said Paul, grinning. "I know who's doing the digging." Then Francis suggested the lupine field itself and shocked them into silence. Paul slowly shook his head. "The *lupine* field?" he repeated, gazing around him at the sacred site.

Charlotte pondered the enormity of it. "Think of all the people who have sat up on that porch looking out at the hills over a pristine field."

"Precisely. It's time to change their view." Francis began to pace. Why hadn't they thought of it earlier? Because they'd been stuck in a rut, trying to follow in the weary footsteps of others. It would be the lupines' last glorious season alone in the limelight. They wouldn't install it until the season had passed, of course; they'd show the proper respect. Perhaps he would even invite Thexton to the opening, show him what the piece was really supposed to look like, introduce him to the simple beauty of a spiral, dazzle him into a rudimentary understanding of what a sited sculpture was all about, and then charge him ten thousand for the privilege of looking at it. He laughed uproariously at the idea. "But the tree's got to go for sure, no matter what." Francis was sighting in on the house along his hand. Charlotte and Paul sighted in, too. "Agreed," said Paul. "Agreed," said Charlotte. He was going to ruin the field, and it didn't matter.

One night when they were out on the porch, drinking iced tea, Francis asked her to tell him about her family. There wasn't much to tell, she said. She grew up in Syracuse, a professor's daughter. Her two sisters were much older; by the time she was eight, they'd both moved away. She was ten when her mother died, and her eldest sister, Rosey, moved back home to help their father look after her. Kitty was already married by then and living in Holyoke. She came to stay with her mother at the end, when she was so sick, and then returned home to Harry. But her two sisters were always there in Charlotte's life, no matter where they lived. They saw themselves as her mothers.

"How did your mother die?"

"She was ill."

"With what?"

"She got the flu."

"She died of the flu?"

"I don't really know. She wasn't well for a long time. She was always very thirsty, and at the end she was very thin. She'd stopped eating, essentially. She wanted to be left alone and it hurt my feelings. Noise bothered her. She had spells, we called them, and took to her bed. At the very end she got very weak."

"Do you think it was diabetes?"

She was shocked. "Why would you think that?"

"Because I'm diabetic. I'm alert to the symptoms."

She remembered what Paul had said about Francis having the "sugar disease." He'd had a low–blood sugar attack the very first day he came by, he told her, after all that work in the barn and not enough food. He'd used up too much of his available energy supply, which was why he'd told her he needed to eat. "I hated to leave, just as we were getting past the introductions. When I said I wanted some supper, you looked offended, as if I'd turned into a rude guest, and I guess I had. Getting hypoglycemic makes me irritable. I didn't want you to think of me as your crabby neighbor."

"Do you take insulin?"

"Yup, the whole nine yards. Was your mother always running off to pee all the time?"

"We couldn't take a long car trip without stopping someplace for her," she said.

"Did she go to a doctor?"

"I don't know, she might have. She went sometimes. I know she lost a lot of weight the year before she died. Then she got the flu, and I guess it was too much for her. I was so young at the time. And anyway, it was my sisters who took care of her."

"She would have been run down."

"I don't think it was diabetes," she said. "I never saw any evidence of it. There were no needles or anything like that around that I was aware of. You know how nosy children are; they're always looking for secrets. I think she just got a bad flu. No one ever said anything about diabetes."

"If you have a certain type, you need insulin."

She asked him why, and he looked at her. "Why I need it?"

"Why you think you need it."

"It's not something I decided in my head, Charley. I don't *think* I need it, I need it. Your pancreas produces enough insulin, and mine doesn't.

It's that simple. It's an amazing business how the body works, how it's made, how things work together. It's intricate and brilliant. With diabetes, the whole process of deterioration speeds up, and all the organs fail together in an amazing, orchestrated way; they all have their own tunes, so to speak, their own parts. The process of our deterioration as humans turns out to be elegant and systematic, like the way we're put together piece by piece—it's beautiful, Charley. It's a work of art, a reason to believe in God."

"You think that deterioration is a reason to believe in God?"

"You wait and see. As you get older, you'll love it. Why do you think everything I make is rusty? Corrosion, deterioration, crumbling, returning, beginning again. It's a hoot." He stopped. "You don't think it's amusing?"

"I'm just wondering if you believe any of it is . . . up to you?"

"I think it's up to me whether I live or die, yes. I can take the insulin, or not. If I don't, I'll get ketoacidosis and go into a coma and die."

She flinched.

"Or I could drink lots of vodka; I could go that way, too. So yes, quite a bit is up to me. It's up to me to control it with insulin shots. It's easy—I could show you if you like."

"No, thanks."

He smiled. "I guess we don't know each other well enough yet."

"I don't think about my pancreas. I don't even know where it is. Or what insulin is."

"It's a hormone."

"I don't really know what hormones are."

"Are you serious?"

She laughed, knowing it sounded ridiculous. "Are they the little things that swim around?"

"Indeed. They swim around and make me crazy and make me want to carry you off to bed."

"So it's not *you* wanting to?" she asked, teasing.

"I *am* my hormones. Who said that? Napoléon?"

"You're saying you can't control them."

217

"Sure, I can—to a certain extent. You want me to resist the clamoring?"

"For a little while," she said.

"But not too long."

"No, not too long."

"How about before the lupines fade? We won't want them to be faded; we won't want to remember it like that."

She agreed. No, it wouldn't be good.

"It's a question of opportunity. No, of necessity."

"Absolutely," she said, and she touched her finger lightly to his lips.

Paul showed up the next day with a handsaw and started to work on the tree, stabbing here and there at the small branches, which he threw into a pile on the grass. She walked out and asked him what he was doing, and he explained that because the tree was so close to the house, he needed to get the limbs off first before attacking the trunk. He worked at a maddeningly slow pace, gradually progressing up the trunk toward the crown with the help of a rickety ladder, calling "TIMBER!" before each small branch dropped to the ground. Despite these random incursions over the course of several days, the tree remained stubbornly intact.

Hoskins took an interest in the project and began lugging the leafy branches around to the back of the house. He tussled with the bigger ones but refused all help; he seemed to have a very specific plan in mind, but they had no idea what it could be. Once the branches were in back, he started arranging them by size and then pulling off the leaves, working long hours at his self-appointed task. When all the branches were bare, he started placing stones at careful intervals between them, being very particular about the sizes and shapes of the stones. Francis was intrigued; he was sure it was a mathematical pattern Hoskins had in mind. "It could be the key to the universe," he told Charlotte. "Or it could be a big joke. Either way, it will be important."

Francis helped Paul jack up the porch, using concrete blocks that they found behind the barn and a tire jack. It was a frightening operation, and excruciating to watch. What if the porch fell with Francis and Paul underneath it? But as the day wore on and she watched both men crawling in and out countless times, unharmed and unconcerned, she felt less worried. When it was done, she walked back and forth across the length of the level porch, arms outstretched, and did a little dance to make Baird laugh.

Francis went to New York for several days to meet with his lawyer, trying to work out a deal with Thexton. His idea now was to offer him something else, some "trinket" as he called it, some cast-off artistic cliché from his youthful career, in storage somewhere, for which he would charge a coincidental ten grand.

When he returned, he no longer looked like a stranger, but a familiar object of her affections, and when they kissed, and kissed again, the last of her meager defenses crumbled for good.

They sat on the porch that evening after the boys were in bed, and Charlotte brought out their iced tea, the clay ashtray, and the package of Gauloises she kept on the kitchen shelf—by now she had learned to inhale the strong cigarettes without fainting. They touched glasses, and fell silent. The only sounds came from their ice cubes as they shifted and clinked, her spoon as she stirred, their swallowing, the small noises one makes during the simple act of drinking liquid. After a while even these sounds ceased, and they found themselves exchanging only waves of acute physical longing.

The lupines had exhausted their season and were starting to fade, turning from indigo to cerulean blue, from deep purple to violet to lilac. Only the whites remained true. There was a new moon, a delicate crescent rising behind the dark outline of pines along the field's edge. The whitest of the blooms glowed in the bands of moonlight. She reached over and took his hand.

"Now give me your heart." He laughed, a low rumbling sound. "The hand is the easy part, isn't it?" She smiled and squeezed his hand. It was warm, and well known, and exciting. "The lupines are starting to fade, Charley."

"I know. I've been watching them."

"I say we wade right into them, Charley, take them unawares, conquer those stiff-necked, pompous blooms. We'll lay naked and close in the pale streaks of moonlight, amid the fading flowers, praising God for their once-perfect brilliance and for their seamless decline."

"They're prickly, you know. We'll need a blanket." She stood up, letting go of his hand. "You won't go away, will you?"

"No chance of that, Charley."

CHAPTER

19

It wasn't worth it to bring in a steam shovel to dig the foundation, Francis explained, because of the way the bucket worked on a slope. The best and most effective tool was a simple shovel; Paul could dig a hole twelve feet square and four feet deep in just a few days if he kept at it. Then they'd pour the concrete, set the rebar, wait for it to set up, and set the structure in place with Bob Finale's crane. They flagged out the square, and Paul removed the sod and topsoil, piling it to one side. It took him half a day of digging to get into the subsoil. Soon after, his shovel hit ledge. He walked up to the house, jacket flapping, and announced to Francis that they were in deep trouble.

They tried again in another place and hit ledge again, and then in five other places. Each time they had to stop and get out the stakes and the string and the levels and the measuring tapes and find another location with the right sight lines. Meanwhile, the aging flowers were being trampled and replaced with ugly piles of dirt. Lupine lovers appearing in their driveway for one last look at the fading blooms turned back in disgust. One couple from Quebec even came up to the house to register their objections; they had been coming for years and were stunned by what they considered a desecration. Charlotte found herself apologizing, then saw them down in the field picking frantically. Francis was in the house with her, watching. "It doesn't matter," he said, giving her a quick kiss on the cheek. "That's where we're going to dig next."

The wandering poet Stodge was hired to help, and quit after an hour. Paul's ex-wife, Billie, called him from the emergency room in QC and pleaded with him to come get her. Her boyfriend had thrown her around and broken her arm, she told Paul, but when he arrived, the same boyfriend was helping her out the hospital door and into his rusty Buick. Billie refused to even look at Paul, and the boyfriend issued some serious threats, telling Paul he'd shoot out his lights if he ever contacted Billie again. When he returned to the Nest that night, in the grip of extreme humiliation, Paul smuggled in a clutch of miniature whiskeys. Stodge found the minis and showed them to Francis, who warned Paul there would be no second chance; if he ever brought alcohol into the house again, or if Francis noticed any signs of his drinking, whether on or off the premises, or heard even the breath of a rumor, the Great Bellini would be booted out for good. Paul disappeared for a week, and when he returned, there was no more mention of the incident.

Francis seemed only mildly annoyed at the lack of progress with the site work and the many setbacks to the project. He didn't mind waiting, he told Charlotte. He wanted to see what would happen. Something was developing; he wasn't sure what, but it was something important. He couldn't tell her, though, in what sphere it was taking place.

For the next few weeks, he spent most of his time working on the final stages of fabrication in his shop, leaving the problem of the foundation unsolved. Then he received word that Thexton had refused his offer, calling the alternate structure a "token work of no historic or artistic significance." Thexton had decided to go ahead with the legal proceedings. Francis marveled at his patron's sudden incisive eye for authenticity. Had he underestimated him all along? Francis returned to New York, and Charlotte settled back into her former routine—picnic suppers on the porch with the boys, long nights reading in bed while swatting jumbo-

sized millers and moths, hours spent making more cards for Hoskins.
She had decided he should learn how to count, and she had made a series
of the blue birthday-cake cards with different numbers of yellow candles.
If she asked him to line them up in order from one to four, he could. If
she asked him to line five up in order from four to nine, he could. If she
asked him to say the numbers aloud, he refused.

The last week of July was looming. The Clatters were planning to
stay for a week, and Rosey was talking about extending her vacation to
include a second week—it depended on her boss and what he wanted—
but she was very excited about coming, about seeing the boys, seeing
Charlotte, catching up, and catching some sun, too. She had bought a
new lounge chair covered with the sweetest chintz fabric; she just knew
Charlotte was going to love it. "I'm going to spend every minute of my
vacation with you. You've been so brave, up there all alone!"

Rosey continued, saying there was something Charlotte should
know. "Kitty's having problems. Harry says she hasn't been feeling well,
and he's worried. She's lost a lot of weight. She spent a whole week in
Boston with her teacher, the one she took classes with at the Mother
Church. There's a clue right there that something's wrong."

"Doesn't she go every year, for the annual meeting?"

"This was different. This was personal. And Mr. Matson, her patient,
died. He had a final heart attack, a big one . . . well, big enough, right?"
Rosey laughed and stopped abruptly. "But we mustn't laugh."

"Of course not." Charlotte felt a sudden rush of love for her oldest sister. There was no one in the whole world like her—as infuriating as she
was at times. She had a certain kind of gaiety that informed her very
nature. She loved to laugh. And cry. She never held back.

"I think it bothers her a lot, but of course she won't talk to me about
it. Harry told me. She won't talk about anything. I'm telling you this,
though, you can take things too far. Kitty says you can't heal through Science if you rely on medicine, too. Mrs. Eddy called it radical reliance, but
Mrs. Eddy herself went to the dentist." Rosey lowered her voice as if Mrs.
Eddy might be listening. "And she had a doctor called in when she had
kidney stones, and she took morphine; think about that. When in Rome,

I say, do as the Romans do. We live in this world, we have to recognize that. Christian Science is all very nice—it makes us all better people—but as far as I'm concerned, when it comes to getting sick, I'm going to a doctor."

"Maybe it's just something temporary," Charlotte said, though it didn't sound like that. It sounded like something might actually be wrong with Kitty. Kitty? How could that be? "Maybe it's not serious."

"I hope not. We can talk about it when I'm there. Aren't you excited about having us come?"

One morning after Francis returned, they overslept and didn't wake up until they heard the boys walking around upstairs. Charlotte darted upstairs in her robe to waylay them while Francis slipped out the back and came around to the breezeway. "Anybody home?" he called, peering into the kitchen at them through the screen door—barefoot, hair tousled, suspenders hanging off his pants. He entered doing a little too much yawning and stretching, she thought. Baird was properly suspicious.

"How come you sleep here?" Baird asked him.

Charlotte and Francis looked at each other blankly; they were ridiculously unprepared.

Baird poured an extra dollop of maple syrup on his cereal. "It's not very far to your house."

"No, it isn't," Francis said finally. "But if I went home at night, I would miss your mother."

"Oh," said Baird.

"Is that a good reason?" Francis asked him.

"Pretty good. Can't you sleep on the couch, though?"

"It's not very comfortable."

Baird scowled but said nothing. Later that day, Charlotte took a pillow and a set of sheets out of the linen closet and laid them conspicuously on the back of the couch, as if awaiting Francis.

She was slowly peeling an orange, watching a spider at work on a web outside the kitchen window, thinking about all she had to do to get ready for the following week and her sisters' visit. The window faced east, and the dew glistened on the delicate strands in the morning sun. When the spider moved, the web bounced ever so lightly. Hoskins was working on his breakfast; Baird was outside, waiting for Francis to come take him to the Town garage. Hoskins wouldn't be going—Francis had made a big point of saying he was too young to go with them, and it had pleased Baird enormously. Not a day had gone by since then that Baird hadn't talked about it.

"I knew your dad," Francis had told him casually one day when Charlotte and the boys had gone to the Nest to watch him weld. They were sitting out on the back patio, on the warm flagstones, and Hoskins was strutting around wearing Francis's welding headgear. Baird said nothing, watching his brother. "Your father was a very talented man. I imagine you know that."

"What's 'talented'?"

"It means there's a lot of things you know how to do and you can do them well." Francis sat down on the bench and invited Baird to sit down next to him.

"No, thanks," said Baird. "I'll stand."

"For one, your father was a very good photographer. He knew an awful lot about taking pictures, how to use the light to advantage, what lens to use to get the effect he wanted, how to compose a picture so that it's interesting. Would you like to learn to take pictures?" Francis turned and looked at Charlotte, mouthing, *Melvin's camera?* and she shook her head. "I understand he was very good at fixing machinery, too. He had a fine old truck. Is that right?"

"He was going to teach me to drive it at the fairgrounds, when nobody was around."

"Really," he said. "At your young age?"

"Yup. This summer, he said."

"I guess you must like engines and trucks and motors and things. It's been pretty clear to me all along, but this seems like real confirmation."

Baird nodded solemnly and Francis told him he knew where there were a lot of things like that, a lot of heavy equipment, and he had the good fortune to know some of the men who operated it, like big Bob Finale, and he was pretty sure that they would welcome a visit from someone like Baird.

The evening before, she'd had to read Mike Mulligan's story twice to the boys. Mike Mulligan and his steam shovel, Mary Anne, had become fixtures in their lives. According to the children's story, beloved by both boys, when steam shovels went out and the new diesel-powered shovels came in, Mike had to fight with all his might against becoming an anachronism. Mike hoped Mary Anne could hold her own against the new machines, with their fancy chrome and sleek construction. As far as he could see, *She could still dig as much in a day as a hundred men could dig in a week—at least he thought she could, but he wasn't quite sure.* Unfortunately, Hoskins had recently taken this lively statement and made it his own.

He spooned up the last little bit of milk in his bowl, and Charlotte picked up the cards lying on the counter. "How old will you be on your birthday in September?" she asked absently, expecting no reply. She wasn't even sure what she was trying to accomplish—the truth was, even if he did say "four," just as he had learned to answer "three," he would only be repeating the answer she fed to him whenever she asked. He never said anything on his own.

"Four," he said.

She sat up straight, suddenly alert. "Four! Yes, four! And how old are you now?" She started to hold up three fingers and stopped—she'd be giving him the answer. He put his spoon in his mouth and let the handle dangle, staring at her with a blank expression. She asked him again, and he shook his head slowly, letting the spoon move from side to side. She held up a fork. "Is this one fork, or two?" He looked blank. "It's a game," she prodded. "You say one or two."

"One or two."

"Just say one."

"One."

"One fork?"

He looked down at his bowl, but she kept going anyway. "Is this one table? Yes or no." He started sliding out of his chair. "Is that one chair?" She was starting to shout. He scowled at her, letting her know he didn't like her game or her tone of voice. She watched him get the washcloth hanging by the sink and wipe his face, swiping at his forehead and cheeks and mouth. Everything he did, he did very, very thoroughly. "Am I your mother? Yes or no!" He wiped his hands and hung up the washcloth, taking great care to center it on the nail, and went outside.

He knew what she wanted, he was capable of answering, and he refused. He was a defiant, willful child, light-years away from Mrs. Eddy's *spiritual idea*. Every day he showed her in so many ways that he had his own business to attend to, and that it was more important than hers. He didn't care what she thought; he didn't care what she felt.

She heard the car door slam, heard Francis greet the children in the yard. He and Charlotte had decided that even if he spent the night, he should continue to go home in the morning, leaving the folded sheets on the back of the couch—it was the least they could do for Baird, Francis said. Baird had been quite the gentleman about it all. Francis had to do his urine test anyway and get his insulin shot. Charlotte had observed him giving himself a shot several times and had been amazed at how small and inconsequential the needle really was, and how easily he did it.

He called out, "Charley?" and walked in, his dark hair still wet from his shower, looking recharged and happy. He wore a plain white T-shirt this morning—no crazy shirt or suspenders today; he'd dressed soberly, for the sake of the men at the garage, she assumed.

He'd made a big decision, he said, pouring himself coffee. He'd finally realized what a stupid game he'd been playing with Thexton; he'd been taunting him like a schoolboy, taunting *himself* is what it came down to. It was a stupid game, and it was time to quit. He was just delighted. It made him feel completely refreshed, completely renewed. Life was once again an exciting prospect. He reached for the cereal.

"You're selling him the stair sculpture after all?"

"Yup. I'm calling him this afternoon—directly, man to man." He laughed. "I'm not even going through my lawyer. It will be my last spiral stairs, end of the line, good-bye and good riddance. Of course, he'll have to take the thing without the contraptions. But he'll come around. I'll sweet-talk him about space and time, throw in a few words like *energy* and *light* and *reverence for the spirit*—he'll love it. Then I'm done. No more bogus stairs to the stars. I've been *blind,* Charley, *blind*. Think about spirals, their endless elevation, their delicate reaching out to one perfect point in the universe. There's only one specific point where they're headed, you know, where solid earth connects to restless air. Yet look at the structure, look at the bloody materials—unyielding steel, for Chrissake. The whole idea is one big wretched, self-mocking metaphor. Is there any milk?" He was already on his way to the refrigerator.

"What about your work in the field? Will you finish that? Will you fill in the holes?" Charlotte could picture her sisters' horror.

He fished the milk out, closed the door. He wasn't really done with it yet, he said very seriously. He wasn't done with the holes and the hills and the mess; he needed to live with his mistake, to put his face in it, learn something. "I've got an entirely different piece for you. I can't say too much about it now, but I'm very excited. You'll love it."

"Shouldn't you consult me? Or are you planning to just throw in a few words like *energy* and *light* and I'll go along with it?"

He stopped in his tracks, milk in midair. "Why, Charley, I hadn't realized you could be so *annoyed*—just like everybody else. *Highly* irritated!" He sat down, poured the milk on his cereal, looked around for a spoon, took hers lying beside her empty bowl. "I thought you'd be pleased. You've been so worried about our Monsieur Thexton and the money and all."

"*So* worried?"

"You've mentioned it fairly consistently, you'll have to admit."

"Is that so dumb, to be a little bit practical?" She felt embarrassed, hearing the echo of Melvin's voice in hers, the voice of the Great Panjandrum.

"Of course it's not dumb to be concerned about the money; it could mean a lot to us—we might want to go to France sometime, or Rio. Have you ever been to Carnival?"

She shook her head. The muscles in her face had assumed a fixed expression and she couldn't seem to move them.

"I mean, if you ever get over your bad mood. But just to be concerned about racking the money up, that's boring, you know, after a while." He gave her a dazzling smile, which she didn't return.

"At the risk of being even more boring—how about consulting your lawyer first, before you talk to Thexton? He might have some good advice."

"She. My lawyer's a she."

"Oh."

"I called her when I got out of the shower. She was already on her way out of the apartment at six-thirty—Liz is a maniac. She was delighted. She's tired of this thing, just like I am. She promised a celebratory lunch, on her. I'll go down next week, and we'll work out the details. Anne-Marie's coming up here from New Jersey, with some friend of hers and her friend's little girl. I told them they could have the house."

"My sisters are coming next week."

"Good, I'll be gone and I won't embarrass you." He put his cereal dish in the sink.

"Why do you say that?"

"Look at your face—you're embarrassed already. I gotta go." He bent down to kiss her, and she pulled away. "What is it?"

"What isn't it!"

"*More* than annoyed? Down in the dumps?"

"Stop making fun."

He sat back down. "All right."

"I have some good news."

"Good!"

"Hoskins said 'four' this morning when I asked him how old he would be on his birthday."

"I hate to say it, Charley, but that's not good news. It's not even news. You've trained him to say it; he's repeating what you say. He's not talking. Now if someday he starts chatting away about his breakfast, his plans for the day, his interest in architectonics, his fondness for sticks and stones, his love of stop signs, his devotion to his zany, proud, smart, sexy mother, then that will be news." He reached for her hand. "Your hair is starting to grow out. Are you going to let it?"

"I like it short."

"Okay. Whatever you want." He picked up the saltshaker and started fiddling with it. He poured some salt onto the oilcloth, arranged it into a small hill, neatened up the sides. "So when do you suppose he's going to talk?"

"He's not ready."

"Do you know why he's not ready?"

"Are you saying you know?" She could hardly recognize her own voice.

"I don't have a clue. But there must be something going on. I think you could find out pretty easily if you were interested."

"Of course I'm interested. It's not that I'm not *interested,* Francis. But I'm not about to ask some doctor for the name of a disease."

"What if you could get information that was helpful? That helped him?"

"What would it be?"

"That's a funny way to think about it, that you have to know what it is before you ask for it. What are you afraid of? I mean, it has to be more than doctors. You're a grown-up; you know they're not monsters. He'll be four soon. It's time to find out what's going on. I've always assumed that your religion wouldn't get in the way of the really important things, that it was just sort of a vague idea that the universe was a beautiful place. Vast and divine and so forth. That's good; there's nothing wrong with that. But I didn't think it would make you blind."

A sharp pain had radiated around to her face from the back of her head. "I'm not blind, and I'm capable of giving him every benefit of the doubt, of loving him as much as a mother can, of caring for him as lovingly as I can. He needs time and patience, and I can give that to him."

"And you do. But he's not talking."

"He's memorized our phone number."

"He's memorized a lot of things. Want to know anything about road signs? That damned steam shovel? Bodily complaints? But I can see we shouldn't talk about it. You're furious."

"I'm upset."

"I can see that, Charlotte."

She was Charlotte now.

"Shall we keep talking? Maybe we can work our way out of this somehow. Baird will wait—he's waited this long. Maybe we can get somewhere if we keep going." He flattened the little hill of salt, licked his finger. "No?"

She said nothing, and he got up. "It looks like we just found something we can't talk about."

She stayed where she was, and he left. She heard his voice outside and then Baird came to the door and yelled "Bye!" and ran off, too excited even to come inside.

Here, said the Porter. Carry my bags.

CHAPTER

20

The Clatters piled out of the car asking a flurry of questions about all the holes and piles of dirt in the field, and Charlotte knew right away that their visit was going to be a disaster. Harry was talking too fast and too much and laughing too loudly, and Kitty looked unhappy. Harry said it looked like the work of giant moles. Kitty laughed gamely, and asked, "Are you looking for oil?"

Though well prepared for this moment, Charlotte launched forth in a voice that lacked authority: The mess, she explained, was only a temporary disruption while a sculpture was being installed in the field. Kitty asked what sort of sculpture, and Charlotte answered, "Abstract," though in fact she still had no idea what it would be, or if it would be at all. Francis was back in New York, no doubt celebrating his decision about Thexton with the smart, sophisticated Liz at that very moment. Charlotte saw her as bright and ruthless, her woman's heart numbed by constant success. She had a brittle laugh; dark, elongated eyes; beautiful breasts. She wore French underwear in court under her suits. Charlotte hated her.

"Abstract?" asked Harry. "You mean blobs?"

"I hope not," she said, trying to smile, and drew Roberta toward her for an awkward hug. Roberta tried to kiss her on the cheek and missed, kissing her nose instead, and turned bright red. She had done something terrible to her eyebrows, replacing them with two thin black lines drawn by a shaky hand. Norman kept a tight hold on the shoebox in his hands, as if he expected Charlotte to wrest it away, and submitted briefly to her embrace before escaping to join Baird on the sideline.

Kitty stepped back from Charlotte after their hug and told her she looked wonderful, though Charlotte saw her doubtful look as she assessed her short hair. "I like it. It's perky."

Charlotte could feel her old defenses coming to life again. "Did you say 'perky'?"

"It's a compliment—I wasn't criticizing."

"I like it a lot," Roberta said. "I think I'll cut my hair like that."

"But yours is straight; it wouldn't look the same," Kitty said, and tried to give her an affectionate pat. Roberta dodged her hand, moving away with a "*Please,* Mother."

"Rosey says you've hired someone to help you look after the place," said Harry.

"Yes. Paul."

"The Great Bellini!" Baird shouted, and bowed extravagantly, making them all laugh.

"He's been a big help."

"What does he do?" Harry asked, looking around pointedly at the house's peeling paint, the remnants of brush next to the maple stump, the unkempt lawn abandoned by Paul when he started the digging.

"Not much," Charlotte said, and smiled, feeling foolish. The whole place seemed to have gone to seed the moment the Clatters drove up. She added somewhat lamely that the porch had been fixed.

"I hope it wasn't too expensive," said Kitty. "An old house can eat up a lot of money." Harry went off with Baird and Norman to take a closer look at the holes in the field. Norman was still carrying his shoe box, and Kitty explained that it housed his precious baseball-card collection and he was probably afraid to put it down. "Everything is about Ted Williams, now that he's coming back from Korea—I apologize in advance. You'll be hearing all about it."

Hoskins, who had observed the Clatters' arrival from the porch, tore past them down the steps and across the lawn, taking a shortcut down to the field by rolling under the barbed-wire fence.

"He certainly seems more grown up," said Kitty. Hoskins was wearing his denim overalls, which emphasized his long legs. "And fast!"

"He's making a lot of progress." Charlotte hesitated. In what sphere? "He hasn't had one of his tantrums in a long time."

"I'm not surprised—he's been in my thoughts constantly. I've been working for him all summer, at least fifteen minutes every day."

"Me, too."

"Of course."

"His vocabulary has grown a lot."

"That's wonderful."

"He knows his numbers up to nine."

"You must be pleased."

"I am."

"I'm not trying to take the credit, Charlotte. I'm only trying to help."

"Oh, I know." Charlotte wanted to change the subject and asked for her news. Kitty told her that Harry had applied for a job with a life-insurance company outside Northhampton. "We're sure he's going to get it."

"Life insurance? You mean, selling?" She couldn't imagine Harry going door-to-door, soliciting strangers.

Kitty smiled. "Opportunities are opening up for him. We're thrilled."

Roberta opened the car's trunk, pulling out a heavy suitcase. "Finally, Harry Clatter goes to work. Like a real dad."

"Please," said Kitty, "you're talking about your father."

"Did I say something wrong?"

"Your tone indicated some kind of disapproval."

Roberta shrugged. "It wouldn't matter what I thought anyway."

"That suitcase is full of books," Kitty told Charlotte. "They're giant tomes with tiny print, and all by Russians."

"I'm a Marxist," Roberta said proudly.

"You aren't any such thing, Roberta!" her mother said.

Roberta started lugging the suitcase up the steps. "The old Russia was corrupt. The peasants were treated like slaves. They didn't own any of the land they worked. Sometimes an enlightened master would give them a small piece of land, but mainly they were just worked to death."

"Such ideas," said Kitty. "I'm sure they tried to be fair."

"Dream on, Mother. Have you read Tolstoy?"

"Heavens, no."

"Then you don't have the authority to speak on the subject. The peasants had miserable lives—like me!" The door slammed behind her.

"It's the crowd she hangs around with at school," Kitty whispered. "They've had a terrible influence on her."

"Why did she do that to her eyebrows?"

"I don't know. I felt sick when I saw it. She thinks it's glamorous, I suppose. Though you wouldn't know glamour was important to her, would you, from the way she dresses?" Roberta had dressed for the trip in her standard trousers and dark-colored shirt. But Charlotte had noticed some cute little saddle shoes peeking out from her trouser cuffs. "She disapproves of everything we do."

Charlotte had always thought of Kitty as such a powerful force, a radiant source of light and energy and strength, always looking for the best in everyone—this worried way about her seemed new and different, and Charlotte wanted to comfort her. "You're all right, Kitty?"

"Of course!"

"You've lost weight."

"Just trying to keep my girlish figure. You've never had any trouble with that, dear, have you?" Kitty was smiling sweetly, but it didn't dispel her drawn, tired look. "But tell me about this artist, the one who's digging up the field."

"It's Francis Roux, from the Nest." Charlotte was conscious of trying to keep her tone friendly and innocent. "Actually, it's Paul who was doing the digging. Francis supervised."

"They're done? They finished?"

"They had to stop for a while because of . . . changes in design. We're not sure exactly what will happen here now."

"It used to be so pretty. It was all part of your lovely view. Now it's so . . . bleak."

The day Francis returned from taking Baird to the Town garage, Charlotte had reminded him again that her sisters were coming and asked him to do something. Did she mean, pretty it up, he'd asked, like a *lawn?* Or cover it with a tarp? He'd thought he was being funny, but she hadn't joined in. She'd said a few things about it being her view; he'd said a few things about her conventional ideas about civilized landscapes, and they had parted, both of them thoroughly unhappy.

The next day, she saw him down in the field retrieving his stakes and tapes and tools, and for a moment her heart had sung out with gladness and relief. She would make him come back to her that night, and they would talk about it and work it out. They would talk about Hoskins; she would confide her terrible fears and he would understand and he would call her Charley again and they would make love and everything would be all right. She watched him from the window, feeling so fond of the way he looked, with his jet-black hair and his big shoulders, his lividly pink T-shirt, his jeans. When he got into his car and drove away without coming up to the house to see her, she'd cried. For two nights she'd sat out on the porch after the boys were asleep and smoked their cigarettes by herself. The first night she drank iced tea; the second night she had a glass of Melvin's whiskey. Why couldn't things be simple again? Why did it have to be so messy and unclear and ragged and awful? The whiskey made her feel drunk, and she thought about driving up to the Nest and singing "Daddy's Whiskers" outside his window. But she hadn't, and he'd left for New York without her seeing him again. She tried now to see the bleakness Kitty was describing as a necessary step toward something wonderful—and couldn't. Without Francis around, the work in the field had turned into an ugly blot on the landscape, an embarrassing symbol of her foolishness.

"I just don't want you to be hurt, Charlotte. You have a reputation to protect."

"What does that mean, my reputation?"

Kitty laughed. "You don't know what it means?"

Charlotte blustered on. "People will think what they like, no matter

237

what you say. You can't control what other people think." She recognized
Francis's words and felt uneasy.

"Well, you can certainly try to influence their views."

"I just wish you would assume that I know what I'm doing."

"Do you?"

Charlotte started to say she did, and then had to laugh at her own
horribly pompous attitude. "Who does? Don't worry, Kitty. I'm perfectly
happy." Though she managed to say it with a confident lilt, she knew that
Kitty knew she was lying. "I like it here. I might even stay after the summer's over. The Berrys would like to rent the house in Syracuse for the
rest of the year—a family is returning for a year's leave from Mozambique. They'd be good tenants, she says. But I don't know—I haven't
made up my mind yet."

"With all the snow, you couldn't even drive up to the house—" Kitty
started to say, and Charlotte walked off, dismissing any further objections.

Rosey arrived while Charlotte and Kitty were preparing lunch in the
kitchen. She drove her big car up onto the lawn and unloaded her new
lounge chair, several straw hats, two bags of groceries, a stack of magazines, and assorted bags and boxes onto the grass.

She trotted into the house with the groceries, past the dim, cool parlor where Hoskins was reading the entries in the dictionary under
opium/orangutan. Roberta was out in back, sitting under an apple tree in
the unkempt orchard, slapping at flies and making notes about the trip.
Her mother and father had had a fight and the dialogue had been particularly dramatic, but then Norman began to torture her with his baseball
facts. "Ted Williams is a creep," she'd told him, "and if you say another
word about him on this trip, I'll pinch you until you cry."

"How about Dom DiMaggio? You want to know his batting average?" he'd asked, and she'd held the end of his nose between her fingers
until he cried for mercy.

At the moment, Norman was upstairs with Baird, who was showing
him the .22 his father had always kept in the bedroom closet. Both of

them were rather frightened of it and laughed nervously as they took turns handling it. Baird said he knew where the ammunition was but he wasn't allowed to tell. His father had told him always to keep guns and ammunition in different places. Norman said, with a lot of authority, that sometimes these things went off anyway, even when they weren't loaded. Especially .22s. Baird said it wasn't true, but he took a step backward anyway from where Norman stood with it.

Rosey set the groceries down and hugged her sisters. Kitty admired her new seersucker suit. So good for travel, Rosey said; it never wrinkles. "You should get one, too," she told Kitty, who was wearing a wrinkled sleeveless shift. "And if I were you," she added with a sideways look at Kitty's loafers and socks, "I'd wear heels when I traveled. You get better service."

"From whom?" Kitty asked, and laughed.

"The man at the pump," said Rosey gaily, "under the sign of the flying red horse!" She turned to Charlotte, saying she just *loved* her short hair, so cool-looking in all the heat, so much better than that old Alice-in-Wonderland look! "But what on Earth is going on in the field?"

Kitty answered for her. "Charlotte's having a sculpture put in." She spoke carefully, as if talking in code.

Charlotte opened a can of tuna and squeezed out the juice into a small bowl.

"Uh-oh! It's the man from the Nest, isn't it?" wailed Rosey. "I know all about that place. Beatriz told me about it last summer." Rolling her eyes, she added, "*Bohemians.*"

Kitty started unloading the groceries.

"Did I say something wrong?" asked Rosey.

"I think Charlotte could probably set your mind to rest," Kitty said, but Charlotte didn't look up. She added mayonnaise to the tuna, stirring, trying to act as if she didn't know they were waiting for her explanation about the Man from the Nest.

Kitty poured herself a glass of water at the sink.

"I'm so glad you like water, Kitty!" Rosey exclaimed. "It's so good for you! Eight glasses of water a day, that's what they say! Did you know that the protoplasm we're made of is more than half water? We have to keep replenishing it."

"Protoplasm!" exclaimed Kitty, laughing. "Why would you care about protoplasm?"

"I want to do right by it, so it will do right by me!"

"What kind of thinking is that? Life comes from God, not protoplasm."

"I'm just telling you what I read." Rosey was lining up cans of deviled ham on the counter. She handed an empty bag to Charlotte. "I don't know where you keep these."

"Just look where that kind of thinking leads you," said Kitty. "Think about what you're saying. *Man is not matter; he is not made up of brain, blood, bones, and other material elements . . .* that's where disease starts, with your assumptions. That's Mrs. Eddy's point exactly."

"I wasn't trying to argue," Rosey said calmly. "I'm just saying water is good for you."

"Mama drank a lot of water," said Charlotte. "She was always thirsty." No one seemed to hear her.

When Kitty walked into the dining room to set the table, Rosey whispered, "Harry's right. She doesn't look good. He says she hardly eats."

They watched her coming back to the kitchen. "You're limping," said Rosey. "What's that all about?"

Kitty stuck out her loafer, laughing. "I stepped on one of Norman's toys last week when I was barefoot. A soldier, I think, with a gun. No wonder it hurts!"

The next day Baird told Roberta that the room she was sleeping in next to the kitchen was the one his mother slept in with Francis when he spent the night. Francis was supposed to sleep on the couch in the parlor, but he didn't. The sheets were never mussed. Roberta told her mother and her mother told Rosey and Rosey said, "I knew it. I knew there'd be trouble if she got mixed up with those people."

The sisters conferred: Charlotte was doubtless confused, certainly

lonely. He was taking advantage of her—everyone knew he was a womanizer. "But you can certainly see why women fall for him," Rosey said.
"He's awfully good-looking."

"Leave it to me," said Kitty. "I'll take care of it."

"Why should I leave it to you?"

"I might be more tactful."

"You think I'm not tactful?"

"I'm not saying that . . . but she's very touchy about him. Or it may be
that the whole thing is over, anyway. She doesn't want to let on, but she
seems sad."

"I know her better than you do, Kitty. Think of the years I spent in
Syracuse looking after her, some of the best years of my life—gone forever. Think of what I gave up!"

"Rosey, please. Let's not talk about Duncan."

"I wasn't going to talk about Duncan!"

"All your subjects lead to Duncan," said Kitty.

"Oh, for goodness' sakes! I can't even talk to you anymore!"

Later that afternoon, Charlotte led an expedition up to the copper
mines, prompted by badgering from the boys. It was a favorite part of the
visit for the cousins. Kitty declined to join them, saying she had work to
do for her patients, and Rosey was eager to try out her new lounge chair,
so Charlotte and Harry went with Roberta and the boys.

They climbed the steep hill slowly, picking and eating blackberries as
they went. The sun was hot, and the grass was so dry it crackled as they
stepped on it. Grasshoppers sprang up all around them. Every so often
Hoskins went off in pursuit of one, and Charlotte and Roberta took turns
rounding him up. Near the top of the hill, they entered a stretch of dense
woods, with hemlocks and firs growing so close together that they had to
walk bent over in places in order to avoid getting hit with their ragged
lower branches. Rotting logs, covered with dirt and leaves, made for
treacherous walking, and their progress was slow. On the other side of
the stand of softwoods they joined up with an old logging road—not
much more than a path that had already started to grow up with saplings
and berry bushes. Rivulets of orange-colored water ran back and forth

across the road and each time they came to another one they all stopped to exclaim over the color. Norman was sure he saw pieces of gold, but Baird, who had been there more often, and was the acknowledged expert, asserted unequivocally that it was only copper ore—and worthless, too. They started to argue, and Harry intervened, suggesting that they race each other to the source. Baird broke into a run; Norman, heavier than Baird, tagged along behind him, struggling to keep up. Then Hoskins shot past them both and all three boys disappeared around a curve.

A dank, sulfurous smell announced that the piles of tailings were just up ahead and Charlotte started to run, shouting at the boys to wait up, but when she rounded the bend, with Harry and Roberta close at her heels, the three boys were standing together on the copper-colored pile, blinking in the bright light. "Stinko!" they yelled in unison, and everyone laughed in relief.

Harry apologized profusely. He shouldn't have told them to run. Charlotte assured him it was fine, Hoskins was safe and sound, but as soon as she could, she took Hoskins's hand and together they climbed the well-worn footpath up the crumbling mound of orange dirt, letting the others follow behind them. Shaft Number 1 was a popular place to visit, and the sparse woods were littered with the remains of human activity: rusty pieces of tin, metal stovepipes and sheeting, an old baby buggy with a crushed frame, tires, shoes, bottles, beer cans. At the top of the incline, the sulfuric smell grew stronger and they entered the narrow concrete passageway that led from the gaping mouth of the mineshaft to the slope where the tailings had been dumped. A stream of cold, dank air rolled out over them, and they grew quiet, listening to the steady dripping of water, awed by the feeling of danger all around them.

"A few more feet and everyone stops," Charlotte said, as they came within sight of the entry to the mineshaft. "Right here," she ordered, "and no farther." They drew up into a cluster and stopped, shivering, as they peered into the darkened tunnel. A rotted vertical beam listed sideways in the stagnant pool of filthy brown water. Water dripped steadily into the pool from in between the rocks in the tunnel's ceiling, creating watery echoes.

"It's spooky," Roberta said.

"I'm not scared," said Norman.

"Me, either," said Baird.

Roberta asked how they'd like it if they were there all alone.

"I'd like it," said Norman.

"Me, too," said Baird.

"I bet."

"Okay," said Charlotte, "I've had enough."

"Spooky," Hoskins said. "Spooky, spooky."

"You're right about that, Spike." Harry reached over and grabbed him and put him on his shoulders, and for once Hoskins didn't object. They passed back over the concrete passageway, talking about the donkeys that had pulled the railroad cars filled with copper ore out of the tunnels and the miners, covered from head to toe with orange dust, carrying their old-fashioned lanterns. It had once been a bustling place, Charlotte said. It was hard to imagine now. It was deathly quiet up there. No birds sang; there weren't even any insect noises. The trees were small, stunted by the poor soil and the chemicals that fed them.

As they started back down the mound of tailings, Baird spotted a young porcupine high in a spindly birch, its weight on the small branch making it wave and sway. The boys were excited and started shouting. They wanted to throw a rock at it, but Charlotte stopped them. "Why would you want to do that," she asked, and Norman replied with amazement at her stupidity, "To make it come down!"

On the way back to the house, they took a different route so that Baird could show everyone a rock he liked. It was large and smooth and had probably arrived in Vermont with the glaciers, Charlotte said, explaining that millions of years ago big sheets of ice had carried huge rocks along with them as they traveled south from the top of the world. Roberta, looking skeptical, asked her how she knew this, and she said, "From reading the newspaper. Mrs. Cake wrote about it in one of her columns. She was comparing the glaciers' arrival to something, I forget what, maybe somebody's out-of-town guests."

Hoskins clambered effortlessly up the huge rock and stood looking down triumphantly as Roberta and the boys slipped and slid, trying to gain a foothold. He sailed back down on the seat of his pants, calling out, "Timber!" Baird and Norman thought it was funny and continued yelling "Timber!" every other minute as the group made its way down the hill.

Roberta led the way, followed by the two older boys, and then Charlotte and Harry, who tried to keep Hoskins in front of them rather than in back, which required that they slow down to a snail's pace, occasionally coming to a complete standstill as they waited for him. During one of these moments, Charlotte asked Harry about Melvin's camera equipment. Had he seen *anything* in the truck at all? Because surely he would have had his camera with him.

"I didn't see anything, Charlotte, but I didn't look, either. Kitty was sure you wouldn't want the truck. The papers were right in the glove compartment—the fellow pointed them out to me—the title was right there, and I was eager to be done with it. I was upset, nervous. I wanted to do things right for you. I always want to do things right—I don't know what happens." He spread his arms out in a gesture of futility. "I just screw up. It comes naturally. Like telling the boys to run to the mineshaft ahead of us."

"It's all right, Harry. Don't get upset."

"That's Kitty's line: *Don't get upset, Harry.*"

"Tell me something. Has she changed? Would you say she's gotten irritable during the last year or so? Does she snap at you?"

"Yup. She seems frazzled. I don't know what's wrong."

"I think I do, Harry. I think she has diabetes, just like our mother did. It can run in families."

"I don't know anything about it."

"If she does have it, and she needs insulin, she'd experience periodic high sugar levels in her blood. A diabetic can't absorb sugar like other people can."

"Have you been going to medical school? How do you know this?"

"From a friend. The field-ruiner."

He smiled at her.

"She may need insulin, or maybe she could just watch her diet, it depends. But she has to have a test."

"She won't see a doctor."

"I know. But I'm going to talk to her anyway. And don't worry about the truck or its contents. It's gone and it's probably just as well."

"Is that the same as *It's probably all for the best?*"

"Right."

"That's Kitty's line, too. What it means is *Forget it, will you?* Or rather, *Let's not talk about it anymore.*"

She laughed at the comical expression on his face. "I hear you're looking for a job, Harry. That's wonderful."

"Well, *finally,*" he said.

CHAPTER

21

Paul Bellini was bearing down on Charlotte and Rosey, grinning from ear to ear with delight. "Hey, look, we've got company!" he exclaimed, shrugging off his jacket as he approached.

"We?" Rosey whispered to Charlotte, handing her a corner of a sheet.

"That's Paul, it's just how he talks. He thinks he belongs to everybody."

Rosey had been lying in her lounge chair in the back, wearing her skirted bathing suit with a built-in push-up bra and tummy flattener, when Charlotte came out with a basket of wet laundry and asked for her help. Paul held out his hand to Rosey. "You must be one of the sisters!"

Charlotte introduced them, and Rosey held out a limp hand. Paul took it and moved it up and down. "You're from New York City?"

"I'm from Kingston, New York."

He raised his eyebrows and widened his eyes, preparing to be riveted. "Where's it at?"

"It's right above Poughkeepsie, if you know where that is."

"Sure I do, sure I do!"

"It's a very nice little town."

"Has its share of pretty women, that's for sure."

"Well, I like it," Rosey said with a little laugh. She handed a wet towel to Charlotte and sat down delicately on the edge of the lounge chair.

Charlotte fished two clothespins out of her apron pocket and hung up the towel. She had asked Rita not to come while her sisters were there but she'd neglected to say anything to Paul. He was apt to say just about anything, and it filled her with both anxiety and glee; she was exhausted by being so careful around her sisters. She hadn't heard from Francis, she didn't know where he was, and she missed him horribly. The ugly holes in the field had become ugly holes in her heart, and all the while she had to pretend.

"What all do you like about it?" Paul folded his arms, assuming a pleasant conversational stance. He was settling in for a nice long talk.

"It's got some very nice stores. And a cultural center. Have you seen *South Pacific*?"

"Guess I must've missed that one."

"It's such a fun musical. It's all about the war."

"I'm a U.S. Navy man myself."

"Oh, my."

"It's where I learned my trade, paid for by the United States government. Best darned school in the country. I've been to Lisbon, Portugal."

"Portugal! My goodness." Rosey dabbed at her knees with the suntan lotion. "What were you doing in Portugal?"

"Goofing around," he said, winking, "on leave."

"I'll bet you weren't goofing around at all. I'll bet you were hard at work defending our freedom."

"Well, sure."

"It must have been quite an experience, Paul."

"Hey, that's good! I like hearing my name spoke by a pretty woman!" He stood a little straighter, producing his most charming smile and fully revealing the gaps in his teeth. Judging from Rosey's expression, the smile more than made up for the gaps. Charlotte decided he was like some washed-out movie star operating with the confidence of his past fame—still able to charm, still confident of his magic. "'A rose is a rose,'" he said. "You know that one?" Her eyes lit up at his vague reference to things poetic, and she asked him if he was a fan of poetry. He nodded enthusiastically.

Rosey motioned to the book beside her. "Do you know Longfellow's *Hiawatha?*"

"Not by heart I don't!"

"I just love it," said Rosey, slowly stretching herself out on the lawn chair and carefully placing her shapely legs on the sun-drenched webbing. "'By the shores of Gitchee Goomee, By the shining Big-Sea-Water . . .'" Her toes were pointed, feet arched, knees slightly raised. Pinup legs. "'Stood the wigwam of Nokomis, Daughter of the Moon, Nokomis.'"

Paul took his bandanna out of his pocket and tied it around his neck. "That straight?"

"Straight?"

"Yeah, knot in front."

Rosey smiled approvingly.

"I got to look my best if you're gonna watch me work." He sat down on the grass right where he stood and began cutting each blade individually with scissors produced from his pocket. Rosey drew her arm up to cover her eyes against the sun, and Paul turned to admire the display.

Charlotte picked up the half-empty basket and took it back into the house.

"He's very nice," Rosey told her later.

"That's the drifter."

"Well, why didn't you tell me what a nice man he is? I pictured some bum! He tells me he has two lovely children, a boy and a girl."

"And a wife with a temper."

"He didn't mention a wife."

"They're divorced," said Charlotte, "but still firmly connected."

"Probably because of the children."

"More likely because of the wife," Charlotte said.

"What's she like?"

"Terrifying. At least, that's what I hear in the village. She's furious and fearless."

"Poor thing," said Rosey. "He deserves so much better."

"I'm surprised at the interest you've taken in him, Rosey. What about his grammar?"

"Grammar isn't everything. I should think you'd know that by now, Charlotte." She paused. "It's the teeth more than anything. How much do you think dentures cost?"

Charlotte tried to warn her: Paul was goofy, unpredictable, unstable. He'd been a heavy drinker for years, and there was some question about it now. He had slipped a few weeks ago, after a run-in with Billie. He was only circumstantially sober. When he was drinking, Leona had told her, he walked on all fours. Rosey recoiled briefly and laughed. "Don't be silly, Charlotte. It's just a little flirtation," she said, but Charlotte could see she was thrilled.

A hot sun baked the earth for days, turning soil to dust and creating waves of heat that wavered above parched ground. Rosey went out to sunbathe every day at 9 A.M., carrying her lotions, oils, towels, glasses, hats, magazines, poetry book, and lemonade, and every day at 9:05, and sometimes at 9:04, Paul Bellini reported to work in a clean shirt, his loafers shined and his hair slicked back. Except for his missing teeth, he looked pretty sharp.

He worked in the garden, watering and weeding, keeping silent watch as Rosey lay in the sun in her lounge chair, her skin glistening, her arm thrust over her eyes. After a while he would come sit on the grass beside her, fanning out his well-worn pack of cards on his sleeves. Or he would read aloud to her from Longfellow's poem in a halting voice, hesitating as he tried to pronounce words like *Wah-wah-taysee* and *Minne-haha*.

Roberta watched from the window in the pantry and took notes. "Do you think she *likes* him?" she asked Charlotte.

"I'm afraid so."

"Why?"

"Maybe because he likes her, and she's flattered."

"That's dumb."

"Dumb? Why?"

"I don't know, it just seems like there should be more to it than that."

"Well, that's not *all* that makes a woman like a man. I thought you read a lot of Russian novels, Roberta."

"Well, sure. But the men aren't goofy."

"What about Prince Mishkin?"

"I've only read *Anna Karenina*. Well, actually, I only started it. I haven't finished."

"The point is, he's goofy but he's a prince, and maybe Paul is a prince, too—underneath. Maybe that's what she's seeing."

"I hope so. Because she's really making a fool of herself."

The plan that afternoon was to go to a lake where the children could swim. After endless rounding up and re–rounding up of children and beach equipment and toys and supplies for their picnic, they were surprised to find that they were nearly the only ones there. The small lake was set in the middle of a forest; the water was beautiful, clear and blue and sparkling clean, with little waves that crested prettily, set in motion by a pleasant breeze rippling across the water's surface. There were two small sailboats out on the lake; colorful rowboats bobbed at the docks in front of a handful of summer cottages.

Hoskins immediately set to gathering small stones along the beach. Norman and Baird started on a castle. Roberta and Rosey flopped down on towels. Harry, fully clothed and wearing Cal McGuffey's old golf shoes, paced along the water's edge.

Charlotte sat down next to Kitty on a rock and looked at the water. How odd it was, she said, that they'd gone to so much trouble to come swimming, yet no one was in the water. It was always like that, Kitty said. There were so many different personalities in any family. She was wearing a jaunty two-piece bathing suit of a gay tropical material, and shoes and socks. Her arms and legs seemed very thin.

"How about if I buy you a soda at the Snack Shack?"

"I don't really need anything."

"Then let's take a walk. Can you walk all right? Is your foot bothering you? You're still limping."

Kitty stood up, smiling. "Of course I can walk. But you look so serious, Charlotte. What is it?"

They walked up the sloping beach toward the parking lot and Charlotte said she'd noticed that Kitty drank a lot of liquids. "Like Mama," she added, keeping her tone light as they stepped onto the gravel path. "I remember that she was always thirsty." Kitty put out a hand on her arm, looking very earnest, but Charlotte forged ahead. "She was a diabetic, wasn't she?"

"I wish you wouldn't. There's no need."

"I'm pretty sure she was."

"She never said that," Kitty said after a while.

"But she was, wasn't she? Even if she didn't say it?"

"She might have supposed she was. I don't know."

"Did she take insulin?"

"If she did, I wasn't aware of it."

"Did she ever go to a doctor?"

"I don't know, Charlotte. I assume she might have seen a doctor once or twice in her life. She wasn't always a Scientist, not until she married Daddy anyway, and I wasn't always there."

"But you were there when she died."

"I don't know what you're getting at, Charlotte."

"I want to know what happened. At the time, I was told only that she was having one of her spells and that she had a bad case of the flu. I was sent away to stay with a neighbor after you came."

"She did have the flu."

"But she didn't die of the flu."

"These are harmful thoughts, Charlotte. There's no reason for you to be dwelling on them now."

"Diabetes sometimes runs in families. It can skip generations, too—our children could have it some day. You seem to have some of the symptoms. I think that's why your foot bothers you. If you're diabetic, your circulation is poor and a wound takes longer to heal. You need to take care of it. Your foot could be infected." Francis had once told her what could happen to him if he wasn't careful about small punctures, especially in his hands and feet. "It has to do with hyperglycemia, which you probably don't want to know about."

"I'm surprised, Charlotte, that you would talk like this." Kitty sounded very sad. "You know how mental malpractice works. Imperfection is the result of an imperfect mind. I can't stress this enough, Charlotte. You'll bring on sickness by dwelling on these things. I'm so sorry that you've strayed so far from your Science."

They were approaching the parking lot and it was already noticeably hotter. "How long had she had the flu?"

"You're talking in terms I can't understand." Kitty was brisk and efficient. "That presupposes I believe she was sick."

"You said she had the flu."

"That's what people said."

"How long was she sick?"

"I can't answer that."

"This isn't a court of law. We're sisters talking about our own mother." A family of beachgoers had spread out a blanket on the asphalt next to their car, even though the lake was only a few hundred yards away, as if they had tumbled right to the ground upon getting out of the car and lost the will to go any farther. "I have a right to know what happened."

"You were there."

Charlotte whirled around to face Kitty. "I was ten years old! And you were in charge! You sent me to stay with the neighbors!" The picnickers stared at them in alarm.

"I can't believe you would talk to me like this."

"I can't believe you wouldn't tell me. I want to know everything, Kitty. Did she throw up?"

"Charlotte!"

"Well?"

"I didn't notice."

"Did she have a temperature?"

"I didn't take her temperature."

"Then how did you know she was sick?"

Kitty stared at her, deciding. "She said so."

"What did she say?"

"She said, 'I'm not feeling well. Will you help me?'"

"What made you make the trip to Syracuse in the first place?"

Kitty walked on ahead without answering. Charlotte caught up with her and followed her into the parklike woods on the other side of the parking lot. "You have to tell me. I won't give up."

"Daddy called me," Kitty said after a while. "He said she was having one of her spells and he was frightened. I came because I needed to communicate a sense of safety to her. His fear was permeating her surroundings."

"He wasn't usually frightened."

"Well, he asked me, and I came."

"Was she in bed?"

"Yes."

"Was she talking?"

"Not much. She just said, 'I'm not feeling well.' And she asked me to help her."

"Help her how?"

"She wanted me to watch and pray with her. To do my work. I wasn't a practitioner yet, but I had already taken the classes by then. I could see that she was relieved that I was there. She soon relaxed, and drifted off."

"She must have looked hot and sweaty and uncomfortable."

"Oh, no, she looked lovely."

"Lovely?"

"She was a beautiful woman, as you will recall. Her hair was still bright—the same beautiful color as yours."

"Did she speak again?"

Kitty shook her head.

"What about Rosey? She must have been there."

"Rosey kept saying, 'She's going, she's going.' She cried and carried on; you know how she is. She wanted me to call the doctor."

"Did you?"

"No."

"Why didn't Rosey call him?"

Kitty didn't answer.

"She did, didn't she? Rosey called the doctor."

Kitty nodded.

"What did he tell her?"

"If I'm correct in remembering, he wanted us to bring her to the hospital." Kitty reached out to steady herself on the WELCOME VISITORS! sign tacked to a white birch. "I asked Mama if she wanted to go to the hospital. She said no."

"She said, 'No, I don't want to go'? Did she open her eyes and look at you and say she didn't want to go?"

"Her eyes were closed. She was very tired."

"Kitty."

"What is it?" She sounded exhausted.

"Why did the doctor want her to go to the hospital? I want to know what he said. Exactly what he said."

"He said he could give her an injection."

"Why didn't he just come to the house and give her an injection?"

"I suppose he thought it was more serious than that. He thought she might go into a coma."

"A coma!"

"It's a belief, Charlotte. I'm not a doctor and I didn't fully understand his thinking. I can't explain it to you."

"She needed insulin and he knew it because he was already her doctor. He'd already diagnosed her diabetes, isn't that so? She knew she needed insulin and so did Daddy and so did you. That's why Daddy called you to come, because he knew what Mama was supposed to do and he was frightened. You can deny it, Kitty, but I'll find out. I can make Rosey tell me, but I want to hear it from you."

"Mama didn't want to be treated by a doctor, and she didn't want to have to take insulin for the rest of her life. She wanted to rely only on God."

"Is that what you're going to do? Rely only on God? Even though you may be diabetic, too?"

"I would never think like that. I don't believe in that way of thinking. I never have. Man cannot serve two masters. There's something else you don't understand. She was ready to go, if necessary. She was ready to pass on."

Charlotte was stunned. "She said that?"

"She said, 'I want to go—let me go.'"

"To the hospital, she meant."

"No! You're getting it all wrong. You're not listening. You can continue to blame me if you like, but I only did as instructed. She didn't want to go to a hospital, she didn't want injections, she didn't want to be dependent on doctors and medicine. She said, '*I want to go—let me go.*' Charlotte, I'm not afraid, either. That's what you don't understand."

Kitty turned away abruptly, and Charlotte watched her walking back toward the beach in her little tropical suit, the very picture of resolute belief, head held high and looking straight ahead, her limp just barely discernible.

CHAPTER

22

The Clatters left early in the morning, two days before their scheduled departure. Rosey decided she wanted to stay an extra week. If her boss didn't like it, he could fire her and find someone to take her place. As far as the spat between her two sisters went, she didn't know what it was about and she didn't want to know—it was her vacation, too, and she intended to stay and enjoy herself.

Kitty had retired to her room when they returned from the lake and hadn't come down for dinner. In the morning, she said very little to anyone. She packed up efficiently, quickly, never lingering in any one room long enough to have an extended conversation, moving quietly around with her little limp. She was the first in the car, packed and ready, waiting in the driver's seat with her forehead in her hand while Roberta struggled to get her suitcase back into the trunk. Norman sat up front with his shoebox, looking glum. He hadn't wanted to leave. He was having a good time, he'd insisted loudly.

Harry lingered nervously, hoping to intercede in the calamitous

argument between his wife and Charlotte, but Charlotte refused to discuss it. She would talk to him later, she said. She just couldn't talk now.
She would call, or write—but not now. Roberta ran back into the house
to fetch something she had forgotten; Rosey ran out to the car to offer a
bag of grapefruit for their snacks, and then they were gone.

Within the hour, Mrs. Eddy came to call.

Charlotte had always had a good relationship with Mrs. Eddy. As a
child she had revered and loved her prim and kindly white haired image
while nevertheless always being aware of her moral authority—she was
Mother, sometimes Our Mother, sometimes Our Beloved Mother but she
was also Leader and Founder and Discoverer, more masculine incarna-
tions that called up images of a younger, tougher Mary Baker Eddy with
a long face and a sharp tongue. In both cases she had snappy eyes, and
under their penetrating gaze, Charlotte grew up knowing she was being
watched.

When Charlotte contracted measles at the age of six, she was deeply
distressed, not so much because of the insufferable itching, headache, and
fever, but because she knew she had done something to displease God.
Why else would she be sick? Her mother tried to persuade her that all
children, no matter how pure in heart and mind, unselfish, and helpful,
got what were called common childhood diseases. Her father, however,
hedged. *Most* children did, he said. Occasionally there was a child so
attuned to Mrs. Eddy's thoughts and wishes and so favored by Divine
Love, and so loyal in her thoughts to the Truth, that she was exempt.
Such had been the case with Kitty, who as a young child had gone forth
to battle with that Goliath of material law, Mortal Mind, and had been
victorious.

But Charlotte was saved from disgrace by Mrs. Eddy herself, who
appeared to her while Charlotte was taking an oatmeal bath. It was in the
middle of the day, and the strong light hurt her eyes. Lillian pulled the
shade and lit a candle, which she set on top of the toilet tank, away from
anything that could catch fire. She also located the cat—a gray cat named
Boris—and shut it in the bathroom with Charlotte for company, telling
her to soak as long as she could and try to lie under the water. It was a
very pretty scene in the little room, except that Charlotte was miserable

in mind and body. She had not *meant* to get spots, but somehow it had happened, probably because she had had bad thoughts and was afraid of quite a few things she wasn't supposed to be afraid of, such as the foxes that lived in the dark space under her bed and the dog that lived at the end of the street and thunder, which had no home. She concentrated on trying to stay submerged in the warm, soothing liquid, as her mother had instructed her to do, fighting the tendency of her body to float upward to the surface. Boris jumped up onto the edge of the sink, settled himself into a regal position, and gazed at her. The candlelight from across the room was reflected in his eyes; he appeared to smile, ever so slightly, and it seemed to her that he looked a lot like Mrs. Eddy, who, according to Charlotte's childish understanding, was all-powerful like God and could do anything she liked and go anywhere, even inside a cat. And there she was, smiling at Charlotte and letting her know she was still one of her favorites despite her ugly, measled body.

When Lillian Baird came in to see how she was doing, Charlotte said she felt a lot better; Mrs. Eddy had helped her by letting her know that she was very special to her, though she didn't mention anything about her going inside Boris, which she doubted her mother would understand. Her mother told her father about Charlotte's healing, and he told Charlotte that she had demonstrated the power of precious spiritual truths and he was very proud. Then he went back to his eggplant, baked just the way he liked it.

After her mother's death, Charlotte was for a time haunted by the idea that the flu was a ball that hovered above people's heads; her mother had *caught it,* by accident, by simply raising her arms, and had died. For several years, whenever Charlotte raised her arms above her head, she experienced a physical sensation of falling in space that was profoundly frightening. She had no one to tell, and so she had turned to Mrs. Eddy, who listened carefully and then referred her to God. God could help her, she told Charlotte kindly, ask Him to help you raise your arms without discomfort. Charlotte had, and although it took several years, the problem finally went away, and she was able once again to hang her clothes up in her closet and play volleyball at school without experiencing the mysterious and embarrassing sensation.

It was at about this time that Mrs. Eddy first started sending her faithful Porter to monitor Charlotte's behavior. The Porter was Mrs. Eddy's own creation—presumably, her beloved and trusted creation. Charlotte assumed that he reported to her and that she had been aware of Charlotte's growing disaffection for some time.

Still, Charlotte wasn't prepared that morning for Mrs. Eddy's fury the moment Kitty left.

Charlotte was in the garden helping Paul weed, struggling with a lacy vine that had insinuated itself around the three remaining tomato plants and at the same time trying to fend off Paul's endless questions about Rosey, who was in the house, baking him marmalade muffins. He wanted to know about her likes and dislikes, old boyfriends, habits. He was most interested in a man named Duncan. It sounded like this guy and Rosey had been engaged, he said.

It was a humid, overcast morning and a swarm of no-see-ums were already struggling to breach the edges of the scarf Charlotte had tied around her head, jostling to be the first to gain the warm crease behind her ears. Hoskins was transplanting the earthworms he'd found under the cucumber leaves to the green peppers, which weren't thriving. Baird was expanding his gravel pit.

Mrs. Eddy appeared out of nowhere, driving a horse-drawn carriage. She wore a dark, shiny dress and held a horsewhip. The Porter, stuffed into a burlap sack and set precariously on the seat beside her, was listing badly. In an expert show of horsemanship, Mrs. Eddy drew the carriage neatly up to the garden and pulled the reins back. The horse stopped abruptly, and the Porter fell out. He landed with a thump on the ground and lay there, inanimate and glassy-eyed. Paul looked up briefly, and returned to his weeding.

Mrs. Eddy wrapped the reins around one gloved hand and sat ram-rod straight, staring at Charlotte. A pretty little cameo was pinned to the lacy collar at her throat. "You have become an ugly person. I have rescued countless humans from spiritual oblivion—but you, I have decided to leave mired in confusion."

The horse exhaled noisily and shook himself. Paul continued weed-ing. Hoskins held a long earthworm up to the light, admiring it.

"Think how disappointed your father would be. I can hardly bring myself to speak of how your mother would feel. We might want to start with the word *besmirched*.

"What would they think of the company you keep? Just look at this idiot in the garden. And the other one, the womanizer. I counsel you to examine the meaning of his name: *roux*, 'a mixture of heated fat and flour used as a basis for a sauce.' *Sauce*. You're aware of the popular meaning of that term, I'm sure. If you wish to die in the gutter, however—and penniless, because you will be, you know—that's no concern of mine. Your Mr. Roux is clearly a follower of that despot, Mesmer. God will arrest him one day, liquor bottle in hand, weaving the dark alleys of exploitation and desire—a felon, a common mental murderer. *Whom the gods would destroy, they first make mad*. Yes, mad. You may quote me. It will be a dark death."

Hannibal shambled around the corner of the house, sniffed at a single daisy. He didn't seem particularly interested in the horse, which lifted its tail at that moment and dropped a pile of steaming dung.

"You've made mistake after mistake. You didn't bother to listen for the still, small voice and tried walking out on your husband. *After marriage, it is too late to grumble over incompatibility of disposition*. I told you that very clearly on page fifty-nine—I TOLD YOU SO. I told you to wait for the logic of events and you didn't *listen!* How much plainer could I have been? And look what happened! It's what you get for not *listening to Mother!* I have lost all patience with you! You've wounded your sister to the core. You thought you understood the cause of your mother's death, but you didn't, really, did you? You had a *hunch*—and what is that? Nothing but a nasty little human theory! Well, now you know the truth. Your mother had a choice, and she decided to follow *me*.

"The fact that Hoskins doesn't talk should come as no surprise, given the fact that you have ignored my WORDS. I *almost* feel sorry for you— almost. Oh, what a wasted life! No wonder you don't understand infinity! And you ask yourself why your babe doesn't talk! Why, he's *ashamed* to talk after the things he's seen and heard.

"You are mortal scum! Look what you've done to my poor Porter— he's useless now. Look at him!"

Indeed, the Porter *was* useless, a mere feed sack stuffed with straw. The straw was leaking out the seams; it would be difficult, dragging him away to dispose of him.

"I hope you're content with dwelling in the lower realms of nature, because that's where you'll stay, ruled by your fickle emotions, your petty feelings. Listen to Mother carefully. You can still reverse yourself. I'm giving you one more chance, but you will have to come back on your knees—an attitude less abject I will not accept. And if you don't, you can be sure I will go out of my way to spite you for the rest of my days— WHICH ARE ETERNAL IN NUMBER!"

With that, Mrs. Eddy cracked her whip and the horse tore off. Charlotte watched as the dust the carriage had raised settled back to Earth.

She prodded the feed sack at her feet with a shovel and more straw fell out. "What shall we do with this?" she asked Paul.

He made a face and frowned, considering. "Mulch," he said.

2 3

Beatriz was standing in the middle of the road, looking like a deportee, pocketbook in one hand and paper bag in the other. "I'm not going to be a bother," she told Charlotte, climbing into the backseat. "I'm going to sit back here and do my handiwork. I won't talk; I got to count rows anyway. You can drive, and I'll do my counting. You don't need me talking at you."

When the phone rang, Charlotte was on her way out the door and knew she shouldn't answer. She'd already been delayed by having to go over her list of instructions with Rosey a third time (peanut butter in pantry cupboard; Band-Aids in bathroom; Rita coming to clean at 9:00; Paul coming to clean the barn; call Leona in emergencies), but she had answered anyway, thinking it could be Francis. Paul had told her he was back from New York. It had been three days now, and she hadn't heard from him.

But it was only Beatriz. When she learned Charlotte was on her way to St. Johnsbury, she'd asked if she could get a ride with her. "Government business," she said. "Got to see some of them government people—

if you don't mind." Charlotte knew of no government agencies in St. J. "Of course I don't mind," she said, meaning *Of course I do,* and it was clear to her, when she saw Beatriz standing in the road like that, looking both anxious and determined, that Beatriz had heard the second meaning in her voice.

She felt greatly put out. It was going to be difficult having Beatriz with her. Even with the noise of the tires on the dirt road, she could hear Beatriz's needles clicking in the backseat. She caught a glimpse of lime-green yarn in the rearview mirror, caught Beatriz's eye. Beatriz looked away.

Beatriz had received another postcard from Ben. The postmark on this one was hard to read, she'd told Charlotte, but it just might be Worcester, Massachusetts, and what was that—two hundred miles? Ben had written: "Hauling Pabst Blue Ribbon beer around the city." Beatriz was sure he was coming back, no doubt about it. In fact, her future seemed so bright, she told Charlotte, she'd said yes to a group of church ladies who wanted to help her spruce up her place. They'd descended on her house and removed the torn green window shades, put the bed back in the bedroom, and washed and ironed and cleaned and tidied until it was spic-and-span from top to bottom. They'd even washed the old Plymouth, and cut the grass around the rear tires and pulled up the weeds. Beatriz said she hardly knew where she was, the place was so beautiful. And all thanks to Charlotte and Mrs. Eddy.

But Charlotte had been in no mood to go along with her fantasy. If Ben was coming back, it was his own doing and it had nothing to do with her, or Christian Science, or prayer, or God's will, or any accidental disposition of cosmic forces. Or did it? She had lived her life by interpreting the significance of signs and symbols, finding deeper meaning in every coincidence, just as Rita did with her ludicrous and crippling superstitions, just as Baird had, with his horse chestnut in his pocket, certain that it would guarantee him the role of Santa Claus. And Miss Gallagher had indeed given him the role, so why wouldn't he think that it worked? If you juggled the facts around enough, you could fool yourself into thinking you could control the whole course of your life—or someone else's. It was just too much responsibility, and the idea wore her out.

"Going to be a hot one," said Beatriz.

"Yup," Charlotte answered.

They drove up Route 5, along the river, and they didn't speak again until Barnet.

The streets of St. Johnsbury's modest business section were festooned with blue-and-white flags; banners were draped across storefronts. There were signs at intersections reading ᴅᴇʀʙʏ ʀᴏᴜᴛᴇ and arrows pointing this way and that off the main street.

Charlotte pulled into a parking space in the middle of the block between two cars. Beatriz said nothing. The day had dawned hot, and though it was only midmorning, the sidewalks shimmered in the heat. The leaves on the trees that bordered both sides of the street were motionless. "It's awfully hot back there. Do you want to get out?"

"Heat don't bother me. It's the cold I don't like."

Charlotte got out of the car and stood on the sidewalk, surveying the scene. Cars were parked diagonally along both sides of the street. It was hard on such a hot day to picture the way it had looked when it was snowing, to imagine Melvin stepping out into the street. Was it here that he'd crossed? Along her side of the street there was a maternity shop, sporting-goods store, appliance store, five-and-dime, a haberdashery. Across the street was a bank and a bookstore. A sign in the bookstore window said ᴄʟᴀssɪᴄs! ᴘᴏᴘᴜʟᴀʀ ɴᴏᴠᴇʟs! ʀᴏᴍᴀɴᴄᴇ! Next to it was an old-fashioned drugstore; a cockeyed mannequin made of prosthetic devices beckoned customers inside with his rubber hand.

Melvin might have parked right where she had and then crossed the street to the drugstore, perhaps to buy pipe tobacco or film or to get coffee at the soda fountain. Or he could have gone to the bookstore. He liked to poke around in bookstores, but not in a snowstorm probably. Unless the defroster was acting up again and he'd decided to try and wait out the storm. Or maybe this is what he wanted a picture of: *A Snowy Downtown in Peaceful Vermont*. Or maybe he was looking for a public phone so that he could call her in Syracuse and ask her to reconsider. Or maybe he didn't care what happened anymore and he just walked out in front of a car.

Charlotte leaned into the open window. Beatriz was busily knitting. Mounds of lime-green yarn billowed over her lap. "I'll be back in a few minutes."

"Take your time. Don't worry about me."

There were two ceiling fans fighting against the sluggish air. A marble-topped soda fountain took up most of one wall; the other walls were lined with wood-paneled glass cases displaying medicine bottles and pharmaceutical equipment. Charlotte slid onto a stool at the fountain.

A tidy-looking man wearing a starched white coat came out from the back to see what she wanted. He seemed to be alone in the store. She told him, very gingerly, that she was looking for some information. He asked if it was about a prescription and she said no, it was a question about something historical, something that had happened out on the street in December.

"I wouldn't really call that historical."

It was an odd word for her to use. She felt flushed. She supposed she must look distraught.

"Can I get you something from the fountain, Miss?"

"I'd like a cup of coffee, please."

"We don't serve coffee."

"Never?" she asked, thinking of Melvin sitting on the same stool, warming his hands on a cup.

"We have sodas, ma'am."

"I'll just have water, then."

"Fizzy or plain?"

"Fizzy, please."

He handed her a glass, and she took a long drink. The bubbles traveled up her nose, and she laughed. Behind the impulse to laugh she detected another, more pressing, impulse to sob. "There was an accident here in December. . . ." She waved her hand vaguely toward the street. "I wonder if you saw it."

"Toward the end of the month?"

"Just a few days before Christmas."

"I thought it was after—it was a bad one. They say the man had been all through the war and without a scrape, either. Just missed it," he said. "I ran out of ones and tens and I had to go next door to the bank. When I came out, the ambulance was blazing down the street, sirens blaring. Fellow was from somewhere in Maine. Had a little dog with him, one of those yappers. The dog was still running around looking for its master when the ambulance pulled away. Fellow was laid up at the hospital in Barton for six weeks; broke his back. Don't know what happened to the dog. The other fellow, the one that rammed the man's car, was local—a farmer. I could put you in touch with him if you like." He smiled grimly. "I'll bet he remembers the accident."

"I think we're talking about two different accidents. The one I'm talking about was right before Christmas. It was Tuesday, December sixteenth."

"I don't work Mondays and Tuesdays; that's my weekend. Gil fills in for me those days."

"Oh."

"The man died in that one, they say."

Charlotte was hurrying now to get out of there. She paid for the seltzer and started to leave, then remembered she needed to ask to see a phone book. She found the listing for Earl's Auto Repair. There had been no address on the bill of sale Harry had given her, which had stated only, "Fifty dollars even, as is, where is." She already had the Epplemans' street address. She'd had it for a long time.

Beatriz wasn't in the car. Charlotte poked her head into the appliance store and the haberdashery, where Harry had gone shopping, she believed. Somehow, he'd gotten the impulse to spruce up and buy new clothes on that awful trip. He left his island of safety and took off into the unknown by himself, despite his crippling, terrible fears, and had come back in brand-new chinos. And a haircut, if she remembered correctly.

She finally found Beatriz in the dime store, standing in line at the cash register. She waved a small paper bag at Charlotte. "I got me a nice crochet hook. For the cuffs."

When they were both back in the car, Charlotte asked her what she was making, and Beatriz looked at her blankly. "It's mostly for practice, you know. Nothing special."

Mrs. Eppleman and her son lived in a brick duplex on a quiet street. There were two blue hydrangea bushes placed symmetrically in front of two picture windows, both of which were covered with lace curtains. The grass in front was close-cropped and brown. No one answered at 119 and Charlotte felt relieved. She returned to the car and scribbled a note: "Boyd—I'd like to see you. I live on McCrillis Hill in Beede. Come if you can—I'd rather talk to you in person." Under her name she wrote directions to her house from the village post office.

Charlotte asked Beatriz about her errand, and Beatriz sputtered something about needing a paper she'd forgotten to bring and then trailed off. She wasn't a good liar. "I suppose that was the boy's house we was at."

"Yes."

"Where to now?"

"Earl's Auto Repair."

"That's the man that bought Mr. McGuffey's truck?"

She didn't ask Beatriz how she knew. Everyone knew everything. Except herself, it seemed. "I believe it's on Summer Street," said Beatriz calmly. Charlotte didn't ask her how she knew that, either.

They found the place at the bottom of a steep hill. Charlotte pulled in and threaded through a jumble of cars; most of them looked like they'd been there a long time. There were no pickups.

Earl Johnson came out of the garage wiping his hands on an oily rag. He was a small man with coffee-colored skin and white hair. He seemed pleasant enough but wary of giving out information. He told her he'd sold the truck, just a few days before, in fact. Foreign fellow, wearing some kind of getup.

"Do you know his name?"

Earl shook his head. "Don't know as I remember."

"Was there anything in it?"

"Don't know as I know."

She asked him how much he had sold the truck for, and he looked shocked. It was clearly private information. "Usually I forget those kinds of things soon as they happen."

"What about the contents? There ought to have been a camera, at least, and some other equipment. Do you know what happened to it?"

He seemed embarrassed. "Was mine to keep, I supposed. I bought it free and clear from the man that come by after the accident."

"That was my brother-in-law."

"Well, could be. To tell you the truth, Miss, I didn't scrutinize the interior."

Charlotte had noticed that when people went to any trouble at all to say they were telling you the truth, they were generally lying. "What about when you sold it? You didn't see anything personal in it at all?"

"I had the boys clean it out. That was 'bout noon, day before yesterday."

"Are the boys here?"

"One of 'em's in the derby. The other's at the hospital. His wife's having a baby."

"Did they put things in the trash?"

He scratched the back of his neck, arranged a thoughtful expression on his face. "I don't know as I know what they did with it."

"Mr. Johnson!" she shouted, surprising herself. "Please help me! Can't you just look around and see if there's anything? Please!" He looked alarmed. "I need your help! That was my husband's truck!" Her voice was shaking. "My little boy would like to have his father's camera!"

He took a deep breath. "Oh, boy. All right. I'll be right back."

He disappeared into the gloom of the shop, and she decided that if he didn't come back she was going to storm in and look herself, turn the trash barrels upside down, rummage through all the wrenches. She waited for a long time, assuming that he was trying to figure out what to do and to say, and how not to admit he'd had the camera all along—which she understood was in fact his to keep if he liked. But if it wasn't there at all, he would have sent her away, wouldn't he? A man walked out of the garage and headed slowly toward a battered black car. He started it, and it backfired with an explosion of blue smoke.

Earl Johnson came trundling out with the camera in one hand and a bundle of Melvin's small brown notebooks, bound up with a rubber band, in the other. "There was some more things, a tripod affair, and I don't know what all. I gave it all to one of my boys, and I was pretty sure he took it home. Would this be your husband's?"

Charlotte reached out and hugged him, and he laughed. "Well, that's quite a thank-you, Miss. You staying for the soapbox derby? People come from everywhere to see it. Hundreds expected. Seein' as you're here and all, you may as well stay and enjoy the fun."

There was a crowd of people blocking the end of the street, and Charlotte turned the car around. There was another crowd at the end of a second street, and a man in an orange vest waving his arms at them. People were lined up along the curb, yelling and whistling. The man in the vest came up to the car and leaned toward her open window. The spiral notebooks, bound together in a worn little bundle, were in her lap. The camera lay on the seat beside her. There was film still inside. "We're trying to get back to the highway."

"You'll have to wait, Miss. Derby's started." She found herself looking at the man's prominent Adam's apple. "It won't be long." The Adam's apple went up and down. "Might as well get out and watch the show," he said. "They'll be coming out of Spring Street in a minute."

There was a tight band stretching from behind her eyes around to the back of her head, and she couldn't move her head but an inch or two without a searing pain. She met Beatriz's gaze in the rearview mirror. "You want to get out?"

"No, thank you, hon. I'm fine where I am. We may just as well rest ourselves here and relax. At least we're in the shade." They'd come to a stop under a big elm. The knitting needles began their rhythmic clacking. People surged around the car, parting like water flowing around a rock. Some carried signs: GO BUSTER! BEAT 'EM, BOBBY! JIMMY'S NUMBER ONE!

She looked down at the notebooks in her lap, so tidily bundled. She slid the top one out from under the green rubber band and opened it. His printing was meticulous, the letters uniform, the spaces in between the words even. Everything he did was so considered, careful, measured. She slipped through the pages to the last entry. *December 16—gas at Mabel's, $14.58 cash. Some light snow, low 20s. Used twelve print rolls 12-15-52. Fourteen exposures of church, one with village girl hauling sled, one from the hill through the iced-over trees, fog lifting. New view—could be pleasing composition.* The rest of the pages were blank. That was all. That was it. There was a receipt for gasoline slipped into the back. She took another notebook out from the little bundle. This one was full, even the last page had something written on it—a shopping list. *Newspaper, film, shoelaces.* He didn't have any messages for her. He was going about his business during those five days, not writing letters to her. She flipped through the other notebooks, recognizing places and dates, their predictions about Hallam.

"You all right?" Beatriz asked from the backseat.

She wanted to say *I'm fine,* but when she opened her mouth a funny sound came out, a kind of a groan or a muted yelp, a moan that caught in her throat, and she realized she was crying. She had to get out of there, turn around, find a place where there weren't crowds of people yelling and shouting, but she couldn't get the key in the ignition; she kept missing the little slot with the key, stabbing at it, missing it. Then it was too late, and the lava flow of tears began in earnest, erupting in wave after wave, shaking her whole body, making her throat ache. She struggled for breath, helpless, and crumpled over, finally giving in to the tears and letting them take her where they would. She heard the car door open, heard the whisper and rustle of someone climbing into the front beside her. Beatriz put her arms around her. It was all right to cry, she said over and over, patting Charlotte's back, her head, her arms. It was good; she needed to cry. Beatriz's voice was melodic. The smell of her powder was sweet.

Charlotte cried for a long time, until the crowds had dispersed, and they drove home unimpeded.

CHAPTER

24

It was Leona who organized the
search for Hoskins. The boy's mother was up in St. Johnsbury, she told
her workers one by one as she called. It was Derby Day up there, and for
all she knew the mother was stuck in the crowds that came for the derby.
Or on her way. At any rate, they had to act—the boy had been gone for
several hours at least, maybe more.

Leona divided the Hill into sections and gave each section a team
with a captain: Eugene Wyndam was in charge of Artie Perkins and the
man who delivered bread goods to the store, who had stayed to help.
Barry and Fred Turley were under Waldo Beal's direction. Walter Turley
she put in charge of Bill Furst (who hung the CLOSED sign on the Moose
Garage within seconds of getting her call) and Walter's hired man, Lucky
LaClair. Bob Finale was directing Amos Andoulette and Ed Thrush and
was hampered by both (Amos was too eager; Ed, a know-it-all). Betsy
Smart was on her own. Leona called the Nest and told the two women
staying there to scour the premises and leave no stone unturned. (The one
she talked to thought it was a lark, it seemed, and kept her on the phone

with silly questions.) Stodge she sent to the burnt-out mill yard, where she didn't think he could do much harm. She told Ben Hightower, arrived that day from Worcester, Massachusetts, after eight months' absence, to go home and stay put; she didn't have time to explain what was going on, but she wasn't going to be responsible for his taking off again before Bea had seen his face. Her husband, Johnny, she sent to retrace the route through the woods from Charlotte's to the Nest. "Must be some traveled by now," she told him. "I'm sure you'll find it easy enough." No one quite understood Leona's reasoning in organizing the search parties the way she did, but nobody questioned her, either. Later on, people would marvel that she had been able to get everybody out in the field within just ten minutes of the time Rita had called her to report the boy missing.

Team captains were to report to Nora Thrush on what they found. "Don't try to call me direct," Leona told them. "I don't want to tie up my line. I'm checking with Nora every fifteen minutes."

Areas covered included the right and left forks of the Hill in their entirety; the McCrillis Copper Mine property; the Roons' pond, which Ted Roon started dragging the instant Paul Bellini ran down there shouting with his pants unbuttoned; all wooded areas, all fields, pastures, meadows, streams, all abandoned buildings. "The boy can climb," Leona told the searchers, "and he can jump, and he can hide. But he can't talk. So don't expect him to holler back at you and tell you where he's at."

Rita Andoulette took off for the mines on her own, after putting the call in to Leona. She didn't think anyone else had the nerve to go there. The place was haunted by the ghosts of dead miners and it stunk to high heaven of rotten eggs and the whole place made your skin crawl. But Rita had spent a night there, camped out at the mouth of Shaft Number 1 on a dare from her brother Amos, and she had survived. She'd brought Axel's army-issue sleeping bag that time, and a flashlight and a rabbit's foot and a kitchen knife, and had nestled herself into a rocky overhang in front of the mouth and had waited for the dawn with her eyes wide open, realizing sometime before first light that what she was really afraid of was live men, not dead ones, and that her mother's kitchen knife was no match for any man with the strength to knock her senseless. So this time,

she took Mr. McGuffey's .22 that they kept in the closet, and the ammunition they kept on the shelf at the top of the basement stairs.

Rosey Baird, who had been busy in the hayloft with Paul when Rita
determined that the boy was missing and issued her alert out in the yard,
immediately became hysterical. She ran to the house and applied ice
cubes to her wrists to calm herself down, then called Kitty in Holyoke,
who promised that she would put everything else aside immediately and
work for Hoskins's safe return.

Baird McGuffey had been playing Ships and Rescue with Alphie
Andoulette on the hill behind the house until a disagreement arose
between them and Alphie walked on home without saying good-bye.
Baird remembered his little brother then, and went to look for him; when
he couldn't find him in the house, he ran down to the field and looked in
all the holes, though they were hardly deep enough to hide a boy. Hannibal followed Baird down to the field, staying for a while before drifting
off on his own business. When Baird finally realized that Hoskins was
really gone, he ran back to the house and called upstairs to Rita, who was
supposed to be vacuuming, but who in fact was modeling Charlotte
McGuffey's nightgown in the full-length bedroom mirror and had to
stop and change her clothes before joining Baird downstairs, thus wast-
ing precious minutes before the search could begin.

Ted Roon had always wanted to drag the pond, and it took only a few
crackling shouts from Paul for him to get out his dinghy and badminton
net, to which he tied his wife's and son's tennis shoes and a few pots and
pans for weight, and set sail while his wife watched, unsmiling, from the
little dock they'd built the first year they bought the place.

Eugene, Artie, and the bread man took nearly an hour to cover the
two miles of road from the photographers' turnout up to the fork.
Hallam, possessed by a sudden fit of garrulousness, had wanted to talk.
"Lot of traffic," he said several times, "lot of dust." It reminded him of
the war. He'd seen Betsy Smart go barreling up the hill in her Jeep, and
he wondered what she thought she was doing, driving like that. Eugene
told him Betsy and her Jeep had been assigned to the logging roads that
crisscrossed the Hill. "She keeps up that kind of speed," said Hallam,
"and she just may find the boy under her tires."

Waldo and the Turley boys were in charge of the right fork from the turn to just short of the mines, which Leona had assigned to Walter's team. Barry and Fred Turley were real acrobats and jokesters, and Waldo, who was naturally dour, had a hard time keeping them in line and on task; fortunately their area was not too demanding. The Nest itself and its premises was being searched by the gypsy girls from the city, according to what Leona had told Waldo, and Waldo told the boys just to walk on by the place and don't get involved—one of the girls was waving at them from the top of Roux's stairs up on the hill and wearing what looked like a harem outfit or something made entirely of see-through scarves, as Waldo told Minna later. "Whatever kind of outfit it was, it looked foreign," he said. "The boys was real interested in meeting those girls," he told her, "and I kept them marching at a brisk pace."

Bob Finale, Amos, and Ed Thrush scoured the left fork, with Amos clambering up and down trees every few hundred yards to take a look around. Bob told him not to waste his energy like that; he wasn't accomplishing anything. Did he expect to see the lost boy in another treetop? They'd almost reached Beatriz's place when Ed determined he heard the lost child groaning in a wooded area off to the side of the road. They ploughed through the underbrush, ducking limbs, and found Betty, Beatriz's ewe, spread out like a limp skirt with her chin resting flat to the ground and barely breathing. Ed said she must've eaten a poisonous mushroom, maybe *omphalotus olearius,* common name of jack-o'-lantern, due to the way it glowed in the dark. "That so," said Bob.

Ed went off to look for the source of the poison, and Amos asked Bob how Mr. Thrush could tell, just from looking at her lying on the ground like that, that she'd eaten a poisonous mushroom, and Bob said, "He can't. Why would a sheep want to eat a mushroom, especially one that glows? Let's get her up and see if she'll stand." They hauled her up on her feet, and she stood for a shaky moment before collapsing again. "They say you can't save a sick sheep," said Bob. "She's always done pretty good on her own—she might want to go out that way, too."

They walked away and left her there, but Amos was unhappy; he was sure the ewe was suffering, the way she was grinding her teeth, and was further burdened by images of coydogs tearing at her exhausted flesh. Ed rejoined them a little way up the road, holding a giant puffball. "Look at this," he said, "Latin name is *Lycoperdon*. 'Wolf fart' is what it means!"

Passing Beatriz's place, they noted a battered blue Chevy parked in the dooryard. They speculated some, and then passed on.

The three of them stopped to help with the pond-dragging at the Roons', which looked pretty fruitless to Amos, as the net was too small and the pond too wide and no one knew what they were doing, and he slipped away unnoticed and returned to the place where they'd left Betty, determined at least to stave off the coydogs until she died. She was still breathing, but there was something about the way she kept grinding her teeth that seemed suspicious. He pried open her jaws and discovered a wad of gum stuck between her tongue and her back teeth. He had to fight with her, but he got it out, and she staggered off down the hill toward one of the many streams that fed the river.

Up at the mines, Rita was walking through the woods near Shaft Number 1, carrying the .22 loosely in her right hand, the way Amos did, stopping every few minutes and listening hard for any unusual sounds, maybe a whispered "amen" from behind some bush, or some other noise that might tell her Hoskins was hiding nearby. It was like when Amos was learning to hunt, and she'd played the stalking game with him and all the little sounds in the woods were sharpened by her fear. First she was the deer, listening. She couldn't move, it was against the rules; she had to wait, listening, while Amos crept up on her trying not to make a sound, learning to be a silent hunter.

When she heard the voices, she froze. Silence, then a twig snapped. Footsteps. She aimed, bracing the rifle butt against her shoulder as Lucky LaClair and Bill Furst stepped into the clearing. Afterward, Lucky denied dropping to the ground with his face in the dirt. Bill Furst yelled, "Hey! Put that thing down!" and she lowered the rifle from her shoulder and stared at him, openmouthed, and turned around and ran. All the way back, she cursed herself for her foolishness. She'd lost her head, got caught up in the fright she always felt when she was the deer. She'd had a crush on Lucky ever since she helped with the milking at Turley's. He'd always ignored her before; now he would snicker. But she had something on him—he'd shown his fear. It was Bill that had acted to save them all.

At 2:00 in the afternoon, Ben Hightower put in a call to Leona and said, "There's a boy here complaining of varicose veins. You know anything about it?" He'd found the child locked in Beatriz's Plymouth out in the shed, he told her. "He must've climbed in and locked the doors on himself. The windows was all closed, and it was damned hot." The boy was nearly unconscious when he found him.

Ben said later that what alerted him first was a slow-moving white dog with a long feathered tail sniffing around the yard. The dog moseyed around, taking his time, checking out the clumps of daylilies, the stack of tires, and the empty cardboard box that had contained the large console TV he'd bought for Beatriz. Ben watched from the window as the dog ambled over to the Plymouth, circled, and began barking furiously. Ben went to see what it was all about and found the boy inside, prostrate. The boy had locked the door from the inside and Ben had had to break a side window to get in. He opened the door and Hoskins tumbled out, flushed and overheated. Ben carried him into the house and doused him with cold water, then called Leona. The boy came to as Ben was dialing and mumbled something about varicose veins.

"Wrap him in cold towels, and get him over to the clinic fast as you can," Leona said. "I'll let Dr. Z. know you're on your way. She's at home, I know that, working in her garden next door to the clinic. I'll see she meets you there."

Entering the village several hours later, Beatriz and Charlotte both sensed something was very wrong. There were more than the usual number of people walking in twos and threes along the sides of the road, as if a big event had just broken up, and there were clusters of people gathered in front of the store and in the Wyndams' yard and in front of Leona's, where Charlotte pulled up. She had not even turned off the ignition when Leona rushed out and told her to get to the clinic as fast as she could. She shouted out the news to Beatriz: Ben's back! He's up at the house! But Beatriz wouldn't even take the time to get out of the car. "Just go," she told Charlotte. "Drive like the devil; I'll hang on."

"Heatstroke," Elizabeth Zetterling said. Hoskins was swiveling around in her office chair, looking a bit dazed but otherwise fine. He was playing with a little skeleton man, bending his dangling limbs this way and that and making him dance. "When they come out of it like this, it's as if nothing happened. No brain damage, no reversals." She held out a hand, and Charlotte felt the many well-defined bones in it. She was a tall, handsome woman with a long face and yellow hair done up in a French braid. She was a collector of antique cars, and Charlotte had seen her driving in Beede's Independence Day parade, scarf flying, wearing some elegant outfit and waving like the Queen Mother at barefoot children. Today she was wearing soiled pedal pushers. "Aren't we lucky, though. His temperature was a hundred and five, just shy of scary. Whoever found him had the good sense to try and bring it down by dousing him with cold water."

Before she left that day, Charlotte told her that she'd like to come back; she had some questions she wanted to ask about Hoskins.

"You mean, about his language deficiency?"

"Yes,"

"It's very interesting. He obviously understands a great deal."

"But he doesn't talk," Charlotte said.

"Oh, he talks, all right. He asked me for a banana."

Charlotte stared at her. "What do you mean?"

"He said 'banana.'"

"You consider that talking?"

"Certainly—it's a kind of shorthand, but effective. And isn't that the point, getting your meaning across? Why waste words? I didn't have any bananas and I told him so, and he said, 'Dammit.'" Elizabeth Zetterling laughed. She shook Charlotte's hand again. "Come back next week, and we'll talk. This is a very interesting little boy."

CHAPTER

25

Baird sat politely in one of the waiting-room chairs, watching a little girl with a runny nose drag a quacking pull toy around the room. Her young mother looked up from time to time, then went back to her movie magazine. Hoskins put the fourteenth wooden block on the tower he was building, taking great care to align it precisely with the one below. The tower wavered, paused, wavered, and settled. The little girl came up behind him and pushed it over with her foot. Hoskins shouted, "Dammit!" and Charlotte leapt up. The little girl ran to her mother and put her head on her lap.

"Sorry," Charlotte told the mother cheerfully, "he's just learned a new word." The mother did not return Charlotte's smile.

They'd been at Dr. Zetterling's clinic for almost an hour—the shabby little waiting room was full of sick people. A man with a dry cough sat with his eyes closed, wavering just a little, like Hoskins's tower; an overweight boy gazed out at nothing, making a small whistling sound as he breathed; a woman with painfully swollen knuckles was reading a tattered *National Geographic* with a shipwreck on the cover.

Charlotte hardly recognized herself in that setting. She might as well be visiting the moon. Still, no thunderbolt had greeted her when she walked into the clinic; no one had asked her to explain herself or expressed even the slightest interest in her presence there. When she'd raced to the clinic with Beatriz the week before, she wasn't thinking about the kind of help she was seeking; she was thinking only of Hoskins, and praying fervently that he was all right. Dr. Zetterling could have been a witch doctor for all she cared. But it had felt very different today as she prepared to leave the house and come here to sit among a roomful of people who turned so naturally to the medical world, instead of to God, for help.

She leaned against the back of the chair, where she had draped her new, neon-green sweater, which Beatriz had presented to her the evening she and Ben had walked up to the house to say good-bye to Rosey. Rosey had gone down to their house to thank Ben personally for saving Hoskins and had stayed to watch *The Ed Sullivan Show* on Beatriz's new TV, and they had gotten to know one another. Seeing Beatriz holding the sweater out to her, Charlotte knew immediately that Beatriz had meant it for her all along. It was very large, and very green, and Charlotte treasured it— just like Hoskins treasured his stones. He'd told her that. It had taken her a long time to understand what he was saying, but when she finally did, she'd been so happy. It wasn't an announcement, it was a real communication; he'd wanted to share his feelings with her, just like any other child.

Baird sidled up to her. How much longer would they have to wait? Charlotte said she didn't know but she hoped it wasn't too much longer. Hoskins was beginning to organize the magazines on the table—he might start yanking them from people's laps at any moment. Baird was anxious to get home, she knew, because Francis had promised to take him to the fairgrounds for his first driving lesson.

When she saw Francis driving Melvin's truck up to the house, she'd understood immediately whom Earl had meant by "the foreign fellow"—*her* foreign fellow, of course, in the *getup*. Baird raced down the driveway shouting for joy; she and Hoskins followed at a run. He opened the door, and she climbed up into the cab into his lap and kissed him.

"Does this mean you're not mad anymore?" he'd asked. "Do I have the body language right?"

"I was sure I'd never see you again!"

"What a crazy kid your mother is," he told Baird, who was climbing in from the other side, followed by Hoskins. "I guess she doesn't appreciate all the secrecy involved in pulling off this kind of caper." Trying his best to look very serious, Baird had said yes, he'd noticed—she was a funny one. Then he reached over and honked the horn again and again, making it ring out from hill to hill.

She asked Francis what on Earth he'd been wearing when he went to Earl's garage, and he said nothing special, just a caftan. Anne-Marie's friend had brought it back from Saudi Arabia.

"You can't buy a truck in St. Johnsbury dressed in a caftan!"

"You're right—well, you can, but it costs extra. He must have thought I was a sultan." He wouldn't tell her what he finally paid for it, but he called it "Thexton's money." The truck was Baird's now. He hadn't called her when he got back from New York because he was after a complete fait accompli, and that was one heck of a completed project. "They wouldn't let me register it in his name over in Montpelier—said he was too young. Can you imagine?"

"Mrs. McGuffey?" the nurse asked. "You can go in now."

"Finally!" said Baird.

Dr. Zetterling wore a capacious flowery sundress. Her crowded desk was littered with papers, and Charlotte liked her very much. The doctor whisked Hoskins up onto the examination table, handed him "Mr. Skeleton," and gave him a thorough going-over, talking to Baird throughout and keeping up a running explanation of what she was doing and what she was looking for. Baird nodded, attentive and serious as a young medical student. Charlotte looked at all the jars and bottles and containers in the glass cupboards, the green autoclave machine, the stacks of towels and scissors and gauze pads, and could hardly believe where she was.

"Who knows?" Elizabeth Zetterling exclaimed heartily after taking down his history, sitting knee to knee with Charlotte. "It could be so many things! He certainly is a healthy child—that we know, in tip-top shape. You must be doing something right!"

Hoskins was occupied with the stethoscope the doctor had handed him. He put the ends in his ears and clamped the cup on the wrong side of his chest, then raised his eyes to the ceiling, listening intently in that posture Charlotte knew so well. Dr. Zetterling leaned over and read-justed the instrument for him, then offered her reflex hammer to Baird. She patted the examination table and told him to hop up—he wouldn't get a nice knee jerk unless he could swing his legs.

"It could be so many things," she continued. "I could make appointments for you for pediatric testing and evaluation at Mary Hitchcock in Hanover, or Mary Fletcher in Burlington, but the testing may be a bit arduous for our young man, and even those folks won't necessarily have an answer. The brain functions in complex ways. Aphasia is one response to a variety of pathologies. Your son exhibits a wide, and I have to say somewhat bewildering, but fascinating, range of symptoms associated with both mental retardation and neurophysiological disorders. On the other hand, he's a very pleasant, obviously very bright little chap."

Baird bonked himself on the knee, but his leg didn't move.

"Rap it smartly," said the doctor. Baird winced and tried again, looking triumphant as his leg jerked forward half an inch.

Dr. Zetterling continued. "An American psychiatrist, Leo Kanner, published a paper in 1943, describing a cluster of behavioral characteristics that has come to be known as Kanner's syndrome, also sometimes known as autism, particularly in Europe nowadays. This young man exhibits many of the characteristics: loves routine, loves order, loves to go his own way, doesn't seem to need affection as much as other children—or at least, doesn't show it. Kanner describes the same pensive look we see here, as well as the advanced coordination and fine-motor control. Although I also note something that is rarely associated with this syndrome—he seems to have a sense of humor. There's something about his look that makes me think he's laughing."

"He doesn't laugh much—occasionally, and then we all rejoice."

"It's an internal sensibility I'm talking about. There's a lot going on internally. I would imagine, if he could tell us, that our lad here knows a number of things unusual for a child his age—he might, for instance, be able to recite the alphabet backward or to skip-count by threes, or he might have memorized everyone's phone numbers, things like that."

"I think he can read," said Charlotte. "I think he reads the dictionary."

"It's certainly possible."

"He loves to be sung to and read to. And he likes to repeat phrases from books. He particularly loves Mike Mulligan and his steam shovel."

"'She could dig as much in a day as a hundred men could dig in a week,'" recited Baird. "'At least he thought she could, but he wasn't quite sure.' That's the part he likes best."

Dr. Zetterling laughed appreciatively. "Ah, don't we all love Mike! It sounds like you're doing all the right things," she told Charlotte, "reading, talking, singing, telling stories, working with your little cards, et cetera, et cetera. You seem to be doing a marvelous job." She scooted back on her rolling chair. "So, to recapitulate: We could have him tested, if you want to go that route, and if we find that he's a candidate for intensive treatment, you could put him in a residential treatment center. You could get the experts at the language center in Boston to train you to do what they do, but I have to warn you that there's a popular theory about 'refrigerator mothers' you might not like. You might not like what they say about you."

"What do they say?"

"They say these children have not developed emotionally because their mothers are cold and unloving. But I think we can discount that theory in your case. It doesn't take me long to size up a mother-child relationship. And look at Baird here—right on track. And what is your chosen occupation for the future, young man? Have you decided yet? Will it be medical school for you? You can get knee-bonkers there, you know."

"I'm going to be a photographer. Like my dad. I have his camera, and I'm going to start using it when I'm twelve."

"Very good!" Dr. Zetterling turned back to Charlotte. "I doubt we would see that kind of personality if you were a refrigerator."

Baird looked worried, and Charlotte said, "She's praising you, Baird. She likes what you told her."

"Or, you could just keep on doing what you're doing and just see what happens. How are we to know about these things? He can't tell us, can he? And he's learning new words all the time, trying out some things. If I were you, I'd wait. He'll be four . . . when?"

"Next month."

"All right. Maybe he'll start babbling like a brook when he sees the cake." Then Elizabeth Zetterling added, "Or you might even try Christian Science. I've heard it does wonders in cases like this."

Francis was at the house when she returned, poring over topographical maps of McCrillis Hill. The configurational sculpture he was planning for her field was like no other he'd done previously and required precise preparations, an approach he was rather enjoying the novelty of, he'd explained. It was a series of cairns, in effect, which he would install at precise locations dictated by astronomical data and solar sight lines; when experiencing the piece, subtle shifts in the grade of the slope and the length of the paths that would connect the cairns would become known to the experiencer. The piece would become a place for running, walking, viewing, crossing, waiting, praying, thinking, talking, and other, more clandestine and exciting behaviors, should the experiencer choose to engage in them during lupine season and in particular when the moon was not yet full. Hoskins's stones, of course, had been a primary inspiration, along with the whole of his own life, of course, and hers, and the light that had dawned when he'd realized how intrusive, how fabricated, how *engineered* his stairs had always been. Analogies, they were. *Like* something! Why would he want to make something that was *like* something? What was wrong with the earth the way it was, only rearranged a little maybe, for clarity? Even God felt free to rearrange—think of erosion and its fabulous power to redesign! The experiential installation— which he would call, simply, *Cairns II*—would be similar to, and function as a model for, the one he was proposing for the Enigmatic Monument Exhibit honoring Brancusi in Budapest the following summer.

She'd asked him, of course, Why *Cairns II?* and he'd shrugged. "Sounds better. Does there always have to be a *I?* Why not jump in running?"

He'd claimed of late that he was busier and happier than he'd been all his life. The fact that he still had to finish the fabrication for Thexton's stupid stairs didn't even bother him. He might even throw in a few bells, what the heck. But no whistles, no alarms, no harnesses. No railings. He was going stark on this one.

He put the maps aside and asked for a report on her meeting with Elizabeth Zetterling. "First of all, Charley, tell me, did you like her?"

"Yes, I liked her."

"She's smart. I knew she could help—did she help?"

"I suppose, but I'm not sure. Everything is a maybe. There's a syndrome with a name, or a couple of names; it sounds like the experts don't know too much about it. He might or might not have it. She thought I should wait a while—he might start talking on his own."

"What do you think?"

"I think she doesn't know. She's feeling her way, partly from information, partly from intuition. Maybe no one knows. It sounds as if, even if he were tested, we still might not know anything, except whether he's retarded—but we have the answer to that already."

"He's a genius, if anything."

She smiled. His championship of Hoskins was always so touching. "In the meantime, I thought I'd start reading."

Francis looked over the titles of the books and pamphlets she'd brought home from the library in West Beede, where she'd stopped with the boys after leaving the clinic: *Your Child's Development Year by Year from One to Five; What to Expect from Your Child as He Grows; The Preschool Years: What You Can Do to Prepare Your Child at Home;* and *What to Do if Your Child Has a Speech Problem.* Francis picked up the latter and started reading aloud: "'Give the child frequent evidence of your affection. The child who simply won't talk may have irrational fears; he needs the feeling of security that can come only from the knowledge that he is loved and wanted. Spend time with your child. If the problem is a cleft palate, even more reason for you to put down that party list and invite him into your lap. Or, your child may be retarded. Or he may be perfectly normal in all respects except in his willingness to talk. In any case, try to eliminate tensions in the home. Avoid fussing over his defect. Never send him to bed in a state of high excitement. Encourage your child to do his best all day long.'" He closed the book. "You think this sort of thing is going to help?" he asked skeptically.

"There might be a nugget or two."

"Somehow the term *speech defect* doesn't seem very useful in his case. You may need better books."

"It's a nice little library. The librarian asked me if I wanted to join a discussion group for preschool mothers. It meets on Wednesdays starting sometime in September."

He leaned forward. "And you said yes?"

"I said I didn't know if I would be staying."

"How can I go to Toronto to install Thexton's piece and not know? It will be torture. What if I come back and this house is empty?"

He was looking very anxious. She didn't think she'd actually ever made him anxious before, and it was undeniably pleasant. "I'll decide before you go, I promise. I won't let you leave without knowing."

He leapt up. "You have a cruel streak, Charley! You know, but you're not telling! What about those church people in Syracuse? Don't they need to know?"

"They said it would be easy to find other arrangements."

"Just think how lonely I'd be."

"You?" Anne-Marie's sylphlike friend in the see-through sari, subject of ongoing and widespread speculation throughout the area, was coming back to stay at the Nest in the fall, "to pull herself together," as she put it, after a devastating review of her New York dance performance. And Liz was coming for the foliage—though Charlotte's visions of Liz and her saucy underwear no longer kept her awake at night. She had asked him, finally, what Liz looked like, and he'd told her: sixties, thickset, chopped hair, terrifying handshake, dreadful shoes, mind like a steel trap. Then there was his sister, whom she'd never met, either, who was threatening to come for what she was calling a protracted holiday. . . .

"I see you have packing boxes in the back room."

"Yes." She'd been picking up boxes to mail things back to Syracuse if she needed to.

"I also see that they're empty. You must be teetering. What can I say to persuade you?"

"If I stay, it will be for a lot of reasons."

"Of course." He was trying hard to look neutral, reasonable, accommodating. "Not just because of me, I realize that. After all, I have commitments; I travel, I'm not always here. The Nest is too full; my life is a mess."

"Right."

"I understand your hesitation."

"There are a lot of things for me to consider."

"Absolutely. There's something else, too, though, and as your friend, I need to point it out. Just so you have a full picture."

"What's that?"

"I'll miss you, Charley, if you go."

She stared at him in silence, wanting to hurl herself at him. Instead, she very carefully explained that she'd make up her mind by the time she returned from Holyoke the next evening. She was leaving early in the morning and would be gone for only one day. Charlotte had written Kitty a long letter, but the only communication she'd received in reply was one short sentence on flowery notepaper—"I'm putting our conversation at the lake behind me, and I hope you will, too. All my love, K." Then Harry had called. Kitty didn't look well, and he was scared. She could hardly walk. She hadn't even been to school to start getting her classroom ready.

"I promise," she told Francis. "I need to think."

"All right, fair enough. It's a big decision."

"A lot could go wrong."

He nodded, looking very serious. "And while you're thinking, I'll be stacking. I've ordered ten cords. Lucky's delivering them this afternoon."

"Ten cords!"

"You don't want to run out of wood when the snow's still flying, do you?"

"Ten cords for the cookstove?"

Francis laughed at the folly of it. "That thing wouldn't heat the place. You need a woodstove in the basement. I've ordered a nice hefty one for you. With enough wood, and the vigilance required to keep on feeding it, it should heat the whole house."

"But what if I don't stay?"

"I believe I have the stamina necessary to return it, if need be." He paused. "I'm counting on you, Charley, you know that. But I'm not all that worried. I'm pretty sure that when you stop thinking, you'll know what you want."

"I already know what I want."

"And?"

"I want to do the right thing."

"Damn! You'll never figure that out, not with your head!"

CHAPTER

26

Charlotte made good time on the highway once she got over the border into Massachusetts. The closer she got to Holyoke, the more anxious she felt; she was rushing pell-mell to the battle at Jericho without the band of angels, without any clear directions, without help from the courageous harlot Rehab, who had hidden Joshua in the stalks of flax. There would be no trumpeting, no shouting, no ram horns to make the thick walls fall down. But she would flail at them anyway, with all her might.

She had only her will, her heart, and the little drawing Francis had made for her the night before of a naked little person with a quizzical expression, wearing socks and shoes. Arrows pointed to his pancreas and liver, the damaged nerves radiating down to his extremities, the sugar molecules trying in vain to penetrate the cells without the help of the hero Insulin, who stood off to one side, wearing a damaged crown. "When able to do its amazing work," he reminded her, "the hero flows through the bloodstream unlocking microscopic doors and allowing sugar to enter the cells. When the level of sugar in the blood is high, the liver stores the excess in case it's needed later. When it's low, the liver converts the stored sugar into glucose and releases it into the bloodstream to keep the blood sugar at exactly the right level. It's always working night and day on your behalf; even when you ignore it, denigrate it, laugh at it, even when you deny its existence, it still chugs away. It's a miracle of the first order—and surely, if anything is, this is God's work. Tell her that, Charley. It just might do the trick."

Francis was in charge of the boys for the day—he would not let Hoskins out of his sight, he promised, and he would not let him climb on the mountain of wood. The ten cords of maple had been delivered—five truckloads in all—and Hoskins had tried to take possession of the mountain immediately, though he'd mystified them by yelling "Pine!" When they finally realized he was saying "Mine!" Francis was very excited. Hoskins wasn't talking about red lights, he pointed out. He was using a word the same way other people did. Amos and Axel were coming to help stack—Francis couldn't both stack and watch, he had decided. He was sorely shorthanded, now that Paul was out of the picture. He'd gone to Kingston to see Rosey. He'd told her he wanted to take her out West to see Yellowstone. "It's always somebody else who does something romantic and never me," Rosey told Charlotte. "Oh, his eyes are so dark and soft," she added, and Charlotte reminded her of what Leona had said about walking on all fours. But Rosey was sure he'd never go back to drinking, now that she'd succeeded in building up his confidence.

At the Clatters' house, Roberta opened the door wearing a hideous orange-flowered sunsuit; the wide shorts stopped just above her pudgy knees and foreshortened her torso, making her look like an overgrown kindergartner. "It's my friend Elaine's," she said, pulling at the crotch. "She's a lot smaller than me. Dad told me to wear something cheerful, and I didn't have anything of my own." Harry had taken Norman to the store, she said. "As if my brother needs one more baseball card. Whereas I need clothes for school. Dad says he'll take me shopping, but can you imagine, going shopping with my father? I'd die of embarrassment!"

Charlotte followed Roberta into the kitchen. She smelled sulfur and saw the pile of burnt matches in a dainty teacup saucer. Roberta lit another and held it up. "Did you know that they all burn for exactly the same amount of time?" She blew it out and added it to the others in the saucer. When she looked at Charlotte, her face had crumbled. "Dad says Mother has to see a doctor, but she won't. Some friends of hers from church were here. One of them told me that the work she has to do now is best done alone and I should try to give her as much privacy as possible. Some nerve."

"Some nerve indeed," Charlotte said.

Roberta composed herself and lit another match. She watched the flame intently. "Maybe I'll make my daughter diabetic."

"You can't make anyone . . ."

"The daughter in my novel. Beata. She has a dog that she loves, little Tipsy, but she can't reach him to scratch his ear because she's stuck in an iron lung. She has polio. Maybe she could have diabetes, too, or do you think that would be too much?"

Charlotte watched Roberta add the smoking match to the others. "Beata's parents must be very sad."

"They're not that sad because it's an awful lot of trouble to take care of her in the iron lung. She has to be fed through a straw and everything."

"Your mother loves you, Roberta."

"I doubt it. Otherwise, why would she want to die? She'd want to stick around and see how I turned out. My character is still being formed even though I'm already fifteen. Norman, though, we know how he's going to turn out. He's going to be a baseball nut all his life and bore everybody to death."

"Your mother's not going to die. Not if she gets help."

"Am I going to get it, too?"

"You could. But I can teach you the signs, and then you can take care of yourself—you're smart and you can do it. It's not such an awful thing, either. My friend Francis is a diabetic."

"He is?"

Charlotte pulled out his funny diagram from the pocket of her skirt. Roberta looked at it and laughed. "I could explain it all to you. Some other time. How is your father doing?"

"He got the job, I guess you know that. He goes *out* to work. I think he hates it, though. He says the system is stacked against the average Joe. He's turning into a revolutionary. Pretty cool, huh?"

"Selling life insurance might not be perfect for him."

"He says he'd rather be selling soap—at least he believes in it."

"Well, are we ready?"

"Yeah, I guess."

Charlotte draped her sweater over the banister as Roberta led her up the stairs. "Mother won't like it that you're here."

"I know."

"She'll be mad."

"That's all right." They stood outside the door. Charlotte hesitated. "Do you think you should prepare her?"

"Prepare her?"

"Tell her I'm here . . . or do you think I should just go in?"

But it was Charlotte who wasn't prepared. She was struck immediately by how frail Kitty looked in her pink armchair, which was facing the window. Her head was tilted against the back at an odd, uncomfortable angle. A thin stream of sunlight crossed the lacy wool blanket covering one of her legs, which was propped up on a stool. The table next to her held her books and papers, pencils and markers, a telephone, an empty glass. On the floor was a pitcher of water. It was a sad, desolate scene and it made Charlotte's heart ache.

Charlotte looked back at Roberta in her orange sunsuit, a bright flower blossoming out of season, and proceeded forward into the room, saying her sister's name.

"What a surprise!" Kitty exclaimed when she saw Charlotte, and quickly straightened herself, repositioning her blanket. She looked drawn and sallow. "I decided to rest today—it's only temporary, don't worry—but I don't like you seeing me like this. I wish you'd called. I would have been sure to be up and around."

"Harry asked me to come."

"I told him not to bother you. Now you've come all this way—"

"It wasn't far." It seemed very quiet in the house. Roberta had either gone downstairs or was standing in the hallway, listening.

"Where are the boys?"

"With Francis. At home." *At home,* she'd said, to hear how it sounded out loud. She'd tried it out in her mind as she drove. Francis had said she'd never be able to figure it out in her head, and she'd tried not to think, just to listen. *On the way back, I'll be going home. When the leaves turn, I'll be at home.*

"Well, it's lovely to see you, dear. You must be getting ready to go back to Syracuse by now. Labor Day is right around the corner."

"We're not going back—well, we'll have to go in order to get our mittens and boots, of course, all our winter things. Baird will be very excited. He doesn't know yet."

Kitty smiled. "I'm sure you know what you're doing. And it will be nice having you closer. You can come again, when I'm better. We'll spend time together. We'll mend our fences."

Charlotte felt a rush of her old affection. How could she have thought of coming here to make trouble for her sister, whom she had always loved so much? The words that had seemed impossible just a moment before came out easily. "I want you to see a doctor."

She held up a hand. "Please, Charlotte. I hope you haven't come to lecture me."

"Well, I have. I've come to plead with you, actually. You could feel better so easily, if you would just get medical help. Mrs. Eddy did, when she needed to."

Kitty withdrew visibly. "Oh, some people say that, but it's not true."

"I can explain exactly what diabetes is and how it works, and why that place on your foot doesn't heal . . . and why you're so thirsty all the time. . . ." Charlotte had left Francis's funny diagram downstairs in the kitchen, but clearly it didn't matter. The idea that Kitty would ever give a sugar molecule even a passing glance, much less believe in its existence, was ludicrous. "It doesn't have to be like this, Kitty. There are reasons why you feel the way you do, and there's something you can do about it. Believe me, it's true."

"Question," said Kitty, suddenly adopting a teacherly air. "Does the brain think? Do nerves feel? Is there intelligence in matter? The answer is decidedly no. God is Truth and mortal man a liar. *God is All and there is none beside Him,* says Mrs. Eddy. So you don't need to explain anything. You don't need to offer me any reasons. And you don't need to tell me what to do. How are the children? Did Hoskins recover from his little adventure? Rosey told me about it."

"I wouldn't know—how can I know? He doesn't tell me anything. Maybe he will someday, after I learn how to ask the right questions. Or he might just start talking."

"All you have to do is ask God to guide you."

Things were slowly turning back around to the way they always were. "I know what you're going to say—that he's already perfect. Please don't."

"All right, then, I won't," Kitty said brightly. "May I ask about Rosey and her beau? She seems to be having a fine time, as unlikely a romance as it is."

"But I want to talk about you, Kitty."

"Well, I'm not interested in talking about me!"

"Let's talk about Harry, then. What would he do without you?"

"Nothing is going to happen to me."

"Not right away, no. But eventually—the same thing that happened to Mama. Any kind of infection—"

"—*like a watchman forsaking his post,*" Kitty interrupted, "*we admit the intruding belief, forgetting that through divine help we can forbid this entrance.* You have forsaken your post. You are letting these ideas direct you."

"I don't want you to die, too!" Charlotte was shocked to hear herself say it. It sounded rude in this room. She hadn't meant to shout. She didn't want to be shouting; she wanted to be calm, persuasive, rational. Convincing.

Kitty was quiet for a while. She closed her eyes, opened them. "Charlotte, isn't my life my own?"

"Only partly."

When she spoke again, Kitty's voice was brisk and efficient. "I am perfectly clear about what my choices are. And you're being overly dramatic. I'm a little under the weather right now, but that's all."

From the way Kitty's back was arched, Charlotte knew it was point-less, but still she paraded out the arguments she'd come prepared with. "What happened to Mama will happen to you. It's not something vague, like a headache or a pinched nerve, that you can overcome—it's like a broken bone! Remember when Norman broke his arm, and you took him to a surgeon to set it? You said it was beyond you—"

Kitty was shaking her head sadly. "You're not a Scientist anymore, I can see that. Otherwise, you would understand that I have all the help I need."

"I guess I'm not, then. Not if it means watching you die. Not if it means I had to lose my mother. Maybe it wasn't so hard for you—I've come to believe you were truly convinced it was the loving thing to do, to let her go. But I didn't want her to go; I wanted her to stay and talk to me. What will happen to your children? They won't have a mother, that's what will happen, and I know what it's like. Roberta wants you to see how she turns out! It's not so much for a daughter to ask. I can't believe God would want you to die for the sake of a principle."

"You're refusing to understand."

"Please let me call a doctor, Kitty. I beg you."

"You know what I'd like you to do for me instead?" She said it so sweetly, for a moment Charlotte almost thought she was going to ask for some little treat, a nice glass of water, a dollop of cream. "I'd like you to think about the wholeness and health and happiness of Man as the per-fect image and likeness of God. Of the great love that God has for us, made in His image. Of Divine Mind, in whom I am putting all my trust."

Charlotte conceded her defeat and gave way to her tears. "But doesn't it hurt? You look like you're in so much pain."

"Not at all. I am perfectly comfortable." Kitty turned her head away. She was crying, too. "Now I have a question for you," she said, not look-ing at Charlotte. "Will you always know that I love you?"

And so Charlotte was dismissed.

CHAPTER

27

It was the last Sunday in August, an unusually hot day for that time of year, when Boyd Eppleman and his mother arrived. Baird and Hoskins were playing under the sprinkler in their underpants. Charlotte was inside making lists. They would be bringing back all their winter clothes, every mitten and boot, so she would have to mail some things back to Vermont. Plus she needed her books and Baird's trucks and all their blankets. Bunny Berry had been delighted to get her news. Though she could have moved the Laplanders into a different rental, she confessed it would be easier to leave them there until the family from Mozambique arrived later in September. For a nomadic people, the Lapps didn't seem to like change very much.

Baird ran inside to get dressed, and Charlotte went out to greet the company. She couldn't imagine who it was, and was shocked to see a tall, gangly boy and a stout, well-corseted woman climb out of the back of a two-toned blue sedan. The car was being driven by a cocky young man with a ducktail haircut—Boyd's cousin, Firman, it turned out. When Charlotte gathered her wits and invited them to come sit on the porch,

Firman quickly declined and returned to the car, where he stayed planted during the whole of their visit, smoking and leaning on it with the insouciant look of a professional chauffeur. She shook hands first with Boyd, then with his mother, and led the way to the porch.

"That's all right," said Mrs. Eppleman when Charlotte asked if she could get them something cool to drink. "Please don't fuss. We don't need anything fancy."

A small pool of water collected around Hoskins's bare feet as the water drained out of his underpants onto the porch floor. He leaned into Charlotte's legs, and she put her arm around his sturdy little body. His bare flesh felt pleasantly cool.

She had no idea what to say. It was clear that Boyd and his mother had no idea what to say, either. Mrs. Eppleman gazed out at the soft hills in the distant haze and remarked on the beauty of the view, pointing out a few trees that were starting to turn. Boyd sat in the hard wooden rocker and looked at his hands. He was wearing a droopy black cardigan over a white shirt, and nice-looking gray trousers—*his Sunday best,* Charlotte thought.

Mrs. Eppleman recrossed her legs; her nylons made a watery sound. "We got your note. It was Derby Day, wasn't it, Boyd, when we got Mrs. McGuffey's note?" Her hair was neatly parted into rows of tight gray curls planted in a bed of pink scalp. Charlotte counted eleven rows.

"It was, Mother. You already know that."

"I appreciate your coming all this way," Charlotte said, trying to include both of them.

"I told Boyd, I said, 'We'd better go now, before Labor Day weekend, or she may be gone.'"

"I'm going back to Syracuse, but just for a few days. We're spending the winter here."

"Oh, well, then. You'll be here over the winter?"

"Yes."

"You may be snowed in."

"My son Baird is looking forward to it." After another silence, in which Charlotte watched Firman rub his cigarette out on the grass, she said it must be nice to have a chauffeur.

Boyd was starting to rock. "I don't drive anymore. I don't care for it."

"He prefers not to," his mother said. "He's high-strung in that way. Driving makes him nervous."

Boyd paused, midair, and asked if she was planning to build a stone wall in the field. There was a pile of rocks down there. His mother strained a little to see.

It was a cairn, Charlotte explained. A cairn was a special pile of rocks that offered a landmark for travelers. It was part of a sculpture that her neighbor was installing in the field. "It's not finished yet, so it just looks like a pile of rocks." *It will also look like a pile of rocks when it's finished,* she thought.

Mrs. Eppleman waited for a moment for a further explanation. "Did you say it was a sculpture?"

"It's a cairn. There will be more of them, and paths between them. It's supposed to blend into the natural terrain."

"It looks like a woodchuck's home."

"Woodchucks make their homes underground, Mother," Boyd said, his tone disparaging.

"All of them?" she asked.

"All woodchucks do the exact same things."

"Oh. I didn't realize that."

"I think what Boyd means is that they don't have individual house styles, like people," Charlotte said. "Their houses are all alike."

"And they don't make them out of stone," he added. "They burrow."

The water sprinkler ticked as it turned. Charlotte couldn't think of anything else to say about woodchucks.

"Boyd didn't want to come," said Mrs. Eppleman. "I told him he'd feel a lot better if he could just see you was doing okay. That's what I said: 'Let's just go down there some Sunday and you'll see she's doing okay.'"

Boyd had started rocking with a little more force. Charlotte started to say she was doing okay but Boyd interrupted, his words coming out in a rush. "My mother had a concussion, but nothing bad happened to me. She had to stay in the hospital overnight. I didn't even bump the window. That's what happens to people when they stop short like that, they hit their faces or they go through the glass, but I didn't even have a bloody nose. Nothing happened to me." He stopped rocking the chair and pointed to his mother. "*She* got taken to the hospital in an ambulance."

"I didn't know half of what I was saying," Mrs. Eppleman said. "I was so upset. I was full of crazy talk. They say it's normal, after a shock like that, you know. You lose your wits."

"I don't know why," said Boyd, "since it was me that was driving."

"Well, Boyd, I was in the car, too. You act like I wasn't even in the car."

Boyd tipped the chair back as far as he could go. Charlotte adjusted her arm around Hoskins, holding him tighter.

"The car skidded out of control; we didn't know what was happening," Mrs. Eppleman said. "I told Boyd, 'It's a tragedy, but it's not something you can avoid.' Maybe he'll believe it if he hears it from you, Mrs. McGuffey. He's a good boy."

"I'm not," he said. "That's a lie."

"Boyd, that's not true. You've always been a good boy."

"How can I be a *good boy,* Mother, if I kill people?" He let go, and the chair rocked forward. He held it there as Baird stepped out to the porch, wearing a pair of wrinkled checkered pants he must have found in the dirty laundry basket. His cowlick stuck up like a rooster comb. He looked around at them as if he knew he'd interrupted something.

Charlotte asked him if he would take Hoskins inside and find some cookies to serve everybody. "Bring them out on a nice plate. You can make up some Kool-Aid, too."

Baird looked at her as if she was truly daft. He was always asking if he could make Kool-Aid, and she was always saying no. "Bring anything else you like," she said.

"All right," he said, rolling his eyes. When the boys were gone, Charlotte told Mrs. Eppleman she'd like to have a few words alone with her son. Boyd shot up out of his chair.

He held the screened door for her, and they went down the steps. "I'll wait here," Mrs. Eppleman called out.

They walked across the lawn without speaking. The spray from the sprinkler was heading in their direction and neither of them tried to avoid it. Boyd wiped the side of his face. "It must have been horrible for you," Charlotte said. "I can't imagine."

"Yeah. It was horrible."

"I asked you to come because . . . because I thought you could tell me something more about the accident. I was desperate for more information. Now I think there isn't any; there are things one never will know. I just have to accept that. I'm so sorry, Boyd. But I want you to know, you didn't do anything wrong. It was an accident, that's all."

"You're probably curious about what happened."

"I don't want to make you talk about it. I can see how painful it is for you."

"You can ask me anything, Mrs. McGuffey, really, but there's not much to tell you. I was driving along; I was taking my mother to the beauty parlor—well, that's not really true. My mother just said that because she thought it sounded better. We were going to the bank to cash a savings bond my father left me, and I was going to buy a guitar, but my mother thought it sounded kind of suspicious. We got to Main Street—I wasn't going very fast, because of the snow, and a man steps out in front of the car. He was trying to catch his hat. I guess it had blown off in the wind." He looked at her, stricken. "It was your husband."

"He was trying to catch his hat?" she repeated, thunderstruck.

"There was a lot of wind and blowing snow—he sort of bent over like this." Boyd demonstrated what he meant, extending his arm outward and hopping along on one foot in pursuit of the imaginary hat like some big, clumsy bird.

"Did you see his face?"

"His face was turned away, toward the hat. He was reaching for it."

"He didn't have any time, then."

"Oh, no, he didn't have any time, Mrs. McGuffey. He never even saw me, I don't think. And then it was too late. I saw him, but I couldn't stop. Maybe I could've stopped, I don't know, if I was a better driver."

"You couldn't have. I can tell, from the way you tell the story."

"You can?"

"It wasn't you that killed him." Just as she hadn't killed him by making him miserable, she thought. What had killed Melvin was a sudden gust of wind in a snowstorm and his impulse to retrieve his hat, and the impact with a car driven by a desperate boy taking responsibility for things he shouldn't. "Your mother's right, you know, Boyd. You just happened to be there at that moment. It was out of your control entirely."

"I wish," he said.

"It's true, Boyd. You should believe me. You've been so kind to come here and tell me this. You've been very brave." He tried to apologize some more, and she tried to divert him with her questions. Had he ever been in one of those soapbox derbys in St. J? What were they like? She'd been there, but she hadn't seen it. Was there a big prize? How many people generally participated? They walked slowly back across the lawn, talking about Boyd's plans for the future, which sounded fairly dismal. He mentioned a course in accounting being held in the school's gym, to which he could walk, he added. And a trip to Canada to see the Montrealers sometime; he wasn't sure how soon he could go, probably not too soon. Firman would have to drive. As they came back around to the front, Boyd's cousin sauntered toward the car, hands in pockets, expression sour. He got in and plunked down in the driver's seat with the door open, his feet splayed out on the grass.

"You'll have to start driving again, Boyd."

"I can't."

"But what if you were visiting your girlfriend and she reached over and kissed you and told you how much she liked you and Firman was bored and told you it was time to go?"

"I've thought of that," he said very seriously. "I can picture him doing that. It would be just like him."

"And there will be other things you'll want to do without him, and without your mother. Like take guitar lessons—or perform for people when you start getting good. I can see you with a guitar. You can't live that kind of life and not drive."

He looked at her and smiled, his face lighting up. "Yeah."

"You just have to do it. You'll have to get in and start driving."

"I'm not sure I remember how."

"Then you'd better tell Firman to get in the backseat with your mother when you take the wheel. You'll remember how by the time you get down to the road. The only thing in your way is a few trees."

He looked at her and laughed, a kind of strangled, gargling sound. "The both of them in back?"

"It's the only way, Boyd. I personally am looking forward to seeing it. I'll be watching as you drive out of here. Will you give me a wave?"

He smiled slowly. "Sure, Mrs. McGuffey, whatever you want."

"Promise?"

"Watch me and see," he said.

Baird and Hoskins brought the refreshments out to the porch and stood with Charlotte as she watched Boyd cautiously inch the car down the drive, its brake lights blinking. It jerked to a stop and an arm emerged from the driver's window, waving wildly. Then it turned onto the road and disappeared behind the trees.

Baird asked who the people were, and she told him they were some people from St. Johnsbury. He didn't ask anything else about them, and they sat down at the porch table to enjoy a private picnic of strawberry Kool-Aid and vanilla sandwich cookies. Baird said that Hoskins had chosen the cut-glass pitcher for the Kool-Aid, and he had chosen the plate for the cookies. They were heaped on one of Melvin's souvenir plates, which she had retrieved from the Beals' store at the beginning of the summer. She had put both of them away on the top shelf of the pantry, where they would be out of the way and safe, and she chose not to ask how they had managed to get them down. The picture on the plate, emerging slowly as the boys plowed their way through the mound of cookies, was of the floating bridge in Brookfield. "It just floats," she told Baird. "It's quite amazing."

"Oh, I know," he said in a rather worldly tone. "I've been there."

"You have?"

"I was there when Dad took the picture! I was helping."

"I see."

"He said he couldn't have done it without me," he told her, and he offered a small smile. "Well, that's what he *said*."

Afterward Charlotte walked down to the field with a small jar and started picking the dried lupine seeds out of their stiff casings. In the spring she would plant them in the bare places where the holes had been. The stone walkways that would crisscross the field and connect the cairns were indicated now only by the lengths of string stretched between stakes. She wondered what Melvin would have thought of Francis's grand plan—not very much, probably, but then again, how could she know? She thought he would probably like it if he knew she was collecting and planting the seeds. Later, when the walkways and the other cairns were added to the field, there would be more trampling, more disturbance, and she would plant the seeds again, and more lupines would grow. It was such an elegant idea, and so simple. In her mind she could see how the lupines would grow up along the edges of the graceful walkways, and she was pleased to think it would always be a place that she had made more beautiful.

CHAPTER

28

"Over two million years ago today," wrote Leona in her September column for the *Beede Opinion,* "our Green Mountain State was buried in ice, some of it more than a mile thick. When that melted ten thousand years ago, it revealed the features of the land we know and love so well today.

"Likewise, when the snows of the coming winter thaw, the mud settles, and the rivers rise, we will see once again what we hold dear: green grass, flowing water, the gentle slopes of the hills around us, buds on barren trees, friends who have been away.

"Not all of our summer friends, however, are leaving. Charlotte McGuffey and her two young sons will be staying at their home on McCrillis Hill during the winter, and we're glad to have them with us. Baird McGuffey, age eight, will be attending the village school. His younger brother, Hoskins, will be staying at home with Mother.

"Mrs. McGuffey has given the First Methodist Church the final beautiful photograph taken of it by her late husband, the renowned photographer Melvin McGuffey. To the surprise of all, it is a whole different view of the church, a cold and wintry scene taken from the hillside above, with both church and village enveloped in mist. Another of his final church photographs has been sold to *Vermont Life* and will appear in next year's winter issue. This one features Miss Amarita Andoulette of Beede going sledding on a bright, sunny winter day.

"In other good news, Miss Rosamunde Baird of Kingston, New York, and Mr. Paul Bellini of South Beede announced their marriage earlier this month in Kingston, New York. They are presently enjoying an extended honeymoon in Yellowstone Park and will take up residence in Kingston when they return. The new Mrs. Bellini is the sister of Charlotte McGuffey. Good luck, Mr. and Mrs. Bellini!"

Mary Hays was educated at Bennington College and at the University of Chicago, where she received her M.A. in humanities. She has written short stories and plays and, until recently, she taught third and fourth grades at a rural elementary school. She lives in Corinth, Vermont, with her husband, Stephen Long. *Learning to Drive* is her first novel.